Moonlight, Tiger, and Smoke

月光
虎
霧

Connie Bailey

Dreamspinner Press

Published by
Dreamspinner Press
4760 Preston Road
Suite 244-149
Frisco, TX 75034
http://www.dreamspinnerpress.com/

Moonlight, Tiger, and Smoke
Copyright © 2011 by Connie Bailey

Cover Art by Mara McKennan

ISBN: 978-1-61372-062-2

Printed in the United States of America
First Edition
July 2011

eBook edition available
eBook ISBN: 978-1-61372-063-9

Part One

WHEN the little boy woke for the second time, he could hear someone else breathing in the darkness. "Who's there?" he whispered. No one answered, and his anxiety grew.

On the night of his first day in first grade, he'd gone to sleep with his bluebird night-light on in his little bed in his little bedroom down the hall from his parents, just like always, but when he had awakened, it was completely dark and he was lying on a hard floor. When he'd tried to get up, he'd banged his head on a low ceiling. Feeling around, he'd decided he was in a box like the ones that refrigerators came in, but bigger and made of wood instead of cardboard. He'd become frightened when he'd abruptly imagined he was in a large coffin. He'd yelled and punched and kicked and done his best to find a way out until he was exhausted. With tears of frustration drying on his cheeks, he'd fallen asleep again.

He rubbed his eyes and stretched his arm up, felt unfinished wood at his fingertips. He was still in the same place, it was still dark, and he was very hungry. Cautiously, he rolled over and got to his hands and knees. Moving slowly in the pitch black, he crawled toward the sound of breathing. In three heartbeats, he touched someone's foot.

"Hello?" he said. "Who are you?"

There was no sound but shallow breathing as he slid his hand up a small, rubber-soled shoe to a bare shin. Halfway up, he ran into the other kid's hand. He could picture the stranger sitting with knees drawn up and arms wrapped around his legs.

"I'm Cheolsu. Are you all right?"

Cheolsu heard a sniffling noise and moved to sit next to the other kid. There was immense comfort in knowing he wasn't alone, so he figured it would make the crying child feel better too. Scooting closer, Cheolsu put his arm around the stranger's shoulders.

"What's your name?" he asked.

"Jae—Jaehan." The other little boy hiccupped. "Where am I?"

"I don't know, Jae. I went to sleep, and when I woke up, I was here."

"Me too." Jaehan took a hitching breath. "I want my umma."

"I think we're all alone. I tried yelling, but no one answers."

"Where is this?"

"I think we're in a big box."

"Why?"

"I don't know."

"I'm scared."

Cheolsu almost said *me too*, but stopped himself. "Don't be scared," he said instead. "Why don't we try and figure out what's going on?"

Jaehan wiped his face with his sleeve. "I don't know what's going on."

"Well, my parents aren't rich, so I don't think someone took me for money."

"People do that? Steal kids for money?"

"Don't you watch TV? It's called kidnapping."

"We don't have a TV at my house."

"Weird," Cheolsu said.

"No it isn't! It's better for you not to watch that stuff! My umma said so."

"Let's not fight, okay?"

"I'm *not* fighting. Fighting isn't nice."

"Do you know how you got here?"

"No. Why is it so dark?"

"I told you. We're in a box."

"I don't want to be in a box."

"I tried to find a way out, but I couldn't." Cheolsu paused at the sound of a soft sob. "Are you okay?"

"I want my umma to come and get me."

"I bet she'll be here soon. How old are you?"

"I'm six. My birthday was in January."

"I'm six too, but my birthday was in February, so I guess you're older. Want to play a game?"

"How can we play a game in the dark?"

"We could play word games." Cheolsu wasn't particularly fond of word games. He preferred kicking a ball or climbing a tree, but neither of those were options at the moment, and he wanted to distract Jaehan. Jaehan's tears made Cheolsu feel bad.

"My umma plays word games with me all the time." Jaehan swallowed, and some of the roughness left his voice. "I know one! I'll say an animal and you tell me what he eats, okay?"

"Okay." Cheolsu would have agreed to anything to keep the sadness from the other boy's voice.

Jaehan said horse and Cheolsu said hay. Jaehan said monkey and Cheolsu said banana. Jaehan said dog and Cheolsu said cat. Jaehan laughed and Cheolsu's heart lifted.

The two little boys played several variations of the game. Each time they started a new round, Cheolsu let Jaehan choose what sort of questions would be asked and who would do the answering. Jaehan always chose to ask the questions and laughed whenever Cheolsu gave a silly answer. They forgot their situation until Cheolsu's stomach growled.

"I think there's a tiger in here with us," Cheolsu said.

"I'm hungry too."

"We're hungry!" Cheolsu shouted at the top of his lungs.

Jaehan flinched at the loud noise and pressed closer to Cheolsu. "Why doesn't somebody come?"

"This sucks!" Cheolsu punched upward, grazing his knuckles on the wood. "Jerks!" Settling back, he brought his fist to his mouth and sucked morosely at the small stinging wounds.

"Who are you yelling at?"

"The people who put us in this box. I hate them."

Jaehan gasped. "You shouldn't ever say that. That's a really bad word."

"They're bad people."

"But you're not." Jaehan took Cheolsu's hand. "Don't be bad, Cheolsu, please. It makes the people who love us very, very sad. My umma said so."

Cheolsu pulled his hand from Jaehan's so he could put his arm around him. "I'm sorry I yelled and scared you. I was mad."

Jaehan turned sideways and put his arms around Cheolsu's neck, seeking comfort the way he was used to—climbing onto his mother's lap when he was troubled. He put his cheek on Cheolsu's shoulder and tried to ignore the gnawing in his belly. For the first time in his life, his hunger wasn't instantly banished by the appearance of food as soon as he acquainted someone with his need. He was slowly realizing what it meant to be on your own, and he was very grateful for Cheolsu's presence. Cheolsu might be rough and a complete stranger, but he was here, sharing this nightmare.

Cheolsu put his other arm around the smaller boy, and Jaehan snuggled in like a puppy. Jaehan's warm presence was welcome as the temperature started to drop, and having someone to protect gave Cheolsu a reason to be brave. He didn't move until he was sure Jaehan had fallen asleep. Burying his face in Jaehan's thick hair, Cheolsu wept until he drifted into disturbing dreams.

THE small cargo ship made port at a privately-owned island west of Japan. At a pier far from any shipyard, three large boxes were transferred from the hold to a freight truck. After a long drive into the country, the truck pulled onto a dirt road and stopped. Two men got out and unloaded the boxes, leaving them on the grass where a trail led into the trees. Having made their delivery, they went on about their business.

Behind the departing truck, a man in monk's robes stepped from the forest. Using various tools he took from a pouch around his waist, he opened the crates and sprayed the contents with an aerosol. In a few minutes, the man heard noises from the boxes and pushed them over. Six small boys—now conscious—spilled out and scrambled to their feet, staring at the stranger.

"Saidzuki desu." The man began speaking in Japanese, and the children found they understood him. "I am Mallet, and I am your master. Each of you is here because his family owes a debt to the Kagehito. When the debt went unpaid, we took a firstborn child, as agreed in the contract. You belong to the Kagehito now... to the Shadow People."

One of the children started to cry. Mallet took two swift steps and gave the little boy a slap that knocked him to the ground. Whirling around, Mallet addressed his shocked audience.

"This is your first lesson, so learn it well. When a master is speaking, you listen. When a master tells you to do something, you obey. Inattention and disobedience will draw immediate punishment." Mallet paused and rephrased his last sentence. "If you don't do as you're told, you'll get a slap, or worse."

Cheolsu leaned over to help the fallen boy to his feet. Mallet didn't interfere, but waited silently until all six boys were facing him again.

"Forget your families," Mallet said. "They know who took you, and they know they'd be killed if they tried to get you back. They've already given you up for dead. You have no family now but the Shadow." He looked around the circle of wide-eyed children. "The sooner you get used to the idea that you're on your own, the less need there'll be to punish you. From now on, all you have will come from us. We feed you. We clothe you. We school you. You're far away from the places you called home, across a sea in another country. Think about that if you think about running away." He met each boy's eyes. "If you run away, you'll be killed. We have no use for stupid children. Do you understand?"

Jaehan's hand crept into Cheolsu's behind Cheolsu's back. He squeezed Jaehan's fingers, but his eyes never left Mallet. The big man's voice held none of the softness most adults used when addressing children. Mallet talked to them as though they were his age, as though he expected them to understand everything he said... and he had no patience at all. He reminded Cheolsu of his stern, heavy-handed father, and maybe he could be appeased the same way: with unequivocal respect.

"*Seonbae.*" Cheolsu used a Korean term of respect as he bowed to Mallet.

Mallet focused on the six-year-old with the neatly-cut, reddish-brown hair. Over the last twenty-seven years, the trainer had seen a lot of boys delivered to Saigo Island and was familiar with all the reactions of a small child dealing with shock. Some cried, some threw tantrums, some shut down, and a rare few accepted the facts and started dealing with them. The latter made the best students... and the most dangerous. They were usually headstrong and harder to control, but if they made it through the program alive, they were peerless soldiers. Mallet saw potential as he looked into this little boy's calm, amber eyes.

"What's your name?" Mallet asked.

"Cheolsu, *seonbae*."

Mallet spun, his right leg sweeping Cheolsu off his feet. "Get up," the trainer told the little boy and waited for Cheolsu to stand. "Don't speak to me in Hangul again. Forget Korea, along with your families. I know all of you were taught Nihongo from the cradle," he said. "If you speak any other language in my hearing, I'll sew your mouth shut."

Cheolsu had never thought to wonder why he'd been taught Japanese along with his native tongue. It was just a fact of life, like visiting his grandparents in the summer or his mother's insistence on turning off the television at dinnertime, but it was useful now. "Hai, senpai," Cheolsu said. *Yes, my superior.*

Mallet gave the little boy a short nod of approval. "I excuse your ignorance this one time. You don't call me senpai; I'm your sensei."

"Yes, teacher," Cheolsu replied with another bow.

"What's your name?" Mallet asked again.

Cheolsu sucked in his bottom lip to keep from blurting out his name again. Desperately, he tried to think of an answer that would please Mallet. "I don't have a name," he said at last.

"Very good." Mallet looked at the other boys. "Forget the names your mothers gave you. You will not have a name until I give you one." He put a hand on Cheolsu's head. "You are Tora, known to your brethren as Tiger."

The newly christened Tiger bowed again and earned another nod of approval.

"We have a long walk to make," Mallet said. "Tiger will lead. Anyone who strays or lags will be punished." The trainer pointed to the trailhead marked by a cairn of stones. "Get moving."

Tiger glanced at Jaehan as he started off. Jaehan looked bewildered, and he hurried to follow when Tiger began walking. The other four boys fell in, too confused to do anything other than stick with the herd.

The pathway was steep and zigzagged back and forth up the face of the grassy hill. It followed the crest for a while and then led up a stony slope dotted with boulders. When Jaehan slipped on some pebbles, Tiger spun and caught Jaehan's hand before the smaller boy could tumble back down the trail. The boy behind Jaehan gave Jaehan a boost as Tiger pulled. When Jaehan was firmly on his feet again, he thanked Tiger and looked over his shoulder to thank the other boy.

"Keep moving unless you want a slap," Mallet barked.

Jaehan gave the boy behind him a quick smile and faced front again. He didn't want to be slapped, or even spoken to in a harsh way. In his home, bad behavior was met with a motherly explanation of why the behavior was wrong and ended with a hug when he promised to be good. Because he loved his mother and never wanted to cause trouble for her, he never repeated an act once he knew it was offensive. Keeping his eyes on the ground in front of him, he concentrated on not falling again.

"No talking among yourselves unless permission is given," Mallet said as they climbed higher. "If you need to speak to a teacher, you will bow and wait for the teacher to notice you. You will do without question any task a teacher asks of you. If you fail to complete the task, you'll be whipped with a strap of leather."

Mallet continued to list causes for punishment as the trail cut through a belt of pines to end at a bridge over a ravine. On the other side, a road followed a dry riverbed carved into the rock of the island's spine. In the shade of an evergreen stood a man in the same dark brown robes that Mallet wore.

"Go on," Mallet said when Tiger glanced back at him. When they reached the other side of the bridge, Mallet told the children the other man's name was Hei, which meant Wall.

Wall gave the little boys a long look before he spoke. "I'm glad this lot is yours," he said in a voice like thunder in the distance. "They look like a bunch of skinned rabbits."

"That's your trouble, Wall," Mallet said. "Your lack of vision holds you back."

Wall chuckled. "It wasn't my lack of vision that earned me this sentry duty."

"No, that was ordinary stupidity. Even if you don't care for the onmyoji's ways, you have to behave as though you respect him."

"I didn't know he would hear my words."

"You never know where the onmyoji has ears," Mallet said.

"True." Wall lowered his voice. "You'd think I'd have more self-control. I don't want a wizard to have a grudge against me."

"That's a wise attitude. I'd better get these rabbits back on the road now." Mallet turned to the half dozen boys. "Walk," he said.

"Cheer up, boys," Wall called out as the children filed past him. "You're almost halfway there."

One of the boys groaned, and Mallet smacked the back of his head, sending him reeling into another boy. Both children staggered as Tiger turned to see what was happening. Tiger lunged, blocking their fall with his body. Jaehan moved beside Tiger, ready to support him if he lost his balance. It was over in seconds, and they started walking again, but Mallet was satisfied by what he'd observed. Though they were from above average stock, it was never certain how they'd perform until tested. These boys showed an inclination to work as a team, to help one another rather than stay uninvolved. This trait would be an asset to them for the next few years, as they underwent basic training. It would be of no help at all once they'd been assigned for specialty training, but that was seven years away.

THE pine forest ended and the road continued through a rock-strewn field to a stone wall three meters high. Behind the wall rose the roofs of several buildings made of the same stone. A metal-banded gate of solid mahogany stood open, and the sentries called greetings as Mallet entered the training compound with his weary charges.

"That's a nice flock of plucked ducklings." A man with a sword on his hip chuckled as he walked past Mallet's group on his way out the gate.

"I'll pluck you someday, River," Mallet said under his breath. "Tiger! Go to the left."

Tiger turned left, walking out of the cobbled courtyard between two large buildings. As he emerged into the open again, the road was lined on one side with small huts. Behind the huts were cultivated fields and tree-shaded pastures, and beyond them, the high stone wall that encompassed the property.

"Stop," Mallet said as they reached a row of mud-brick huts. "You will live here. Two to a hut." He pointed at Jaehan. "You live in this one with Tiger."

Jaehan looked up to meet Mallet's eyes. "Are you my appa now?"

Tiger tensed as he waited for Mallet to slap Jaehan for using the Korean word for father, but the sensei didn't raise his hand.

"Are you touched?" Mallet said, gazing intently into Jaehan's sweet face. "You're not supposed to have defects, but it's so hard to tell with kids. You're all full of moonshine until life knocks it out of you." He cupped Jaehan's chin on his palm, studying the boy's pale features. "Your name is Tsukikage now," he said as he let Jaehan go. "It means moonlight, and you'll be Tiger's kohai."

Moonlight's smooth brow wrinkled in a miniature frown.

"You want to say something, Moonlight?" Mallet asked.

"Yes, teacher. Tiger should be kohai. I'm older than him."

"Someone has taught you well," Mallet said.

"My umma is a teacher," Moonlight said proudly. "She taught me my letters and numbers."

Once again, Mallet refrained from reprimanding the little boy for not speaking Japanese. "The senpai/kohai relationship is not always defined by age, and in this case, a few months don't matter. All of you are six years old." He turned to the other boys. "You and you," he said pointing to another pair.

"Teacher," one the boys said as he bowed.

"What is it?" Mallet asked.

"I'm not six. I'm seven."

Mallet stared at the little boy like a hawk spotting a mouse. "You sound very proud of that. It's very rare that a novice chooses his name, but from now on you are Shichi—Seven. Now get into your hut." He pointed to the remaining pair. "You go in that one. The sun will set in half an hour and you will go to sleep. Since you're exhausted, that shouldn't be a problem. I'll be back for you at sunrise."

Tiger bowed.

"What is it, Tiger?"

"Are we going to eat, teacher?"

"That's up to you." Mallet turned and marched away, leaving the children alone.

Tiger immediately started toward his designated hut. Glancing over his shoulder, he held out his hand to Moonlight. Moonlight took Tiger's hand and went with him.

"Wait a minute," said the boy who'd steadied Moonlight on the trail. "Don't you want to talk about what's happening?"

Tiger turned, pulling Moonlight around with him. "You should go where the teacher told you. He said not to talk to each other."

"He can't hear us now." The little boy brushed a drift of heavy bangs out of his eyes. "Are you just going to do what they say? Don't you want to know what's going on?"

"Do you know?" Tiger challenged, looking at the other four boys. "I didn't think so. So why talk about it?"

"So you're going to go along with it?"

"We can't fight them. We're just kids," Moonlight spoke up.

"Then can we be friends? I'm Junho."

Moonlight bowed. "I'm Moonlight, I guess."

The boy dubbed Seven bowed also. "I'm Eunki, but I guess you can call me Seven."

The last pair bowed and introduced themselves as Hwangbo and Kyuhwan.

"You've already heard my name," Tiger said. "Now let's go inside, like the teacher told us." He went into the first hut, drawing Moonlight along with him.

The small building had one room with a dirt floor. In one corner was a stone fire pit with a vent hole. At the back wall was a pallet made of stacked squares of felt. Otherwise, the place was bare and windowless. As Tiger and Moonlight entered, Moonlight sniffed loudly.

"Noodles!" Moonlight exclaimed, letting go of Tiger's hand to dash across the short space to the hearth. His goal was an earthenware pot with steam escaping around the edges of the lid.

For no reason Tiger could name—other than the nature of everything that had happened since he woke in the box—he felt a stab of fear. He shouted a warning, but he was too late. As Moonlight neared the fire pit, his foot came down on a booby trap. A wooden rod sprang out of a groove in the floor and smacked Moonlight between the eyes. Moonlight stumbled back, blinking rapidly, both hands flying up to cover his face. In a moment, blood began to pour through his fingers.

Tiger pulled off his shirt and put a hand on Moonlight's shoulder. "Sit," he said. "And put your hands down so I can see."

Moonlight sat and looked dazedly at Tiger. "What happened?"

"There was a trap. They knew we'd go straight for the food."

"Ow!" Moonlight jerked away when Tiger pressed his jersey to Moonlight's nose.

"You hold it then," Tiger said. "But you have to press hard to make the bleeding stop."

"How do you know?"

"I broke my nose playing soccer a few months ago. Coach made me sit with my head back and hold a towel on it filled with ice." Tiger paused. "I don't have any ice though."

"Ow!" Moonlight said again. "I don't want to be a baby, but it really hurts."

"I know." Tiger squeezed Moonlight's shoulder. "It's going to hurt for a while."

"Why would they do that? Why do they want to hurt us?"

"I don't know." Tiger shook his head as he walked cautiously toward the hearth. "To make us tough, I guess."

"They're mean."

"I know," Tiger said again as he carefully lifted the lid off the pot. Picking up a set of plain bamboo chopsticks from the hearth, he pushed them around in the soup. When the pot didn't explode, Tiger lifted out a skein of noodles and sniffed them. He couldn't smell anything funny, and he was so hungry that his mouth was filling with saliva. If the food was poisoned, there was nothing he could do about it, but he had to eat. After stuffing his mouth as full as possible, Tiger pushed the pot across the room to where Moonlight sat. "Open," he said, pulling out more noodles and offering them.

"Thank you," Moonlight said when he'd swallowed the mouthful of food. "I think my nose is getting bigger."

"It's going to swell a lot. You'll have to breathe through your mouth."

Moonlight nodded and opened up for more noodles. Tiger obliged, alternately feeding Moonlight and himself. When the noodles were gone, they took turns drinking the broth until the pot was empty. By that time, the sun was going down and shadows began to gather in the hut. A search of the room yielded nothing that could be used for light.

"Maybe if we went to those fields, we could find wood," Tiger said.

"But we can't make a fire. We'll get in trouble."

"I don't think that rule works here, but anyway, we don't have a lighter or anything."

"We should just try to go to sleep, like that man said. I don't want him to be mad."

"Me either." Tiger look across at Moonlight, at the way the smaller boy's skin glowed in the dimness. "Moonlight," he said. "It sounds funny, but it's a good name for you."

"My name is Jaehan."

"You should get used to being called Moonlight."

Moonlight sighed. "Okay." He tilted his head down to look at Tiger. "My umma's not coming, is she?"

"I don't think so."

Tears welled up in Moonlight's dark eyes and ran down his cheeks. "She'll be so sad when she can't find me."

Tiger pressed his lips together and set his jaw, determined not to give in to his tears. "Since our families are gone, we'll have to be each other's family."

"Okay." Moonlight took the shirt away from his face and smiled shyly at Tiger. In the midst of this nightmare, he was getting the thing he'd always wanted. "We can be brothers," he said.

Tiger held up his fist, and after a moment, Moonlight bumped his knuckles against Tiger's.

"We stick together, right?" Tiger said.

Moonlight nodded solemnly.

"Now neither of has to be afraid because we'll take care of each other," Tiger said as he took his blood-soaked shirt from Moonlight. "Looks like the bleeding stopped. Wait here. I'm going to see if there's water somewhere."

"I want to go with you."

"Okay, but walk slow and don't bump into anything. You could start bleeding again."

Some distance behind the hut, the boys found a brook by the sound of water flowing over stone. Tiger dipped his shirt and wrung it out several times while Moonlight lay on his belly and drank directly from the stream. The ice-cold water numbed his face and relieved a little of the pain of the broken nose. After a few moments, Moonlight sat up and took the shirt from Tiger.

"I can do it," Tiger said.

"I'm the one who got it dirty," Moonlight replied. "I should clean it."

"You have a lot of rules," Tiger said as Moonlight put the shirt back in the stream.

"There's nothing wrong with having rules."

"I didn't say that. I know we need rules, like how we should look for cars before going across a street."

"You go across the street by yourself?"

"Sure." Tiger shrugged. "What's the big deal?"

"It's dark now," Moonlight said as he wrung out the shirt and handed it to Tiger. "We should go in."

Each boy had another drink of water, and then they walked back. Tiger hung his wet shirt over a tree branch outside the hut and entered the dark room behind Moonlight. When he closed the door, he couldn't see the other boy just a few feet in front of him.

"Where are you?" Tiger asked. "I don't want to bump into you."

"Here's my hand," Moonlight said.

Tiger swept his arm around in the direction of Moonlight's voice and hit Moonlight's hand. He caught hold of Moonlight's fingers and shuffled forward. "We'll just walk slow until we run into the wall," he said. "Let me go first so you don't hit your nose again."

"What if there's another trap?" Moonlight stopped and tugged on Tiger's hand to stop him too.

"We have to go to sleep," Tiger said. "I'd rather sleep on those pads than the floor. I'll check them out before we lie down."

It was hard to tell in the dark, but after running his hands over the large squares of thick felt, Tiger was reasonably sure there were no spikes or scorpions or anything but lanolin lurking in the layers of pressed wool.

"Come on," Tiger said, patting the pallet. "I think it's safe."

Moonlight crept over on hands and knees and sat down. Methodically, he pulled off his shoes and socks, tucking the socks neatly into the sneakers. He unbuttoned his white, short-sleeved shirt and folded it. Slipping off his navy blue shorts, he placed them on the shoes, and then stacked the shirt on the top. Keeping his underwear on, he stretched out on the pallet. "Can I sleep next to the wall?" he asked.

"Sure." Tiger moved and Moonlight rolled to the other side of the sleeping pad. Settling back down, Tiger toed off his sneakers and let them drop to the floor.

Both boys were so exhausted that they fell asleep as soon as they were horizontal, only to wake with chattering teeth in the middle of the night. Tiger spooned up against Moonlight's back, and they huddled together for warmth until they dozed off in fitful sleep. They didn't rest well, and morning came very early, bringing their unforgiving new life with it.

TIGER sat up, jerked from sleep by a loud, clanging noise. He froze when he heard Mallet's voice.

"Get up!" the sensei shouted. "Put on the clothes by the door and get out here."

Tiger shook Moonlight's shoulder, amazed that Moonlight could sleep through the racket. Moonlight flinched and squirmed as though burrowing into nonexistent blankets.

"We have to get up," Tiger said.

"Don't want to. Too early."

"We *have* to."

Moonlight opened his eyes, alarmed by the stress in Tiger's voice. "What's wrong?"

"The teacher is calling us. We need to get up and go outside."

"I want to sleep more." Moonlight pouted.

"Me too, but we can't. Come on. Get up." Tiger took Moonlight by the upper arm and pulled him up.

"Where are my clothes?" Moonlight said as soon as he was on his feet.

Tiger went over to the pile of clothes by the door. "The teacher said to put these on," he said, holding up a knee-length tunic of heavy cotton.

"That looks like a dress. A really ugly dress."

Tiger shrugged. Moonlight was right—the tunic was shapeless and the gray color of old gum that you found with the bottom of your shoe. It was also coarse and bulky and looked like it would itch. Tiger didn't like it either, but there was no other choice. They could put on the tunics or go out in their underwear. "Just put it on," he told Moonlight as he pulled one of the tunics over his head. "Come on. You can do it."

"Of course I can." Moonlight snatched the garment from Tiger's hand. "I just don't want to." He got into the tunic, his pout even more pronounced. "It smells funny."

Mallet shouted again and Tiger bolted out the door, dragging Moonlight by the wrist. The other four boys stood abreast in front of the sensei, watching him warily with sleep-crusty eyes. All of them were dressed in the loose tunics, and they looked like a line of small prisoners. Tiger pulled Moonlight into place at the end of the row and bowed his head to Mallet. Mallet put his palm on the back of Tiger's head and pushed it down farther.

"Be quicker tomorrow morning," the sensei said.

"We will, master," Tiger answered.

"It was my fault," Moonlight said.

"I know," Mallet said, his eyes on Moonlight's face, his fingers digging into the muscles of Tiger's neck. "Whenever a kohai does something wrong, his senpai will be punished for it."

"That's not fair. It...." Moonlight's voice trailed off as Mallet squeezed Tiger's neck harder. He bowed and stepped back into line.

Mallet released Tiger, meeting the boy's eyes in silent approval of Tiger's acceptance of the rebuke. "All of you follow me," he said. "Tiger first."

The sensei tucked the ends of his robe into his belt and began to run. After only a moment's hesitation, the boys followed their master up the dirt road. On their left was the wall and on their right the planted fields that stretched to the pine forest. Mallet stopped at a stone shed and opened the door.

"Take one hoe each," Mallet said. "You're going to weed and water crops this morning and every morning until they're harvested. If you don't know how to use a hoe, I'll show you. You're here to work, not to eat. Do you understand? If you're caught eating the crops, you'll be punished."

After a few minutes' practice, each boy could use the hoe as it had been intended. As the sun climbed toward its zenith, they weeded the rows of strawberries, mouths watering at the sight of the ripening fruit. Inevitably, one of them picked a strawberry and slipped it into his mouth. Seven grimaced at the tart taste, and then the red and white pulp flew out of his mouth as Mallet smacked the back of his head.

"Idiot!" Mallet spat, yanking Seven up by his hair until they were face to face. "Foolish child! Do you think the rules are just made up to torment you? The rules keep you safe. Eating green fruit on an empty stomach will make you sick. If you're sick, you can't work. If you can't work, you're of no use to us. And Kagehito don't keep what we don't use."

Seven clenched his teeth against the pain of his burning scalp, but he didn't cry out. Tears rolled down his cheeks as he endured it until Mallet let go of him. "I'm sorry, teacher," he said. "I won't do it again."

"I should make all of you eat a handful so you'll know how severely the pain of stomach cramps can affect you." Mallet shook his head. "Take your hoes to the shed. Do I need to tell you to stack them neatly?"

Tiger was the first to move, and the other boys followed him in single file. When they reached the shed, Tiger stood at the door, taking the implements from the others and leaning them in a corner. "Are you okay?" he whispered as Seven handed over his hoe.

Seven nodded.

"Then stop being stupid. You'll get us all in trouble."

Seven nodded again and moved aside to let Junho turn over his hoe.

Mallet stood back and watched. Half his job consisted of observation, and he was good at it—so good that when he'd completed his training, he'd been chosen to remain on the island as a teacher. Coupled with his keen senses was an empathy that allowed him to see into the thoughts and motivations of those around him. He had an intuitive gift for seeing the prime potential in others, and the best way to prepare them for the time when the onmyoji decided which clan they were best suited for... the way the onmyoji had chosen him as Tetsuzoku, a warrior of the Iron Tribe.

The last thing he'd expected while waiting for his first mission was an inner calling to the Denkouzoku, the Lightning Tribe. It was rare that the outer calling to Iron didn't match the inner avocation, but Mallet had to accept that he was a teacher, no matter how much he wanted the life of a soldier. He knew that training future Kagehito was even more important than going on missions, but secretly he still longed for adventures in foreign lands. For more than twenty-seven years—from six to thirty-four—he'd spent every minute on this island, and though it was the home of his heart, he dreamed of leaving it at least once before he died. However, it was not up to him where he went or stayed. He was Kagehito, and he did as he was ordered by his superiors.

As his students did as he ordered them.

Mallet watched Tiger put the last hoe in the shed, satisfied with the progress this group was making. He expected them to be precocious, otherwise they wouldn't have been harvested, but these six were especially quick. "Line up," he said, as Tiger latched the shed door without being asked. "We're going to run back and Wall will show you how to make porridge."

Spirits rising at the possibility of food in their future, the boys ran with a will. They passed the cottages and stopped at a one-story stone building with a porch as long as it was. Under the shelter were rows of wooden tables and benches.

"This is where the teachers eat," Mallet said. "Follow me into the kitchen."

The boys weren't given much time to gawk at the lack of refrigerators and electric stoves before the sensei called Wall started his lesson. Swiftly, using the bare minimum of words and ingredients, he showed the six boys how to make porridge in a pot over a fire. After each boy nodded that he understood the procedure, Mallet herded them back outside. On one of the tables sat six bowls of porridge topped with sliced strawberries.

"Eat," Mallet said, and the boys wasted no time following his order. "This is your last free meal, so enjoy it. When you return to your cottages, you'll find a pot, two bowls, two cups, two small spoons and one large, and two sets of chopsticks. These belong to the kohai. The kohai will use them to cook with and feed his senpai. If they're broken or lost, the kohai must replace them." He glanced around the table. "Since you're all finished eating, let's move on."

Mallet led his class to another stone building. This one had two metal-bound doors guarded by a pair of men with swords. The sentries nodded to Mallet and opened the doors.

"This is the armory," Mallet told the boys as they walked into the cool dimness.

The boys were allowed several minutes to look around the room full of weapons that gleamed softly in the scant light: racks of swords, maces, and axes, bows and quivers hanging from wooden pegs, spears leaning together like shocks of hay. Among all these implements of death, there was nothing more modern than a crossbow.

"There's another room with body armor," Mallet told his wide-eyed charges. "You'll see that in a few years. Now, come outside to the practice yard." He led the boys into a stone square sprinkled with sand and surrounded by a tall fence of thick, wooden planks. "This is where you'll learn to fight," he said. He nudged the small pile of wooden swords with his toe. "Each of you will take one and get back into line."

When the boys had done as Mallet ordered, he faced them. "I told you yesterday that you belong to the Shadow now. You're slaves, but if you train very hard, you can earn a place with us. There is no greater honor, as you will learn. The Kagehito exist in secret to keep balance in the world. We remove those who would tip the scales too far toward evil. This is a difficult and dangerous task, and only those with the talent and proper training can do it." Mallet drew his sword. "Shall we begin?"

On Mallet's last word, Wall burst through the gate of the practice yard with his sword in hand. Without a word, Wall attacked Mallet in flurry of strokes so fast they were blurred. Mallet mirrored each blow, blocking Wall's blade with seeming effortlessness. The duel took on the form of a courtly dance until Mallet switched from defense to offense. In a series of five moves, Mallet had forced Wall to give ground and driven him to the fence.

"Thank you," Mallet said, bringing his weapon to a neutral position.

Wall bowed. "Always a pleasure to spar with you." He focused his gaze on the spellbound faces of Mallet's novices. "If you listen to your teacher and do as he says, you might be this good someday." With a salute to Mallet, Wall sheathed his blade and walked away.

"Pair off, kohai with senpai, and let me see if you have any natural talent for this," Mallet said to the boys. "You've all pretended to have sword fights before, haven't you?"

The boys paired off: Junho and Seven, Kyuhwan and Hwangbo, Tiger and Moonlight. After a couple of nervous seconds, the clacking of wood on wood echoed in the enclosed area as four of the boys play-fought.

"Why are you just standing there?" Mallet asked Tiger and Moonlight. "I told you to fight."

"Come on, Moonlight," Tiger whispered harshly. "Try and hit me."

"I don't want to," Moonlight said.

Mallet smacked the middle of Tiger's back with his sheathed sword. "Attack him," he said.

"He's not fighting back, teacher."

"That will make it easy for you to win, won't it?"

Tiger blinked. Never in his life had an adult said such a thing to him. The notion of fighting with someone weaker was so alien to him that he was stunned for a moment. There was no honor or sense of satisfaction to be gained here. There was only obedience. Slowly, he lifted his head and met Moonlight's eyes. "Please," he said. "Just hold the sword up for me to hit."

"I might hurt you," Moonlight objected.

"You have to fight," Mallet told Moonlight.

"No! I'm not supposed to fight. My umma says it's not nice."

"If you don't learn to fight, you'll end up dead."

"I'd rather be dead than hurt somebody."

Mallet looked at the stubborn pout on the little boy's face and stopped arguing with him. Pulling his sword, he put the point against the bottom ridge of Tiger's left eye socket. Deliberately, he drew the razor sharp blade down Tiger's cheek in a shallow cut.

"Don't! Please!" Moonlight cried out.

Mallet lowered his sword. "Did you forget that it is your senpai who suffers when you disobey?"

Tears streamed down Moonlight's cheeks as his fingers clenched into fists. In all of his six years, he'd never been presented with such a dilemma. He didn't want to hurt anyone, but he didn't want Tiger to be hurt either. Seeking guidance, he met Tiger's eyes and saw the trickle of blood that dripped from Tiger's jaw.

"I'm sorry," Moonlight said.

"It's okay."

Moonlight swallowed hard and brought his wooden sword up parallel with his swollen nose. "I'm sorry," he said again and swung the sword at Tiger.

Tiger blocked Moonlight's half-hearted blow and countered it. His blade hit Moonlight in the ribs and knocked the wind out of him. Moonlight stumbled backward and landed on his butt, looking up at Tiger in surprise.

"Follow up your advantage," Mallet barked, swatting Tiger across the backs of his thighs.

Tiger smothered his natural impulse to help Moonlight up and pounced on him. Knocking the sword from Moonlight's hand, Tiger pinned the other boy's shoulders to the ground. "Fight me," he said in Moonlight's ear. "If you don't, teacher will beat me."

Fresh tears welled up in Moonlight's eyes. Why didn't Umma come and make everything all right? Why was he being forced to do things he knew were bad? He needed to get away from here. With a cry of frustrated rage that emerged as a squeak, Moonlight pushed at Tiger with all his might. Tiger went sprawling, the gritty stone sanding skin from one of his elbows as his sword went flying.

"Good," Mallet said softly as Tiger recovered his sword and Moonlight scrambled after his. The teacher had his doubts about Moonlight, but was glad to see that the boy could be driven to violence. Without a fighting instinct, a novice was worthless and soon consigned to perpetual slavery or the depths of the sea. Mallet wouldn't like to see that happen; he had high hopes for Tiger, and he could already see that Moonlight would be the best means of keeping Tiger under control until Tiger learned to control himself.

Satisfied with Tiger and Moonlight's progress, Mallet turned to the other pairs. Of the four, Junho showed the most potential. He was scrawny, all flapping hair and sharp elbows, but he was quick and surprisingly agile for a six-year-old. Though he wielded the sword with no greater skill than his partner, he was easily able to avoid Seven's attack. After watching Junho bend backward at the waist to let a wild swing pass harmlessly overhead, Mallet put a hand on the little boy's shoulder, stopping the fight.

"You are now Kemuri, known to the Kagehito as Smoke," Mallet said. "Because you're as hard to get hold of as the mist."

Junho gave the sensei his wary, sidewise glance, but bowed respectfully, accepting the name.

"Enough practice for today." Mallet raised his voice. "Follow me." He took the boys to a room like a closet off the armory's main weapons room. One by one, the novices placed their practice swords in a notched rack. "You'll use these every day until I decide you're ready for a different weapon. Treat them well."

Mallet led the group out to a well in one of the few unpaved squares in the main compound. He showed the boys how to lower the bucket and draw up the cold, clear water. Each drank a dipperful and was told to sit under the branches of an ancient pine. When all six were sitting in the shade, Mallet leaned back against the well and spoke to them.

"You aren't the worst group of novices I've ever had," he said. "Some of you show real potential." Mallet took a long drink of the fresh water. "Your lessons with me are over for a few hours. It's time for you to go to a class where you learn from books. You'll have some time to eat again, and then you'll return to the practice yard. When you're too tired to stand up, you'll be allowed to sleep. This is how your days will go from now on, so I hope you were all paying attention today. I won't be there tomorrow to wake you like little babies. You're expected to be in the field at the same time as today. If you aren't at work before I get there, you'll be sorry."

As the days knotted themselves into weeks that lengthened into months, the boys got used to the routine of life in the Kagehito crèche. They rose at daybreak, dressed, ate whatever the kohai prepared, and worked in the fields until ten. After another mouthful or two of porridge with fruit or vegetables, they exercised their minds and bodies with River or Wall, but always overseen by Mallet. They learned to read and write, to add and subtract, how to hunt and dress game, how to make vessels of clay and fire them, the many ways to use a knife as a tool or a weapon, and countless other things that they didn't see the sense of yet. Each minute of each day was accounted for until the boys lay down to sleep. They were constantly reminded that they were slaves who existed only to serve the Kagehito and that their continued existence depended upon their usefulness. Only in dreams were they free, and in time, even those dreams faded.

The boys ceased to speak of their families among themselves and soon ceased to think of them unless reminded. Only the one called Moonlight still missed his mother so much that he often cried himself to sleep. His senpai consoled him when he wept, but neither spoke of the reason for the tears, and by the time they turned nine, the tears had stopped. Life with the Kagehito had become the reality, and everything that came before was a vague collection of moving images like episodes of an old television show. Mallet was the constant adult presence in their lives, and they naturally wanted to please him. The only thing that pleased Mallet was when they worked hard and excelled at their lessons, so that's what they did.

Tiger, son of a traditional, competitive man who prized status, fell easily into the name and the role that Mallet had assigned him. He took the lead in everything, making sure no one was ever late or lazy, in addition to doing everything the instructors required of him. Fiercely protective of his group, he nevertheless showed little mercy when one of them broke the rules.

Seven fell into the routine almost as easily as Tiger and became a sort of second-in-command, following the leader the way he'd followed his older brother in his crowded family home. He was used to living barracks-style with a pack of boys and helping out with household chores without being asked. Perhaps he was a bit of a complainer, but that trait was soon discouraged and rarely made an appearance.

Moonlight came from a single-parent home, his unwed mother concealing the fact with a pawn-shop ring and a story about a soldier husband who died abroad. She was an elementary school teacher who'd taught him to read and write by the time he was four, and he found himself far ahead of the rest of his crèche in the classroom. It was Moonlight the others came to when they needed help with bookwork or just a sympathetic presence when they were troubled about something. Moonlight always had something warming in a pot on the hearth, and he never made anyone feel like they were being a baby if they needed a hug.

Kyuhwan, son of two factory workers, was Ichi-Shonen, Boy One, until he was given the name Tako for being all over the place like a kite in a windy sky. He all but crackled with nervous energy, but he could take a chunk of wood or a lump of clay and turn it into a bowl, or a spoon, or any number of useful objects that actually worked.

Hwangbo, who claimed to not remember his parents, was known as Ni-Shonen, Boy Two, for almost two years, until he earned the name Kagi, Key, because he could unlock the answers to anything, whether it was how to move fire from one hearth to another or the way the vanes of a feather worked. Endlessly curious, he was always a hair's-breadth away from being punished for tardiness.

Junho, now called Smoke, grew up poor in a household where everyone worked several jobs just to keep food on the table. He was the most aloof of the group, but he was always there if his help was needed. He was less inclined to high spirits than the other boys, preferring to sit quietly and observe, but the rest of the group had learned to listen when he spoke. He'd prevented them from getting into much more trouble than they would have without him.

By design, the six boys had attributes that complemented each of the others. By chance, their personalities meshed perfectly into a seamless unit. They bonded so quickly that Mallet had already made a bet with Wall and River that all six would still be alive when their basic training ended. Privately, he suspected that this group would produce at least one champion, and when he had this thought, his eyes went to Tiger.

The boys had made it through the crucial period when most groups lost at least one member, and they'd suffered nothing worse than some bad scrapes, deep bruising, and one broken nose. Mallet didn't count colds, pulled muscles, exhaustion, or bouts of depression; those were to be expected and worked through. Kagehito learned to endure pain, were inured to discomfort of the body or mind; weakness was not acceptable and soon winnowed out. After three years on the island, the boys in Mallet's charge had been forged into something harder, and the preliminary work of shaping them for use began.

"TIGER, Moonlight, Seven, Smoke, Key, Kite." Mallet tapped each boy on the head as he walked down the line. "Today you are ten, a decade of life on Earth. You're lucky. You were chosen by the Kagehito to become more than ordinary humans. You'll be swifter, stronger, tougher, smarter. You've walked a few steps on a long, hard road, and at the end, I think you'll agree that every tear, every drop of blood and sweat was worth it."

Tiger didn't turn his head, but his gaze darted around the clearing as Mallet spoke. They'd gone into the woods many times for many reasons and were as comfortable outdoors as they were in their huts. He wasn't nervous, but he was curious, and he scouted unfamiliar territory out of habit now.

The meadow was small. The blanket of green was thin, with rocks poking through the grass here and there. Behind Mallet were the stony knees of the mountains that divided the island in half. To the birds, Tiger imagined that the island looked like the back of a dragon swimming in the sea. Moonlight touched his hand, and Tiger realized he'd been inattentive. Immediately, he focused on the sensei again.

"Until now, the mountains have been forbidden," Mallet was saying. "But today you will climb that face." He pointed up. "Tonight you'll sleep in a cave or whatever shelter seems best to you. Tomorrow you'll hunt and bring your kill back for the commander's table."

Tiger's eyes narrowed at the mention of the man who ran the military side of the fortress. Unlike the reclusive onmyoji who oversaw the school, the commander was sometimes seen striding in or out of the gate that connected the two halves of the compound. Commander Broom had no authority over anyone or anything at the school and never had contact with the novices, but he was a definite presence in their lives. Tiger was impressed by the man's self-assured bearing and the black, double-breasted suits with metal buttons that were Broom's uniform. The tailored garments and polished boots were a sharp contrast to the gray, shapeless clothing Tiger wore every day, and even at ten, Tiger could see that this was a privilege of rank.

"We'll make sure the commander eats well tomorrow evening," Tiger said.

"I know I can count on you, Tiger," Mallet said. "Collect all the bows and knives and give them to me."

"We need them to hunt, teacher," Tiger said reasonably.

"No, you don't."

Tiger bowed and turned to collect weapons from his group without further argument. He returned their questioning looks with a little shake of his head before taking the weapons to Mallet. Mallet strapped the bows together and put the arrows and knives in his knapsack.

"Be back before dusk tomorrow," Mallet said and began the walk back to the compound.

"Let's get hiking," Tiger said, starting off in the opposite direction.

Moonlight bounded after Tiger to walk at his side, and the others followed in no particular order. It was a pretty day in the country and they were boys without adult supervision for several hours. They had a grim night and grim task ahead of them, but at the moment, the sun was shining, the tuft-eared squirrels were chattering and leaping from pine to pine, and they had a mountain and permission to climb it.

They took their time and several detours in reaching the section of cliffs that sheltered a few shallow caves. Tiger threw off the mantle of leadership, and no one was scolded for straying from the group or for running down a strange lizard to show everyone else. Even pine-cone-throwing fights were winked at.

"Hey," Moonlight said as he picked a pine needle from Tiger's hair. "If we collected bunches of this, we could spread it on the floor of the cave to make it warmer."

"You want to build nests?" Tiger grinned.

"It's a good idea." Smoke walked up, shaking pine straw from his tunic. "Don't you think?"

Tiger nodded. "It's a good idea. Prickly, but good."

"And we have each other," Smoke said. "If we're all in a nest with some of the pine needles over us, we'll sleep warm tonight."

Kite heard them talking and joined the conversation. "If we can find vines, we can tie the straw into bundles and make a snug little shelter. If we can't find vines, we can unravel some thread from our tunics."

"Then let's do that," Tiger said. "Everyone start gathering pine straw and bring it to Kite."

"I need—" Kite began when Tiger interrupted him.

"There are vines on the cliff behind you."

Kite turned and began pulling strands of greenery away from the stone while the others went to gather pine straw. Tiger didn't give instructions, but worked alongside the others, leaving Kite to act as foreman. By the time the boys were starting to feel hungry, they had built a hut in the back of the deepest cave and hauled in wood to build a fire later. After drinking from their leather canteens, they broke into pairs to hunt for dinner.

"Look! *Pyogo!*" Moonlight looked back at Tiger with a beaming smile.

"Mushrooms," Tiger said firmly as he took the shiitake from Moonlight's hand. "Nice ones too." He smiled. "Great find."

Moonlight had already untied the cloth sash around his waist and formed a sling from it. Kneeling, he picked the mushrooms, laying them carefully in the improvised shopping bag. "There are enough for everyone, and we can take some back to school with us."

"That's a good idea." Tiger knelt beside Moonlight and helped pull the fleshy fungus from the rotting wood of the fallen tree trunk. "Moonlight, you have to be more careful. You still use Korean words when you get excited."

"I'll be more careful," Moonlight said without dissent. "I wonder how the others are doing."

Tiger shrugged. "We'll know when we see them."

Moonlight turned to look at Tiger, the sunlight dazzling his eyes for a moment. "Don't you ever wonder about anything? Like what we're going to be doing in a couple of years? Or where we'd be if we hadn't been kidnapped?"

"Not really. I just want to deal with what's happening right now."

"Deal with this," Kite shouted as he leaped from behind a tree trunk.

Tiger dodged Kite's lunge easily, grabbed the back of the other boy's tunic as he hurtled past, and swung him around. When Tiger let go, Kite went flying, tumbling across the mossy ground.

"I heard you sneaking up on us," Tiger said when the would-be attacker rolled to a stop. "Where's Key?"

"He's already back at the cave. Probably starting a fire and waiting for me to clean the fish."

Moonlight looked up as a tiny piece of bark fell onto his shoulder. Without thinking twice, he threw himself to the side, cradling the mushrooms with one arm. Key landed in the spot Moonlight had just vacated, bending his knees to absorb the impact of jumping from a branch almost four meters above the ground. He launched himself after Moonlight, but an arm around his neck yanked him back.

"Join your noisy senpai," Tiger said as he flung Key down beside Kite.

"Sorry," Kite said to Key. "I'm still no good at stealth."

"Keep practicing," Tiger advised. "By the way, Key, how did you get up in that tree without me noticing?"

Key unwound a lasso of handmade rope from around his waist and held it up.

Tiger raised his eyebrows. "Later you can show us all how you did it. Moonlight found mushrooms. Did you really catch some fish?"

Key held up the lasso again.

Tiger cocked his head at the other boy in an incredulous expression, and Key couldn't keep a straight face.

"We made spears from a couple of saplings," Kite said.

"We're not supposed to use weapons," Tiger said, turning as Smoke and Seven walked up.

"We could hear you for miles," Seven said.

Smoke smiled at his kohai. "Seven's right. We tracked you down with our eyes closed." He turned to Tiger. "And I think the teacher meant we couldn't use weapons to kill whatever we bring back for the commander's table."

"You have a gift for making words say what you want them to," Tiger answered. "I don't. If teacher asks me if we used weapons, I won't be able to lie to him."

Moonlight put a hand on Tiger's forearm. "It's done," he said. "No point in talking about it." He looked around at the others. "I think everyone understands how serious this could be."

Smoke nodded. "But I really do believe teacher was only talking about tomorrow's hunt."

"He took our bows and knives," Tiger said.

"But he knows we can make weapons," Kite spoke up.

Tiger thought for a few moments before he replied. "All of those things are true." He looked at Smoke. "You must be right." He turned his head to meet Moonlight's eyes. When Moonlight nodded, Tiger spoke again. "What did you do with the spears?" he asked Key.

"They're part of a tripod that our catch is hanging from."

"You and Kite make three more. We might need them tonight. Teacher says there are still boars on the island, even if we haven't seen them."

"If a boar comes to visit, invite him to dinner," Moonlight said. "I'd love some crispy pork."

Smoke groaned. "Don't talk about food. I'm starving."

"Let's go back to the cave and have something to eat," Tiger said as he extended a hand to Moonlight.

With Tiger's help, Moonlight stood and checked to see that the mushrooms hadn't been crushed. "As soon as we get a fire going, I can roast these, and the fish won't take long to cook." He glanced at Smoke and Seven. "Anything to add?"

Smoke reached into the front of his tunic and pulled out some pale roots that had been scraped clean of dirt.

Moonlight's eyes glowed as he snatched the wild daikon from Smoke's hand. His friends grimaced and made disgusted noises when he took a big bite of the crisp radish.

"I don't know how you can eat it that way," Smoke said.

"It's good."

"I know it *tastes* good, but I can't stand the way it squeaks on my teeth when it's raw."

"Me either." Kite shuddered as the others nodded agreement.

"Then you must not really be starving," Moonlight said before taking another bite.

"You sound just like a mom," Key teased.

Moonlight stopped chewing as he stared at Key. He swallowed and bits of radish stuck in his throat. A coughing fit bent him double and Tiger patted him on the back, helping dislodge the radish.

"Nicely done," Tiger said, glaring at Key.

"I wasn't thinking," Key said. "Sorry, Moon."

Moonlight looked up with watering eyes. "It's okay. I know you didn't say it to make me feel bad."

"Are you okay?" Tiger asked.

Moonlight nodded. "It just came out of the blue. I haven't thought about my mom for a while, and when Key said that, it hit me really hard." He met Tiger's eyes. "I've completely given up on the hope that my mom is going to come and get me some day."

"I'm sorry." Tiger paused before he spoke again. "But I think it's better if you *don't* hope that."

"Me too," Smoke agreed unexpectedly. "The most important thing is to make it through this training alive. We need to concentrate on that instead of trusting that we'll be rescued."

"Thanks," Tiger said. "I really wish I could explain things the way you do." He put an arm around Moonlight's shoulders. "You ready to go back to camp?" he asked.

When Moonlight nodded, Tiger led them back to the cave, with Smoke acting as point scout. By the time they arrived, Smoke had built a fire and used his flint and steel to ignite it. Moonlight sent Seven to gather large leaves and wet them in the stream. Wrapping the fish, mushrooms, and chunks of radish in the leaves, Moonlight placed them directly on the embers to cook. After they ate, Seven showed them how he'd used the rock-weighted lasso to swing from tree to tree. When it got dark, they banked the fire and went into the pine straw hut. Settling down like puppies in a basket, they fell asleep.

Morning arrived, chill and misty, and the boys sat around the fire until the fog dissipated. Leaving the spears in the cave, they moved higher up the slope as quietly as possible. Above the tree line, they found an area with small patches of grass growing from cracks in the rock. Grazing on the damp green was a small flock of wild goats.

A goat or two would make a fine offering for the commander's table, but without cover, there was no way to get close to them. They would have to separate at a safe distance and encircle the flock. When the goats got wind of them, odds were that one of the animals would run toward one of them. Silently, they crept away, up and down slope, leaving Tiger in place to give the signal. Tiger lay down on his belly and watched the herd, counting off the seconds in his head. When he reckoned everyone had had time to get into place, he stood. All around the perimeter of the herd, the other five popped up, one at a time.

Unnerved by the appearance of danger on multiple fronts, the goats milled about for a few moments before the first one bounded off toward the pines. Another followed, but the rest took off in different directions. The boys began to move toward the animals nearest them, trying to intercept their flight. Seven and Kite's quarry eluded them, and they took off in pursuit. Smoke flung himself at a zigzagging goat and bowled it over. As he got to his feet, Key ran to help him corral the dazed animal. Tiger's target evaded him by making a series of suicidal leaps up the cliff face, but Tiger's attention had been snared by motion along the top of the ridge. Bleating in panic, a kid ran blindly along the edge of the cliff.

Directly behind the frightened animal was Moonlight. Tiger didn't stop to think. He scaled the rock in front of him, using the same route as the goat that got away. Reaching the top, he shouted at Moonlight to let the kid go.

Moonlight was taking insane chances as he tried desperately to herd the small animal away from the precipice. Arms outspread, darting and dodging without looking down to check his footing, he danced with death.

"No!" Tiger shouted as the terrified little goat ran directly at Moonlight.

Moonlight pivoted on one foot and reached down to grab at the kid.

"Let it go!" Tiger screamed.

Moonlight's muscles jerked in response to the order from his senpai, but he dove for the goat anyway. He got his hand around a hind leg and held fast as the small creature bounded off the cliff. Anticipating the weight of the falling goat, he dropped to his belly and groped for something to hang on to. He grunted as his arm was nearly jerked out of the socket, and then he was sliding over the edge. Digging in with his toes, he willed himself to be heavier as he was dragged inexorably downward. At the end of his arm, the flailing goat added lightning bolts of pain to the fear that was jamming his thought processes.

"Umma," Moonlight whispered as he lost the battle with gravity. As he went over, he clutched desperately at the rocks that scraped his skin.

Tiger threw himself forward, landing belly-down at the cliff edge, reaching frantically for Moonlight. He caught hold of Moonlight's wrist just as Moonlight's fingers slipped. Moonlight fell another foot and stopped with a shoulder-wrenching jolt. Tiger slid forward, his head and chest hanging over the edge, his hand locked on Moonlight's wrist.

"Let the goat go," Tiger said in a strained voice.

Moonlight's eyes were fastened on Tiger's, but he didn't answer, and he didn't let go of the kid.

"If you don't let it go, it's going to pull both of us off."

Tears shimmered in Moonlight's eyes and ran down his cheeks. A calm voice in his head put forth the opinion that it would be better if he and Tiger were dead and out of the Kagehito prison. For just a moment, Moonlight considered yanking Tiger off the cliff with him, and then his hand opened and the kid fell to the rocks below.

"Give me your hand," Tiger said, a drop of sweat falling from his chin to splash on Moonlight's forehead.

Moonlight reached up, his shoulder screaming in agony. "I can't," he panted.

"You have to."

"I hurt my shoulder. It won't work right."

"Make it work." Tiger stretched his free hand as far down as it would go. "Come on!"

Moonlight tried until every muscle was trembling and coated with sweat.

With horror, Tiger felt Moonlight's wrist start to slide in his grip. "Moon, you have to do this. You can't die and leave me alone here."

Tiger inched a little farther forward and pulled with all his remaining strength. Moonlight ignored the excruciating pain in his shoulder and stretched until his fingertips brushed Tiger's. Tiger locked the tips of his fingers with Moonlight's and raised his kohai a little higher, but he was almost out of power.

"You're slipping," Moonlight said.

"Shut up." Tiger focused all his will on crawling backward.

"Let me go."

"I can't."

"No one's going anywhere," Smoke said as he took hold of Tiger's legs and anchored him.

"Smoke," Tiger said breathlessly, "I can't hold him."

Smoke didn't take the time to reply. Lying down on Tiger's back, he moved forward until he could see Moonlight. He wrapped his hand around Tiger's forearm and pulled. Moonlight came up another few inches, far enough for Smoke to get hold of his wrist. Slowly, awkwardly, Tiger and Smoke hauled Moonlight up in tiny increments. By the time Moonlight was back on the top of the cliff, all three were drained, unable to do anything but lie in limp heaps on the stony ground. They were still lying there when Key found them.

"I got a goat, if anyone's interested," Key said. When no one spoke, he continued. "No thanks to you, Smoke. You took off and left me with that hell-beast. I got kicked in the head and—" He stopped and looked at each of the others in turn, at the red faces and the mouths gasping for air. "What have you been doing up here?"

"Moonlight got a goat too," Tiger wheezed as he sat up.

Key looked around. "Where is it?"

Moonlight went on hands and knees to the edge of the cliff and looked down. The kid lay among the red-splashed rocks, limbs splayed, neck turned at an impossible angle. Moonlight stared at the small corpse for a long moment before turning away. Scrubbing his hands over his face, he got shakily to his feet.

"Thank you," Moonlight said to Tiger and Smoke before he began moving away along the top of the cliff.

"Where are you going?" Tiger called out as Smoke told Key what had happened.

"I'm going down to fetch my kill."

"You don't have to do that. We have Key's goat."

"And leave it to rot?"

"Something will eat it."

Moonlight shook his head. "I'm going to get it."

"Why risk your neck again?"

Moonlight didn't answer, and Tiger hurried after him. After a hair-raising scramble to the bottom of the gorge, Moonlight led the way to the carcass. Tiger looked up and saw Smoke and Key looking down.

"Go on to camp," Tiger told them. "We'll meet you and go back to the school from there." When Smoke and Key's heads disappeared, Tiger turned to Moonlight. "What do you want to do?" he asked.

"I have the urge to bury him, but I know how stupid that is." Moonlight took a deep, halting breath. "He wasn't a person or anything. Just a dumb goat, but—" His voice broke and he started crying again. "He was just so frightened. Imagine it. He was playing in the sunshine, and then we came along. The worst day of his life." Tears overflowed his eyes again.

"Why'd you chase him then?"

"I wanted to save him. I wanted to make it right somehow."

Tiger put his arms around Moonlight and hugged him. Moonlight leaned into the hug, resting his wet cheek on Tiger's shoulder.

"You have to stop thinking like that," Tiger said. "The goats are food. Food makes us strong. You want to be strong, don't you?"

Moonlight nodded, his hair tickling Tiger's neck. "When I'm strong enough, I'll leave this place."

Tiger sighed. "I really wish you wouldn't say things like that."

"But I always tell you the truth."

Tiger sighed again. "Maybe you could lie once in a while. I'm kidding," he said when Moonlight looked up at him in reproach. "I just don't want anything to happen to you."

"I don't want anything to happen to me either, but I can't help how I feel."

"I know. I just wish you were better at pretending."

"My umma says...." Moonlight's voice trailed off. "It's just better to be yourself," he finished.

Tiger held Moonlight tighter. "You go ahead and be yourself. I'll protect you."

"Because you're the best senpai in the world." Moonlight made himself let go of Tiger. The comfort he got from physical closeness was hard to give up.

"What do you want to do with the goat?" Tiger asked again.

"Let's take it back with us. When we get our knives back, I'll make jerky or something."

Tiger patted Moonlight's shoulder approvingly and helped hoist the dead kid into Moonlight's arms. They met the others at the cave and ate more roasted mushrooms before hiking back to the compound, carrying the carcasses.

"I'm really sorry I hurt your feelings," Seven said to Moonlight on one of their rest stops.

"You already said you were sorry."

"It's been bugging me though." Seven moved a little closer to Moonlight. "It bothers me that I forgot my family so easily."

"No, you're just smarter than me," Moonlight said. "Tiger's right. The sooner we forget everything else and concentrate on surviving our training, the better it'll be for us."

"And then what?" Key stopped blatantly eavesdropping and joined the conversation. "What do they want us to do after we're trained?"

"Don't you ever listen in class?" Smoke interjected. "We're the future keepers of the balance."

"That's what the teachers say," Moonlight conceded. "They tell us that we're going to keep bad people from having too much power." He paused. "It sounds a lot grander when they say it."

Smoke smiled at Moonlight. "It's kind of like a comic book, isn't it?"

Moonlight smiled back. "Like a superhero-ninja cartoon."

"What's wrong with that?" Tiger said, sitting down next to Moonlight. "Sounds like a great job to me."

"You'd be a great superhero," Moonlight said. "I'm not sure I'd be as good at it."

"You can be my sidekick if you want," Tiger said. "All superheroes have sidekicks."

"Tiger and Moonlight," Moonlight murmured. "It doesn't really work together, does it?"

"You can pick another name when we start fighting evil. We could be Tiger and... Dragon!"

Moonlight giggled and the conversation grew lively as the boys speculated on the names under which they would do battle with the forces of evil. They were laughing as they resumed their journey, taking turns carrying the goats and staging mock fights between fictional arch-enemies. Moonlight was quiet, but everyone assumed he was still shaken by his fall from the cliff—an incident that hadn't been mentioned since Smoke's brief explanation of the event. It was not their way to dwell on unpleasant subjects, though everyone cast at least one look of hero worship in Tiger's direction before they sighted the walls of the fortress.

Mallet was waiting in the compound mess when the boys showed up to ask Wall for help with dressing out the goats. The sensei handed his students their knives and told them their bows and quivers were in their huts. Tiger heard the tone of dismissal and led his troop away. Before they left the kitchen, Wall called out, thanking them for the meat. Mallet rolled his eyes at Wall, as the boys continued on their way with heads held higher and more energy in their steps.

The next morning, Mallet brought the boys some of the roasted meat and told them that the commander had enjoyed his dinner. He told them that they'd done well, especially Moonlight, since he frankly didn't think Moonlight was capable of killing with his bare hands. He told them they were progressing well, but they needed to work even harder in the future. He didn't tell them that they were the fastest learners he'd ever worked with, or that the onmyoji himself was keeping a close eye on them. He'd been doing this too long to make the mistake of clouding the purity of their focus at this point.

Mallet could see that the latest test had had a profound effect on Moonlight, but he wasn't surprised. Ending a life when you could

feel it warm between your hands was no easy thing. Most humans
had to be driven to extremes to commit such an act, an act that the
Kagehito expected their operatives to perform routinely. It wasn't
always possible to bring a weapon into the presence of a target. Nor
was it always possible for the operative to escape with his life, but
that was something else that Mallet didn't tell the boys. He was
pleased with his pack of wolf cubs, and predicted that this crèche
would add extra luster to his reputation as a trainer.

Tiger showed definite signs of becoming the perfect field
agent. He had all the right traits: razor-sharp reflexes, great physical
strength, superb hand/eye coordination, and a talent for adaptability
that extended to his sense of morality. All Mallet had to do was keep
nudging the boy down the paths that would form his adult psyche
into a configuration streamlined for the Kagehito's purposes.

For the rest of the novice stage of training, Mallet continued to
work tirelessly, and worked his charges just as tirelessly. The days
blurred together in a nonstop regime of exercise, weapon practice,
and classroom lessons. Seasons rolled by, rounding into smooth
years unmarked by birthdays or holidays. The boys grew stronger,
swifter, and harder, and also taller and broader, without noticing the
changes. Three years on, the twelve-year-olds were a solid unit, each
automatically doing what he was best suited to and making up for
the others' weak spots without being told. They were friends,
comrades, brothers-in-arms.

It was time they started learning true self-reliance.

 # Part Two

MOONLIGHT dipped the wooden bucket in the brook, filling it with clear, cold water. Before he started back to the hut, he took a moment to turn his face to the sun and breathe deeply of the crisp, piney air. Despite the chill of the dawn breeze, the twelve-year-old wore nothing other than a thigh-length tunic belted at the waist. The tunic and a wool cloak were the only garments he had, but he didn't need anything else. He was inured to extremes of heat and cold by seven years of exposure to both. He could go for days with nothing to fill his belly but water. Pain was just a fact to him, a signal that his body was damaged and needed seeing to. He was strong, quick, and clever, and no more self-conscious than the wild animals in the forest. After scooping up a mouthful of the water, he hoisted the pail and carried it home.

As Moonlight looked in the door of the hut, he saw that Tiger had started a fire in the crude hearth. In fact, the other boy was still squatting on the dirt floor, feeding straw and twigs to the greedy flames.

A smile crept over Moonlight's face as he moved stealthily across the floor. Lifting the bucket, he slopped some of the cold water on Tiger's neck. Tiger leaped up with a shout, making a grab for Moonlight. Laughing, Moonlight dropped the pail and skipped backward. Nimble as mountain goats, the young men dodged, spun, and lunged as Tiger pursued Moonlight. Tiger made a lucky swerve and caught Moonlight with an arm around Moonlight's waist.

Pivoting on his heel, Tiger swung Moonlight around and let go. As Moonlight reeled, flailing for balance, Tiger pounced, tackling his kohai and taking them both to the ground. They rolled across the floor until they hit the wall, with Tiger topmost.

"Now you pay." Tiger grinned as he pinned Moonlight's wrists, letting his full weight rest on the other boy.

Moonlight bucked, but couldn't dislodge his senpai. "All right. You win."

"You're giving up this easily?" Tiger's face revealed his shock.

"Just let me up." Moonlight abruptly arched his back, trying to take Tiger by surprise.

Tiger subdued Moonlight again. "I knew you weren't done," he said with delight. "Give me a real fight."

"Let me up!"

"Make me."

Moonlight bit his bottom lip. If he didn't get away right now, Tiger was going to discover what Moonlight was trying so hard to hide. "Get off!" he said in frustration. "Today isn't just another day, you ass. We need to get ready."

"I didn't forget." Tiger grinned at Moonlight, clearly enjoying his friend's annoyance. "Your face is all red," he said.

"I said get *off*!"

"I said make me."

Moonlight gritted his teeth as a bubble of rage burst in his brain. Calling up every reserve of strength, he threw Tiger off and scrambled to his feet. Quickly, he turned away so Tiger wouldn't see the bulge at his crotch.

More and more often when they wrestled, Moonlight would get hard, and it worried him. He knew the rules; the sensei had listed them when he'd explained about sex. Masturbation was normal and healthy, and Moonlight wasn't supposed to feel odd about doing it. He didn't; in fact, the boys often jerked off together. However, it was strictly forbidden for trainees to use one another for sexual pleasure. So the way Moonlight felt when he and Tiger touched frightened him as much as it excited him. Mallet had a way of seeing into the minds of his students, and Moonlight was afraid he'd be punished for the thoughts he'd been having.

"Calm down, kohai," Tiger said as he got up. "What's up your butt this morning?"

"You know how important today is!"

Tiger picked up the bucket and poured some of the water into a pot. "You need your tea," he said. "Why don't you braid your hair while I make some?"

Moonlight took several calming breaths, letting the tension drain away. "Some senpai you are. Look at you waiting on me."

Tiger chuckled. "I'm a disgrace."

Moonlight snorted. "You're the best of us," he said as he divided his long hair into three equal parts. He wove the glossy strands into a thick rope as he watched Tiger working at the hearth. "You do let your kohai get away with being lazy though."

Tiger chuckled again. On their first day here, Mallet had explained that the senpai protected his kohai and the kohai took care of his senpai. Mallet had detailed the duties of each, but Tiger couldn't bear to watch Moonlight struggling to carry the water bucket by himself, and it didn't seem fair that Moonlight was expected to do all the washing, cooking, and maintenance of the hut. Moonlight gladly accepted Tiger's help and, in return, hunted with Tiger for meat to add to the vegetables and grain they had learned to grow. The instructors didn't interfere; each pair learned something different from their time in the symbiotic arrangement. So Tiger and Moonlight were allowed to find their own balance, and they shared duties on an alternating basis rather than dividing them.

"Are we eating sometime this morning?" Tiger asked, adding, "I made the fire."

Moonlight tied a leather lace around the end of his braid and tossed it over his shoulder. "Are you going to let me near this fire you made?" he retorted.

Tiger moved to stand in the doorway, where he could pretend to watch the road while he stole glances over his shoulder. Lately, he found himself watching Moonlight as if he expected the other boy to do something unprecedented. If Moonlight laughed, Tiger's heart leaped. If Moonlight was angry, Tiger's heart shrank. If Moonlight was sad, Tiger's heart ached. It had been like this almost since the beginning, but in the last months, Moonlight was all Tiger could think about; he viewed everything in light of how it related to his kohai. Tiger told himself to be strong, to ignore the distraction as the sensei had instructed, but he just couldn't resist. Moonlight drew his eyes, and before long he found himself having punishable thoughts. With an effort that was fast becoming a habit, he pushed away the vague imaginings of what might happen if he touched Moonlight in certain places.

Turning his thoughts to the ceremony ahead, he reviewed what he knew. Today the half dozen boys who'd arrived together seven years ago would leave novice class behind and become initiates. Today they would find out what discipline they would study for the next five years. Today the onmyoji would look at them and assign the roles they would fill for the rest of their lives. Today they would be claimed by their clans. Tiger was excited, but more than a little nervous about being face to face with the onmyoji. Magic made him uncomfortable.

"Hey, Tiger!" Moonlight called. "This porridge isn't going to eat itself."

Tiger smiled as he went back inside to take the clay bowl from Moonlight's hands. Bringing it to his lips, he tilted it to let the warm, honey-sweetened mush slide into his mouth. Gulping and swallowing continuously, he finished his breakfast almost before Moonlight finished filling another bowl.

"Tiger! Moonlight!" Smoke called from the doorway.

"Come in, Smoke," Moonlight called back.

The gangly boy shook his head, dark rippling hair brushing his shoulders. "Me and Seven are going to the square early to see if we can see the onmyoji before the ceremony."

"Why?" Tiger asked as he cleaned his bowl in the bucket.

"Aren't you curious? He runs our lives, and we haven't had one sight of him in seven years."

"That's not really surprising, considering we're forbidden to enter the area where he lives," Moonlight said.

"What do you think he's been doing all by himself in that tower?" Smoke asked.

Tiger rolled his eyes. "I don't think he's been up there for the entire seven years. I'm sure he has his own way on and off the island."

Smoke grinned. "Like what? A dragon?"

"Dragons aren't real." Tiger gave the other boy a suspicious look.

Smoke had earned the name Smoke because he was so hard to get hold of in the combat ring, but he was elusive in many other ways. It was hard to tell when Smoke was being serious and when he was mocking you. Limber as a sapling, with the rangy frame of an adolescent cat and a dauntingly sharp brain, Smoke could shred an opponent physically or verbally, and though he was a comrade, Tiger had learned to be wary of him.

"Oh dear, is Tiger grumpy again this morning?" Smoke asked.

Moonlight shrugged. "He's Tiger," he said.

"Don't tease me," Tiger said. "You know I can't keep up when you two start joking around."

"I have to go anyway," Smoke said, smiling impishly. "I'll bet the onmyoji is at least a hundred years old, with a beard that looks like spider webs."

Moonlight laughed. "And he walks all bent over with a cane that looks like a branch he picked up off the ground."

"You're both disrespectful," Tiger told them.

Smoke grinned at Moonlight. "See you in the square then," he said.

"We're right behind you," Tiger said as he took Moonlight's empty bowl and dropped it in the bucket.

Smoke and Moonlight bowed to each other, bumping heads in their customary good-bye, and Tiger was surprised by a stinging flash of resentment. He bent his head over the bowl he was cleaning, afraid Smoke would see his anger in his eyes. Guilt swept over him. Smoke was a brother, one of a handful of people that Tiger trusted; he had no reason to be mad at Smoke for a brotherly gesture he'd seen many times. Still, he didn't like the idea of anyone but him touching Moonlight.

When Smoke left to catch up with Seven, Tiger pushed the bucket aside and drew his knife. "Trim my hair for me?" he asked.

"Why don't you just let it grow?" Moonlight asked, as he always did when Tiger requested this favor.

"It gets in my way," Tiger answered, as usual.

"Turn around then." Moonlight ran his fingers through Tiger's thick mane of autumn-brown hair. "So many snarls," he chided. "You should use the comb I made you."

"I do."

"More than once a year."

Tiger sat still as Moonlight tugged on locks of his hair and ran the razor-sharp blade over them. Moonlight started to brush the clinging wisps off Tiger's shoulders, but he stopped abruptly when his fingertips began to tingle… along with his groin. He stepped back and told Tiger to put his tunic on.

"Thanks," Tiger said, brushing away the rest of the hair himself. He pulled his tunic over his head and tied the knotted cord belt, oblivious to the way Moonlight's eyes lingered on his naked skin before it was covered. "I'm ready," he said.

"Race you to the square!" Moonlight shouted as he broke into a run.

Tiger was fast, but Moonlight was faster, as swift as the deer they sometimes hunted. Long, smooth legs flashing under the short tunic, Moonlight reached the square's western arch several strides ahead of Tiger and stopped to wait. Neither boy was anywhere near winded, but they'd learned, to their pain, to never enter a situation without scouting it first.

"Look at Smoke," Tiger said in Moonlight's ear.

Moonlight's gaze went to Smoke, who was standing with the other three members of Mallet's crèche. Smoke kept rising on his toes and swiveling his head around to search the courtyard. "He isn't usually so obvious when he's interested in something," Moonlight said.

"He's really curious about the onmyoji." Tiger shook his head. "For such a smart guy, Smoke can be really foolish sometimes."

"He's not foolish. He's just…. He cares about different things than you do," Moonlight said.

"So do you, but you stay out of trouble."

"That's because I have a good senpai." Moonlight smiled over his shoulder at Tiger.

Tiger smiled back, but his eyes were on the other boys. "Have you ever wondered why there are only six of us?"

Moonlight shrugged. "I'm just glad we're all still here. How many stories have the sensei told us about boys who died in the first year of training?"

Tiger ignored the comment. "Maybe there are other schools on other islands."

"I think you're right. We can't be the only ones. The Kagehito must have a lot of power and wealth. Like you said, there are only six of us, but there are always at least fifty other people in our area, counting the teachers and the commander's men, and then there's the onmyoji's household. We don't grow enough food to—"

Whatever Moonlight was going to say next was lost as Mallet entered the square and barked a command. The boys were already lining up in the order that had been established their first day on the island. All talking ceased as they faced front, eyes staring straight ahead, awaiting their master's bidding. They drew up a little taller when they heard the sound of boots on the stone pavement. Only those with high rank wore shoes here; all others went barefoot except in the dead of winter. It was a tribute to their training that the novices' heads didn't move a fraction as a small group marched into the courtyard and stopped behind Mallet.

Two guards flanked the commander and the onmyoji, who was dressed in clothing from the distant past. His long robe of muted rose brocade was belted with a sash hung with hundreds of silver amulets, which chimed when he moved. He wore a shoulder-length head covering of ivory silk, making it impossible to see what he looked like, but his bearing was that of a great emperor from ancient times.

"Slaves of the Kagehito, I am Aki, known as Autumn among the clans, and I am your judge." The onmyoji's voice was as beautifully modulated as a well-played woodwind. "You have completed the first round of lessons and have all been deemed worthy to move on to further training. Today you will learn your first destiny, the fate your body is matched with. Your soul has a destiny also, but that inner calling will not be decided today. It reveals itself in its own time, and when it occurs, you will not mistake it for anything else.

"Today you will learn which clan will claim your physical being. Your teachers have told you that warriors belong to the Tetsuzoku, the Iron Tribe, and they are the weapons of the Shadow People. Those who are quick-witted and persuasive of tongue go to Hanezoku, the Feather Tribe, to be trained as our representatives in the outer world. Those who are clever with their minds and hands become members of the Saruzoku, the Monkey Tribe. Those chosen for Denkouzoku, the Lightning Tribe, have the greatest honor for they become teachers and illuminate the darkness." Autumn paused. "Once in a generation, a slave might be judged apt for the Ryuzoku, the Dragon Tribe, the guides of Kagehito destiny, but this is almost always a second calling." The magician's gaze was caught by Moonlight's profile. "Almost as rare is an assignment to the Barazoku, the Rose Tribe."

The words drifted from the onmyoji's mouth like incense on a warm breeze, and Moonlight looked at the wizard as though his name had been called.

"Turn your head to the side, slave," Autumn commanded, pointing at Moonlight.

Moonlight cringed inside. His broken nose had healed well but had a higher bridge than was typical of the people around him, and he liked to blame this difference on the injury. He knew he was odd-looking, but he really hoped the onmyoji wasn't going to call attention to his beak in front of everyone.

"Walk to the end of the line and come back to me," Autumn ordered. "As you approach, smile as though you are pleased to see me."

Moonlight bowed and stepped out of the line. Taking a calming breath, he pretended he was on his way to the brook for a splash. He didn't dare glance at his friends for fear the urge to laugh would infect him and he'd be humiliated. Despite his nervousness, walking naturally wasn't too hard until he turned and started back. He saw the onmyoji watching him and froze between one step and the next, staring at the wizard with a bewildered look on his face.

The onmyoji made a regal gesture, beckoning to Moonlight to come closer.

Conditioned to obey a superior automatically, Moonlight started forward again. Before he could think about it, his gaze flicked sideways to Tiger. Tiger gave a tiny nod of encouragement as Moonlight's eyes returned to Autumn. Moonlight's lips curved upward in the shy smile that Tiger's approval always provoked.

"Beautiful," the onmyoji said. "Come here, child."

Moonlight stopped in front of Autumn and bowed. Autumn cupped Moonlight's chin on his palm and tilted Moonlight's head up. For several long moments, the onmyoji stood this way, seeming to fall into a trance.

"You look like no one else I have ever seen," Autumn said dreamily. "Your beauty is your own, and you draw the eye the way the moon draws the tide."

Moonlight swallowed hard. The onmyoji's words seemed like praise, but the tone was eerie. Autumn's voice sounded as though it came from far away, like the sound of the ocean in a shell.

"You will go to the Rose Tribe because, like the rose, you delight all the senses."

Moonlight's eyes met Autumn's again as the onmyoji took a step back. In the boy's gaze was a question... in the wizard's, a mystery.

Mallet cleared his throat and signaled to Moonlight to get back into line. Moonlight bowed and stepped back, keeping his eyes on the ground. The onmyoji put his hand on top Moonlight's head briefly, and then moved on to the next boy.

Tiger stood at attention, none of his confusion over Moonlight's assignment showing in his resolute gaze. He had no doubts about which tribe he belonged to; he was only waiting to have it confirmed. However, he was disturbed that he and Moonlight hadn't been chosen together. For seven years, they'd done everything as a team, been together constantly, both awake and asleep. How could they be assigned to different clans?

"Tetsuzoku," the onmyoji said, clapping a hand to Tiger's shoulder. "You are an Iron Tribe initiate now. Some day you may be a weapon in the hand of the Kagehito."

Tiger bowed as Autumn turned his attention to the next in line.

Smoke clenched his teeth and resisted the urge to drop his eyes when the onmyoji stopped in front of him.

Autumn looked deep into the boy's ink-dark gaze for a long time. "Feather Tribe," he said at last. "One of the hardest placements I've ever made. You would do well in any clan, Smoke, but you will best serve the Kagehito as Hanezoku."

The onmyoji moved on, placing Seven with the Tetsuzoku, Kite with the Saruzoku, and Key with the Denkouzoku. There was no ceremony, no fanfare; Autumn made his choices, and then left the courtyard with his escort.

"Don't just stand there with your foolish faces hanging out," Mallet said, a bit miffed the onmyoji had paid so little attention to Tiger. "If you hurry, you won't be late for your first classes as initiates."

Tiger bowed and waited for Mallet to nod at him. "We don't have to work in the fields this morning?"

"No. That job falls to someone else now. Your tasks will be explained to you by your new instructors." Mallet stared at each boy in turn. "You take with you all I have taught you. Don't embarrass me." Putting a hand on Kite's shoulder, Mallet gave directions and sent him off. Next went Key, and then Smoke. Mallet gazed at Moonlight for a long moment, giving the boy's shoulder a squeeze before letting go. "You're the first of my students to be selected for the Rose Tribe," he said. "As you train, remember that all you learn has a purpose and that your purpose is honorable. Now go."

Moonlight obediently trotted off to find his new teacher, but glanced back once before he turned the corner of the armory building. His gaze sought Tiger, and their eyes met. Another step and Moonlight was out of sight.

"And you unfortunates have another five years with me," Mallet said to Tiger and Seven. "Wall, River, and I will continue your weapons and classroom training. What is it, Tiger?"

Tiger straightened from his bow. "Will Moonlight's classes be over by dinnertime?"

"It doesn't matter. You'll be eating with the other Tetsuzoku from now on."

"So I won't see him until bedtime?"

"You won't see him for five years, *if* you ever see him again. That part of your life is over."

Tiger's face didn't change, but his heart dropped straight through the ground under his feet, through the molten core of the planet, and plummeted into the freezing void of outer space. This couldn't be happening. It couldn't be true that he would never see Moonlight again. He hadn't even said good-bye.

"Do you have any more questions?" Mallet asked.

Tiger shook his head, numb with disbelief, unable to imagine life without Moonlight. When Mallet began to walk, Tiger automatically fell in behind him. Once again, his life had been severed into two pieces without warning. And this time, he didn't have his companion to make it bearable.

"ATTENTION!" Mallet shouted as he walked into the combat ring.

Tiger and Seven ceased their conversation and faced their sensei.

"This morning we will decide which of you is granted warrior status and which of you will do the warrior's menial chores." Mallet held out two wooden staffs and waited until Tiger and Seven took them. "When I give the signal, you will fight until one of you can fight no longer. The one still standing will be given the privileges of a Kagehito soldier. The loser will serve him as you undergo the next phase of training."

Tiger and Seven exchanged a glance.

"I hope you're a good cook," Tiger said.

Seven bared his teeth in a fierce grin.

"Begin!" Mallet said sharply.

For almost fifteen minutes, the only sounds in the courtyard were the rapping of wood against wood, the thudding of wood against flesh, and the grunts, growls, and panting breath of the combatants. Both young men were battered and bloodied, with busted knuckles, skulls, and staffs, streaming with sweat and staggering with exhaustion, but neither would give up. They'd been fighting barehanded since breaking their cudgels, fists sliding on slick flesh, unable to land a knockout blow.

"It looks as though you'll both be servants," Mallet called out.

Blowing like winded horses, the two young men locked eyes and fought with renewed vigor for a few seconds. When the flurry of strikes ended, they hit the ground, with Seven topmost. Tiger reached up, grabbed a double handful of Seven's hair, and pulled down. At the same time, he brought his head up and smashed his forehead into Seven's face. Blood began to pour from Seven's broken nose as he fell sideways. Tiger twisted in the dust and slammed his fist into Seven's jaw. Seven brought an arm up to block the next blow, and Mallet called a halt.

"Tiger is the winner," the sensei said as he knelt next to Seven.

While tending the injuries of both his students, Mallet continued the day's lesson. "I needed to see how far you would go to win honor, and you didn't disappoint me. You fought until the end," he said, wrapping Tiger's broken fingers with tape. "And so you are both accorded the status of warriors-in-training."

"Yes!" Seven exulted under his breath as he held a compress to his nose.

"You'll have to fight to keep it," Mallet said. "Now that you are warriors, you'll fight every day for the privilege of rank, against one another and against initiates from other Iron clans." The sensei handed each young man a cup of herbal tea. "Drink it down," he said, unnecessarily—both warriors had already swallowed the bitter liquid.

"Why does something that's good for us have to taste so bad?" Seven wondered.

"If it was easy, everyone could do it," Tiger quoted one of Mallet's favorite sayings.

Mallet hid his proud smile. Tiger and Seven obeyed orders without question, made light of physical pain, and took pride in their accomplishments. They were also tough, strong, and ruthless in battle. Mallet didn't anticipate them losing many challenge matches, as individuals or as a pair. He looked forward to the grudging praise of other trainers. In theory, there was no rivalry in the ranks of the Shadow; all Kagehito worked selflessly to achieve a greater good. However, in practice, it was a proven fact that competition sharpens skill, and Kagehito were still human after all.

TIGER stood perfectly still, though every nerve was humming with anticipation, every muscle tense with readiness for action, and every sense so keenly honed that he was practically vibrating on a submolecular level. He could see nothing through the blindfold, but he could hear the small crowd of initiates and their trainers, the excited breathing, the shuffling of bare feet on hard-packed dirt, and the occasional hushed voice giving last-minute instruction. He could smell his opponent a few feet away: the musk of dried sweat, the radish on his breath, and a scent Tiger had no name for that marked the bearer as a worthy rival.

A veteran now of dozens of matches, Tiger had learned that most people will give up when a certain amount of damage has been inflicted, but there were others—like him—who ignored the pain and kept fighting. He'd learned to recognize them among the members of visiting crèches, the troops that manned the island garrison, and those who trained him. This barrier of pain and the will to break through it fascinated him, and he wondered if one day he'd find something he couldn't endure. He was sure that his dedication to the way of the Iron warrior would sustain him through anything, and he feared no test, but he wondered… and it annoyed him. It called into question the purity of his faith in the Kagehito mission. Lack of belief was a short road to failure, as Mallet often reminded him.

"He's called Wind," Mallet said softly, as he moved behind Tiger to remove the blindfold.

The sensei's tone confirmed what Tiger's senses had already told him. His opponent was one of those who'd fight to his last breath.

"Don't embarrass me," Mallet said as the chosen referee threw a pebble across the space that separated the combatants.

As Tiger and Wind charged toward each other, time seemed to slow for Tiger, each moment a snapshot, like stop-motion animation. He saw everything separately and clearly, allowing him to make split-second decisions without panicking. Tiger knew he had two choices. He could fight Wind to a standstill while suffering injuries that would take a long time to heal, or he could end it before it got started. He saw the infinitesimal dip of Wind's shoulder that told him Wind was going to duck in an attempt to get under him and throw him. Tiger let his body take over, pushing off with his back foot in a leap straight at Wind. He planted his right foot on his opponent's bent thigh and climbed him like a wall. Wind got a hold on Tiger, but it was too late. Tiger's arm was around Wind's neck, and Tiger was dropping to the ground behind Wind. Wind's spine snapped under the load of Tiger's full weight, and it was over. Tiger let Wind's body settle to the ground as the referee arrived with Mallet and Wind's trainer.

"He's gone," the referee said after checking Wind's vital signs.

Wind's sensei clenched his jaw as he turned from his dead fighter to Mallet and Tiger. "That was a brilliant move," he said.

Mallet nodded and Tiger bowed deeply in acknowledgment of the compliment. Neither spoke until the other man walked away.

"Congratulations," Mallet said as he and Tiger returned to the barracks. "You went up a level today. You made a truly pragmatic decision."

"It seemed wasteful to spend any more time in recuperation."

"You could have choked him to unconsciousness."

"And I'd meet him again someday."

"Logic stripped of all sentiment. Remember how it felt when you made the decision to eliminate your opponent. It's useful, but from now on, try not to kill any of our own."

"It's not against the rules of the challenge."

"No, it isn't, but the Shadow needs soldiers."

"And they should be the best."

"That's why I'm here." Mallet smacked Tiger on the back. "Run the rest of the way. And give Seven some surprise physical therapy when you get there. A dislocated shoulder shouldn't take this long to heal."

Tiger grinned. "He'll never know what hit him."

"I don't want him missing another challenge match."

"He won't."

Tiger trotted off down the wooded slope that ended at the dirt road bordering the crèche compound. He picked up speed as he passed the row of small huts on his way to the garrison. It was stupid to take this route, but he always did. Maybe he was testing his ability to endure pain, or maybe he was hoping that repetition would help dull it.

As always, a ghost appeared in the doorway of the first hut, the ghost of a small boy with the blackest hair and the whitest teeth, smiling as he beckoned to Tiger. Tiger turned away, and then he was past the hut, but he could still see those shadowed eyes, the eyes of someone who'd trusted him, someone he'd promised to protect, someone he'd let down.

Tiger ran faster, pushing himself to do better, determined not to fail again. He would excel. He would win the respect of his superiors. One day, he would be one of the powerful, and no one would take anything away from him again.

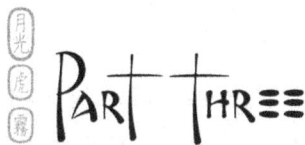 PART THREE

"EXCELLENT," Mallet said as Tiger finished his stroke, neatly cleaving the cadaver from right shoulder to left hip.

Tiger bowed and sheathed the katana. "Thank you, teacher."

"You've passed the final test of arms with edged weapons. You can call yourself a master of the blade... as far as technique goes."

"I hope I make you proud."

"Let's see how you do as you move on to more modern weapons." Mallet paused as though remembering something. "You're seventeen today."

Tiger raised his eyebrows. "Is it my birthday?"

"It is if I say it is. You've nearly attained the status of a man, but you have one more rite to undergo. Are you ready? Yes? Then let's go visit River."

Tiger bowed and put himself in Mallet's hands as he was used to doing, following the sensei to the armory. River was waiting for them, and he directed Tiger to sit in a chair with his back to the open window. River took up needle and ink and tattooed the sigil of the Iron Clan between Tiger's shoulder blades. The unsheathed sword stood on point, the top of the hilt coming to just below Tiger's nape.

When the design was finished, River slapped Tiger on the back. "To make sure it sticks," River said solemnly.

Other than a tightening of facial muscles, Tiger didn't react to the stinging pain. He got to his feet and bowed to River. "Thank you, teacher," he said.

"It's a proud symbol," Mallet said. "Don't disgrace it."

"I won't." Tiger bowed to Mallet.

"I believe you," Mallet said, slapping Tiger's back as hard as River had. "Let's go have our dinner. You'll need your strength for your final manhood ritual."

They had dinner with Seven, drinking a cup of rice wine before starting on the grilled meat and rice. Like any young man, Seven looked forward to the night he would be initiated into sex, and he teased Tiger with good-natured envy. Sex with a partner was the great unknown for Kagehito slaves. While masturbation was approved, even encouraged, sexual relationships with other trainees or teachers were strictly forbidden. The potential for jealous violence was too great a risk in a place where pubescent hormones were combined with martial arts training. The rumored punishment for "fraternizing" was so horrible that no one talked about it above a whisper. However, everyone agreed it involved the slicing off of certain bits. Among the crèches, making love acquired a mystique that bordered on religious.

"You're a lucky man," Seven said as Tiger rose to follow Mallet after dinner.

"I'll tell you all about it later," Tiger smirked.

Mallet spun and took hold of Tiger by the throat. "I didn't see it, but I heard a smirk in your voice. Is that how you were taught to view sex? With snickering arrogance?"

Tiger shook his head. Mallet's grip on his windpipe made it impossible to answer in words.

"There may be times in the years ahead when you'll have to fuck for advantage, and after the training you receive you'll be able perform superbly. But tonight you'll have the privilege of making love with a virgin trained to give pleasure. Tonight is a rite of passage for you, and you will not stain it with juvenile grubby-mindedness." Mallet let go of Tiger.

Tiger coughed and rubbed at his throat. "Sorry," he said hoarsely.

"It's all right." Mallet grinned. "I want you to have the proper respect, but I also understand that you're a seventeen-year-old who's never had sex. I remember what it was like. I'm taking you to the baths, and I recommend you yank it at least once while you're washing up. Otherwise, you'll shoot off the second your cock feels the touch of someone else's hand."

Tiger swallowed hard at the mental image Mallet's words called up. "You've always given me good instruction," he said.

"You'll be fine, Tiger." Mallet stopped outside the bathhouse. "Go on in and wash off the dust and sweat. When you're done, go to the building out back."

"That's the private—"

"I know what it is," Mallet interrupted. "Do as I say."

Tiger hurried through his bath, balancing his desire to smell pleasant with his desire to see what was waiting for him. He rubbed his chin with his fingertips and felt stubble, but he couldn't take the time to use the straight razor. It was just a small patch of whiskers, barely noticeable. Finger-combing his thick hair back from his face, he left it standing in damp tufts as he trotted out of the bathhouse in his loincloth. He strode down the short path bordered by raked gravel, his brain conjuring countless images of what lay in store. By the time he stood in the archway of the temple-like building, his heart was thudding against his ribs like a blacksmith's hammer on the anvil. Soon, *soon*, he would know what *it* was like.

Tiger put a hand on the door and slowly pushed it open. There was a fire on a marble hearth, and candles shed their buttery light from every corner of the room. A slender figure in a white silk robe knelt in front of the fireplace, staring into a pot suspended over the flames. A fall of raven dark hair shimmered against a cheek like a snow-covered slope.

As supple as a hunting cat, the visitor rose and turned toward Tiger. His face was tilted down, and he looked up at Tiger through lush, sable lashes. The expression was demure, but the gleam of his eyes was suggestive of mischief. "I'm home, Tiger," he said softly.

Tiger's shocked look turned into a grin of delight. "Moonlight! I've missed you so much," he said as he crossed the room, arms spread wide to hug his friend.

Moonlight stood his ground and was engulfed in Tiger's enthusiastic embrace. With his arms trapped between them, there was little Moonlight could do until Tiger loosened his hold briefly. Moonlight got an arm around Tiger's neck and one around his waist and hugged him back. For a long time, they stood there, absorbing the reality of one another's physical presence.

"Wow, muscles!" Moonlight said at last. "You're as hard as a rock."

"You're in great shape too," Tiger said, squeezing Moonlight's biceps. "Let me look at you," he said, taking a step back. "What's with the white robe?"

"It's traditional."

"For what?"

"Just a minute." Moonlight turned and lifted a small, thick-sided jar from the pot of hot water. "Don't want this to get too hot."

"I already ate."

"It's not food." Moonlight smiled fondly at his friend over his shoulder. "I was shocked when I heard your voice, but now I'm glad it's you."

Tiger gave his friend a perplexed look.

"It really hasn't hit you yet?" Moonlight's smile widened to a grin. "I'm still quicker than you are."

"Your head is still full of moon dust. I'm really happy to see you, but you're probably going to have to leave soon. I'm supposed to—" Tiger's words broke off at the look on Moonlight's face. "What?"

"I'm not going anywhere," Moonlight said. "I'm going to stay with you all night."

Tiger's eyes widened. "You? You're my... my... my first time?"

Moonlight nodded, the dark fringe of his hair brushing his nape with each small movement. "After tonight, I'll be a true member of the Rose Tribe."

Tiger swallowed hard. "I never thought...." His voice trailed off.

"Me either. When they took off my blindfold, I didn't know where I was, but I started preparing as I'd been instructed... and then you walked in. For a second, I was sure I couldn't go through with it, but when you hugged me, I knew I could. I hope this is okay with you."

Tiger took a deep breath. "Are you kidding? It's perfect." He blew the air out of his lungs in relief. "I was so worried a woman was going to be waiting for me, and that I'd perform poorly."

"I think our masters know you better than that." Moonlight tested the temperature of the little jar, and then picked it up and set it beside the soft mattress.

"I'm glad." Tiger paused. "And I'm a little nervous."

"Because of what we're going to do? Or because you're going to do it with me?"

"Both," Tiger said honestly.

"Would it make you feel better if I told you that I'm supposed to teach you about pleasure? All you have to do is enjoy."

"It's a little embarrassing to think of you that way."

"Would you like to kiss me?"

"Yes," Tiger said instantly.

"I thought so." Moonlight turned away from Tiger and knelt to arrange the silk cushions on the soft mattress.

Puzzlement drew Tiger's features together in a mild frown. "Are we going to kiss?"

"That's up to you," Moonlight said softly, glancing over his shoulder at Tiger.

Tiger had heard those taunting words from Moonlight before and he'd seen that challenging look a thousand times, but this time it was different. There was a new element to the teasing that made his heart race like it did when he spotted game, but Moonlight was no deer to be brought down with an arrow. For the first time in ten years, Tiger wasn't sure what to do next.

"What do you want, on this night that you become a man?" Moonlight asked as though he could read Tiger's mind.

"You." The word emerged as a croak from Tiger's dry throat. He swallowed hard. "I want you. I've always wanted you."

"I've always belonged to you." Moonlight stood and turned to face his friend, breaking from the script. "From the moment you took my hand in that box, you cared for me like I was the most precious thing in the world. It was so hard being parted from you. I felt like I'd been ripped in half."

"So did I. It hurt so bad for such a long time. I asked Mallet where you were, but he never answered me. One night I sneaked out and went to the inner wall. I was going to climb over and see if you were in the fortress or the onmyoji's tower."

Moonlight's eyes widened. "What happened?"

"Mallet was waiting for me. He didn't say anything. He just stared at me until I turned around and went back to my bed. I expected a thrashing the next morning, but he never mentioned it."

"You were always his favorite."

"Because I never slack off." The conversation had helped Tiger calm down a little and he felt more at ease. Taking a step closer, he looked into Moonlight's eyes. "Show me how to kiss," he requested.

Moonlight smiled with delight. "Nothing you could've said would've pleased me more." Putting a hand around the back of Tiger's neck, Moonlight drew him forward until their lips touched.

Tiger's heart surged at the feel of soft lips against his, at the thought that he was touching Moonlight so intimately. He was so lost in the dreamy feeling that he just stood there and let Moonlight kiss him. When Moonlight pulled back, Tiger made a sound of complaint.

Moonlight smiled at Tiger's eagerness. "Open your mouth just a little," he said.

Tiger did as he was told, parting his lips. For a second or two, he and Moonlight hovered on the edge of a kiss, their mouths millimeters apart, their breath mingling, and then Tiger closed the gap. He'd meant to wait for Moonlight to make the next move, but instinct took over. Covering Moonlight's full lips with his, Tiger pressed a little harder, but broke the kiss when he felt Moonlight's tongue.

"Relax," Moonlight murmured. "You'll like this."

Framing Tiger's face between his hands, Moonlight brought their lips together again. Delicately, he drew his tongue along Tiger's bottom lip before darting it into Tiger's mouth. He was gratified by Tiger's little moan of pleasure and the way Tiger's arms went around him. Boldly, Moonlight explored Tiger's mouth, inspiring Tiger to reciprocate. For several minutes, they kissed, letting their hands stray farther and farther.

"You're right. I like kissing," Tiger said, as he paused to catch his breath.

"And it gets better." Moonlight let the wide neck of his robe slide off his shoulder. "There's so much more to be kissed."

This time Tiger didn't hesitate. Wrapping his arms around Moonlight, he kissed him deeply before his mouth strayed down the long neck to the smooth, pale shoulders. With each taste, he wanted more, and found himself tugging at the silk robe in an attempt to bare more flesh. The sound of tearing fabric and Moonlight's laughter spurred him on until the gown was in shreds at Moonlight's feet. Tiger took one look at Moonlight's naked body and didn't need anyone to tell him what to do next. Taking hold of Moonlight's shoulders, Tiger lowered him to his back on the mattress.

Moonlight knew he should regain control of the situation. It was up to him to guide this young warrior through the sexual initiation. His appointed task was to give the soldier as much pleasure as possible and show him how the Kagehito rewarded excellence. Tiger should emerge on the other side of this experience feeling gratitude to his masters and an intensified sense of purpose. However, when Tiger threw a leg over Moonlight's hip and leaned in to kiss him, Moonlight slipped the leash of conditioning and gave himself completely to the experience.

Eagerly, Moonlight returned Tiger's kisses as he stroked and squeezed everything he could reach, relearning the contours of his friend's body. The stringy, whip-thin boy had grown into a tall, young man with the lean, rock-hard muscles of a long-distance runner. Moonlight's physique was sculpted as well, but more with an eye toward pleasing proportions than practical purpose. There wasn't an ounce of fat on either, but Tiger was deeply tanned, with the rangy, cobbled frame of someone who works hard outdoors. Moonlight was as pale and as smooth as an ivory statue of a young god. Each was delighted by the changes in the other and expressed their approval with constant caresses that discovered new wonders in every inch.

Moonlight's mission—much-planned and rehearsed—should have been accomplished in a series of well-timed steps that heightened the subject's state of arousal as they led up to the moment of climax. Right now, Moonlight should have just finished accustoming the warrior to the feel of another's hands on his cock. He should be easing into the oral sex and introducing the idea of penetration. All he wanted was to feel Tiger moving inside him, to be connected physically with the one he'd loved almost all his life. He wanted to ride the wild feeling rising rampant within him until it threw him or took him somewhere he'd never been.

"Wait," Moonlight said between kisses. "Just a minute."

"I don't want to stop." Tiger ran his tongue over Moonlight's upper lip. "It feels too good."

"I'll make you feel even better. Hand me that pot."

Tiger reached out and picked up the small clay jar, sniffing at the contents. "Sweet," he said.

"It's oil, and it'll make the penetration easier for me."

Tiger's feelings wavered between lust and concern as Moonlight's words sank in. "Easier?"

"It's nothing to worry about. Just grease."

"How can I help?"

Moonlight smiled up at Tiger. "Put some of the oil on your cock."

Tiger smiled back. "You oil the keyhole, not the key," he said.

"True." Moonlight pulled his knees up. "I can do it if you want."

Tiger shook his head as he dipped two fingers in the warm oil. Letting the excess oil drip onto Moonlight's dusky rose cleft, Tiger ran his fingertips around the crinkled entrance. When Moonlight moaned softly, Tiger looked up at him. "Okay?"

Moonlight nodded. "I'm just really excited. It never felt like this in training."

Tiger pushed a finger into Moonlight and his state of arousal went into overdrive. Abruptly, he couldn't wait to feel Moonlight's tight heat wrapped around his cock. "Is that enough?" he asked.

Moonlight's instructor had always spent several minutes on this step, using fingers and a slim dildo. The sensei had told him that without the stretching, the initial penetration would hurt. Moonlight didn't care. Pain was temporary. He was as eager for his first time as Tiger was. "I want you inside me now," he said.

Tiger dropped the pot onto the floor, smearing the oil from his fingers onto his cock. Trembling with eagerness, he slid his thighs under Moonlight's ass and shifted around until he was in what he considered a good position.

Moonlight looked up into Tiger's eyes and urged him on. His heartbeat doubled as the tip of Tiger's dick nuzzled his ass cheeks and pressed against his hole. He braced himself, and then the head was inside him. Moonlight took a deep breath, and before he could let it out, Tiger thrust again. Biting his lip to hold in a groan, Moonlight willed his muscles to relax.

Tiger sagged forward, lost in the powerful sensation, sinking another two inches into the velvet vise. "So good," he breathed.

Moonlight's heart expanded until it crowded the cage of his ribs. The ache in his lower half faded in the force of his love for the one joined to him. He still felt the pain, but it was a small thing next to his passion and soon forgotten. The only thing that mattered was that he and Tiger loved each other. He didn't know why he'd been sent to Tiger as his first mission, but he was sure that the only pertinent factor in the decision was how the outcome benefited the Kagehito. Moonlight didn't care. He was just glad he was here in this moment, sharing this splendor with the one he loved most in the world. This was worth any price.

"Do what you want," Moonlight said tenderly. "For your first time, I want you to have the freedom to do just as you feel. Try not to think. Let your instincts guide you."

"I feel like I'm going to explode," Tiger panted as his full length sank into the clinging sheath.

Moonlight reached up to brush back the uneven bangs that hung over Tiger's forehead. His full lips curved up in a sweet smile as he gazed into his lover's eyes. "Don't hold back," he said.

A shiver ran the length of Tiger's spine as the entrance to Moonlight's sheath tightened around his cock. His eyelids fluttered and a soft groan leaked from between his lips. "So sweet."

Moonlight anticipated the burn as Tiger withdrew. When Tiger thrust back in, Moonlight relaxed as he'd been taught. The oil eased the friction, making the penetration tolerable for him until he was stretched enough to enjoy it physically as well as emotionally. Lifting his butt, he tilted his pelvis so that Tiger's next thrust passed over his prostate.

Tiger opened his eyes at the sound of Moonlight's soft moan. He thrust again and Moonlight met him halfway. Tiger's excitement rose another notch, and the intimations of something wonderful just ahead spurred him on. Wrapping his hands around Moonlight's hips, Tiger thrust in short, quick strokes as he watched Moonlight's carved features go soft with pleasure. When Moonlight reached down to take hold of himself, Tiger got there first. Taking a firm grip on Moonlight's hardening cock, Tiger stroked it from root to tip in rhythm with his thrusts.

"Tiger!" Moonlight gasped as a powerful climax crashed through him like an avalanche. He knew it was coming, but its magnitude shocked him. Not once in all the times his instructor had made him come had he felt like this. To compare the experiences would be like spitting into a waterfall. Breathless and shaking, Moonlight clutched at the silken coverlet as the flood of pleasure crashed through him, spreading outward to every fiber of his being.

Tiger felt Moonlight's cock pulse against his palm and watched the stream of milky fluid spurt from the tip. An answering pulse behind Tiger's pubic bone triggered his climax. Leaning forward, he pushed Moonlight's knees farther apart and thrust deeper. Savoring the look of transported bliss on Moonlight's face, Tiger plunged in and out a handful of times as he released his seed. The feeling that suffused him had a mystical element that he didn't question as he reveled in the fleshly pleasure of his sated cock ensconced in the snug sheath. He couldn't get close enough to Moonlight and bent his lover double so he could kiss him.

Moonlight was exceedingly limber and had no trouble with the position. He reached up to weave his fingers into Tiger's hair and returned the kiss, drawing it out, easing them both through the aftershocks and into the afterglow. With unhurried caresses, he coached Tiger on when to pull out, and then coaxed him down to lie chest to chest. He could feel Tiger's galloping heart begin to slow its pace as they exchanged several more short, sweet kisses that melded into another long, slow one.

"I've never felt anything like that," Tiger whispered into Moonlight's ear.

"Me either."

"I want to do it again, but I want to rest a few minutes first." Tiger shifted until he was on his back with Moonlight against his side. His voice was grainy with exhaustion, but he didn't want to sleep. He wanted to lie here with Moonlight in his arms until the world ended. "So what have you been doing all these years that you've been neglecting your senpai?" Tiger asked in what he hoped was a casual voice.

"The same thing you've been doing: improving."

"Good job." Tiger stroked his fingertips down Moonlight's neck to his navel.

Moonlight's lips curved up in a pleased smile. "I'm glad you approve."

"Seriously though, what sort of lessons did you have? I don't think they were the same as mine." Tiger's lethargy helped him keep his voice calm. While they were doing it, he'd managed to avoid thinking about the fact that someone had taught Moonlight about sex; the thought of anyone else doing those things with Moonlight bothered him. He didn't want to ask questions, but he couldn't stop himself.

"What have *you* been learning?" Moonlight's tone had a slight edge, an unconscious response to the tension in Tiger's voice.

"Most of the same things we were learning when you were here, just more… intense, you know? I know how to use dozens of weapons. I know how to study my opponent and think like he does. I've started learning strategy on a bigger scale, but—"

"I've trained with weapons and strategy too," Moonlight interrupted. He fell silent for a moment, reminding himself that his calling was as honorable as any other before he spoke again. "But you're right. My lessons were different."

"Tell me," Tiger said.

"I learned how to sing and dance, how to arrange flowers and write poetry." Moonlight paused. "They taught me how to look at paintings…." His voice trailed off.

"What else?"

"I don't know how to say it. My new teacher taught me about beauty. How to… appreciate it in many forms. How to… create it. I doubt I'm making sense now."

"You're beautiful," Tiger murmured into Moonlight's hair. "That's all I need to know."

"Tiger? Remember the first time we met?"

"Of course."

"Do you remember your mother?" Moonlight took a deep breath. "I can't remember what my umma looked like. I can hear her voice sometimes, but nothing else."

"What's the point of trying?" Tiger stroked Moonlight's hair.

"You're right. I just feel like I've lost something that…." Moonlight hesitated. "Do you ever feel like we're different from normal people?"

Tiger snorted. "Of course, we are. We're *better*. Don't you listen when your teacher is talking before meditation?"

"They tell us we're more than human, but I wonder if that's true. I wonder if we aren't less than human."

Tiger rolled onto his side so he could look into Moonlight's eyes. "What do you mean?"

"They teach us not to feel when we're doing certain things, you know?"

Tiger nodded. "If we react emotionally, we might hesitate when it's time to act."

"I know they trained us to be like this so we can serve better, but it feels wrong."

"This doesn't feel wrong, does it?" Tiger asked as he tightened his arms around Moonlight.

"This is the one thing that's always felt right to me." Moonlight kissed Tiger's jaw. "Last year, I got a new teacher, named Mink, who taught me about the beauty of physical pleasure. He made me feel very good, but he never made me feel anything for him. He praised me for that when I confessed to him."

"I don't see the problem." Tiger contained the surge of relief at the news that Moonlight had felt nothing for this Itachi who'd trained him.

"I *want* to feel something."

"I felt something when *we* did it," Tiger said. "I thought you did too."

"Of course I did. Because it was with you. I… love you."

"I love you too. I always have, I just never… we've never needed to talk about it. But we can if you want to. I wouldn't mind," Tiger babbled.

"I'll be leaving in the morning," Moonlight said abruptly, ending the stream of words.

"No. They wouldn't bring you back just to take you away again."

"Why wouldn't they? Is it too cruel?" Moonlight met Tiger's eyes. "When has that ever stopped them?"

Tiger shifted. "Don't talk like that, okay?" He kissed Moonlight's forehead. "Five years ago, they told me I'd never see you again, but here you are. If we both keep training hard and doing well, maybe—"

"Do you think this is some kind of reward?" Moonlight paused. "Well, it is, I guess, but make no mistake. They put us together tonight for their own reasons. Everything they do is for the Kagehito. You and I don't matter at all."

Tiger held Moonlight closer. "Shhh," he soothed. "Please don't be upset. It breaks my heart."

"You're right again," Moonlight said. "I should be enjoying every moment we have together instead of ruining it with my whining." He managed a smile. "I was supposed to be the silken seducer, beguiling you with pleasure until I could mold you to whatever shape I desired. That's what my teacher told me. As soon as I saw you, I forgot all his words. I failed the test."

"I don't think so." Tiger kissed the tip of Moonlight's nose. "You did turn me into jelly."

Moonlight's face heated up in a sudden rush of blood. "Don't make fun of me please."

"I'm not joking. There were several moments when I would have promised you anything to keep you from stopping what you were doing."

"Truly?"

"Truly."

Moonlight relaxed again. "It's nice to hear you say it. I'm proud of my skill, but I know that some people won't see seduction as an honorable tactic."

"Strategy," Tiger said.

"What?"

"If you plan to seduce someone, it counts as strategy. If your strategy fails, then you turn to tactics, which can vary with the situation as it changes."

"You sound like Mallet."

"Well, I've been with him longer." Tiger ruffled his fingertips through the fringe at Moonlight's nape. "Your hair was always so pretty, so long and black and shiny."

"It was really long before they cut it last year—down to my waist. Now they keep it like this." Moonlight blew out a breath, lifting the heavy bangs that came down to his eyebrows.

"I love it." Tiger turned Moonlight until he was pressed against Moonlight's back. Lowering his face, he grazed his lips against Moonlight's bare nape. He licked the stylized rose and thorns tattoo and blew a cool stream of air over it. "I love the way you shiver when I do this." He sucked hard at the curve of Moonlight's neck, leaving a burgundy brand behind. "I love the way you moan." He nipped at the sensitive skin. "The way you whimper." He circled Moonlight's waist with his arms, pressing his palms flat against Moonlight's lower belly. "I love the way the curve of your ass fits perfectly against my crotch. I love the way you make me feel like you can't wait for my touch."

"I *can't* wait," Moonlight said breathlessly. "When you touch me, I catch fire."

"I want you so much," Tiger groaned.

"You have me."

Tiger rolled again, putting Moonlight face down on the soft mattress. He caressed the long muscles of Moonlight's arms, as he stretched them out on the silky bedding. Taking hold of his hard cock, he slotted it between Moonlight's ass cheeks, still slick with oil. He spread his knees, forcing Moonlight's thighs wide apart. The sight of Moonlight's glistening opening made Tiger's entire being clench with need. Pushing the tip of his shaft into Moonlight, he leaned forward onto his elbows, sinking into the tight, wet heat in one long, slow thrust. "You're mine," he said in Moonlight's ear. "I'm yours. Nothing anyone can do can change that. You know it's true."

Moonlight turned his head as far as he could to meet Tiger's gaze. "I know," he whispered.

Tiger bent farther and covered Moonlight's lips with his. Flexing his buttocks, he shifted his cock in Moonlight's sheath.

Moonlight ended the kiss on a gasp, stealing the air from Tiger's lungs. "More."

Tiger withdrew, trailing his hands up Moonlight's back. Seating his cock again, he stroked Moonlight's velvet-skinned lower cheeks as he eased in. He paused when Moonlight's interior muscles clamped down, and he adjusted his angle when he thrust again.

"Sweet, so sweet," Moonlight breathed as Tiger set a rhythm.

"It feels good?" Tiger asked in a strained voice.

"So good...." Moonlight's voice trailed off in a series of gasps and moans.

Tiger's teeth sank into his lower lip as Moonlight tightened and relaxed, clinging to his hardness with wet friction, kindling the sweetest heat at Tiger's core. He felt as though he was holding back a wall of lava with his bare hands, but he could sense that Moonlight was close to climax, and even more than he wanted to come, he wanted Moonlight to come. He wanted to hear Moonlight cry out and know that it was his cock, his hands, his mouth that had given Moonlight pleasure.

"Tiger!" Moonlight choked out. "I'm coming."

Tiger continued to thrust as Moonlight came apart under him. With a bone-deep shudder, Moonlight arched up from the mattress, pressing his spurting cock into the covers. His head tilted back and a long sigh of utter fulfillment purred out through his parted lips as Tiger sank into him to the hilt and pulled out again. Boneless, Moonlight whimpered in helpless arousal as the head of Tiger's shaft stroked delicate tissue that was now hypersensitive.

"Is it good?" Tiger groaned.

Moonlight nodded, fingers clutching at the satin pillow. "Come in me," he said breathlessly.

Every knot, every snarl that had stiffened Tiger's body and soul since he'd been shut in a box eleven years ago loosened all at once. What he'd said to Moonlight was the truth. They had something that no one—not even the Kagehito—could take from them. This one thing belonged to them alone. No matter what else happened, they'd always have this, this love that was all-consuming, that set the rest of the world at naught and made them a nation of two.

Tiger leaned in as his seed unspooled deep inside his beloved. Wrapping his arms around Moonlight, he pressed kisses to Moonlight's back, murmuring sweet, vulgar poetry into the satin skin. Not until his sated shaft softened and began to slide from the slippery channel did he move.

"Where are you going?" Moonlight mumbled a half-awake complaint.

"Just letting you breathe, Moonlight."

"Don't call me that when we're like this, okay?"

"Jaehan," Tiger murmured, brushing the bangs away from the other young man's forehead. "You'll never learn, will you?"

Moonlight closed his eyes again. "Hold me."

There was no order Tiger would rather follow. Gathering Moonlight close, he cradled him to his chest, stroking his back until he fell asleep again. He held his love safe in his arms, but he couldn't still his fears. One thing that hadn't changed about Moonlight was his recklessness with his thoughts and his words, and sooner or later, the wrong person would take notice. There would be nothing Tiger could do to protect Moonlight. He wished Moonlight would just accept things and make the best of them. Even now, Tiger knew the Kagehito wouldn't hesitate to cut their losses by consigning Moonlight to eternal slavery, or to the grave.

Tiger didn't know what his life would be like if he hadn't been kidnapped eleven years ago. He didn't know what his life would be like if he had tried to escape. What he did know was that his life was a lot better when he followed the rules and worked hard to please his teachers. Seeing Moonlight again changed all that. Now the most important thing in the world was pleasing Moonlight. Tiger didn't know how he'd balance this new priority with obedience to the Kagehito, but he knew he'd find a way. No matter what happened, he'd find a way.

MOONLIGHT cleared his mind of useless worries and composed himself once again in the Barazoku manner. Few things could provoke him into showing emotion, but today he was summoned to the onmyoji's presence. Though he'd racked his brain for most of the night, he couldn't think of any reason for the meeting. With a sigh, he set about clearing his mind again as he let his gaze travel up the bare walls.

The onmyoji's quarters were comprised of an L-shaped dwelling of tile and dressed stone, a courtyard, and a square tower three stories in height, set among small gardens. Moonlight stood on the ground floor of the tower, looking up at the ceiling about ten meters overhead. The stairs were stone and climbed up the inside wall until they ended at a door banded in strips of metal. There were no arcane symbols painted or carved in the tall chamber, no curtains on the high narrow windows, nothing to break the curved lines of the smooth blocks of limestone. There was nothing to catch the eye and distract the brain. With nothing else to focus on, the visitor's mind consumed itself with speculation about the summons.

With an effort of sheer will, Moonlight brought his mind to bear on a subject of his choosing. Bowing his head, he closed his eyes and pictured Tiger. Even if he never saw Tiger again, he would have the memory of their night together to warm him for the rest of his life. Almost a month had passed, but Moonlight still felt a glow at his core, a light and heat that had been sparked by Tiger's touch, banked in smoldering embers. He was a slave with no rights, but he had known love, real love, the true love his mother used to talk about. He'd been transformed, lifted up and spun around until he and Tiger were one, and he knew that Tiger would always be with him, no matter how long fate separated them. He also had faith that he and Tiger would be together again one day. A love this strong would find a way through all the obstacles.

The door at the top of the stairs opened. "Moonlight, you may come up now."

Moonlight recognized the onmyoji's voice, though he'd last heard it five years ago. The vibrant tenor was as pleasant as a mellow flute, whether issuing an invitation or pronouncing the doom of a child slave.

The stair had no rail and the trip to the top usually kept a visitor's mind on his next step. Moonlight bent and took hold of the hem of his long robe. Draping the heavy fabric over one arm, he climbed to the top with an acrobat's equilibrium. The door stood open, but he knocked anyway as he let the folds of the robe slither back into place.

"Please come in."

Moonlight kept his head bowed as he pushed the door open and entered a round, airy chamber. All of the many windows were open, letting in the breeze and sunlight. Through the window directly opposite, Moonlight glimpsed the tops of flowering trees on the other side of the outer wall.

"Welcome," Autumn said as he rose from a bench under another window.

The onmyoji was not wearing his veil, and Moonlight's training was barely sufficient to keep him from staring. He'd never seen anyone with hair as red as river clay or eyes as gray as rainwater.

"It's an honor to speak with you, master," Moonlight managed to say.

"Come and look." Autumn gestured to the view.

Moonlight did as he was told, crossing the room to look out of the large window.

"Does it please you?"

Moonlight nodded. "It's very pleasing, master. The blossoms on the wild fruit trees look like snow." He looked up at the onmyoji from under his lashes. "Behind the walls, it's easy to forget that it's spring."

The onmyoji smiled. "Very good, Moonlight. I must remember to praise your instructors when I speak with them again. Your dissatisfaction with your lack of freedom was slipped quite gracefully into the conversation. And you display admirable self-confidence for one so young."

Moonlight bowed.

"Really, you're most remarkable," Autumn went on. "Even in that colorless sack, even standing still, your quality is evident. You shine with grace, beauty, and power."

"All the credit goes to my teachers."

"That's for me to decide." The onmyoji gestured to the cushioned bench, and Moonlight sat down with him. "It wouldn't surprise a smart boy like you that I've been keeping a close eye on your progress. I'm very… intrigued by what I've seen, and I wanted to observe you face to face. You're very good at maintaining the serene-fisherman mask. It's the perfect tension between unobtrusive interest and expectant patience. I'm not surprised that it's your chosen public persona. It gives nothing away while drawing the prey in close. Ah, you don't like the word prey, do you?"

"It has a certain directness that grates, master."

"Excellent answer. You're still very young as the outside world counts such things, but you have the spirit of an adventurer. Nothing frightens you, does it?"

"I don't particularly like being alone," Moonlight answered honestly. "That scares me a little."

"We'll see what we can do about that later. Right now, I'm offering to be your guide. My first calling was to the Rose Tribe. My inner calling to the Dragon clan came when I was sixteen, so I never went on a mission for the Barazoku, but I completed the training, and I remember my lessons well.

"I feel a kinship with you, Moonlight. You're young, and beautiful, and intelligent, and the people around you want to use you for their own purposes." Autumn paused, and when he began speaking again, his words had the cadence of a practiced speech. "I see something of my younger self in you, and I feel a compulsion to help steer you through the next few years as a full-fledged but inexperienced member of the Rose Tribe."

"I can't refuse such an offer, master."

"No, I suppose you can't." The onmyoji gazed out over the wall. "I know you don't trust me and that's all right. Caution is good. Now I'm going to do something to try to win you over, but first, you must tell me about your final test as an initiate."

Moonlight took a long slow breath, and then another.

"Why do you hesitate?"

"I was summarizing. I don't want to waste your time with a lot of details."

"And if I require details?" The onmyoji turned to face Moonlight. "That blush is very charming. Can you do it at will?"

"I don't seem to be able to control it, master."

"Well, it's charming and a very minor flaw. You can stop trying to put the wonder of your manhood ritual into a few tidy paragraphs. I don't need to hear about it. I just wanted to see how you reacted to my order." Autumn reached out and pushed back the hood of Moonlight's robe. "That's better," he said. "After observing the manhood ceremony, it was clear to me that you are at your best when you're with your senpai from your training crèche."

Moonlight could see Autumn's mouth moving, but he couldn't hear the words over the pounding of blood in his temples. His heart was beating hard and fast as it tried to climb into his throat. *The onmyoji had watched him with Tiger.* The ice forming in Moonlight's belly began to spread along his veins. Despite all he'd experienced since being kidnapped, this violation had the power to shock him into immobility.

"Moonlight?"

Moonlight snapped out of his paralysis. It wasn't easy to face the onmyoji now that he knew the man had watched him make love with Tiger, but he managed it. "Yes, master?"

"I can arrange it so that you have free time to spend with Iron Tribe's Tiger. Would that please you?"

"You know it would, master," Moonlight said calmly.

"*Very* good answer." Autumn leaned forward, bringing with him the sharp scent of citrus and the smoke of sandalwood. "I see something in you that I can't put a name to yet. I think that with proper guidance you'll bring glory to the Kagehito. Shall we begin?"

Moonlight bowed his head. "When you are ready, master."

The onmyoji unfurled a scroll from among the many on his desk.

"Come and sit here and make a copy of this for me."

Moonlight sat down at the writing desk and pulled a sheet of rice paper toward him. Picking a bamboo pen, he dipped it in ink and drew the first few characters.

"Good," Autumn said. "You have a talent for this. With a little practice, I'm sure you could reproduce this writing perfectly."

"If I may ask, will I be your secretary?"

"Yes, I think so. It will give me a reason to keep you here. Unless you'd rather be going on missions for Rose Tribe, seducing lecherous crime lords or entertaining high-ranking Kagehito officials. It's up to you."

"My answer hasn't changed. I'm honored to have you as mentor."

"I can only imagine." The onmyoji put a hand lightly on Moonlight's shoulder, allowing the edge of his thumb to rest on the skin of the boy's collarbone. "Now you may go and pack whatever you need. I'll send a message to Mink, informing him of the change in your status. By the time you're ready to leave, I'm sure you'll find him very cooperative."

"Thank you." Moonlight bowed and left the onmyoji's tower.

Autumn let him go because he knew Moonlight would return, bringing with him that radiant excess of energy. The onmyoji congratulated himself again on the success of his notion to put Moonlight with Tiger for their sexual initiation. He had sensed the pretty boy's potential when he'd assigned him to Rose Tribe and had manipulated his progress ever since. Today, he'd confirmed that his intuition was still reliable. Moonlight was ripe and glowing with energy, energy that Autumn could tap and use. And if Moonlight needed a recharge, it would be simple enough to arrange, at least while Tiger was still in training. Once the Iron Tribe soldier was assigned to a fire team, it would take a bit more work to arrange an assignation.

The onmyoji's train of thought was interrupted as an idea occurred to him. Perhaps there was someone else whose life force would mesh with Moonlight's as completely as Tiger's did. Autumn stared at the scroll without seeing it as his mind hurtled down this track. He would have to induce Moonlight to couple with likely candidates and observe the results. That would take time, but he had time while he waited for the perfect alignment of the stars. And now he had a powerful source of arcane energy.

 Part Four

MALLET smacked the back of Tiger's head as he came up noiselessly behind him.

Tiger didn't move. He stood with his head bowed, his weight perfectly distributed between his feet, his hands hanging loosely at his sides. He'd been standing like this since the honor guard of two Iron Tribe soldiers had escorted him into the compound half an hour ago.

"Nothing to say?" Mallet stopped in front of Tiger. "How were your field trials?"

"There were a lot of tests."

"Tell me about them."

"You've undergone them yourself. I don't know what I could add."

"Don't be so modest. I've already heard how you impressed the bosses." Mallet smiled. "Your scores in marksmanship and martial arts were the very highest."

Tiger finally abandoned his straight face and smiled at his sensei. "I couldn't really tell how I was scoring while I was shooting and fighting, but it all felt good. I felt like I was doing really well." He paused. "I did everything exactly as you trained me, without thinking about it. I trusted my body to react correctly and everything fell into place. I even felt as though I knew what my opponent was going to do next."

"I shouldn't say this, but you're the best student I've ever had. Out of all the boys I've trained, you're the best."

"I'm honored, teacher."

"We're equals now. You call me by my name."

Tiger looked up in surprise. "I still have mission op training to complete before I'm—"

"You've only just passed your field tests and already you're arguing with me."

"No, I'm not." Tiger shook his head. "I guess I am. I'm confused."

"Not surprising. Are you hungry?"

"I'm starving."

"Answer me again, but this time use my name. Try it just once. After that it gets easier. I speak from experience."

"I'm starving, Mallet."

"Then let's go get something to eat and I'll tell you about the message I received from the onmyoji this morning."

"What's the wizard got to do with me?"

"Don't look so worried. All my news is good."

"You're a lot nicer to be around now that we're equals," Tiger observed.

Mallet chuckled. "As the pupil excels, so does the master. You're very good for my reputation *and* you've given me a way into active service."

"How?"

"If it works out, I won't have to explain it to you, and if it doesn't, I won't have wasted my breath. What's important is that you're skipping right to active missions. You'll be getting your training on the job, right across the water in Tokyo. And there's one more thing." Mallet stopped as they came in sight of the barracks.

"You have your own room now and your dinner is waiting for you there." He held up a key and dropped it into Tiger's hand. "The third door."

Tiger found his room, marveling at the luxury of a door that locked. The space was a square about four meters to a side with a shelf bed, a hearth, and a desk and chair. It was the same bare floor and simple wooden furniture he was used to, but the fact that he could call it his and lock the door if he wanted privacy made it a palace. He'd guarded a small spark of hope in his heart that Moonlight would be waiting for him, but he knew how foolish a dream it was.

However, the knowledge that his dream was far-fetched didn't keep him from having it. They had let Moonlight come to him once; maybe he could perform a service for the Kagehito so exceptional that they would grant him one wish. If he could have Moonlight beside him for the rest of his life, he would give the world to the Kagehito on the point of his sword.

Tiger bent to unlace the thongs that bound his scabbard to the side of his backpack. Gripping the inlaid hilt, he drew the blade a few inches from the sheath. The scant light ran like water along the silky steel and highlighted the incised symbols of his clan. He kept it sharp, and though he'd never used it in a real battle, he kept it close. Sliding it back into the scabbard, he set it on the wooden hooks in the wall above the bed.

He ate the meal set out on the hearth while he read the manual for an automatic handgun. After taking the dishes to the mess, he visited the bathhouse and then got ready for bed. Pulling the blanket up to his chest, he let his hand slide down to cup his crotch. His mind went back to novice days—before they'd turned twelve and Moonlight turned suddenly shy about his body—when they used to yank it together. He could picture the way Moonlight's front teeth caught at his lower lip when he was about to squirt. Slowly, he stroked himself as he let newer images of Moonlight flash through his mind. Of course, he knew now why Moonlight had abruptly stopped wanting to wrestle, and he had to laugh at himself for being so oblivious. Then again, he'd been hiding his own secret from Moonlight. Ironic that they'd been concealing the same thing, both too frightened of exposure and punishment to even mention it when they were alone.

Tiger brought his thoughts back to the night he'd been initiated into the realm of sexual pleasure, or more precisely, to the morning after. He pictured Moonlight kneeling between his feet, arms resting on his thighs. He pictured Moonlight looking up at him as Moonlight's perfect lips neared the head of his cock. He remembered how it had felt when Moonlight had taken him into his mouth for the first time, and his fist moved faster on his hard shaft, the pulses of pleasure in his groin speeding up until they merged into one glorious explosion. Picturing his cock sliding into Moonlight's sheath, he came. Fingers clutching at the sheet and the head of his spurting dick, Tiger rode out the climax as strings of cum oozed between his knuckles. He let go a deep sigh into the darkness as a warm wave of lassitude crept through him. "Jaehan."

After a few minutes, he reached for the underwear he'd dropped at the side of the bed and cleaned himself up. Exhausted from the field tests and the trip, pleasantly drained by the orgasm, and with his head filled with images of Moonlight, he fell asleep.

When he woke, he reported to Mallet and learned he was being sent away for fire team training. Disappointed that he hadn't seen Moonlight on his visit, he packed a bag and left.

"THIS is ready for your seal," Moonlight said when the onmyoji gave permission to speak.

"Bring it." Autumn's long, slender fingers moved in an imperious gesture as he turned to watch Moonlight walk toward him. "Who chose your wardrobe today?"

"I did, master."

"I know." Autumn looked at the document that Moonlight put before him. "But I love hearing you assert yourself. You look very alluring, very elegant, and yet approachable." He rubbed the thin leather of the document between thumb and forefinger. "You did a very good job on this, too. If the ink wasn't fresh, it would look exactly like one of the original scrolls."

Moonlight bowed his head. "I'm glad it pleases you."

"It does please me." Autumn spun around on his stool. "You please me, Moonlight."

"Thank you, master."

"Why do you think I favor you?"

"I believe you said I reminded you of your younger self."

"You do." The onmyoji tilted his handsome face to the side. "You're beautiful, intelligent, and strong-willed. Quite a potent combination. It must be carefully channeled." He cocked his head the other way. "And who channeled me? Is that what you'd like to ask?"

"I'd never be so disrespectful."

"Not while I'm holding the carrot anyway." Autumn smiled. "Don't pout. I'm one of maybe three people in the world that could read your body language at this stage of your training. Your poise and control are remarkable for someone of your age. However, it's obvious to me that the thought uppermost in your mind is that it's been several months and you haven't seen Tiger, as I promised you would."

A pink stain spread over Moonlight's cheekbones.

Autumn made a noise with his tongue against his teeth. "So much control except when it comes to this one thing. You cannot hide how you feel about your old senpai."

"I'll be mindful of it, master."

"Yes, it's good to recognize one's weaknesses," Autumn said. "Tiger is away training to become part of a fire team. When he returns a month from now, you may see him."

"Thank you."

"While you're waiting for him, I have something to help you pass the time."

"How may I serve you?"

"It's time for Smoke's manhood ceremony. I want you to initiate him as you did Tiger." Autumn paused. "Is something wrong?"

"No, of course not."

"Yes there is. I can see it in your eyes. The thought of having sex with anyone but Tiger repels you." Autumn shook his head. "Remember that you are Barazoku. Sex is your sword, and the more you wield it, the more skilled you become."

"I understand." Moonlight bowed his head.

"No, you don't, and this is why you fascinate me so. How did you reach this point in your training with your romantic illusions intact?"

"I don't—"

"Silence." The onmyoji stroked Moonlight's hair. "I'm not in the mood for your stubborn side today. If you want to see Tiger, you'll do as I say."

"I'd rather not see him, then."

"You answered very quickly."

"I'd rather never see Tiger again than betray him."

"You do realize how impractical that attitude is, don't you?"

Moonlight kept his voice to a pleasant murmur when he answered. "I know what I am... what you've made me. I'm trained to seduce and conditioned to obey, and I know I'll do as you say, but my heart will always be mine."

Autumn smiled. "You are so young," he said in a voice as soft as Moonlight's. "There is nothing you have that the Kagehito do not own."

Moonlight took a calming breath. "When would you like your tea?"

"Didn't I tell you to be silent?" Autumn turned back to his writing desk and sat. "I've changed my mind about sending you to Smoke." He paused. "I'm going to send you to each of the former members of your crèche for their initiation into manhood."

"Why, master?"

"Because I believe it would create a unique bond that would—" The onmyoji broke off in mid-sentence. "I'd like my tea now," he said.

Moonlight bowed and left the room, glad to escape the sense of hanging doom in the chamber. He never knew what the onmyoji might say or do, whether he would be cruel or kind, dispensing slaps or pats on the head, and it was wearing on his nerves. For once, the ritual of tea-making failed to calm him. He knew he'd be going on missions eventually, and that he'd have to use his training to seduce strangers, but the thought of initiating his friends made him uncomfortable in a way he couldn't describe.

When the leaves had steeped enough, Moonlight put the pot and a cup on a tray, arranged his face into the serene-fisherman mask, and went back into the onmyoji's study. He smiled pleasantly as he set the cup down in front of Autumn. It would gain him nothing to antagonize his patron, and it was always possible that the wizard would change his mind again and appoint some other Barazoku to initiate Smoke and the others. It was even possible that someday the Kagehito would no longer rule Moonlight's life. Sometimes the only thing that kept Moonlight from screaming until his throat was raw was the thought of a future free of the Shadow People, with Tiger at his side. If he ever lost that hope, he was sure he'd go mad and leap from the top of the wizard's tower.

Autumn took a sip of the tea and smiled. "Very good." He set the cup down. "You think I'm cruel, don't you?"

"Master?"

"You think the Kagehito way is cruel."

"I don't—I never—" Moonlight stammered for the first time in over five years.

"Didn't I remind you not fifteen minutes ago of how well I can read you?"

"How do you do that? Master Drum says I'm the best actor he's ever trained."

Autumn smiled. "Unlike most of the people you will meet in your life, I'm not interested in making you fall in love with me."

"I don't understand."

"I see *you*, Moonlight, not some idealized love object. There will be many who will fight for one of your smiles, but I won't be among them. I'll never be swayed by your grace or your charms because I know them too well. I've been you."

Then why don't you have more compassion? Moonlight quickly dropped his eyes before the wizard saw his thoughts in them.

"I'm no crueler than the hammer that strikes the hot metal on the anvil," Autumn said. "I smelled the forge on you the day I chose you for the Rose Tribe—steam and hot steel. I could feel your destiny beating against my soul like the wings of a dragon. I can't yet see your fate, but I know it will be interesting. That's another reason to keep you close... and of course, there's your power, which I'm harnessing for our people."

Moonlight didn't agree with the onmyoji's analogy—metal didn't have feelings, after all—but he understood what his master was telling him. He was being fashioned according to very specific design into some sort of spy for Autumn's personal use, and Autumn would stop at nothing to achieve the result he wanted.

THE morning after Tiger returned from the mission prep program, he went with Mallet to meet the man at whose beck and call he'd be for an undetermined amount of time. Tiger's new superior was a stocky, middle-aged man of average height, known to the outside world as Hasigo and as Ladder among the Kagehito. Normally, a lower-level official would have given Tiger an orientation, but Ladder had seen Tiger at the fire-team field trials and was happy to meet with the young man and his trainer.

"I'm pleased to add you to my team," Ladder said. "Any ill effects from the trip to the base?"

Tiger looked to Mallet, and then remembered he didn't need permission to answer questions any longer. "None, sir. I rode in a helicopter to the field trials and I enjoyed it, but the airplane was more comfortable."

"It feels a bit odd in those clothes after wearing traditional for so long, eh?"

In fact, Tiger stood as though he'd been wearing white oxford-style shirts and crisp new jeans all his life. From his clothing, demeanor, and hairstyle, you'd take him for an athletic college student.

"They're very comfortable, sir," Tiger answered. "And I have complete range of motion." He demonstrated with a slow-motion roundhouse kick.

"I see you have your priorities in order." Ladder turned his gaze on Mallet. "I understand you wish to work in the field. I'd think dealing with packs of young male humans would involve enough hazards for anyone, but the onmyoji recommended that your request be given consideration. He suggested that you would be suitable for the role of handler. I appreciate that you know Tiger better than anyone, but you don't know anything about running a field agent. So until you learn, you'll be an apprentice to one of our best."

"I'm sure I'll learn a lot from him," Mallet said.

"Your liaison on the outside is a member of Feather Tribe. Smoke is a secretary at the Korean Embassy in Tokyo. He's a sort of clearinghouse for messages between our headquarters and our active agents. He's new, but very sharp." Ladder smiled at Mallet. "It seems that all the members of your latest crèche are exceptional, teacher."

"I only had Smoke until he was twelve," Mallet said. "His Feather teachers deserve credit as well."

"No doubt, but between us, I don't think it's coincidence that your first calling was to the Iron Tribe and that your students always number among the finest. Of course, I'm double Iron, so I might be a bit biased." His eyes twinkled. "Of course, *most* Iron clanners are doubles, and we're always being accused of having too much pride. Can you imagine? Too much pride? How can you have too much pride?"

Tiger shook his head. "I don't know, sir."

"Exactly. You can't." Ladder slipped his hands into the pockets of his suit jacket. "I don't have anything against the Feathers, but they can be a little too… cautious sometimes. That's not how you win wars. And we're in a war, make no mistake about that."

"I won't, sir," Tiger said.

"Are you ready to fight to keep the balance?"

"Yes, sir."

"It's been decided that you'll best serve the Kagehito as an adjuster. Do you know what that means?"

Tiger's gaze went to Mallet again.

"If I may," Mallet said. "I've worked with Tiger for twelve years, and I'm certain he's ready to do whatever needs to be done to keep the balance. He'll follow the orders of his superiors without question, and he won't blink when the time comes to pull the trigger. He understands that he's helping the Kagehito keep the world from turning into a cesspool, and he'll make whatever sacrifices are asked of him."

Ladder nodded at Mallet, and then turned his gaze on Tiger again.

"You want me to kill people," Tiger said. "Evil people. I'm ready for that."

"You've never killed anyone, though."

"Only once, sir. In a challenge match."

"Well, you'll get lots of experience with killing. There are a lot of evil people in the world, each of them tipping all of us a little closer to the slime pit. No shortage of targets at all." Ladder stood, and Mallet and Tiger got to their feet. "You're going to get the rest of your training on the job," he said. "I'm putting you on the active roster as of now."

"I don't mean to question your decision, but—" Mallet began.

"Yes," Ladder answered before the sensei could finish the question, "it's unusual to put a beginner on a fire team right away, but Tiger already has physical skills that match any of my top adjusters. All he needs is experience, and there's only one way he's going to get it."

"Thank you, sir." Tiger bowed. "I'm pleased to hear I can go right to work."

"Rain is waiting for you in the outer office. He'll act as your supervisor from now on."

As Mallet and Tiger left Ladder's office, a man broke off his conversation with Ladder's aide.

"I'm Ame. You call me Rain," the man said. "You're Mallet and Tiger. Follow me."

As Rain turned and walked out the door, Tiger glanced at Mallet. "They don't waste time here," Tiger said. "I like that."

"Oh, I have a feeling you're going to fit right in," Mallet replied as they trailed Rain. "Our guide could be you just a few years from now. You're both in peak condition and have no-nonsense attitudes."

"Perfect assets for a secret agent," Rain said over his shoulder as he stopped in front of a pair of doors. "We've already heard how the amazing Tiger scored the highest of any initiate during his field trials and how he's going to be the best operative in Kagehito history."

"He did very well," Mallet said. "But you don't have to worry about him being conceited."

Rain gave Mallet another look over his shoulder as he opened one of the doors. "I wondered what you were doing here. So you're an interpreter. Does Tiger speak at all?"

"I'm not particularly good with words," Tiger said.

Rain smiled unexpectedly. "Not a problem. That's what Feathers are for." He pushed the other door open. "Welcome to headquarters."

The three men passed through an empty room with lots of chairs around a long table and entered a slightly smaller room filled with electronics equipment and multiple screens of varying sizes.

"This is Tanpopo, our intelligence expert. You call him Dandelion," Rain said as a young man looked up from his keyboard.

"I prefer Lion, but everyone calls me Dandy. I know who you are."

"You already have your second calling," Tiger said. "I noticed you have a monkey paw *and* feather tattoos."

"Yeah, and I have this great job that lets me be both."

Tiger's brows drew together at the faint mocking tone in Dandy's voice, and Rain spoke before the conversation could go any further.

"My office is this way."

"May I ask you something?" Tiger said when Rain closed his office door.

Rain sighed as he sat in the chair behind the desk. "That's what people say when they're about to ask a very personal, embarrassing question. Go ahead," he said, gesturing impatiently for Tiger and Mallet to sit down. "And you don't have to use your formal manners around here."

"I was wondering what's wrong with your arm," Tiger said.

"What makes you think there's anything wrong with either of my arms?"

"You favor your right. Not much, but you do things with your left hand more often than most people."

"Maybe I'm left-handed."

"If you were born left-handed, you'd be less... awkward."

Rain met Mallet's eyes. "Is he like this a lot?"

"Were you any different at eighteen?"

"You have a point." Rain sat forward and rested his forearms on the desk. "Let's be crassly truthful. I don't like having a co-handler forced on me. When my arm was injured," he glanced at Tiger, "I had to stand down from the fire team until I healed. After a while, it became obvious that I was never going to be one hundred per cent again. By taking the position of handler, I was able to stay on active duty, and guess what? I'm good at it. But the handler/operative dynamic is like senpai/kohai, so you can see why I'm a little puzzled and not exactly happy that my new kid comes with a nanny."

Mallet nodded. "Understood. It's always been my dream to be part of a mission team. The onmyoji feels that my best use is as a teacher, but I've been given this chance to experience active duty. Even if I only work on one mission and go back to the island, I'll have the memory."

"There's nothing glamorous or glorious about missions. There's a lot of intelligence-gathering, which means hours and hours of research. A lot of mundane details like flights and time zones have to be organized. The actual hit is over in a split second. The aftermath and everything leading up to it can take days, weeks, months, sometimes years." Rain paused. "The worst part is the waiting. You're all geared up to do your job, but you have hours of time to kill, and yet you have to stay focused."

"I can stay focused," Tiger said.

Without warning, Rain braced his palms and sprang onto his desk like a frog. Without pausing, he launched himself at Tiger. Tiger lifted his feet and kicked at the desk, throwing himself backward. As his chair hit the floor, he rolled to the left, away from Mallet. Rain twisted in midair, as supple as an otter, and avoided the legs of the overturned chair. While Tiger scrambled to his feet, Rain lashed out with his foot and hooked Tiger's ankle. Tiger let himself fall back onto his hands and pushed off the floor, popping to his feet in a squat.

"Don't wait for him to make a move," Mallet barked at Tiger. "Forget that he's your superior. He attacked you."

The next time Rain aimed a kick at Tiger, Tiger reached out with eye-blurring speed. Grabbing Rain by the calf and ankle, Tiger spun, twisting the limb in his grip. Rain was flipped facedown when Tiger released his hold, sending Rain crashing into the wall. When Tiger leaped to follow up, Rain held up a hand.

"Enough," the handler said. "I've seen all I need to." He grinned. "You're very strong."

"I've worked hard to make myself strong."

Rain nodded. "Come on. I'll show you your quarters, and then we'll talk about your first mission with the fire team."

THE express penthouse elevator opened on the gleaming glass and stainless steel of the apartment building's lobby. Yamada Wataru stepped out, accompanied by four members of his security team, and strode across the highly polished marble. They reached the front entrance, and Yamada's round face curdled in displeasure when the doorman was slow.

"Out of my way, useless fool," he barked.

Yamada's bodyguards shoved the doorman aside and made a human tunnel for their boss to walk through. The limousine was idling at the curb, disregarding the no-parking zone. Yamada considered that his wealth put him above the rest of society and that the same rules didn't apply to him. Most of Yamada's employees followed their superior's custom of ignoring the law when it suited them, counting on his influence to keep them out of trouble. With a number of government officials in his deep pockets, neither Yamada nor his associates feared ordinary policemen.

Pulling his Russian sable collar closer around his neck, Yamada stepped out onto the sidewalk, fully confident in the abilities of his hired muscle to keep him safe. He walked toward the car, glancing at one of his men as a cell phone rang in the bodyguard's pocket.

The minder ignored the ringing as he scanned the surroundings for signs of danger, but everything looked as it should on the busy street. Cars and taxis crawled to the light at the intersection, hindered by the pedestrians that crossed the road wherever they pleased. The plate glass windows of a designer clothing store directly opposite gave the bodyguards a mirrored view that allowed them to see what was going on behind them, and all movement in the area was normal for the time of day.

The head of security motioned to the chauffeur to let him know everything was optimal just as a bicycle courier flashed by the limo on the street side. Attracted by the sudden burst of activity, the bodyguards reached for their guns, but the messenger was already turning the corner, causing oncoming traffic to slam on brakes. The man who'd jumped in front of Yamada turned to say something about the suicidal couriers in Tokyo and saw his boss on the sidewalk. Yamada had a surprised look on his face and a small hole in his forehead.

"Man down!" the minder called out as he knelt beside Yamada and his colleagues surrounded him, guns pointed outward.

The head of security quickly determined that his charge had been shot by a weapon with a very effective silencer. Yamada was carried back inside and an ambulance was called while two men chased the courier. As they waited for emergency services, the bodyguards did what they could in the way of first aid. However, it was apparent that Yamada had died instantly.

"No one was tracking that messenger?" The security chief angrily berated his men, and the crowd that had gathered took several steps back. "Not one of you saw him approach?"

One of the men spoke up. "I didn't see him until he was parallel with the limo, and then he was gone. I don't know where he came from."

"He must have come out of the alley between this building and the next one," another man said.

"It happened so fast," said the team's rookie.

The head of security held up a hand for silence and listened to a report on his ear bud. "Damn!" he said under his breath, and then raised his voice. "We lost the shooter."

Several blocks away, atop a high-rise parking garage, Tiger dismounted from the racing bike and unsnapped the chinstrap of his helmet. He heard the unmistakable sound of blades chopping at the air and looked up to see a small, wasp-like helicopter descending. The sleek craft alit on the roof of the structure and Tiger walked over to it. The bike was loaded and Tiger got in. Buckling the harness around him, he nodded to the man in the copilot's seat.

"Good job," Rain said.

Tiger took the compliment with outward calm, but his pulse was still racing, and he had the urge to punch a fist triumphantly into the air. "Thank you, sir," he said, proud of the steadiness of his voice. "Were you able to see the entire procedure?"

Rain nodded. "The helmet-camera worked perfectly." He held out a hand and Tiger passed him the colorful headgear. "It was quick and clean and no one knew anything had happened until it was all over. You're an amazing shot. I was dubious, as I said several times, that you'd be able to make the hit from a moving bicycle, but you did it."

"Yamada was a large target."

"True." Rain chuckled. "But still, you had to hit him on the fly. Not an easy thing and you drilled him right through the forehead. We watched his men carry him inside before we came to pick you up. Yamada won't be selling any more children into slavery."

"Good." Tiger glanced at the pilot. "When are you going to let me take this chopper for a spin?"

"As soon as we get back to base, if that's what you want," Rain said.

"I'd like that," Tiger said. "I've had basic flight instruction with rotors, but not much chance to fly them."

"That can easily be arranged." Rain reached back and tousled Tiger's hair. "You're making me look good, Tiger."

"As if you needed me for that." Tiger grinned.

"I know we're not in this business for the glory," Rain said. "But it's nice to have a good reputation and the respect of your peers."

Tiger nodded. "What's next?"

"So eager," Rain said.

"And effective," the pilot added.

"True." Rain rubbed his chin, looking speculatively at Tiger. "Maybe we should just turn you loose and let you sort out all of the Kagehito's problems."

"I'd like that," Tiger said.

"I'm sure you would." Rain chuckled. "Are you sure the only reward you want is a helicopter joy ride?"

"Well… there is one other thing." Tiger paused. "But it may be too much to ask."

"Tell me your wish, and I'll tell you if it's too much."

Tiger quieted his misgivings and told his team leader what he really wanted: a few days on Saigo Island.

"WELL done," Mallet said as he met Tiger at the helipad on Saigo Island. "You're a full-fledged Iron man now."

Tiger grinned in pleasure at his sensei's approval as they started walking toward the west side of the compound. On the way, he described the mission and answered Mallet's questions. They reached the dividing wall, and Mallet paused.

"I'll say good-bye here," the instructor said.

"Aren't you going to celebrate with me?" Tiger asked.

"Another time. I wanted to greet you, but now I have other obligations."

Tiger was actually relieved when Mallet said good night and walked away. He looked forward to being alone for a while so he could think about Moonlight. Maybe now that he'd been promoted, he could find a way to see his friend.

When Tiger reached his new room, the door was already open. Cautiously, he pushed it wide and looked into the small chamber.

"Sorry to keep surprising you like this," Moonlight said, rising from his seat on the narrow bed.

Tiger crossed the room in two strides and swept Moonlight into a fierce hug. "You're really here," he murmured, his hands moving on Moonlight's back.

"I'm not the one who was away." Moonlight kissed Tiger and couldn't stop until he'd kissed everything he could reach with his mouth.

"I missed you too." Tiger drew back a little to look into Moonlight's eyes. "When I wake up in the morning and don't see this face, the sun doesn't shine for me."

Moonlight ducked his head, smiling shyly. "So you're a poet as well as the best Iron Tribe recruit in a thousand years?"

"What?"

"I hear you did very well on your first mission."

"That's what I hear too." Tiger kissed Moonlight. "And here you are. Now will you listen to my theory about being rewarded for good work? Hey, don't pout. It was just a bad joke."

"It would hurt me if you thought of me like that."

"Of course I don't." Tiger kissed Moonlight again. "I love you."

Moonlight kissed him back and it was several moments before either spoke again.

"Do you want to eat first or—?" was as far as Moonlight got before Tiger's tongue was in his mouth, effectively killing the conversation again.

Turning Moonlight around, Tiger crowded him up against the wall. With shaking hands, he pulled Moonlight's loose trousers to his ankles and ran a hand over the perfect curves of Moonlight's ass. His other hand was busy freeing his cock, which was getting harder with each beat of his heart. Through the weeks and months of separation, he'd fantasized about this moment so many times that it was now a prophecy fulfilled.

Moonlight braced his palms against the cool stone of the wall and waited breathlessly. He heard Tiger spit and then he felt Tiger's hard, slick cock slide between his cheeks. He gasped as Tiger reached around to take hold of him.

Leaning hard against Moonlight, Tiger pulsed his hips, dragging his hardness up and down Moonlight's crack. He stroked Moonlight's cock to the same urgent rhythm, his other hand splayed across Moonlight's taut lower belly, keeping Moonlight's round butt tight against his crotch. Letting his head drop back, he breathed in great gulps of air.

Moonlight pounded a fist silently against the wall, biting his lip to hold in a cry of ecstasy as he came. Reaching over his shoulder, he caught a handful of Tiger's hair and pulled him forward.

Tiger fastened his mouth on Moonlight's neck, sucking strongly as Moonlight's cum oozed between his fingers. He continued to shuttle his fist slowly on the sated shaft as he ground harder against Moonlight's ass. His climax caught him between one thrust and the next, and his seed squirted along the soft delta of skin at the top of Moonlight's cleft. Still holding tight to Moonlight's cock, Tiger leaned harder, nuzzling at Moonlight's nape as the orgasm rolled through him and began to fade.

"Wow." Tiger let out a big breath.

Moonlight smiled as Tiger kissed his ear. "I couldn't wait either, but after we eat something, we're going to do it again. Several different ways."

"I'm not really that hungry."

"Trust me. You're going to need your strength." Moonlight leaned closer to whisper in Tiger's ear, and Tiger waited with a gleeful smile of anticipation for whatever erotic fantasy Moonlight was about to outline. "This room is probably bugged," Moonlight murmured. "Don't say anything you wouldn't want the onmyoji or the commander to hear."

Tiger nodded his understanding and went to sit where Moonlight pointed. When Moonlight asked, Tiger repeated his account of the mission while they ate. As soon as Tiger had wolfed down some food, he pulled Moonlight into his arms and made love to him among the remains of dinner.

The next morning, Moonlight kissed Tiger good-bye and returned to his lessons with the onmyoji, but he was allowed to come back the next evening. And the next and the next until Tiger was assigned to another mission. When the mission was over, Tiger came back to the island again. Again, he and Moonlight were allowed to see each other. Over nearly a year's time, this became their routine as each fulfilled his role within the Shadow and looked forward to the breaks in the battle when they could be together.

"HAVE you heard about how well Smoke's doing?" Moonlight asked as he sprawled in a post-orgasmic haze across Tiger's bed.

"Well… yeah," Tiger said uneasily as he rolled onto his side. He cleared his throat. "I sort of work with him." As he'd feared, Moonlight's reaction was instant and reproachful.

"Why didn't you tell me?"

"I'm not supposed to talk about anything that's mission related. Everything a fire team does is secret. I'm sorry."

"I've never kept one secret from you."

"That's why I'm sorry." Tiger ran a finger down the line of Moonlight's throat to the divot between his collar bones.

"But you're telling me now." Moonlight clamped down on the wild stirring in his groin as Tiger's fingertip traced patterns on his skin.

"Isn't that how it's supposed to work?" Tiger chuckled. "You soften the agent up with mind-blowing sex and then get him to tell you all his secrets?"

Moonlight's temper flared even as the vibrant, baritone sound of Tiger's laugh was setting off warm vibrations in his crotch. Suddenly, Tiger's solid self-assurance looked like crass cockiness. "You don't have the first idea what it's like to be Barazoku," Moonlight said.

Tiger heard the new note in Moonlight's voice and his hand stopped moving on Moonlight's inner thigh. "You're right. I don't. No one does... except maybe another member of Rose Tribe." He met Moonlight's eyes. "Do you want to tell me what it's like?"

Moonlight's delicate features bore a complex expression as he gazed back at Tiger. "I was all ready to be mad at you for being such a clueless, arrogant brute." He reached up to lay his palm against Tiger's cheek. "But the truth is that you just have a terrible sense of humor."

Tiger looked blank for a couple of seconds, and then broke into a full-bellied laugh. "That's true," he said when he caught his breath. "My attempts at jokes have always failed. I always envied the way you and Smoke could be funny without trying."

Moonlight smiled. "He's so smart. Of course you already know he's been promoted to liaison in Tokyo."

"Yeah." Tiger bent his elbow and rested his head on his hand. "But how did you know?"

"The onmyoji told me."

"He shares that kind of thing with you? I didn't realize he was teaching you the business. I thought...." Tiger's voice trailed off.

"What?" Moonlight grinned as he gave his lover a mock slap. "You're so predictable. You thought the onmyoji was teaching me all sorts of secret sexual techniques, didn't you?"

"Something like that." Tiger sighed as he rolled onto his back.

"Does it bother you that I have sex with other people?"

"Does it bother you that I kill other people?"

Moonlight closed his eyes. "I really wish things were different."

"Look, I know I'm a jerk with only one thing on my mind at a time, but I love you."

Moonlight rose far enough to drape himself over Tiger's chest. "I love you too," he said. He knew Autumn was probably recording every word they said, but he was willing to deal with any consequences. Right now, he wanted to be as close to Tiger as he could.

Moonlight kissed Tiger's unshaven chin, nuzzling the small patch of stubble. Barazoku underwent a permanent electrolysis procedure that eliminated all hair follicles except for eyebrows and eyelashes, the top of the head, and the groin. Moonlight would never grow a mustache, never have to shave, and Tiger's sparse whiskers were a turn-on to him.

"You think you Iron Tribe men are tough?"

"We're tough," Tiger answered.

Moonlight snorted. "Roses are tougher than Iron."

"How?"

"Our training requires more strength of will."

"Really."

"Yes, really. My will is stronger than yours, because there are things you wouldn't be able to make yourself submit to."

"You've always had a strange way of looking at things." Tiger wrapped his arms and legs around Moonlight. "How is it stronger to submit?"

"You already know the answer." Moonlight flexed his buttocks, rubbing his crotch against Tiger's. "It's how we survived our first year on the island. It's the lesson the Kagehito have been grinding into us since we got here."

"If you say so." Tiger's breath caught as Moonlight reached between them and grabbed his revived erection.

"I say so." Moonlight got to his knees and shifted until the head of Tiger's cock was pressed against his hole.

Tiger replaced Moonlight's hand on his shaft, and Moonlight let his hands rest on Tiger's chest. Slowly, Tiger lifted his ass as Moonlight sank down. Residual lubricant and recent activity eased the penetration, making it a smooth glide that had both men holding their breath.

"Fuck. That feels so good," Tiger breathed as Moonlight's opening flexed on the base of his cock.

At a languid tempo, Moonlight pumped his hips, palms pressing hard against Tiger's chest as he rocked on Tiger's shaft. Tiger ran his hands over Moonlight's hard pectorals, rubbing the sensitive tips of the rosy nipples with the rough heels of his palms. Moonlight moaned at the exquisite sensation, kneading Tiger's shoulders with his fingertips, digging into the firm muscles. Tiger took Moonlight's nipples between thumbs and forefingers, pinching, twisting and rolling them until Moonlight was shuddering with pleasure. When Moonlight began to ride Tiger's cock faster, Tiger let one hand slide down his lover's cobbled abdomen. Taking hold of Moonlight's leaking shaft, Tiger shuttled his hand up and down. Moonlight's mouth fell open on a gasp of sheer bliss as he thrust into Tiger's fist. Tiger gazed up at the earthy angel that danced atop him, performing a tarnished miracle, transmuting lust to something finer with the alchemy of love. So close now, both so close to the moment when the exciting but almost unbearable tension was broken in a hot rush of ecstasy. Tiger yearned toward that moment, willed Moonlight to reach it with him, every fiber of his being crying out in need, and in a flash of insight, finally understood why this was dangerous… why it was forbidden to novices. It was simply too powerful.

"Come for me," Tiger gasped.

A shiver ran through Moonlight's frame as Tiger lifted his pelvis and began to thrust in short strokes. Moonlight's cock was forced through Tiger's fist to a faster pace, and the extra stimulation drove him over the edge. He came with a hoarse cry, sinking down on Tiger's shaft as he began to spurt. Tiger churned his hips, bouncing Moonlight's ass as Moonlight's cum landed on his belly. The sight of Moonlight's face beatified by bliss launched Tiger's release. Sheathing himself to the hilt, Tiger clutched Moonlight's slim flanks as his seed unfurled. Gasping for breath, hearts beating like thunder, they held on to one another as the echoes of the orgasm gradually faded.

Tiger ran his hands up and down Moonlight's back as Moonlight relaxed completely against his chest. Gently, he eased out of Moonlight's sheath, and Moonlight stretched his legs out, twining them with Tiger's. Tiger turned his head to kiss Moonlight and was snared again by his lover's profligate beauty and the luminous soul in the fathomless depths of his eyes.

"I love you so much," Tiger said, his voice breaking in the middle.

"I know." Moonlight returned Tiger's kiss. "And there's nothing in this world I love as much as you," he said. Let Autumn hear where his true loyalties lay. He knew he was being reckless, but while he was in Tiger's arms, he felt so safe. Snuggling into the solid warmth, he fell asleep.

Tiger stayed awake for a while longer, cradling Moonlight in his arms while he thought about how deep the bond between them ran. It was a little disconcerting to realize how much power his feelings had over him, but he wouldn't change them if he could. Moonlight was his, and it was only right that he love and protect him. Having made a temporary peace with his fears, Tiger dropped off to sleep.

LADDER gestured to Tiger to come in to his office and sit.

"Instead of telling Rain so he can tell Mallet so Mallet can tell you, I'm going to tell you myself." Tiger's top boss tapped his breast pocket. "I had a call an hour ago from Talon."

Tiger nodded in respect. Tsume, called Talon by his brethren, was Iron Tribe's chief enforcement agent.

"We're finally going to go full-scale in Russia," Ladder said. "The field office currently in operation there is going to be replaced by an elite team that will crack Moscow like a nut."

"Good."

"Yes, it is, and long overdue." Ladder smiled. "Talon wants you on the team—you and Rain."

Tiger stopped himself before he could ask about Mallet. "Will I be going back to the island before Russia?"

"I don't know." Ladder looked a bit taken aback. "Do you have any other questions about the assignment?"

"No, sir."

"Somehow I thought you'd be more excited about the posting."

"I am excited, and proud to be chosen, sir."

"Well… then I suppose you can go back to what you were doing."

"Thank you, sir." Tiger left the office.

Two days later, to Tiger's great relief, he returned to Saigo Island in one of the Kagehito's sleek helicopters.

"TIGER!" Moonlight rushed to throw his arms around the other young man, drawing him into an alcove that wasn't bugged. "I know it's only been a few days, but I missed you so much."

Tiger let himself be swept into a kiss that threatened to melt his bones. "Wait," he said when Moonlight let him have some air.

"You must be joking. I'm oiled up and ready to go."

"Shit." Tiger embraced Moonlight fiercely.

"What?" Moonlight pulled back to look into Tiger's eyes. "What's wrong?"

"I'm going to Moscow."

"For how long?"

"A long time."

Moonlight closed his eyes a long moment before opening them again. "You're part of the elite squad."

Tiger nodded.

"I'm so stupid. Why did I believe him?"

"Who?"

"The wizard, of course." Moonlight grimaced. "I knew about the team that's going in to take Moscow, but the onmyoji let me believe that you'd be kept on the Tokyo team."

"I can't figure him out. Sometimes he treats you like his favorite, and sometimes he's so cruel to you that I can't help thinking he hates you."

"I don't think he knows either." Moonlight chewed his lower lip. "He can't decide what to do with me. Sometimes it's like he's grooming me to take over his duties; other times he orders me around like his house servants. He'll send me back to the Roses for a mission and then keep me here for weeks, ignoring any messages asking for me. And of course, no one calls him on it. Everyone's completely terrified of him."

"Does he put spells on them?"

"I wouldn't rule it out. I think most of them are worried about how much he knows about them. He has a lot of spies among the clans." Moonlight didn't elaborate on the onmyoji's spy network or the sort of missions he did for the Barazoku. He didn't talk about how sick he felt when other men touched him or that sometimes his rage was so great that he was afraid he'd choke on it. He didn't mention any of these things or a thousand others that were destroying his hopes and his sanity. Instead, he stuck his head out of the niche and looked up and down the barracks hall. "Run with me," he said when he turned back to Tiger.

"What?"

"The helicopter's still here right?"

"Yeah… probably."

"You can overpower the pilot, can't you?"

"The whole crew, if I need to."

"And you can fly it."

Tiger nodded.

"Then let's just go."

"That's crazy."

"Then be crazy with me. Come on. Don't let this chance slip away."

"We can't." Tiger went over the route in his head anyway. "Too many troops between here and there."

"They won't question you, and if they do, you just say you left something on the helicopter."

"What about you?"

"I'll get there my own way." Moonlight grabbed the front of Tiger's shirt. "We can do this."

"No, we can't. The best we could hope for is to be blown out of the sky."

"We could fly low, head for the coast, and bail out with parachutes. They'll go after the wreckage, and we'll—"

"Stop!" Tiger wrapped his hands around Moonlight's upper arms. "You're scaring me."

Moonlight froze, staring into Tiger's eyes. "*I'm* scaring you?" He broke Tiger's hold and pulled away. "It doesn't scare you that you're being ordered to leave and you don't even question it? Do you question anything?"

"You sound angry."

"I am."

"I know, but it's been a long time since you raised your voice."

"Don't change the subject. Will you go with me or not?"

Tiger shook his head. "They'll kill us if we run. I can't stand the thought of anything bad happening to you."

"Bad things happen to me every day."

"Moonlight, please." Tiger's voice held a note of desperation. "You know how large and powerful the Shadow is. We can't fight it."

"You won't even try!"

"Because I know it's pointless. I've seen what they can—"

"You think I haven't seen things too?" Moonlight cut him off. "Or am I just a little dimmer than you?"

"Of course not, but I don't think you understand—"

"I understand that you're too scared to do what you know is right."

"And you should be too."

"The Kagehito told us we were slaves and you believed them. You gave up a long time ago."

"I'm not moon-brained enough to believe we can fight them."

Moonlight's face went blank. "Then I don't have anything more to say to you." Turning on his heel, he hurried away, disappearing around the corner.

"Wait!" Tiger took two long strides and entered the main hall, stopping in surprise. Moonlight was nowhere in sight. Tiger questioned the Lightning Tribe initiate coming in the front door, but the messenger hadn't seen anyone leaving. Though Tiger searched until it was time for bed, he found no sign of Moonlight or anyone who had seen him. Knowing he wouldn't sleep, he sought out Mallet.

Mallet looked up from the book he was reading when Tiger stopped in front of him. "What can I do for you, Tiger?" he asked.

"I can't find Moonlight."

Mallet put down his book and invited Tiger to sit.

"I can't stay," Tiger said. "I need to find him."

"You will or you won't, and your entire life will be different depending on which occurs. And the hell of it is... you'll never know if the other would have been better or worse for you." Mallet glanced out the window of the Denkouzoku dormitory's common room. "I know you boys wonder what your lives would have been like if they hadn't been forfeit to the Kagehito." He met Tiger's eyes again. "You will never know the answer to this question. You *were* taken in by the Kagehito, and that can't be changed."

"I know this."

Mallet nodded, conceding the point. "But neither of us has been able to teach this lesson to Moonlight. I would stake my life that, in his heart, he still hopes to find his family and make everything the way it was before he was brought to the island."

"I don't know about that," Tiger said evasively.

"Of course you do. You know him better than anyone, even me. You know he's never truly accepted that he belongs to the Shadow."

Tiger was quiet for a few moments before he spoke again. "Do you know why the onmyoji allows Moonlight to visit me?"

"Incentive would be the obvious reason, but the wizard is seldom obvious." Mallet shook his head. "I don't pretend to understand why he's breaking so many traditions lately, but I'm not the man to question someone of his stature."

"Maybe someone should."

"I've never heard you talk this way." Mallet looked up in surprise. "If I were in charge, you would not have seen Moonlight again after your crèche was broken up. He was useful for controlling you when you were boys, but now his influence is weakening you."

"You're wrong about that. My love for him makes me strong."

"Only a very young man is blind to the way love weakens him." Mallet sighed. "Moonlight's getting a reputation for being the onmyoji's ears... among other things. I'd caution you to be careful with him."

"He wouldn't do anything to hurt me."

"It's not what he might do, but what he *is* that should frighten you."

"And what's that?"

"Roses cannot be trusted. Deceit is their way of life. Everyone knows this."

"Moonlight would never deceive me."

"You don't think so? Have you kept things from him?"

"Only if I thought they would hurt him."

"What makes you think he hasn't done the same?"

"I know him."

Mallet sighed. "I guess you've stopped listening to your old teacher. I knew it would happen one day, and you've certainly made your mark with the Blue Iron fire team. Maybe you don't need my advice anymore."

"Don't try and play on my sympathy. I don't have any. You made sure of that."

Mallet smiled. "Just try not to make too big a fool of yourself out there in the world without my guidance. I wouldn't care except that it would reflect badly on me."

Tiger aimed a mock punch at Mallet and dodged the return swing. "I'm going to run a circuit," he said. "See if I can tire myself out enough to fall asleep. You want to come?"

"No. I'd like to stay here and finish my book. Tiger... be wary."

"Aren't I always?"

"Except when it comes to Moonlight."

"I'm going to ask Ladder if Moonlight can come to Russia with me."

"That's not what I'd call being cautious. Do you really want to call attention to your... relationship with him?"

"Other Kagehito have formed couples. It isn't forbidden."

"Maybe not for men who've been in service for years and have earned privileges. You're barely twenty and at the beginning of your service."

"The quality of my service will make up for the lack of quantity," Tiger said over his shoulder as he trotted away.

Mallet shook his head as the young man disappeared behind a screen of trees. In his way, Tiger was as much of a dreamer as Moonlight. Mallet had recognized how potent their pairing could be back when they were soft six-year-olds, but he'd counted on the secondary training to break that childhood bond. Instead, their separation made their longing to be together even stronger. Down that path lay obsession, and it worried Mallet to see his best pupil taking the first steps in that direction. It was true that this craving could be used to control Tiger, but it could just as easily impair him.

Without much hope that his words would be heeded, Mallet took up his pen and wrote a letter to the onmyoji. He was surprised to receive a reply and even more surprised when he was sent back to Blue Iron as a team member. However, the wizard's carefully worded command to keep an eye on Tiger cleared up the mystery. Mallet intended to do exactly as the onmyoji suggested, but for his own reasons this time. Humming tunelessly, he began to pack.

 Part Five

"YOU know what this team really needs?" Tiger asked.

Over the top of his monitor, Dandy gave Rain a look of incredulity at Tiger's audacity.

Rain smiled and glanced over at the fire team's junior member. "Enlighten us, Tiger," he said.

"A Rose."

"A Rose?" Dandy echoed.

"Yeah. Wouldn't it have been nice on that last job to have a Barazoku to seduce that gay head of security? A Rose would have brought us the key to the building, and we wouldn't have had to use all that climbing equipment."

"That's true," Rain admitted. "You know, it used to be standard for all fire teams to have a Rose as a member. Wonder why we don't anymore."

"Because they cause too much internal strife," Dandy said. "It's a matter of historical record that when you have a Barazoku on the team, it leads to a breakdown in integrity."

"What?" Tiger looked over at Dandy.

"Just having one of those witches around causes tension that causes division that causes team members to be at one another's throats."

"That sounds like crap to me," Tiger said. "We're Kagehito. We don't get distracted by the things that distract ordinary men."

Rain and Dandy exchanged a glance. "If you feel strongly about it," Rain said, "I can mention it to Talon and see what he thinks."

"I'm just trying to improve the team," Tiger said. "When do we meet Talon?"

"He'll be here soon. The plan is for him to run a mission with us before we leave for Russia."

"I'm looking forward to working with him. He's a legend."

"Someday someone will say the same thing about you," Rain said. "If you live that long."

"I love your motivational speeches," Tiger said.

Something that sounded like a giggle came from behind Dandy's monitor.

"What are you simpering at?" Rain said. "You encourage his cockiness with your hero worship."

Dandy gasped. "That's not true!"

"Then why is there a picture of Tiger under your pillow?"

"There isn't!"

"Don't be embarrassed, Dandy," Rain said. "It's only natural that you'd look up to a guy like Tiger and that you've have some feelings for—"

"If you're just going to be ridiculous, I'm not going to listen," Dandy said, slipping on a pair of headphones.

"He loves you," Rain told Tiger.

"Impossible," Tiger replied. "His heart already belongs to you."

Rain chuckled. "I'm glad the whole team is going to Russia. I'd hate to have to go through the process of getting comfortable with a group of strangers again."

"I'll miss Ladder," Tiger said.

"He'll miss you too," Rain said. "He really looks on you as a son, or at least a nephew."

"Well, I still have Mallet to mother me."

Rain started to chuckle, but his reply was preempted.

"Someone just landed in a G-5 jet," Dandy said, pulling one of the earpieces away from his head. "Inbound from Saudi Arabia. It could be Talon." He listened to the headphones and then spoke again. "It's him."

"This team is about to go into hyper-drive," Rain said.

"Don't forget to ask him about—"

"I won't," Rain said. "Dandy's piqued my interest with his dire warnings. Now I *have* to know what it's like to work with a Rose."

Tiger bit the inside of his cheek to keep from saying anything. Besides Mallet, only Ladder had any inkling of Tiger's connection with Moonlight, and only in the vaguest of terms. Tiger's boss knew only that his new recruit was allowed to return to Saigo Island from time to time, that he met someone there, and that he had the onmyoji's approval. Tiger didn't want this special treatment to drive a wedge between him and the members of his team. It occurred to him that taking Moonlight to Russia might tip his hand, but he'd have to trust that he and Rain and Dandy knew each other well enough now for them to accept the relationship.

Tiger reined in his thoughts. There was no guarantee that they'd be taking a Rose with them to Russia, or even if they did that the Rose would be Moonlight. He needed to stop worrying about problems that might never come up and focus on the work in front of him.

"I'd like the opportunity to work with a Rose too," Tiger said as Rain stood up. "Can I go with you to meet Talon?"

"He requested that you be there when he arrived," Rain said. "Your hotshot reputation is really getting around."

Tiger jumped to his feet and followed his superior, determined to make a good impression on Blue Iron's new team leader. He didn't even have to try.

Talon had not only read the standard dossiers on each of his new team members, he'd done his own research, and he liked everything he'd learned about them, particularly Tiger. He took Tiger's hand when they were introduced and pulled him into an Iron clan warriors' embrace. Loudly stating that he was looking forward to leading a team of like-minded men, he called an immediate staff meeting. Once inside the tactical room, Talon's demeanor became markedly milder. There was no question that he was in charge, but it was at a lower volume. He listened more than he spoke, and within a half hour had won the goodwill of his new team. One of his first acts was to expedite Rain's request for a Rose.

"LISTEN to this," Autumn said, turning the letter a little more toward the light as he read aloud. "'I was wondering, as was Lord Mahogany, whether you had some overriding reason for keeping such a valuable asset out of circulation.'" The onmyoji sniffed disdainfully. "No one knows how to deliver a veiled insult these days. Talon's heavy-handed reference to the chief of Iron Tribe is supposed to throw a scare into me."

"Has he never met you, master?" Moonlight wondered.

Autumn chuckled. "Mahogany certainly has, but not Talon." He paused. "Maybe Talon should meet *you*." His eyes widened slightly as they focused on a point somewhere between him and Moonlight. He appeared not to breathe as he stood unmoving for several heartbeats. "Yes," he said slowly. "Yes, Talon should meet you."

"Master?" Moonlight said as Autumn went to his writing desk.

"Quiet. I need to compose a letter and I have to strike just the right tone. Talon will get what he wants, but I want it to be clear that it's only by my generosity." He turned his head to look at Moonlight. "Are you still here? Go and pack. You're going on a mission."

Moonlight blinked. Again the onmyoji had caught him off balance. "Yes, master," he murmured and glided from the room. He had just finished filling a large backpack when Autumn entered his room.

"Yes, master?"

"You'll be gone for an indefinite period of time," the wizard said. "I feel as though I should give you some timeless piece of wisdom." He tapped his lips with his forefinger. "But that would be pointless. You won't listen. The only thought in your head is that you'll be spending more time with Tiger. I defy you to tell me I'm wrong."

"You're not wrong, not at this moment anyway."

"I see you packed sparingly. Good. You'll be given whatever clothing you need for the assignment when you get to Tokyo."

Moonlight nodded. "When do I—?"

"Leave?" The onmyoji laughed. "You can't wait to be away from here, can you?"

"A change of scenery can be very pleasant and mind-broadening," Moonlight answered.

"Clever child." Autumn smiled his humorless smile. "I want you to do something for me while you're with the Blue Iron fire team."

"You want me to spy on Iron Tribe's top enforcer," Moonlight guessed.

"I want Talon humbled."

Moonlight gave his master an inquiring look.

"You heard me, Moonlight. I want you to break him down."

"I'm not sure what you mean by that."

"Why do you pretend that things you find unpleasant simply don't exist? It's better to deal with life's little miseries head-on. Look the trolls in the face and cut their heads off." Autumn put a hand on Moonlight's shoulder. "You will seduce Talon and turn him into your lapdog."

"I'd really rather not."

"I'm sure." Autumn dug his fingertips into Moonlight's muscles. "I don't care how you feel about it. Just do it."

"I might not have enough time."

"Then cheat, do whatever you have to, but make Talon your creature... and by extension, my creature as well. When he advances, he'll be very useful." Autumn looked into Moonlight's eyes. "You will do this for me. I will tell you how." He leaned closer and began to whisper in Moonlight's ear.

"THE Barazoku is here," Dandy said as he took off his headphones and set them down. He looked across the ready room at his new boss. "I told security to send him down."

Talon nodded from behind his computer. "Good. He can meet everyone at once."

A short time later, the outer door to the fire team's quarters opened, and everyone present turned to look as a slender figure seemed to flow into the room.

Moonlight's hair was a nest of soot-black tendrils that emphasized the marble smoothness of his skin. He wore a pair of snug pants of some soft-looking, nubby material and a thigh-length shirt of a fabric as pale and filmy as a cloud. His dusky coral nipples and the chiseled musculature of his pectorals and abdomen were clearly visible through the mist-colored fabric. Around his hips was knotted a length of red silk that trailed gracefully as he moved. Each step was accompanied by the jingle of the metal discs sewn to the tops of his ankle boots. His every motion drew the eye, and the attention sat easily on him; he was neither embarrassed nor vain, but projected an air of self-possessed serenity.

A shiver ran down Tiger's spine as Moonlight's gaze skipped over him as though he was a piece of furniture.

Moonlight homed in on Talon and bowed to him. "I'm Moonlight. I present myself for service."

Talon felt an odd shock as the Barazoku's gaze met his. He couldn't tell what color Moonlight's eyes were, and found himself staring into them a bit longer than was polite. "I'm Talon. I look forward to working with you."

"So do I." Moonlight held Talon's gaze.

"These are the members of your fire team. Rain, Dandy, and Tiger."

Moonlight nodded to each man as he was introduced. "I know Tiger," he said. "We were crèche mates."

Tiger blinked. He hadn't expected a hug, but he was hurt by Moonlight's coolness toward him. "I look forward to working with you too," he said.

"Would you like to see where you'll be staying while you're here?" Talon asked.

Moonlight shook his head. "I left my bag with security. I don't need to see my bed until it's time to sleep. I'd like to be up to speed, if I have a choice."

"Excellent." Talon sat back down at the head of the long table scattered with papers and electronic devices. "Our target is this man," he said, turning a screen around so Moonlight could see a picture of a middle-aged Japanese man with a wispy mustache and goatee. "Obato Shige is the head of the Port Authority. He was a wealthy man before he was appointed to this powerful position, but I guess having money only made him greedy for more. He takes big payoffs from the Yakuza in return for allowing the shipment of drugs into the country. Mr. Obato is very corrupt and very paranoid. Because of a series of political assassinations a couple of years ago, no one thinks it's odd that he never goes out without a bulletproof vest and helmet or that he's always completely surrounded by bodyguards."

Rain spoke up, and Moonlight turned toward him. "We were having a hard time finding a way to get to Obato until Dandy found online evidence that he visits Internet sites that are nothing but libraries of pornography. Obato prefers films that feature young male 'performers' who have a certain... delicacy of features and well-developed bodies."

"He's going to love you," Dandy said, looking at Moonlight over the top of his glasses.

"Let's hope so," Talon said. "But first we have to introduce them. We've yet to come up with one idea that—"

"*Nantaimori*," Moonlight murmured.

"Excuse me?" Talon raised his eyebrows at being interrupted.

"Have you thought of using *nantaimori* as a way to attract Obato's attention?"

A smile formed slowly on Talon's lips. "We'd have to set up a legitimate business, but that's no problem. Neither is publicizing it where he'll hear about it. He's bound to be intrigued by the concept of eating his dinner off a naked man."

"He'll jump at this bait," Rain predicted.

Talon looked around the room. "Well?"

"We'd need a classy menu," Dandy said. "With classy photos of the... tables."

"I was asking what you thought of the idea, but I think I can assume that you think it's a good one," Talon said. "I'd like to see your virtual mock-up for the menu as soon as it's finished."

"I think you'd make a very convincing restaurant owner," Moonlight told Talon. "And you should be the one who handles the arrangements. If Obato is paranoid, his people are probably suspicious of everything. They'll sense your authority and it will soothe them."

Talon smiled at Moonlight before he turned to Dandy. "Tell Smoke what we need," he said. "The sooner we adjust this scum, the sooner we get to Russia and earn our reputations. We're on a roll now. Let's keep the ideas coming."

Tiger sighed. "Doesn't it go without saying that I'm going to be a waiter with a hypodermic containing a lethal dose of potassium chloride solution under a napkin on my tray?"

"And that I'll distract the bodyguards long enough for it to be administered," Moonlight added.

"It'll look like Obato's choking or having a heart attack," Dandy said.

"I'll call for emergency services," Tiger said. "But they'll be too late to save him."

Talon nodded. "I think it'll work. The authorities will ask you and Moonlight a lot of questions, and they'll probably call me, but they'll let you go and there'll be nothing the bodyguards can do to stop you with the police on the scene. I like a plan where everyone lives."

"Except the target," Tiger said, and looked surprised when everyone laughed.

"Then let's move like we have a purpose," Talon said.

MOONLIGHT opened the door to his room and let Tiger in. As soon as the door was closed, he threw his arms around Tiger.

"What a relief," Tiger said. "I thought you were still mad at me for not running away with you."

"I was sad, not mad."

"Don't be. We can be together now." Tiger grinned. "I'm the one who suggested that the team needed a Rose."

"And now you have one."

"You don't sound happy."

"Think about it. Why would the onmyoji give in to Talon's request?"

"Because he had no choice."

Moonlight shook his head. "The onmyoji sent me here for his own purpose. He wants Talon in his pocket, and you gave him his chance."

"Are you saying the wizard wants you to… influence Talon?"

"Definitely."

"Once we're in Russia, you won't be taking orders from him anymore."

Moonlight held Tiger tighter. "I wish that was true," he said softly. "How long can you stay?"

Tiger pressed his lips to Moonlight's in a sweet kiss. "As long as you want me to."

"My heart floats when you say things like that, but we have to be practical. We've done really well so far, keeping a professional distance in public, but if we start sneaking around like this, someone's bound to figure it out. These aren't stupid people we're working with."

"I don't care if they know." Tiger's lips moved against Moonlight's throat.

"Yes, you do. If our superiors here knew we were lovers, they'd reassign one of us."

Tiger left off nuzzling Moonlight's collarbones to wrap him in a tender hug. Gently, he rocked from foot to foot as he stroked Moonlight's hair. "I had to see you," he murmured. "It's really hard to be around you all day and not be able to touch you or even smile at you. I didn't come here for sex. I came here to be alone with you."

"I hate the Kagehito," Moonlight said in a choked voice. "I hate what they've done to us. I hate that we can't love out in the light. I hate myself for what I'm doing."

"Shush." Tiger kissed Moonlight's forehead. "That's your conditioning. You have to follow orders. You don't have a choice."

"My orders include seducing Talon."

Tiger's heart clenched with a sharp pain. "Does that mean you have to sleep with him?"

"I don't see how it can be avoided. Of course, I'll stall for as long as possible, but eventually, I'll have to deliver on all my implied promises of sexual ecstasy."

"I'm sorry," Tiger said, holding Moonlight a little tighter.

"I thought you'd be angrier."

"What's the point? I can tell you that it flays my heart to think of you with Talon or anyone else but me. I can tell you that my first impulse was to find Talon and kill him. I can tell you that I want to scream at you to ignore your orders. But what good does any of that do? Anger is not a luxury I can afford yet."

Moonlight made a sound like a strangled sob and his voice was squeezed thin when he spoke. "I just want to be free to feel the way I feel. To not have to hide my real emotions. I'm so tired of wearing my face like a mask."

"I really am sorry. It's easier for me. Outside of film and photos, I usually only see the target once or twice before the adjustment, if at all. I don't have to interact with them the way you do. If you ever need to talk about it, you can talk to me."

"Really?" Moonlight wiped at his eyes with his fingertips. "Are you sure you'd want to hear about it?"

"We should be able to talk about anything."

"We should… but we're Kagehito."

"Don't be cynical with me. I'm the one who loves you," Tiger said, holding Moonlight at arm's length before pulling him back for a kiss.

Moonlight poured himself into the kiss, embracing Tiger as though he meant to absorb him. Slowly, he drew away, sucking Tiger's lower lip into his mouth as he ended the kiss. Sliding down to his knees, he let his hands trail over Tiger's chest, stroking and squeezing. He rubbed his face against Tiger's crotch, against the growing bulge, as he unfastened Tiger's trousers. Kissing the soft skin of Tiger's lower belly, Moonlight reached through the fly of Tiger's shorts and pulled out his cock.

Tiger sucked in a big breath and widened his stance as Moonlight's lips touched the head of his dick. He moaned with pleasure as Moonlight sucked at the tip while teasing it with his tongue. Two seconds into the blow job and Tiger knew he was going to come hard and fast. Looking down, he met Moonlight's eyes, and the small degree of control he didn't realize he was hanging onto was burned away in a rush of volcanic heat. His knees went weak and his vision blurred as he climaxed in three powerful surges of all-consuming pleasure. Slowly, he sank to the floor, his sated cock sliding from Moonlight's mouth.

"I love you so much," Tiger said, covering Moonlight's mouth with his in a sweet kiss while pushing aside his robe.

Moonlight whimpered as Tiger's hand closed around his hard dick. He would do anything for this man, to feel his touch, his love, and each time they were together like this, he came undone. Only with Tiger could he drop all his masks and defenses. Only to Tiger could he give himself completely. Only at these times did he feel like a real person.

Tiger gazed on Moonlight's beloved features, softened by the heat of passion, and knew he'd never see anything half as beautiful in this life. Sliding an arm under Moonlight's lower back, Tiger leaned in, and the kiss grew fevered as his hand shuttled up and down on Moonlight's arousal. Lowering his lover to the floor, Tiger eased a finger into him, searching out his prostate. With little teasing thrusts, Tiger toyed with the small, pliable bump, eliciting louder moans and pleas for more. Reading Moonlight's body like a sailor with a weather eye, Tiger caressed him until the cumulative power of each stroke reached critical mass.

Moonlight gasped as the sweet tension in his groin exploded, overloading his system with pleasure so intense it made his muscles ache. Shuddering in reaction, his abs contracting in waves, he lay helpless in Tiger's arms for the brief eternity before the climax started to subside. Echoes of sheer bliss were still rippling outward from his core when Tiger moved between his thighs and entered him.

Tiger's cock pulsed in answer to Moonlight's abandoned cry of pleasure. Holding Moonlight's thighs against his chest, Tiger rocked in and out to the meter of his lover's wordless poetry. From the moment they'd met, he'd never felt so connected to anyone, and he was grateful that this affinity extended to lovemaking. He was more comfortable expressing himself physically, and being able to bring Moonlight to this state of oblivious grace meant a lot to him. And so he thrust, tirelessly and at various angles, depths, and speeds, until Moonlight grew hard again. Wrapping his fingers around Moonlight's revived erection, Tiger stroked him inside and out until he crested again. Easing his control, Tiger climaxed at the same time, pulling out to press his spurting cock against Moonlight's. As Moonlight's legs slid down Tiger's sweat-slick shoulders, Tiger pressed himself to Moonlight, kissing his way up to Moonlight's lips.

"My stars," Moonlight cursed mildly in a voice grainy with exhaustion.

Tiger stopped nuzzling long enough to reply. "It was good?"

"I forgot where I was. Lost my mind completely." Moonlight could feel Tiger's mouth curving into a smile. "And that's how we do it."

"What?"

"You're always wondering what it's like to be Barazoku. I'm illustrating a point for you. Making a man feel like he's the world's greatest lover is a key element of—"

Tiger sat up. "You were playing me?"

"Of course not." Moonlight stroked Tiger's cheek. "I'm always honest with you. You know that."

"Well… your timing really sucked on this one."

"I'm sorry. I always manage to ruin things somehow."

"You make life worth living for me. If I thought for a minute that you were pretending… it would kill me."

"I'm really sorry. It's just that my whole life is deception now. The only time I can lower my guard is when I'm with you."

Tiger kissed Moonlight in forgiveness. "It won't always be like this," he said. "If I keep getting promoted so quickly, I could be a boss in a few—"

Moonlight put his hand over Tiger's mouth. "No. You don't want that. To become a boss, you have to really become one of them… and then I couldn't love you anymore."

Tiger shut his eyes for a moment, and Moonlight uncovered his mouth. "I'm just being realistic," Tiger said. "And it would be nice if you had a little more faith in me. Isn't it possible that I could become a chief without being corrupted?"

Moonlight shook his head. "They'd sniff you out right away and quietly destroy you."

"Who?"

"The ones who hold the *real* power. The ones who use the organization for their personal agendas. If you're not one of them, you have no influence. They'll freeze you out."

"What a pessimist."

"I'm just being realistic."

Tiger chuckled and kissed Moonlight again. "I don't like reality," he said as he got to his feet.

"It's all we've got to work with." Moonlight accepted Tiger's offer of a hand up. "For now."

"What's that mean? Is the onmyoji teaching you magic spells now?"

"Mostly herbal concoctions so far," Moonlight said as he went into the small bathroom. "Autumn's magic seems to consist of a very strong will and the power of suggestion."

Tiger lay down on Moonlight's single bed. "He's got real influence though."

"He's the only one who can read the stars and interpret their messages." Moonlight flushed the toilet and went to the sink. "So few Kagehito are called to the Dragon Tribe. The only other living onmyoji is eighty-nine and senile."

Tiger got up as Moonlight exited the bathroom, kissing his ear as they passed. "You have an incomparable ass," he said over his shoulder.

"I could say the same, and mean it." Moonlight turned to throw a hand towel at Tiger.

Tiger snatched the towel out of the air and took it into the bathroom with him. "I think I'm going to like working with you," he called over the sound of his splash.

"I really hope so," Moonlight murmured.

Tiger came out of the bathroom and put on the clothes Moonlight tossed at him. "Are you trying to tell me something?" he joked.

"Yeah. Wipe that well-laid look off your face before you leave."

"Is it *that* obvious that I had sublime sex a few minutes ago?"

Moonlight grinned. "Yeah. What about me?" He framed his face between his hands and looked up at Tiger.

"You look absolutely amazing. Are you sure you're from this planet?" Tiger pulled Moonlight into a hug, holding him tightly.

Moonlight poured himself into the embrace, absorbing each second spent in Tiger's company, laying the shining moments away for when he was alone again.

"Enough." Moonlight's training made it easier for him to pull away first. "Go get some sleep. We've got to go to work in the morning."

TIGER swallowed hard when he walked into the private dining room and saw Moonlight lying on a low table, wearing nothing but cleverly-placed morsels of sushi. Moonlight's perfect body and flawless skin outshone the artfully-assembled hors d'oeuvres and flower arrangements. Obato Shige, the target of this operation, was going to melt like wax in a furnace when he got a look at his dinner.

The justifiably paranoid man who controlled the flow of imports in Tokyo's harbor had elected to come to a restaurant rather than have strangers in his home for his private birthday celebration.

On the short guest list were two prominent political figures and a bona fide gangster. These were the only three people, aside from Obato's personal staff, who'd made the cut. They were here by virtue of the fact that they were homosexuals... like Obato.

"Tiger," Mallet called out, and Tiger joined his sensei at the service cart.

"Nice work," Tiger said, watching Mallet fold a linen napkin into a lotus.

"There is no task so small that it is not worthy of being done well."

Tiger glanced at Moonlight. "I'm glad I'm not playing his part," he said. "He's going to be in that position for at least another hour."

"I'm trying not to imagine what it would feel like to have an octopus draped over my *chinko*."

"I'm not deaf," Moonlight said. "And it feels like a rubber glove full of cold jelly."

Tiger walked over to Moonlight, highly aware that Talon's eyes followed his every move—as they followed anyone who got close to Moonlight.

"I wish I could warm you up," Tiger whispered as he reached the table.

"Go away. Talon's watching us."

"Mallet says Talon's infatuated with you."

"That *was* the plan."

"Mallet is probably going to report Talon for laxness and favoritism."

"Our sensei always was vigilant."

"Can you meet me later?"

"A lot later. After midnight."

"I'll be waiting."

Tiger walked away, content with his near future, and Moonlight went back to staring at the ceiling. He had nothing to do at the moment but think, and his thoughts revolved around the onmyoji's plan to enthrall the Iron Tribe's chief enforcement officer. Armed with his training and Autumn's inside information on Talon, Moonlight had seduced him and played upon his natural possessive tendencies. The Blue Iron fire team leader was now in imminent danger of letting his jealousy undermine his authority. Talon was still in control of himself in public, but he was shaky, and he was standing on the edge.

Moonlight took several long, deep, calming breaths. He hated what he was doing to Talon of Iron Tribe. Talon was a good man, not some morally degenerate criminal that deserved to be destroyed. Countless times when Moonlight was alone with Talon, he had nearly blurted out his deception, but each time he'd refrained. As long as Tiger lived, the onmyoji would always be assured of Moonlight's cooperation. It would be all too easy for the wizard to order Tiger's death, as he'd implied more than once.

Moonlight reminded himself to stay focused on his ultimate goal. He could endure anything for the chance that he would one day escape with Tiger. Right now, he needed to concentrate on the task of beguiling a proven bad guy so his colleagues could take the man off guard.

At precisely 8:29 p.m., Obato's aide called and spoke to Talon. Three minutes later, the rear entrance to the rented restaurant was thrown open to Obato and his party.

"We're live," Talon murmured to his crew as the guests were seated.

Tiger nodded as he took the drinks tray that Mallet handed him. He suppressed his distaste at the way Obato and his cronies drooled openly over Moonlight's naked form. Unobtrusively, Tiger placed water beside each man's plate and took their drink orders. By the time the guests finished their second round, the combination of alcohol and the Barazoku's allure had dulled their awareness.

Obato announced that it was time to eat, and his guests reached eagerly for the feast spread before them. The attention of everyone seated at the table was fastened on Moonlight. Tiger leaned over Obato to refill his water glass before moving on to the next man. As Tiger listened to a request for a straight Scotch, Obato made a choking sound and began to twitch.

One of the four Obato bodyguards in the room hurried over to his boss.

"Is the wasabi too hot for you?" one of the guests joked.

Obato was shaking violently, like a man in the throes of a seizure. Talon reached into his pocket and all four bodyguards trained guns on him.

"I'm calling for an ambulance," Talon said, and the weapons were lowered… slightly. At least they weren't pointed directly at him anymore.

"You!" The chief of Obato's security pointed at Tiger as Mallet went through the motions of performing the Heimlich maneuver on Obato. "You were the last one near him."

"I filled his water glass," Tiger said calmly. He'd already palmed the small hypodermic and stashed it under a napkin on the table.

"Take it easy," Talon said. "No need to let our concern for Obato-san get the better of us. The ambulance will be here soon."

"He's not breathing," Mallet said, lowering Obato to the floor. He began giving the man CPR, but one of the bodyguards displaced him.

"There's a heartbeat," the guard said as he began compressions, alternating with mouth-to-mouth breathing.

"If I find out that my boss was poisoned, I'll skin all of you," the chief bodyguard said.

"Calm yourself," said one of Obato's politician friends. "That sort of violent threat only increases the tension."

"I don't need your opinion on the matter, sir," the bodyguard answered. "As far as I'm concerned, you're a suspect for suggesting this restaurant."

The politician made a show of swallowing the food in his mouth before picking up his napkin to dab at his lips. Light winked on glass and metal as the syringe tumbled to the floor, and the head bodyguard's gaze fastened on it, identifying it in a split second. His head came up sharply and he pointed his gun at Tiger. Tiger was already on his way to the floor.

"It's a setup," the chief bodyguard barked.

As Obato's men opened fire, Tiger rose from behind Obato's gangster friend and knocked the gun from a man's hand with a tray. Somersaulting over the low table—and Moonlight—Tiger landed on his feet in a squat. Leaping forward, he crashed into another guard and took him to the floor, where Mallet bashed his skull in with the teapot. Talon had grabbed the gun that Tiger had dislodged, and he took aim at one of the two remaining Obato soldiers. Obato's guests had wisely taken what minimal cover was available, as the pair of bodyguards shot at anything that moved. Moonlight still lay atop the table, as motionless as an ice sculpture.

"Don't move," Tiger murmured as he began crawling on elbows and knees around the table. The room was clean of weapons, as specified by Obato and enforced by an inspection earlier in the day. However, there were many items lying around that could inflict physical damage. Groping around the exposed corner of the table, Tiger felt the slim outline of a dropped chopstick. He gripped it like a throwing knife, popped up to his knees, and did a lightning visual assessment of the scene.

"Stay down," Mallet shouted.

As the bodyguard near the door turned toward Mallet, time slowed for Tiger. As he prepared to throw the chopstick, he watched the hired gun take aim at Mallet. As he cocked his arm, he caught the attention of the other gunman. Ignoring the pistol coming to bear on him, he was poised on the cusp of the strike when Moonlight sat up, blocking his field of vision.

"No!" Tiger shouted frantically. "Get down!"

Moonlight flung himself to the side, and Tiger threw the chopstick. The slim bar of silver entered the left eye of the man pointing his gun at Moonlight. The other bodyguard fired, and his bullet took Mallet through the throat.

Talon ferreted out the disarmed bodyguard and shot him through the head. "All of them," he shouted to his team.

Tiger looked up from Mallet's lifeless body and met his leader's eyes. After a moment, he nodded and got up to kill the two surviving members of Obato's party.

"Sounds like the paramedics are here," Tiger said after he finished breaking the sobbing politician's neck. "For all the good—" He paused when he saw the smile exchanged by Talon and Moonlight. "But those aren't real paramedics, are they, Talon?"

Talon shook his head as Rain and Dandy came in the door at a trot. "Moonlight came to me with a scenario eerily like the one that played out here. I made the decision to order a sweep crew. I don't pretend to understand the way of the Rose, but Moonlight's 'premonition' was correct."

"And you didn't tell the rest of us?" Tiger said.

"It was last-minute, and the team was honed to such a fine edge that I—"

"Our leader made a decision and that's the end of it," Moonlight said as he joined them.

"Maybe things would've gone differently if we'd had more information," Tiger said.

"There was no way to plan for a random occurrence," Talon said. "All that happened is that Moonlight had a doubt and expressed it to me. Because he did, we managed to avoid complete disaster." He glanced to where Rain knelt beside Mallet. "We lost a good soldier today, a teacher who trained champions of the Kagehito."

"Well said, Talon." Moonlight surreptitiously stroked Talon's arm. "Out of respect, we should refrain from quarrelsome words."

"Out of decency, you should put on some clothes." The words were out of Tiger's mouth before he knew it.

"And you should look around this room if you imagine you have any right to lecture me on decency."

"I didn't mean it." Tiger dropped his eyes. "Please forgive me, for I am a graceless oaf."

"Don't flatter yourself."

"Both of you are behaving like cranky children," Talon said. "Moonlight, you can get cleaned up now. Tiger, help the sweepers, or go to the van with Dandy."

"I'll go to the van," Tiger said. On his way out, he lifted Mallet's body to his shoulder. "I'll take him with me," he said and carried Mallet out to one of three vans. "Ride well," Tiger whispered, brushing Mallet's forehead with his fingertips before he joined Dandy in another van.

He was stunned by the thought that Mallet would no longer be present in his life, and he was hurt by Moonlight's coldness. The mission had gone horribly wrong: instead of an absolutely mundane heart attack that would scarcely cause a ripple, the Kagehito apparatus was now tasked with the clean disposal of the bodies of a dozen people who would appear to have simply vanished. It was *not* an ideal situation.

"I WASN'T sure you'd come," Tiger said when Moonlight slipped into his room around 1:00 a.m.

"I wasn't either, but I realized I wasn't mad at you. I was mad at the world."

"You can't fight the world."

Moonlight snorted. "Me and the world have been at war for a long time."

"If by 'world' you mean 'reality', I'd have to agree."

"If you're going to be a jerk...." Moonlight put a hand on the doorknob.

"No! Absolutely not. Not going to be a jerk. Come sit down." Tiger patted the mattress.

Moonlight settled next to Tiger and put his head on Tiger's shoulder. Tiger put his arm around Moonlight, and they sat there for a while in sweet silence.

"Why did you move?" Tiger asked softly.

"What?"

"During the firefight today. You sat up and drew that bodyguard's attention."

"He was going to shoot you."

"How could you see that from flat on your back?"

"I didn't have to see it. I knew it was happening."

Tiger turned his head to look into Moonlight's face. "If you want to play the mysterious, spooky Barazoku for the others, that's fine, but don't do that hocus-pocus number on me, okay?"

"I'm not screwing with you. Why are you so worked up?"

"Mallet died."

"I'm not going to pretend to be sad. He made my life hell."

"It wasn't *all* horrible."

"All that matters is that we had no choice. The Kagehito made us slaves."

"And if you hadn't sat up, Mallet would still be alive."

"Would you rather be dead?"

"Of course not. It's just that...." *You knew he was going to report you and Talon for misconduct.*

"Just what?"

Tiger pulled Moonlight into his arms. "Nothing. *Ya lublu tebya.*"

"I love you too." Moonlight kissed Tiger. "Your Moscow accent is getting really good."

"I have a great coach." Tiger kissed Moonlight. "How many languages do you speak now?"

"An even dozen."

"You're amazing." Tiger tucked a lock of jet-black hair behind Moonlight's ear. "I can't wait to see you in one of those Russian fur hats."

"You're very silly sometimes… and I love you for it. Please don't ever grow all the way up."

"I promise." Tiger fell onto his back and pulled Moonlight with him. "I hope we leave for Moscow soon. The farther away we are from the island, the happier I'll be."

"The bigwigs aren't going to be impressed by Blue Iron's first mission under Talon's leadership."

"Sometimes things just go wrong, no matter how well you plan."

"Yes, they do." Moonlight threw an arm across Tiger's chest and a leg over Tiger's thigh. "You're the only thing I wouldn't change about my life after age six."

"I wish you were happier." Tiger sighed. "I wish I could make you happy."

"You *do* make me happy. If I could be with you twenty-four hours a day… well, no point in talking about it. I'll just have to savor the moments."

Tiger kissed Moonlight's forehead and hugged him tight. "You mean more to me than all the rest of the world put together. Never doubt that."

Comfortably entwined, they drifted into sleep. Moonlight woke three hours later and kissed Tiger without waking him. Carrying his shoes, he walked the deserted corridor to his room.

"Good morning," Rain said, pushing away from the wall beside Moonlight's door. "You have an early, super-secret meeting with Talon?"

"If our leader wanted you to know, I'm sure he'd tell you," Moonlight said, neither confirming nor denying as he reached for the doorknob.

"Hold on." Rain moved to block the door. "I waited a long time to talk to you. Can I have a few minutes?"

"What do you want to talk about?"

"What is it with you Barazoku?" Rain looked deep into Moonlight's eyes. "You're good-looking, but I could go out and find twenty more people just as pretty. What is it about you that has Talon behaving like an empty-headed schoolboy?"

"If I knew what you were talking about, I might have an answer for you, but since I don't—"

"Tiger's under your spell too."

"Are you coming to any sort of point?"

"I'm just curious. How do you do it?"

"Years of training." Moonlight shoved Rain aside and opened the door. "Good night."

"Is it the sex?" Rain said as he started to follow Moonlight into the room.

Moonlight turned and Rain stopped suddenly. "What do you really want?" Moonlight asked. "Did you come here thinking I'd sleep with you?"

"It's what you do, isn't it? It's why Talon and Tiger follow you like puppies."

"Are you testing *me* or *yourself*?" Moonlight turned away. "Get out and don't bother me like this again, or you won't like the consequences."

"I told you, I'm just curious." Rain went to the door. "Good night, Moonlight."

Moonlight shut the door on Rain and went to lie down on his bed. It had been a very long day, but his nerves were singing at too high a pitch to allow him to sleep. He stared at the ceiling until the adrenaline from his encounter with Rain drained away and he was able to relax. His mind finally grew weary of chasing its own tail and he was able to focus on a single image.

Moonlight imagined that he was back on Saigo Island with the light of the fire pit embers casting a bronze glow on the humble objects in the hut. Tiger was pressed against his back, warm and solid. Tiger's arm was around his waist, holding him securely. He imagined he could feel Tiger's breath on his nape just as he drifted off. His sleep was deep and untroubled until his phone rang at 5:00 a.m.

TIGER walked into Blue Iron's ready room and looked around. The place was deserted except for Dandy, who was—predictably—in front of his massive computer screen.

"Where's Rain?" Tiger asked, knowing that Dandy could locate anyone in the complex within a matter of seconds.

"He's meeting with Lord Mahogany."

"Lord Mahogany's here?"

"A conference call," Dandy clarified.

"Where's Talon?"

Dandy looked at the time in the corner of the screen. "Somewhere over India, I imagine."

"Is he going to Russia ahead of us?"

"He's not going to Russia." Dandy swiveled his chair around to face Tiger. "While you were sleeping, Talon got new orders."

A thought occurred to Tiger and his stomach filled with ice. "Have you seen Moonlight?"

"He left with Talon."

"Where were they going?"

"I shouldn't even know this, much less be telling it to you." Dandy paused and then continued. "The powers-that-be sent Talon to Paris to meet with some other bosses. I don't know what the meeting is about exactly, but it looks like admin is concerned about some kind of rogue outfit, or maybe a rival network of some sort. Of course, I could be completely wrong."

"If there was another organization like the Shadow, we'd know about it."

"I'm sure you're right." Dandy looked at Tiger over the top of his glasses. "I hear Rain is being promoted to team leader."

"He'll be a good one. Do you hear if I'm still on the team?" The words continued to come from Tiger's mouth, but he couldn't hear himself over the screams in his head. *Moonlight was gone.*

"Looks like you'll be the youngest second-in-command in the field."

Tiger nodded to acknowledge that he'd heard Dandy.

"We'll probably be shipping out tonight or tomorrow morning. The equipment is already being crated up. Our electronics will be the last to go."

Tiger nodded again.

"I thought you'd be more excited." Dandy studied Tiger's face. "You look a little shocky. Have you had anything to eat today?"

"I slept too long. My head feels like it's filled with wet cement."

"You needed the rest." Dandy tapped his monitor. "I watched the tapes of the mission this morning. You were a fireball when everything fell apart."

"I can't believe I was so stupid. It wasn't in the plan to put the syringe on the table, but that bodyguard was too suspicious of me. I had to get rid of it."

"You were smart to ditch the hypo." Dandy shook his head in sympathy. "It's just beyond belief that clown thought to use his napkin with a gun pointing at him."

"And that sharp-eyed bodyguard homed right in on it."

"It's done," Dandy said. "Hey! You want to see some really hot footage of the Barazoku? I edited a few minutes of film out of the video that feature him getting decked out in sushi."

"Maybe later." Tiger swallowed hard as his growing nausea threatened to empty his already empty stomach. "I should get something to eat."

"Tiger! Bring me a snack," Dandy called out as Tiger left the room.

Tiger shouted something unintelligible and kept walking. The tiles seemed to twist under his feet and his stomach was still on the roller coaster. He couldn't believe it had happened again. Once more, the Kagehito had pulled the rug out from under his life. And though he'd been careful not to hope for too much, his hidden heart had counted on having Moonlight in his daily life again. Not only was Moonlight gone, it appeared he'd been given to Talon, like an accoutrement of Talon's new rank.

Halfway to the mess hall, Tiger ducked into a toilet and locked the door. After several minutes of struggle in the dark, he conquered the urge to go on a rampage, swallowing his grief and rage back down like the bile that rose in his throat. He turned on the light, splashed his face with cold water, and exited the men's room.

From that moment, his exterior became one of unshakable composure. Those who worked with him for even the shortest period of time invariably remarked on Tiger's poise. His bearing had the gravity of a man three times his age and experience. No matter what arose, he continued to move forward, as relentless and emotionless as a shark.

 Part Six

THE wind that blew down the Moscow backstreet found its way into every chink of Dandy's clothing, chilling him to the bone. All he wanted was to end this conversation quickly.

"Look, I know you're a tough guy, but—" Dandy broke off as the Vory soldier he was talking to pulled out a dagger. "Easy, now. All I want is some information."

"Who do you imagine you are?" Grigori Zaytsev growled as he threatened Dandy with the blade. "We've all seen you sniffing around. Did you yellow fellows think you could move into our house without a fuss?"

"Of course not. That's why I want to talk with Mr. Novikov, but he won't return my calls or my messages. My boss has been very patient, but— Ow!" Dandy brought his hand up to his neck as he flinched away from the Russian. "No need to get physical."

"That was just for a start, pretty boy." Grigori grabbed for Dandy's shirtfront, but stopped short when he felt the chill of metal against his throat.

"Why so unfriendly, Grisha?" Tiger said in the Russian's ear. He held up the straight razor so Grigori could see it. "We're going to be neighbors, and I'd hate to have bad blood between us."

"What do you want?"

"My colleague already told you. He wants to see your boss."

"You can kill me, but my boss won't talk to a messenger boy. Maybe if your boss came here—" Grigori stopped speaking when the cold steel pressed against his Adam's apple.

Dandy smiled. "Come on, *droog*. You've tried freezing us out. You've tried burning us out. Mr. Rain is not coming into your den so you can do away with him at your leisure."

"What would you suggest then?"

"Never mind what he'd suggest," Tiger said. "You call your boss and set up a meeting right now."

"I'm not afraid of you, and I'm not afraid to die."

"Are you afraid of living the rest of your life as a eunuch?" Grigori grunted as Tiger grabbed him by the crotch and squeezed hard.

"If you had any honor, you'd never threaten a man's jewels," the thug wheezed.

"I don't have any honor... or sympathy... or scruples." Tiger unzipped Grigori's pants and reached into the fly.

Grigori reacted, and the razor drew a line of red across his throat.

"Easy, Tora," Dandy said softly. "We want him alive."

"Tora?" Grigori slid his eyes to the side. "You are Tiger?"

"That's right," Tiger said. "Have you heard of me?"

"I heard what you did to Kurechenko."

"He tried to kill my boss."

"Your retaliation was... creative."

Tiger felt a shudder run through the soldier's frame. "Have you changed your mind about us?"

"Let go of my *khuy*, and I'll make the call."

"I just got comfortable," Tiger said. "I think I'll hold on to it while you talk."

"*Suka*," Grigori muttered as he carefully took his phone from his pocket.

"Call me bitch again and I'll make you mine," Tiger said.

Grigori called his boss and spoke for a very short time, uttering no more profanity. "Okay. Mr. Novikov will see you," he said when he hung up. "I'll take you there."

Tiger released his grip on the thug's cock and gave him a shove. "I'm glad you've decided to stop wasting our time," he said.

Slightly less than two hours later, Tiger escorted Dandy back to the fire team's headquarters. Dandy was cheerful, talking brightly about the successful meeting, all but bouncing off the walls of the buildings as they walked to their car.

"Rain's going to be very pleased," Dandy said.

"I think everyone involved is pleased... with the possible exception of Grigori."

"Don't remind me. I knew you were backing me up, but I still nearly pissed my pants when he pulled that knife."

"He's a pretty scary character," Tiger agreed. "His skills are third-rate, but he's vicious and has poor impulse control. Crazy and cruel make a formidable combination."

"I think you had him pissing in *his* pants before it was over."

Tiger shook his head. "If he'd been pissing, I would've known it. My hand would've been warm for the first time since we got here."

Dandy chuckled. "You're pretty amazing," he said, giving Tiger a sidelong glance.

"Because I threatened to deprive a man of his balls if he didn't do as I asked?"

"No. Not specifically. You're just...." Dandy sighed. "You're never going to be interested in me, are you?"

Tiger looked over at his companion. "You're not making a joke," he said.

"No, I'm not. I like you, and I thought maybe once we were in Russia...." Dandy's voice trailed off. "Never mind. It was stupid of me to bring it up."

Tiger stopped and pulled Dandy into the mouth of an alley. "Are you trying to tell me that you're attracted to me?"

Dandy nodded. "I was hoping that you might—"

"No. Sorry, but no. I'm not looking for anyone."

"Aren't you lonely? I know I am."

Tiger looked up at the gray sky between the rooftops. "I'm lonely, but...."

Dandy interrupted, speaking quickly. "I know it's technically against the rules to fraternize without sanction, but no one on the team's going to report us. And I'll bet if we asked, we could get consent."

Tiger sighed. "Why is this so hard to say?" In a rare gesture, he put his hand on Dandy's shoulder. "You're very good-looking, and you're smart and funny, but I'm not...."

"It's the Barazoku," Dandy guessed. "I can understand why you'd want him, but that's just a fantasy, Tiger. I want you, and I'm right here."

Tiger was quiet for a long moment before he spoke again. "I've been in love with Moonlight since we were boys in the same crèche. We've been lovers since my manhood night. My only ambition is to serve the Kagehito so well that they'll let me have him and leave us in peace to live out the rest of our lives together."

Dandy recovered from his shock at Tiger's abrupt confession. "That's... incredible. Why would your superiors allow you to have a sexual relationship as initiates?"

"For their own reasons, I imagine. They never explained it to me, and as long as they let us be together, I never questioned it."

"I can see why you'd want him. He's...." Dandy's voice trailed off. "He's indescribable."

"He saved me. He's my world."

Dandy shivered at the devotion implicit in Tiger's tone. His fondest wish was for someone to feel that way about him. "Listen...

don't worry that I'll mention this to anyone. We're speaking frankly, in confidence, and I'll respect that."

Tiger's sharp, handsome features were devoid of expression as he stared down the street past Dandy's shoulder. "That's good to know," he said.

Dandy shivered as though the words were an explicit threat. "I'm not exactly a company man, in case you hadn't noticed."

"I've noticed that you use a lot of sarcasm when you talk, and you're what my sensei liked to call irreverent."

"I give my respect when it's earned, not because some rule says I owe it to someone. I'm smarter than half of the—"

"I understand," Tiger interrupted.

"Don't worry. We're not being recorded."

"Are you sure?"

"Not one hundred percent, but I'm *reasonably* sure." Dandy glanced both ways as they reached a cross street. "Damn, this is an ugly part of the city."

"I hadn't noticed."

"Everything is gray concrete and dirty snow."

"Welcome to my world," Tiger said.

"Damn, you're a bleak fucker." Dandy shook his head. "Just my luck that I'm attracted to gorgeous, brooding men who could snap a neck with one finger."

"Why don't we concentrate on doing our jobs so we can get out of here faster?"

"Once Novikov's taken out of the equation, the others will see the sense of dealing with us directly."

"I intend to make that adjustment at the meeting."

"I thought you might. Try not to die, okay?"

"Got it."

Dandy chuckled as they approached their car. "I almost pity the Vory. They think they're such badasses, and now they've run into people who truly have the will to do whatever it takes to get what they want."

"It's true that Iron men are the baddest of all asses," Tiger said with a straight face as he got into the driver's seat of the Lada Niva. The small SUV had four-wheel drive, and needed it in some parts of the city.

"Woof! It smells like ass in here. Very bad ass." Dandy rolled down the window as soon as Tiger turned the ignition key.

Tiger sensed movement and glanced at the rear-view mirror. "Close the window," he yelled as he dropped the transmission into drive and hit the gas.

The vehicle accelerated slowly, tires slipping in the slush and garbage. Tiger cursed and shouted again for Dandy to shut the window. Dandy had his finger mashed down on the control button, but the window rose at a snail's pace. Tiger's gun was in his hand, and he turned to fire through the back window. Glass shattered and the wind invaded the cabin of the Niva. Tiger fired again, and then a small object flew in through Dandy's window. The man who'd thrown it flung himself to the ground and squeezed between the wall and an industrial garbage bin.

"Get out!" Tiger yelled at Dandy, already halfway out his door.

With a sound like brief thunder, fire bloomed in the alleyway and shot upward. Pieces of the Niva slammed into the walls and bounced off to land on the remains of the chassis.

Tiger picked himself up from where the blast had thrown him and stared at the wreckage in a world gone suddenly silent. Movement attracted his attention, and he raised the gun he'd never let go of. As Grigori broke from cover, Tiger shot him through the back of the right knee. Adjusting his aim, Tiger shot the enforcer in the left kidney. As he walked toward Grigori, Tiger continued to fire rounds into selected parts of the bomber's anatomy. Reaching the wounded man, Tiger put a foot on his back and held him facedown in the muck.

"Big mistake, Grisha," Tiger said, his ears still ringing from the explosion. "The man you just killed was a friend."

His face a frozen mask, Tiger knelt beside the Vory killer and made Grigori's last few minutes of life very unpleasant.

MOONLIGHT put down the hairbrush and glanced out the open balcony doors. The stars were a profligate spill of tiny diamonds glittering against the midnight-blue velvet of the Parisian sky. The moon was almost full, glowing like a dragon's prize pearl, a lover's lamp above the streets of the City of Lights. The air was the perfect temperature and lightly scented by the roses in the garden below. Moonlight was alone, as had become his preference, and had nothing more difficult on his agenda than distracting a few men while Talon conducted business… the onmyoji's business.

Even here, far away from Saigo Island, Moonlight felt Autumn's presence and the weight of Autumn's will like a constant draft of cold air. He was convinced he would never feel warm again unless the wizard was dead.

Ashi, the eerily quiet butler with the feather tattoo, knocked once at the bedroom door and announced himself. "It's Reed, sir. Everyone is here."

Moonlight called out his thanks and the butler left as silently as he had come. The phone rang and Moonlight controlled the impulse to jump. He answered and spoke with the onmyoji for a few minutes before hanging up.

Rising from his chair, he walked naked to the balcony and looked up at the constellations. "Cheolsu," he whispered, wondering if Tiger was looking up at the Russian sky and thinking of him. It was only two hours later there and Tiger might be out on the street, on his way to a meeting with some Muscovite crime lord. Moonlight closed his eyes and hoped with all his heart that Tiger was well and wouldn't die tonight.

Turning back to the bedroom, Moonlight dressed in the clothes he'd laid out before his bath. The snug trousers were made of a stretchy, cream-colored material with the soft shine of satin that hugged every contour of his round backside and long legs. Over the pants, he wore a chocolate-brown sweater trimmed with glossy fur at the neck and wrists. The dark-brown, flat-heeled sheepskin boots were only suitable for indoor wear, but he wasn't planning on going out and they were terribly comfortable, besides fostering the image he'd built in Paris. Those acquainted with him knew him as a gorgeous, childlike clotheshorse, elegant and adorable, open yet unattainable.

His life revolved around shopping and his role as Talon's companion. Mostly, he planned and hosted parties or attended parties on Talon's arm, using the social occasions to further the onmyoji's plans. It wasn't that difficult to sway high-ranking Iron men to Autumn's political viewpoint; most of them were already halfway there. Like the three who were visiting tonight.

Moonlight passed by the mirror again and ran his fingers through his hair to tousle it a bit. When he was satisfied that his rumpled appearance suggested he'd been well-loved recently, he left the bedroom and moved unhurriedly down the hall. He could hear voices and knew Talon had invited his guests into the lounge for a drink. It was time for his entrance. Loosening his stride, Moonlight entered the lounge as though it was empty and kept walking toward the entertainment den.

"Moonlight," Talon called out.

Moonlight feigned startlement and turned toward the group of men seated in front of the bar. "Oh! Please forgive me. I didn't know you had company, Talon."

"No need to apologize." The white-haired chief of transportation for Western Europe raised his glass. "We're just having a friendly drink."

"I really didn't mean to interrupt." Moonlight looked up from under his lashes. "I hope it won't bother you if I watch the television in the next room. I'll wear headphones."

"Of course it won't bother us." Iron Tribe's East European head of weapons acquisitions smiled at Moonlight.

"Maybe you'd like a drink." A junior enforcement operative glanced at Talon as he spoke.

"That's so sweet of you," Moonlight said. "But the Armani runway show is being broadcast in ten minutes, so I need to get set up in there."

"Enjoy your show," Talon said.

Moonlight smiled and went into the next room. Talon smiled too as his guests' eyes remained glued to the Barazoku while Moonlight bent over a cabinet in search of his headphones. Finding them, Moonlight went to the couch, but had to bend all the way over when he knocked the remote off the coffee table. Finally prepared, he plopped down on the big, over-stuffed piece of furniture, hugged a big overstuffed teddy bear to his chest, and turned on the giant flat-screen television.

Over the next hour, Talon enlisted the loyalty of three key men while they were mesmerized by Moonlight's artless enthusiasm for the fashion show and the nearly life-sized plush bear. If Talon hadn't been aware of the calculation behind Moonlight's bouncing and unabashed cries of delight, he would have sworn they were genuine. At first, he hadn't put much stock in the value of the Barazoku's methods, but Moonlight had proven an invaluable asset. Though it was a bit disillusioning to find out how susceptible most Shadow men were to this innocent slut act, Talon was not above letting Moonlight use it. He'd even learned to control his jealousy when other men showed an interest in Moonlight. He knew his Rose saved his real love for him. They had a genuine connection; they *meshed*, and together they were an unbeatable team. The onmyoji was very pleased with their progress, and tonight was another victory.

"You're a lucky man," the transportation chief said as he was leaving.

"I know," Talon said. "But were you speaking of something specific?"

"The Barazoku. Very few men can brag about having such a companion."

"I've earned the onmyoji's generosity."

"I see. Good to talk with you, Talon. Autumn can count on me when the time comes."

"I'll mention it in my next report."

"Thank you." With a bow, Talon's last visitor left the penthouse.

"Moonlight," Talon called as he walked away from the front entrance. He caught Reed's eye as he passed the kitchen and nodded cordially to the multi-tasking butler. Moonlight met him in the doorway of the lounge, and he put his arms around him. "Good job," Talon murmured, kissing Moonlight's forehead.

"More converts?"

"Your backside is powerfully persuasive."

Moonlight pushed Talon away. "Autumn will be happy."

"I'll send a report before I go to sleep." Talon eyed Moonlight's silhouette as the Barazoku walked away from him. "It really is amazing... that airhead act of yours." He followed Moonlight to the kitchen, looking around to make sure the butler was gone. "I know most Kagehito are conditioned to find both men and women attractive, but it never fails to surprise me how you can get them drooling over you just by walking into the room." He watched Moonlight pour coffee and declined the silent offer of a cup. "I don't believe you can completely subvert a person's basic nature, but I haven't run across a single Iron clan agent that's immune to your charm. It seems odd to me to build a weakness like that into the system. Effective though."

Moonlight shrugged as he blew on the surface of the black coffee. "Like you said... conditioning. It's a powerful thing." He took a sip. "I'm not attracted to women at all. Not sexually anyway."

Talon's lover rarely spoke of himself, and Talon made a confession of his own in hopes of keeping the conversation going. "When I was in my early twenties, I slept with a few university women in Seoul. My superiors set me up with them and encouraged me to seduce them. I know now that I was participating in some kind of program, but at the time, I was convinced that I was making myself into a real man. Sometimes I didn't take no for an answer, and my superiors covered it up if the girl made trouble." Talon paused. "That was over a decade ago. A different life."

Moonlight kept his eyes on his coffee. When he'd first met Talon, the man had owned a calm nature as deep as the sea. Now that calm was a paper-thin layer over something that seethed quietly in the shadows. "You're not an adjuster now," he said, as though Talon needed the reminder. "You're Iron Tribe's chief of enforcement. A very important, very powerful man."

Talon focused on the Barazoku. "No," he said. "I'm middle-management at best." He came across the room to put his arms around Moonlight's waist from behind. "But not for much longer. When I'm Chief of all Iron Tribe clans, it will be against the law for anyone but me to look at you."

"You're in a whimsical mood." Moonlight shivered as Talon kissed the side of his neck. Talon reminded him of Tiger sometimes—tall, self-confident, and sensual—but when Moonlight closed his eyes, the smell was different. Moonlight couldn't delude himself that Talon was Tiger, no matter how hard he tried.

"I'm just horny." Talon chuckled. "Do you know how long it's been since we—?"

"Of course I do. I keep track of things like that." Moonlight turned to face Talon, meeting the eyes so close to his. "Are you asking because you've lost count? Or are you making some kind of point?"

"Neither." Stung by the sharp edge of Moonlight's words, Talon drew back a little. "I was just going to suggest that we go to the bedroom."

"And instead you chose to criticize what you perceive as my lack of desire for you."

"No."

"That's what it sounded like to me."

Talon clenched his fists in frustration as the exchange of words slid further out of control. "I wasn't criticizing you."

"How else am I supposed to interpret your question?" Moonlight put down the coffee. "Why did you feel the need to point out the length of time between fucks?"

"Because I miss making love with you."

"So you *were* making a complaint."

"I don't know how this turned into a fight, but could we stop?"

"It's not a fight, Talon. You're allowed to express your dissatisfaction. Though, if there's something about my performance that you find inadequate, it would do you more good to complain to my master."

"Why are you acting like this?"

Moonlight's voice was emotionless when he answered. "Because this job is over. The onmyoji has called me home, and not just for a visit."

"You're leaving?"

"Those are my orders."

"I'll negotiate with him."

"I don't want to stay with you."

"I thought we were going to the top together."

"Because that's what my master wanted you to think."

Talon was silent for several moments while he tried to make things slow down. How had they progressed from the peak to the pit so quickly? They had just cemented their position in Europe, and Talon had been looking forward to a celebration and a shining future of successive triumphs with his angel at his side. How was it possible he had lost all of that in a few words of conversation? Surely there must be some way to go back just a few seconds, to the time before Moonlight said he was leaving. There had to be something he could say to restore the world he'd built. There had to be some way....

"Did you ever feel anything for me?" were the words that finally emerged from Talon's mouth.

"I don't think you want me to answer that question honestly."

"You were only with me because the onmyoji ordered it?"

"How could you not know that?"

"I thought it was more than an assignment to you."

"It was part of my assignment to make you think that."

"You're good." Talon shook his head. "Really good."

"Thank you."

"I have to know. Are you proud of it? Do you get a sense of accomplishment in knowing you did your job so well?"

"I serve the onmyoji."

"Is that your answer?"

"It's the best apology I can make." Moonlight met Talon's eyes. "You had your mission and I had mine. We're Kagehito. What else is there to say?"

"I thought you felt something for me."

"If you insist on knowing, what I felt mostly was resentment. When I was ordered to accompany you to Paris, I hated you for a little while, though I knew it wasn't your fault."

"All this time…." Talon paused. "Every time I touched you, you resented it?"

"It's not your fault."

"You never wanted me? Every smile was fake? Every moan?"

Moonlight sighed. "You're a good lover, Talon. You're just not the one I want."

Talon snatched the chance to respond to something he understood. "You're in love with someone else," he said. "Who is he?"

"You're joking, right?"

"This isn't funny to me. Tell me his name."

"I'm not discussing this with you." Moonlight turned away. "I need to pack."

Talon grabbed Moonlight's arm and yanked backward. Moonlight spun as he was pulled, sweeping the cup of coffee off the counter into Talon's face. Talon twisted the arm he held and Moonlight didn't resist, continuing to pivot on his heel. Stiffening the fingers and wrist of his free hand, Moonlight drove it into Talon's diaphragm. Deprived of air, Talon leaped backward, letting go of Moonlight's elbow.

"Want to try that again?" Moonlight asked softly.

Slowly, Talon raised a hand to wipe the coffee from his eyes. "No… thank… you," he panted.

"I was going to wait until morning, but I think I'll leave tonight. Would you ask Reed to get the car ready?"

Talon nodded and watched warily as Moonlight left the kitchen. His silken kitten had transformed into a wildcat with slashing claws and sharp teeth, and for all his experience, Talon was a little shell-shocked. Knowing that Rose Tribe members had the same basic combat training as all Kagehito was not the same thing as facing one in a fight. Moonlight's retaliatory strike had been swift and severe, instantaneous, with no thought beyond disabling his opponent. Talon wondered how many times Moonlight had lain next to him in the dark and imagined killing him.

Resolutely, Talon pushed the thought away. Leaving the mess for the butler, he went to his study. By the time Moonlight brought his luggage to the foyer, Talon had made several calls and changed into pajamas and a robe.

"The car's ready," Talon called out as Moonlight passed the open doorway of the lounge. "Do you have time for a last drink with me?"

"Not the very last, I hope," Moonlight said as he walked to the bar. "We'll work together again, don't you think?"

"I'm not sure how I'd feel about that. Vodka?" Talon held up a bottle.

"And a dash of—"

"Grenadine," Talon finished for him.

"Actually, I'd rather have grapefruit juice."

"Even your favorite drink was a lie."

"Can we keep this pleasant?"

"Sorry," Talon said as he poured Moonlight's drink. "I'll try to hold the sarcasm to a minimum."

"I'd appreciate it. It wasn't personal, after all."

Talon swallowed the retort that rose to his lips. "You were following orders. I understand. Did you manage to book a flight?"

"I called the chief of transportation. He was surprised to hear from me again so soon, but quite happy to do me a favor. There's a jet waiting for me at the Charles de Gaulle."

"I wouldn't be surprised if you find him stowed away on the jet."

Moonlight sipped his drink. "I doubt it. He didn't get to his position by being impulsive."

"I called Autumn," Talon said, his eyes on Moonlight's face.

"I know. Autumn called me," Moonlight said coolly.

"Well, that kind of ruins my surprise, doesn't it?"

"I gave him my flight information, and he wished me a safe trip. We didn't talk about anything else."

"Would you like to hear my surprise?"

"Of course. Just because I'm not in love with you doesn't mean I'm not interested."

"When Mahogany joins the Inner Council, I'm to be elevated to Chief of European Operations."

"Congratulations. It's a great honor."

"Then why do I feel like it's a consolation prize for losing you?"

"Because that's how the onmyoji wants you to feel." Moonlight finished his drink. "If you'd just remember that, you wouldn't have to ask so many questions."

"I never knew you at all, did I?" Talon asked as Moonlight put down his glass.

"I'm sorry," Moonlight murmured. "You're... you were a good man."

"Good-bye," Talon said and watched Moonlight walk to the door. "Moonlight!" he called.

Moonlight paused in the doorway.

"I'd like to get to know the real you someday."

"Good-bye, Talon."

The butler held the front door open for Moonlight and bowed as he approached.

"Good-bye, Reed," Moonlight said.

The butler bowed again. "Your luggage is in the car, sir. May I ask how long you'll be away?"

"I'm not coming back."

"What a pity. Such a pleasure to serve someone who appreciates it. My best wishes for the future."

"Thank you, Reed." Moonlight bowed to the butler and walked to the private elevator. Emerging in the parking garage, he crossed to the Jaguar sedan idling in a nearby slot. The driver got out and opened the back door. "Hello, Bat," Moonlight said as he got into the car.

The chauffeur bowed and got behind the wheel. A short time later, Moonlight got out of the car at the airport and checked his luggage at the curb. He said good-bye to Bat and, with the help of airport personnel, was soon sitting in a Shadow-owned aircraft, taxiing down a runway. Once they were airborne, Moonlight found it more difficult to avoid thinking about his destination. Up until now, he'd been able to distract himself by picking a fight with Talon and arranging the details of his sudden journey, but up here there was nothing but the night sky and magazines he'd already seen.

Moonlight didn't want to imagine what was going to happen when he returned. He'd learned that anticipation led to disappointment and did his best not to speculate, unless it concerned mission strategy. It did him no good to try and predict the onmyoji's actions, and it hurt too much to wonder if he'd ever see Tiger again. Yet, these were the two subjects his thoughts revolved around when they were given free rein. Maybe he was a masochist, as the onmyoji sometimes hinted.

"But I don't enjoy the pain," Moonlight whispered.

"Did you call, sir?" An Iron Tribe crew member appeared beside Moonlight's seat.

"No. I'm fine. Thank you."

"Are you sure? We have a fully stocked bar as well as an espresso machine. I'd be more than happy to whip up whatever you'd like."

Moonlight wasn't imagining it. This soldier in a flight attendant's uniform was flirting. "I'm afraid I'm the one who's whipped," he said. "I'd really just like to close my eyes for a while."

"Of course. I'll dim the cabin lights and try to keep it to a dull roar in the cockpit."

"Thanks." Moonlight gave the crewman a grateful smile. Tilting his seat back, he gazed out the small window and tried not to think. When he woke, the jet was landing at Akita. His luggage was transferred to a helicopter, and he was in the air again, headed back over the Yamato Basin. As the sun rose, he touched down on Saigo Island once again.

AS SOON as the house servant closed the door, the onmyoji removed his head covering and gestured to Moonlight to come closer. "You look different," Autumn said after studying his protégé's face.

"Breaking a man's spirit will do that."

"Do you refer to Talon or yourself?"

"An interesting question." Moonlight let his gray wool cloak slide from his shoulders. "You still keep it too warm in here. You'll thin your blood."

"You sound different too."

"I may have picked up a trace of a Parisian accent."

"You're so... vibrant." The onmyoji removed his glove and touched Moonlight's cheek. "Like a string on a violin that's been wound to a perfect pitch and played for too long. You're so full of emotion that you practically resonate. It's a good thing you came back now."

"Let's continue the analogy. Are you saying I would've snapped?"

"Inevitably and soon, but you're here now, and I know how to take care of you."

"I was surprised to receive your message. Granted, Talon and I moved several key pieces into place, but I would've thought you'd want us to continue—"

"There are other operatives I can use to widen the network. I have more important work for you." The onmyoji picked up a length of pale silk from his writing desk. "For you," he said.

Moonlight took the cloth and saw that it was identical to the wizard's veil. "You want me to wear this? I'm not Ryuzoku."

"I want you to get used to it." Autumn stood and walked to the window. "Come here and imitate my walk."

"Of course I can imitate your walk... and your voice, and your mannerisms, and handwriting, but why? Do you want me to be your decoy?"

"Of course not. I want you to be my proxy. It doesn't suit me to leave the island, but I'll need to meet with certain people on their own territory."

"Certain people?"

"Tribal Chiefs," Autumn clarified. "Men too important to be summoned. Men who'll be familiar with me from Inner Council meetings."

"Aren't you worried that I'll use this position to my advantage instead of yours?"

"I trust you, Moonlight, because as long as you do as I say, Tiger continues breathing." The onmyoji sighed. "I'm getting weary of reminding you."

"Is he still in Russia?"

"Yes, and he's doing very well. By all reports, he's a very intimidating presence in the Russian criminal underworld. The Shadow now has much more than a toehold in the drug trade, and we're making inroads into the black market."

"I'm pleased to hear it."

"You miss Tiger."

"I can't help it."

"I wish I could arrange for you to see him, but he's become very valuable to Iron Tribe. I think it will be some time before they let him slow down."

"You could send me to him."

"I need you here."

"Not for yourself, of course, but for the greater glory of the Shadow." Moonlight's reply was a perfect mimicry of the tone, pitch, and cadence of the onmyoji's speaking voice.

"Very good," Autumn said. "Work hard now and who knows what rewards the future will bring."

"What's my first mission?"

"First, I want to be sure you can impersonate me well enough."

"Test me," Moonlight said, wrapping his head in the long veil. "I'll fool anyone you like."

While the onmyoji observed from hiding, Moonlight convinced various servants, a sentry, and the camp's commander that he was Autumn. The real Autumn was impressed and saw no reason to delay in sending Moonlight back into the field. During the week that the onmyoji briefed Moonlight on the individuals he would be meeting, he steadily siphoned the deep well of the young man's pent-up emotions. By the time Moonlight left the island, the onmyoji had stored enough stolen energy to keep him potent for several months.

Moonlight flew away from Saigo again, sparing the island a single glance as the helicopter climbed away from it. He had a dangerous, complicated job ahead of him, but he preferred it to spending time in the onmyoji's presence. Every time he saw the wizard, it left him feeling inexpressibly drained and depressed. Moonlight was beginning to fear he'd never be allowed to see Tiger again, that Tiger would die alone in some Moscow backstreet, his last breath rising like smoke in the frigid air.

"Tokyo." The pilot's voice was loud in Moonlight's headset.

Moonlight rolled his eyes as the pilot pointed. Did the man really think it was possible to miss the largest city in the world?

"We'll be setting down on Shinjuku's government complex helipad."

Moonlight nodded to show he understood and held on to his breakfast as the sleek craft heeled over and dove toward the rooftops. One exhilarating swoop later, he stepped out onto the flat roof of Shinjuku ward's city hall. He thanked the pilot and moved his bags away as the chopper prepared to take off.

The door opened in a small structure on the opposite side of the roof and a man emerged. He lifted a hand in greeting as the helicopter rose into the air and flew away. The man's thick, shoulder-length hair blew around his face in the wake of the chopper's departure, and he shielded his eyes with his hand. It wasn't until he stood in front of Moonlight that Moonlight was sure he seemed familiar for a good reason.

"Smoke!" Moonlight dropped his bag and held out his arms.

Smoke stepped into the hug, wrapping his long arms around his crèche-mate. "It's good to see you again, Moonlight."

"YOU make an excellent cup of tea," Moonlight said as he set his bone china cup back on its saucer.

"One picks up certain skills in diplomatic circles," Smoke answered archly before taking a sip of his tea. "Oh how I wish I was still at the Korean Embassy." He sighed. "It was a much more refined form of politics than they play here. My boss is practically a mobster."

"A powerful, well-connected mobster."

"Yes, well, there is that. Sitting close to the throne is handy." Smoke let his eyes rest on Moonlight for a few more minutes. "So, I was told to meet someone and extend that someone all courtesy, which means a great deal, by the way. I never thought that the someone would be you. I have to say it once—you look amazing."

"Thanks." Moonlight smiled. "You look pretty amazing yourself."

"It's the suit. I have them tailored."

"You make the suit look good."

"All part of the service, right?"

Moonlight nodded. "I never think of my clothes as just clothes. They're costumes, you know?"

Smoke leaned over his desk and lowered his voice. "I don't think this room is bugged, but be careful what you say anyway, okay?"

"No, I can't wait to go shopping in Tokyo," Moonlight said loudly. "And I want to stroll around Harajuku too."

"I'll be happy to show you around. What else can I do for you?"

"My cover is an entertainer, a bit avant-garde, but not outré. I'll need introductions to agents, promoters, contracts if you can manage it. I'll need costumes, a portfolio, and of course, I'll need a place to live that's not too posh but not too dreary."

"Bohemian?"

"Exactly, but not too coffee-house."

"More torch singer than beat poet?"

"Exactly."

"You just got back from Paris, didn't you?"

Moonlight nodded. "It shows?"

"I love the beret." Smoke nodded at Moonlight's cap. "And I think a blues singer with a French flair would go over well in Tokyo right now."

"No singing unless I have to. I'm an interpretive dancer. It lets me keep more of an emotional distance from the audience than singing would."

"All right. How about modeling? Do you do that?"

"Of course. I'll need to have a visible source of substantial income."

"I can set you up." Smoke picked up his phone. "What's the cover for?"

"I can't talk about my primary mission."

Smoke held up his hand as someone answered on the other end of the line. By the time he said good-bye, Moonlight had a garden apartment in an older part of the district. "Come on," he said as he stood up. "I'll take you over to look at it."

"You have work, and I can find my own way."

"Let me rephrase. I'd like to drive you to the apartment and have dinner with you, if you like."

"So we can talk about old times?"

"Yeah, why not?"

"Seems kind of sad."

"What about the time Kite covered himself with mud to sneak up on me, and Key pointed out that he was also covered with leeches?"

Moonlight smiled. "True, that wasn't sad. At least for those of us who were leech-free."

"So there *are* things we could talk about that aren't painful."

"And after those ten minutes are up?"

"I think I'd best give up now," Smoke said wryly. "Give me a minute, and I'll call the real estate agent back and have him meet you with the keys."

"No, it's okay. I'd like it if you drove me."

"Are you sure? I'm here to make things easy for you, not the other way around. My orders are very clear."

Moonlight smiled again. "Yes, I'm sure. And please make reservations for dinner. Somewhere low-key, but with a dress code."

"I know just the place." Smoke took out his phone again as he went to the door.

"THIS is nice," Moonlight said as he looked around the tastefully-designed restaurant of fieldstone, glass, and wood. They advertised authentic Korean food, and to judge by the brands of *soju* on offer, they were telling the truth. He tossed back a third shot and watched Smoke fill his glass again. "Sometimes nothing satisfies like childhood food."

"Wait until you taste the ribs in bean sauce. It's an orgy in your mouth."

"They should put that description on the menu."

Smoke grinned. "What a scandal!"

"I've spent the last fourteen months being scandalous."

"You think I haven't heard tales of Talon's Rose?"

Moonlight leaned back against the tobacco-brown mohair banquette. "Oh really?" he drawled. "What sorts of dreadful things are people saying?"

"You're practically a legend, my friend. People say you're so beautiful that it can't be natural. That you have the power to bewitch men."

"No one actually says that. You're making it up."

"I haven't even told you the most ridiculous one yet."

"What are you waiting for?"

"I don't think I'm going to tell you. You don't really want to know. You think it's crap."

"Of course it's crap. Tell me anyway."

"No, it's too ridiculous. I'll feel foolish repeating it."

"You already sound foolish. What have you got to lose?"

Smoke chuckled, ducking his head as he felt his cheeks grow warm. He was amazed, but thrilled at the speed and ease with which he and Moonlight had fallen back into their comfortable relationship of affectionate teasing. They were older, true, but they still fit together as naturally as a baseball and a mitt. They were two of a kind, birds of a feather, from the same mold, and all the other clichés that meant they understood one another without having to explain anything. Smoke hadn't realized how much he'd missed this camaraderie.

"All right, I'll tell you, but don't let it go to your head." Smoke drank his shot, drawing the moment out, savoring the sparkle of anticipation in Moonlight's chatoyant eyes. "Some say the onmyoji created you out of moonlight, snow, and the perfume of white roses."

"Very poetic. If any of those people could have seen me at nine with scraped knees and a dirty face, I wonder what they'd think."

"People believe what they want to believe." Smoke refilled the glasses.

"Easy there," Moonlight said. "We'll be drunk by the time the first course arrives."

"That's my plan."

"Well, it isn't mine. I don't like my senses impaired."

"Are you really that paranoid? Relax a little. I'll take care of you tonight."

"Thank you. That's a lovely offer, but I think I've had enough to drink."

Smoke signaled their server and food began to arrive. The dishes were delicious, and it wasn't until halfway through the second course that either man spoke.

"This is really excellent duck," Moonlight said. "How are your scallops?"

"Try one."

"I can't eat shellfish."

"How could I forget?" Smoke shook his head. "I vividly remember the day we found the mussels and made stew with them. You stopped breathing, and then your lips turned blue. It was really scary. Even scarier when Tiger brought the sensei and Mallet cut a hole for you to breathe through."

Moonlight touched the tiny scar at the base of his throat. "The good old days," he murmured.

"Since you're determined to be gloomy, did you hear about Seven?"

"What about him?"

"He's gone. He was driving for a fire team in Bangkok and his car was T-boned by an oil delivery truck. Burned down a fairly large section of the city."

"I didn't hear about it."

"Well, you know how good the Shadow is at covering up anything embarrassing."

"What else do you hear about our crèche-mates?" Moonlight asked.

"Kite is working at the ordinance and explosives branch of Monkey Tribe's experimental lab facility at LaHore."

"Weird. He liked building things, not destroying them."

"I understand he has an affinity for unstable compounds."

"And the Kagehito don't care what we want. All they care about is how we can be useful to them."

"Them?" Smoke met Moonlight's eyes. "We *are* them."

"Speak for yourself."

"All right. Do you want to hear about Tiger?"

"Tell me everything."

Smoke smiled wryly. Moonlight had never been able to hide how he felt about his senpai. Tiger was the sun that brightened and warmed Moonlight's world. "Tiger's building a reputation too. The words I most often hear associated with his name are ruthless, fearless, relentless… in short, the perfect adjuster."

"Is he still in Moscow?"

"Blue Iron team is based there, but Tiger's done jobs in Hong Kong, Berlin, and a dozen other cities. He's the guy the big bosses call on when the target is high profile and mistakes aren't acceptable. I predict he'll be chief enforcer in a couple of years."

"He'd like that," Moonlight said casually.

Smoke put his hand on the table, palm up. "It's me… Smoke. We've been friends forever. You can drop the blasé act." He smiled. "I see right through it anyway."

Moonlight put his hand over Smoke's. "I've forgotten what it's like to have a friend."

"I'm here to remind you."

"For now."

"I'll always be here for you."

"I know you mean what you say, but I've had my life rearranged too many times to believe in 'always'. We live at the whims of our masters. They move us around like game pieces."

"Do you think it's that different for people who aren't Kagehito? Ordinary people do what they must to survive, just like us."

"They have a choice."

"Not much, from what I see."

"You know it's different."

"I know that you want it to be different." Smoke squeezed Moonlight's fingers. "Let's go back to talking about Tiger, okay?"

Moonlight's smile was wistful. "It's nice having a friend," he said.

BY THE second night of Moonlight's first show, he was an icon of Tokyo's gay community. By the end of the second week, he was a leading light of the avant-garde set. Young Tokyo hipsters with a surplus of disposable income and a taste for the fringe flocked to the clubs featuring the indefinable performer known as Gesshoku, Eclipse of the Moon. Eclipse's shows—part dance, part acrobatics, part sleight of hand—were uncomplicated, elegant, erotic, and enthralling. Two months after arriving in Tokyo, Moonlight was an underground star and used his status to gain entry to the right parties to meet useful people. As soon as his cover was solid, he began his real work.

Over the next half of the year, the onmyoji's reputation grew as he appeared before Inner Council meetings in various parts of the world without ever seeming to leave his palace. His calm speeches counseling the chiefs to examine the direction of the organization fell on receptive ears. And his secret meetings added to his list of allies. The onmyoji felt optimistic, but he resisted the urge to speed up his plans. There was too much to gain to risk it by being hasty. He'd been patient for over half a century; a few more years were nothing. His vision was coming true and, while he waited, he had Moonlight to keep him strong and vital.

"Of course," Moonlight said into the phone. "When?" He chewed his lower lip as he listened, and then spoke again. "I'll see you then." He hung up and looked over at Smoke.

"What was that about?" Smoke asked.

"The onmyoji wants to see me. I'll fly over to the island on Monday."

"A briefing or does he just miss you?"

"It's as if he *has* to see me every three months or so, but after a few days of constantly being in my company, he sends me away again. He's odd."

"Wizards are supposed to be eccentric." Smoke looked around the small apartment. "Why won't you let me move you to a larger place?"

"Find a place as charming as this one and I'll consider it."

Smoke watched Moonlight walk toward him, haloed by the setting sun shining in through the atrium. In contrast to Smoke's traditional black dress suit, Moonlight wore a long white shirt with a red velvet vest over tuxedo pants tucked into knee-length boots. He looked as though he might break into an aria at any moment.

"Are you ready to go?" Smoke asked.

"I suppose. " Moonlight picked his floor-length white fur coat off the back of the love seat. "Honestly, I'd rather stay here, but I need to catch the eye of that promoter from Osaka."

"You could have your agent contact him."

"I could, but this way, bumping into me at a party, he'll feel like he discovered me. Men always like their own ideas best."

"And once he's handling your bookings, you'll have a nice, aboveboard reason to travel to Osaka for an extended stay, which I assume is your goal."

"You assume correctly."

"I heard there's a meeting in Osaka soon of the enforcement chiefs from each tribe."

"You mean you burrowed like a ferret until you found that nugget of information."

"You liken me to a ferret?"

"If you don't like it, pick another slinky, supple mammal with a glossy pelt."

"I think I know why the onmyoji can't do without you."

"And why is that?"

"You're never boring."

"What a lovely thing to say." Moonlight kissed Smoke's cheek as he brushed past him in the doorway. "I'm glad you're my friend."

"I'm glad too." Smoke followed Moonlight across the small sitting room and out the front door into the courtyard.

Moonlight waved at his only neighbors, an elderly couple industriously weeding the shared garden. Stopping to accept a white rosebud from the woman, he waited for her to pin it to his vest before joining Smoke at the stone arch.

"If they only knew," Smoke said as he held open the gate.

"They survived two wars; I doubt I could shock them."

"I think they think that I'm your lover."

Moonlight smiled as he got into the black limo with city government plates. "Let them think what they like," he said as Smoke slid in next to him.

"I wouldn't mind if it was true."

"That would be nice, but I don't think you'd want to be my lover unless I loved you back."

"That would be nice," Smoke repeated.

"I'm sorry."

"You don't have to be sorry. You can't help it if you don't love me that way."

"I am sorry, though. Why did the onmyoji send me to you?"

"You mean now, or when we were teenagers?"

"You know what I mean. He plays with people just to see what will happen."

"I think it's a little more calculated than that."

"You're right. That was my frustration talking."

"If you need to let off some steam…." Smoke let the words hang.

"What do you have in mind?"

"I was wondering if it was appropriate to ask you for a few favors in between your missions."

"What sort of favors?"

"Just what you usually do. I'd like my boss to move up a little faster, and if certain officials were out of the picture, he'd be able to step into their places."

"Sure, as long as I don't have to kill them myself."

"I was thinking more along the lines of blackmail."

"Child's play."

"I appreciate it."

"You're my friend, and you never ask me for anything. I'm happy to help you out."

The car stopped in front of a members-only nightclub and the driver opened the door.

"Are you sure you're not a little overdressed?" Moonlight said as he entered the club with Smoke.

Smoke glanced around at the crowd of actors, rock stars, agents, and promoters dressed in their glitzy best. "Don't you mean underdressed?" Smoke shrugged. "I'm comfortable in the suit. You can get away with diamonds and fur, but I'd feel too showy."

"You're the best-looking man in the room," Moonlight said ignoring the eyes that followed his every move. He was used to being stared at and it bothered him no more than the constant slap of the waves bothers a figurehead. "Do you see Nagase?"

"Don't worry about it. He'll see you." Smoke took Moonlight's hand. "Let's get a drink."

"No thanks. I want to dance."

Smoke caught Moonlight's coat and passed it to one of the wait staff. His gaze never left Moonlight as his friend strode onto the dance floor and promptly owned it. It didn't take long for the other dancers to realize there was someone extraordinary in their midst, and they stopped to watch. Moonlight was lost in the music, oblivious to the fact that he danced alone in a cleared space. True to Smoke's words, Nagase, the promoter from Osaka, sought Moonlight out and offered him a booking on the spot.

"A successful evening, wouldn't you say?" Smoke asked as he and Moonlight got back in the limo shortly after midnight.

"I would." Moonlight sat back, stroking the lapels of his coat.

"I'm glad you came to Tokyo. I like working with you."

"You've made it so easy for me. Of course, the onmyoji knew you'd take a personal interest and do your best for me."

"And that's why he sent you to me on my manhood night. He was planning ahead." Smoke looked out the window. "He didn't have to bother. I was yours already." When Moonlight didn't answer, Smoke spoke again. "Fate's a funny thing. Why did you end up in a box with Tiger instead of with me?"

"I try not to think about things like that. I keep moving forward until I can see Tiger again."

"How do you know you'll see him again?"

"Because he told me I would."

Smoke nodded, humbled by the faith implicit in Moonlight's voice. "I hope so. I'd like you to be happy, as happy as the day of your first birthday party on the island. Do you remember? You were so sad the whole week leading up to your birthday. I almost told you about the surprise a hundred times."

"It was such a nice surprise."

"Tiger bullied us for weeks until we came up with presents for you."

"I remember. Kite made me a big wooden bowl. Seven gave me a pretty rock that was as smooth as glass. Key made me arrows and restrung my bow for me. Tiger brought me a chunk of fresh honeycomb, and I had to put mud on his beestings. You made me a bracelet woven of dried grass. I wore it until it was too small for my wrist." Moonlight smiled. "You all made me very happy that day."

"I remember that it felt good to band together and do something just because it was the right thing. Not because the sensei ordered it, but because we wanted to. And your face when you walked into the hut and saw us waiting for you…. You glowed like star."

"That's a good memory. Unfortunately, it's far outweighed by bad ones."

"I know it's different for you… messier," Smoke said. "But the boy I remember would let the bad memories slide away like mud at bath time. I always admired the way you never let any of it touch you, even when you had to submit to the sensei's orders. You didn't let it change who you are."

"That was a long time ago, and a lot has happened since then." Moonlight took a deep breath. "I took a good man and twisted him into the onmyoji's creature. Not an evil man who needed adjusting, but a soldier of the Shadow. A man whose only offense was that he occupied a position that was advantageous to Autumn. How does that live side by side with the Shadow's stated mission?"

"We were talking about you, not the organization."

"The subjects are directly connected. I'm symptomatic of the disease that's rife in the organization. You're not blind."

"No, I'm not, and I do what I can to counteract corruption when I find it."

"You can't fix it. It's too widespread—and worse, it looks legitimate."

"What exactly are we talking about? Are you speaking in general, or is there some plot—?"

"Of course there's a plot," Moonlight interrupted. "It must be obvious to someone with your brains that the onmyoji is securing a power base and a network of influence that spans the globe."

"He's a wizard. It's the kind of thing they do, right? Does he have any plans to raise the dead?"

"This isn't business as usual, Smoke. Autumn is sincere about becoming supreme head of the Shadow People."

"Does he do the evil cackle when he announces this ambition?"

"Fine. Joke all you want. When the onmyoji is sitting in the Highest Chair at the Inner Council, it won't be so funny."

The car pulled to the curb in front of Moonlight's house.

"May I come in for a while?" Smoke asked.

"I have to get eight hours of sleep tonight so I look my best tomorrow afternoon. I'm having new publicity photos shot for my Red Eclipse show."

"Will I see you before you leave for Saigo?"

"Breakfast at Uri Natsu at seven, Monday morning."

"I'll be there."

"Good. I'll call you when I'm coming back." Moonlight got out of the car and stuck his head back in. "Bring a list of the people you find inconvenient. I have a feeling I'll be in the mood to wreak some havoc. Tasteful havoc, of course."

"Of course. Good-bye for now. Tokyo's going to be dreary without you."

"Ha! You think a week with the onmyoji is going to be a day at the carnival?"

Smoke laughed and told the driver he was ready to go. "I'm a weak man," he murmured as the car pulled farther away from the place where Moonlight was. It was appalling how quickly his happiness had come to depend on Moonlight's continued presence in his life. Even now, the thought of a week, maybe even two, without Moonlight's company made Smoke feel a dull panic that leached all color, light, and harmony out of his life. He'd vowed it wouldn't happen, but he might as well have promised to stop breathing. Moonlight was his unicorn, his Holy Grail, and all the other wonderful, shining things the world hides from us until we're worthy of them.

Even if Moonlight never loved Smoke the way Smoke loved him, Smoke would still do everything in his power to insure Moonlight's happiness and health. Smoke would give all he had to Moonlight, including his life, and never ask for anything in return. He wasn't motivated by the thought of any reward he might receive; he simply couldn't conceive of standing idle if the one he loved needed his help. Even if the loved one was never aware of the help. Smoke had no doubt that Moonlight was attending the enforcement chiefs' meeting for some reason known only to the onmyoji, and he was just as sure that the situation could become dangerous.

Secure in the bug-free cabin of the limousine, Smoke took out his phone and dialed a number he rarely used. "Of course it's me," he said when his call was answered. "Who else has this number?" He paused. "That wasn't a joke. If you've given this number to anyone else, tell me before I hang up. Are you sure no one else has it? Good." Smoke sat back and watched the city slide by in the side window. "I assume you'll be in Osaka next week?" Smoke listened for a few minutes. "Keep an eye out for my friend." A minute later, he ended the call, satisfied that Moonlight would have an angel on his shoulder in Osaka.

"LORD TALON, Iron Tribe's Chief of Enforcement, requests a private meeting, my lord."

Moonlight's veil rendered the messenger's face into a pinkish bean shape. The head covering disguised his identity, but he couldn't read the nuances of expression that allowed him to virtually read minds. He had to pay careful attention to vocal inflections to maintain the façade of a powerful wizard.

"He will see me at the meeting," Moonlight answered in Autumn's chilly tones.

"I'll see you now," Talon said as he strode into the room.

Moonlight suppressed the urge to stand. He was the one in the position of power here. "I see you're as rude in person as you are by phone."

"How fortunate for me that I'm useful to you."

"Indeed you are. What is it you wish to discuss?"

"Moonlight."

Moonlight resisted the urge to fiddle with the small objects on the desk. "I'm listening."

"What will it cost me to get him back?"

"You think you can buy Moonlight?"

"I was hoping we could speak frankly."

"We are speaking frankly. Moonlight has become too valuable to me to give away like a toy." Moonlight lifted his chin in Autumn's imperial manner. "You can always apply to Rose Tribe for a companion, although I understand the waiting list is quite lengthy."

"I want Moonlight."

"I wonder if you realize how obsessed you sound. I'd advise you not to let others overhear you speaking this way if you want to keep your position."

"You have me right where you want me, don't you, you evil bastard?" Talon controlled himself with an effort. "Are there any circumstances under which you'd consider letting me see Moonlight?"

"I'll ask him if he wants to see you. Is there anything else you'd like to talk about?"

"You remind me of him a little."

"I trained him." Moonlight leaned forward in his chair. "If you want some good advice, you'll forget about Moonlight. He's moved on. He's a different person now. The Moonlight you knew doesn't exist. He never did."

"How can you use people like that?"

"It takes talent, intelligence, and skill." Moonlight turned his head toward the messenger. "Escort Lord Talon out," he said firmly.

"I'll see you at the meeting," Talon said.

"Where I expect you to support me wholeheartedly."

"You know I will." Talon stalked out of the room, brushing the messenger aside.

When Moonlight was alone again, he lifted his veil and soothed his dry mouth with a glass of water. "I guess I can fool anyone," he murmured as he washed the copper-penny bitterness of adrenaline from his tongue. After a few minutes, his heart slowed to its normal rhythm and he felt steady enough to attend the meeting.

Talon followed Moonlight's lead on every proposal, and the other chiefs took the example of Iron Tribe's head of enforcement. It was agreed that there was a need for more soldiers and that immediate steps should be taken to institute a program to allocate more money and land to foster crèches and to produce more potential inductees. The men around the table swore to bring this matter before their Tribal Councils, and the meeting broke up.

As soon as Moonlight was certain he was alone, he went to the bathroom, removed his veil, and lost the contents of his stomach. Pale and shaking, he turned on the cold water in the sink and rinsed his mouth. He splashed more water on his face and reached for a towel without looking in the mirror. The thought that he'd just enabled the kidnapping of more innocent children made him retch again, but he had nothing to bring up. It was getting harder all the time to balance his feelings with what he was being forced to do. If he had an ounce of real integrity, he'd kill himself before he did one more thing to help the onmyoji.

Soft and low, Moonlight heard Tiger's voice chiding him for his thoughts. He heard Tiger whisper to be strong for a little while longer. He heard Tiger's promise that they'd be together again someday.

Moonlight dropped the towel on the floor and went to pack up his luggage. He summoned the Saruzoku messenger and requested a car to the airport. By the time the car was ready, Moonlight had changed his flight, cancelled the next night's booking, and changed into the onmyoji's habitual traveling robes. Silent as a ghost, he departed the Kagehito's VIP lodgings in Osaka and returned to Tokyo. There was no reason to stay here. Autumn would be pleased with the outcome of the meeting, and Moonlight missed Smoke. He needed the sympathetic ear of a friend right now, and a sympathetic shoulder would be welcome too.

Moonlight called Smoke en route, and Smoke met him at one of their favorite restaurants. He didn't protest when Smoke kept filling his glass with *soju*, and he quickly felt the disorienting effects of so much alcohol. His equilibrium was compromised and his tight control was considerably loosened.

"I shouldn't be in public." Moonlight's statement came out as a lazy drawl that stroked all of Smoke's erogenous zones.

"Dinner's on the way, and you need to eat something."

"In France, they give you bread to soak up the alcohol. It's very practical."

"Sounds counterproductive to me."

"Seriously, I think we should get our food to go."

"Why?"

"I feel as though I might become very emotional at any moment."

"Like breaking down in sobs emotional or breaking the furniture emotional?"

"A fifty-fifty mix would be my prediction."

Smoke settled the bill and collected the boxed-up dinner while Moonlight went to wait in the car. When Smoke reached the vehicle in the parking garage, the top was down and the radio was on at full volume. He set the bags in the tiny back seat and slid in on the driver's side. Turning down the radio, he cranked the ignition, and the Italia's engine responded with a throaty purr. He glanced at

Moonlight and got the look that said this situation called for an inordinate amount of speed. Shifting up, Smoke put his foot down on the gas and careened out of the parking space. He tapped the brakes long enough for the sensor to read his permit and open the gate. Once the way was clear, he gunned it and took Moonlight on an exhilarating, zigzagging ride that blurred the neon and the street lights into smeary streaks of color against the night. They were both tousled and breathless by the time Smoke pulled up to the curb outside Moonlight's house.

"Much better," Moonlight said as he got out.

"Fresh air usually works." Smoke grabbed the bags and followed Moonlight through the garden to his apartment. "You need any help with the key?"

"No, I got it." Moonlight opened the door and stood aside for Smoke to go first.

Smoke put the bags in the miniature kitchen and came back out to find Moonlight sprawled on the pink satin love seat. "Can I make you a plate?" he asked.

"I don't think I could swallow. Every time I think about what I'm doing, I feel sick."

Smoke sat down next to Moonlight and pulled him into a hug. "I'm sorry," he said, stroking Moonlight's hair.

"It makes no sense, but knowing you understand makes it a little better."

"Just knowing you exist makes it better for me." Smoke kissed Moonlight's forehead. "Do you want to tell me what made you so upset?"

"I can't tell you everything." Moonlight put his head on Smoke's shoulder. "But I ran into Talon. It wasn't a pleasant meeting. He's obsessed with getting me back."

"Which gives the onmyoji more power over him."

"The onmyoji may live to regret ensnaring Talon."

"That sounds very ominous. I'm not doing a very good job of cheering you up."

"And I've taken advantage of your friendship once again. You're too good to me."

"I'll be as good to you as I like," Smoke said mock-sternly.

"Will you stay until I'm asleep?"

"Of course. Would you like me to tell you a story?"

Moonlight snickered and cuddled closer to Smoke. Smoke let Moonlight lie down in his lap, slipping a cushion under his head.

"Do you have that list of inconvenient people?" Moonlight asked drowsily.

"As a matter of fact, my boss has become terribly inconvenient. Would you mind pretending to seduce him and giving him poison? Real poison, not pretend."

"Anything for you." Moonlight's eyelids fluttered and stayed down. "So tired," he sighed.

Smoke held Moonlight until his friend was deep asleep. Easing Moonlight off his lap and onto the couch, Smoke spread Moonlight's coat over him and leaned in to tuck it around him. He couldn't resist tracing the curves of Moonlight's lips with a fingertip, and jumped when Moonlight murmured something in his sleep.

"Have sweet dreams," Smoke said as he straightened up. With a last look at his sleeping friend, he left, locking the door behind him.

Moonlight snuggled into his pillow, lost in a dream of a summer's day in a mountain meadow, napping after a swim, the sun warm on his skin and Tiger's lanky frame pressed against his side. The stalk of grass was sweet on his tongue and the drone of the bees in the wildflowers was a potent lullaby. His belly was full and he had nowhere to be. For a few fleeting hours, life was golden.

"COULD you at least try and look like this means something to you?" Rain nudged Tiger with his shoulder as they approached the door to the Great Hall of the Shadow.

"I thought I had a respectful look on my face."

"Bored is closer to the mark." Rain stopped when a sentry held up a hand.

"There they are!" A heavyset man rose from a divan to the left of the entrance to the Hall.

"My lord," Rain murmured as he bowed to Iron Tribe's new chief.

"A pleasure to see you, sir," Tiger said, bowing as well.

"It's my pleasure to have two such remarkable men in my service," Ladder said. "How was Russia? I hope you didn't freeze your *kintama* off."

"I think Tiger has an extra set," Rain said.

Ladder chuckled. "I wouldn't doubt it."

"Is the Chief Enforcement Operative here?" Tiger asked.

"Talon's here." Ladder made a sour face. "He's as pleasant as a wasp's nest, and he's made it no secret that he wants my job." Iron Clan's chief lowered his voice. "Some say he's made a fool of himself over a Barazoku that rejected him and that's why he's so touchy."

Tiger's heart lurched, but his expression didn't change.

"It had to be the Rose that worked with us on the naked sushi adjustment," Rain said. "Pretty thing, but I didn't trust him. You never knew what was going on behind that beautiful face. You remember him, Tiger."

"How could I forget?" Tiger gave the answer the other men expected to hear, waving his fingers as though he'd burned them.

Ladder and Rain chuckled.

"Barazoku is a strange clan with strange customs," Rain said. "I'd have thought their methods would be obsolete by now."

"Sex as a weapon will never be obsolete," Ladder said. "But I understand your attitude. I've never run a team with a Rose on it, and I never will. I find the entire system... distasteful." He cleared his throat. "However, conditioning runs deeper in some, and the big bosses have to have their playthings, right? I wouldn't want to deprive them of their Rose concubines."

A bell pealed, and Ladder cleared his throat again. "We've stood in the hall long enough. Are you ready to receive the gratitude of your clan?"

"If I had a choice, I'd skip the ceremony," Tiger said.

"Wouldn't we all," Ladder commiserated. "I miss working with you directly, both of you. I asked that you be assigned to Tokyo since you're familiar with the area, and Lord Mahogany agreed to it. Rain, you'll continue to act as Blue Fire team leader. Tiger, you'll be his second-in-command."

"Thank you, sir," Rain said as Tiger bowed to Ladder.

"No need to thank me." Ladder nodded to the sentries and the doors swung open. "Welcome back. Now allow me to escort you to the High Table."

 Part Seven

"YOU sure this is the heaviest place in town?" Rapper Shoog-G Six tilted his shaved head down to look at his bodyguard over the tops of his diamond-studded sunglasses. Fluffing the collar of his floor-length faux fur coat, Shoog tapped his foot impatiently. "Because I'm not gettin' out of the limo if this place is as lame as it looks."

"It's the shit," said Shoog's road manager, former British pop star Gilly Blaise. "I'm tellin' ya, mate. This is where the Yakuza come to let their hair down."

"Wasn't talkin' to you." Shoog fixed his tar-pit eyes on the bodyguard. "This the one s'posed to know Tokyo like a native, yo."

"You asked about a place where there are no rules." The bodyguard jerked his chin at the warehouse behind him. "This is that place."

"I asked around a bit," Gilly said. "This is the wildest scene going. Hardly anybody knows about it except for randy pols and their owners."

"Bo-ring, but since we here, we might as well step in."

"That won't be necessary." The bodyguard gave the driver a nod and a large piece of machinery came to life with a loud ka-chunk. A whirring noise filled the interior of the long car as it began to descend smoothly into an underground parking garage.

"Now this is dope," Shoog drawled, giving the bodyguard a gem-encrusted grin.

The security agent's face didn't change. It wore the same impassive expression that it had for the twenty-six hours Shoog had been acquainted with him. Shoog figured it was an Eastern thing. Shoog liked Eastern things: Chinese food, kung fu movies, and geisha lady-boys. He hadn't seen any of these things since he'd landed at Narita Airport yesterday for the first concert of his Asian tour, and he was getting a little peeved, in spite of the excellent selection of booze in the limo's bar. However, the cloak and dagger entrance to the club soothed his nerves. It looked as though he was in for an interesting evening, and that pleased him.

"You done good, Tiger," Shoog said as the guard got out to hold the door for him. He glanced at the single elevator door that was flanked by two large men. "That way?"

Tiger bowed slightly. "We're expected," he said and turned to lead the way.

Shoog hung back a couple of seconds before he followed the bodyguard. Though Tiger wasn't Shoog's type—too tall, too aggressive—Shoog appreciated a handsome man who moved like a wolf across a clearing. Shoog watched Tiger deal with the sentries, and then sailed into the open elevator as though he came here every day. Tiger bowed briefly to the pair of guards and got into the lift with Shoog and Gilly. Shoog counted four floors up before the doors opened again.

Tiger stepped out and extended a hand. "Welcome to the Tea Room," he said without a trace of humor.

Shoog and Gilly got out of the elevator and paused to look around the intimate-sized lounge. "This is the warehouse tower, isn't it?" Gilly said.

Tiger nodded. "Another club is below, but this one is special."

"Damn sure better be." Shoog took off his sunglasses. "I like the atmosphere so far, now how about a place to set my ass down?"

The bodyguard gestured, and a host appeared from behind a red silk screen to the left of the elevator. Dressed in a tight black leather version of a military school cadet's uniform and with a demeanor to match, the host raised an imperious hand and summoned a waiter. The waiter's short hair was a rich burgundy color that contrasted nicely with his creamy Edwardian shirt. Adroitly, the trim man led Shoog's party through the scattering of low tables and cushions arranged on tiers around a semi-circular stage.

"Is this to your liking?" the waiter asked as he stopped beside a black-lacquered table.

Tiger looked around the dimly lit room, gauging the prominence and the proximity of the other guests. "This will be fine," he said. "Bring sake, and then we will order drinks."

"You seem to know your way around," Gilly said to the bodyguard. "Come here often?"

"Not often. It's not every day that I escort someone of Mr. Six's stature. Only the most famous—or infamous—are permitted in the Tea Room."

"Some heavy dudes in here," Shoog said as he arranged himself on a large red cushion with as much dignity as possible. "You can smell the gun oil over the expensive aftershave."

Gilly nodded, taking a surreptitious look around at the other tables. "That gent with the tall bird in the red wig looks like the real deal to me. You reckon he's a Yakuza assassin?"

"He's got the stone-cold killer look to 'im," Shoog said as the waiter arrived with a pot of sake and three cups.

Tiger turned his cup upside down as the waiter served the other two men.

"Anyone famous in here tonight, lad?" Gilly asked loudly.

The waiter recoiled slightly and then answered in precise English. "The man across the room drinking champagne is an important government official, the mayor of Shinjuku ward."

"Wonder if he's spending the taxpayers' money?" Gilly elbowed Shoog. "I count five bottles of very expensive bubbly."

"His date is hot," Shoog said, eyeing the slender young Asian man seated to the politician's left.

Tiger ran his mild gaze over the politician's companion again, from the heavy waves of dark hair that shadowed a pair of depthless bedroom eyes to the handmade boots that completed the tailored suit. "He's most likely an aide or a social director, but he's definitely a facilitator of some sort. He might be having sex with his boss, but I doubt it."

"The mayor of Shinjuku, huh?" Shoog tossed back his cup of rice wine. "Should that mean somethin' to me?"

"Shinjuku is a very rich ward: lots of skyscrapers, biggest train station, and largest foreign population in the city," Tiger said. "Also lots of red-light districts, you know? Clubs with gambling and strippers. Prostitutes. Drugs."

"Is that right?" Shoog gave the heavyset politician a long, speculative look.

"Don't stare," Tiger said. "His bodyguards will notice you. You don't want that."

"Shit, I ain't afraid," Shoog said. "Anyway, that's what you here for. Your rep says you hung with the Russian Mafia, so you should be able to handle some local flavor." He looked up at the waiter. "Bring me a Seven and Seven," he said.

Gilly took a sip of the sake and ordered a martini.

"When the show start?" Shoog asked, glancing at the stage.

"Soon," Tiger said.

"Better be good." Shoog crossed his arms over his broad chest. "I appreciate that you brought me to a place where the heavy hitters hang out, but I like a little more action, you dig?"

Gilly chuckled. "What if that Yakuza hit man had a row with that red-headed tart? Picture her with that bosom heaving, eh?"

"That man works here as a domestic during the day. He comes back at night because he gets his drinks at a discount. The redhead is neither his date nor a woman. That's one of the performers in the drag show." Tiger rattled off these facts as if reading them from index cards.

Before anyone could speak again, the lights dimmed further and the waiter returned with the drinks. As he glided away, gold-embroidered red curtains pulled back from the small stage. Soft lights illuminated the half circle with a silver-white spotlight beaming down on the shrouded figure standing like a figurehead on a prow. Head tilted up, face veiled, body draped in flowing fabric that trailed on the ground, the performer held the pose as the silence stretched out.

A few plaintive notes played on a reed flute drifted from behind the curtain. The figure onstage bowed, and the translucent silk headscarf drifted down to pool against the boards. As the performer straightened up, pale, perfect features framed by glossy, raven-black hair were revealed in a wash of light that mimicked moonlight. Smooth skin drank in the fragile radiance, glowing like alabaster. Large eyes outlined like a pharaoh's gazed tranquilly out into the middle distance. A pair of full lips poised somewhere between a sulk and the prelude to a kiss were subtly highlighted by a layer of clear gloss.

Shoog leaned over the table toward Tiger. "You gonna tell me that's a dude too?"

Tiger didn't answer right away. His breath caught in his throat the way it always did, the way it always would, when he caught sight of this man. "Of course he is," he said when he could trust his voice. "He isn't trying to fool anyone, which you'll see for yourself if you take a longer look."

Shoog reassessed the frame under the multiple layers of diaphanous silken robes. "I see what you mean. Looks like a brother gets to the gym now and again. Check the bubble butt. Bet he's a trained dancer."

Tiger nodded. "You'd win that bet."

The unseen flutist played another few notes. In a move that was part ballet and part martial arts, the performer half-turned, lifting an arm over his head in a graceful arc. Another length of delicately tinted silk floated to the floor, revealing a hand and forearm as perfect as anything sculpted by Michelangelo.

When the Kagehito had called Tiger back from Russia, he had let himself hope that he'd see Moonlight, but so far he hadn't. Now Moonlight was here, at the same club where Tiger was scheduled to make an adjustment to the population. Tiger couldn't see any point in their superiors withholding the knowledge that they were on the same job, and that worried him.

Beginning to get the concept of the floor show, Shoog lounged back against the cushions to enjoy the performance-art striptease. He started to say something to Gilly, but the room had fallen silent except for the occasional clink of glassware and the discreet rattle of ice. Shoog recognized respect for an artist and held his remarks for now. Sipping his drink, he gave the performance his full attention. Even when the dancer was down to the last modesty-preserving swatch of fabric and Shoog could see what was coming, he held his tongue along with the rest of the crowd.

The dancer did a slow spin on one foot. While his back was to the audience, he loosened the black string that ran between his shapely buttocks and around his slim waist. The crotch-covering length of red silk that hung from the string dropped to the stage. With no vulgar, teasing pause in between, the performer completed the spin, arms stretched behind him, poised on the toes of one foot as though he was going to leave the ground any second. Every toned muscle in the lithe body stood out in satiny relief, and the fans that blew the curtains at his back gave the billowing scarlet fabric the semblance of vast fiery wings. When the stage lights abruptly went out, Shoog held his breath just like everyone else until the house lights came up again.

"Hoo-wee," Shoog said softly. "That's what I call art. Invite him to have a drink with us."

"I think someone has beaten you to it."

Shoog turned in the direction of Tiger's gaze and saw the mayor's aide disappearing behind the stage curtains. "Why don't you do somethin' 'bout that?"

"Not worth it." Tiger leaned over to light the cigar Shoog stuck in his mouth. "The mayor really does have Yakuza connections. It's well known that he's ordered law and code enforcement officials to ignore the Yakuza sweatshops in his ward.

"The Yakuza ship in poor Koreans, luring them into immigrating by promising them good jobs. The Yakuza pay for the tickets and arrange the paperwork, telling the workers they can pay it back later. When the Koreans get here, they find out they're working long hours for low pay in the knock-off industry. Then the interest begins to pile up on their debt to the Yakuza, and they begin to realize that they can never pay it back. The Yakuza own them. They're slaves and their children will be slaves."

"Daaaaamn," Shoog said on a long exhale. "That's real underworld, man."

Tiger nodded. "Well put, Mr. Six."

"Just so you know… I'm against slavery."

"Not according to Tres C, Rajeena, and MacDonna."

"What do my backup singers have to do with…?" Shoog looked over at the bodyguard. "Did you just make a joke?"

"It's only a joke if it's funny." Tiger's head turned as a door opened in the far wall.

The mayor's aide emerged and turned to hold the door for his companion. The dancer walked through, clad now in snug, black pants and a high-necked tunic of bright red knitted silk. He'd removed the dramatic makeup and brushed out his hair, softening the geometric lines of his hairstyle. The smile he gave the aide for his courtesy was an electrifying contrast to the cameo-like mask of his onstage persona.

"He's a stone fox," Shoog said. "Hate to see him wasted on some fat-cat politician."

"Does he deserve someone more like you?" Tiger divided his attention between Shoog and the dancer.

"I'm just sayin'…." Shoog watched the aide introduce the mayor to the performer. "Damn shame."

Across the room, the dancer bent at the waist like a reed in the current and spoke into the mayor's ear. The politician looked up, his explosive affirmative fluttering the feathery sheaf of hair that curved around the young man's left cheekbone. The mayor got to his feet and followed the dancer back down the steps as the aide sat down at the table. One of the mayor's bodyguards got up and trailed his boss backstage.

"That didn't take but a minute," Shoog said as Gilly nodded in agreement. "Looked like a setup to me."

"If it was a setup, the aide would simply have taken the mayor backstage." Tiger winked at Shoog. "You're right though. It's damn shame. Still want me to do something about it?"

"What you got in mind?"

"Nothing is stopping us from requesting a few minutes of the dancer's time." Tiger rose. "Are you coming with me?"

"Hell yeah!" Shoog reached into his fur jacket, but his customary sidearm wasn't there. "Shit! For a second, I forgot I was in Japan with no permit to carry."

Tiger reached under his vest and slipped an automatic handgun into Shoog's hand. Shoog nodded his thanks as he stood up.

"What about me?" Gilly said.

"Finish your drink while you wait for us," Tiger said.

With Shoog at his back, Tiger moved purposefully down to the stage and kept going into the right wing. Shoog didn't hesitate, slipping behind the curtain at the bodyguard's heels, reveling in the chance to live the thug-life fantasy.

There were two doors in the tiny backstage area, and in front of one of them stood one of the mayor's bodyguards. "Off limits," the burly Chinese man said as Tiger approached at a brisk walk. "Turn around and go back the way you came."

When Tiger didn't slow down, the mayor's bodyguard went for his gun. Tiger took a step to his left and spoke over his shoulder.

"Cover him," Tiger said to Shoog.

Shoog pointed his pistol at the sentry and the man held his hands up. "Smart move," Shoog drawled.

"Keep him here," Tiger said, putting his hand on the doorknob.

"He ain't goin' nowhere," Shoog answered.

The door was locked but yielded to a twist of the bodyguard's wrist. Tiger pushed the door open and sprang inside, shutting it behind him. From across the room, the dancer locked eyes with the bodyguard.

"Moonlight," Tiger said.

"Tiger!" Moonlight let the mayor's limp body fall to the floor and crossed the room. "I don't believe it!"

"When that curtain pulled back and I saw you...." Tiger put his arms around Moonlight and hugged him fiercely. "I've missed you so much."

"Am I forgiven?"

"You were following orders. I of all people understand that. I'd never blame you for what the Kagehito make you do." Tiger paused. "You're not with Talon anymore?"

"No, but he's allowed to visit me when the onmyoji wants to reward him."

"Someone needs to kill that wizard."

"If only that was possible."

Tiger hugged Moonlight tighter. "Is he dead?" he asked, glancing at the mayor.

"Not yet."

"How's it goin' in there?" Shoog called through the door.

Tiger grimaced. "I was supposed to make it look like the mayor was hit by a stray bullet when a decadent Western rap star started a gun battle."

"I'm doing a favor for Smoke. I was supposed to make his boss's death look like a heart attack during vigorous sex."

"We can still do something like that," Tiger said. "It could look like the mayor had a heart attack when he heard gunshots. Smoke could still escape suspicion of having anything to do with his boss's death."

"And he'll keep moving up in the government and grow more useful to our masters. Did he see you in the lounge?"

"Probably. I saw Key out there too, but he didn't acknowledge me."

"Key? Really? I thought he was an instructor." Moonlight retrieved a small case from the makeup table and opened it. Inside was a gleaming syringe filled with clear liquid.

"He was my waiter." Tiger watched Moonlight remove the hypodermic from its cradle and kneel beside the unconscious man. Taking Moonlight's hand, he took the syringe away from him. "I'll do it."

Moonlight tried to moisten his dry lips, but his mouth was just as arid. "Thanks," he whispered.

Tiger pushed the needle in, depressing the plunger. The deadly chemical entered the mayor's bloodstream, and he died of cardiac arrest without regaining consciousness.

"Tiger?" Shoog called out.

"It's cool," Tiger called back. "Thanks for having my back."

Moonlight looked up from the corpse and met Tiger's eyes. "Run with me," he said, as he'd said five years ago.

"What?"

"You're going to start shooting right? Gunplay will get everyone excited. More people will join in. The police will certainly take an interest. While it's all being sorted out, you and I could just take off and keep running. I'm not even supposed to be here tonight, not officially. It'll be a while before they realize I'm gone."

"When they do, they'll come after us."

"We're smart and strong and fast. They won't catch us." Moonlight took Tiger's hand. "I can't live like this any longer. Please, Tiger. Come with me."

Tiger thought about his life without Moonlight and made his decision. Turning his head toward the door, he shouted, "Help!" Pointing his gun above head height, he pulled the trigger as Moonlight flipped off the lights. A shell splintered the wood of the doorframe as it passed through into the hall. Two seconds later, the door banged open, and Shoog fired a shot into the ceiling from his position on the floor. Tiger was already out the window, following Moonlight across the warehouse roof, when the mayor's bodyguard joined the shooting party.

Moonlight picked up speed as he neared the edge and leaped the gap to the slightly lower roof of the neighboring building. He didn't slow down, racing across the flat surface to the other side and jumping another alley onto the sloping roof of another warehouse. At the other end, he stopped and pointed.

Tiger looked down at the train tracks, and then at the light of the train approaching from the left. "How fast do you think it'll be going?"

"It has to slow down for the curve. We can do it."

Tiger nodded and reached for Moonlight's hand. Moonlight threw his arm around Tiger's neck. They leaned together, and their lips met. Passion flared with an intensity that negated the rest of the world for the space of three heartbeats, and then the sound of the train recalled them to real time.

"I love you," Tiger said, his eyes on the engine, gauging its speed.

"I love you," Moonlight answered.

"Get ready." Tiger squeezed Moonlight's hand. "Count of three. One. Two. Three."

Tiger leaped, throwing himself into space as the train hurtled beneath him. Moonlight jumped at the same time, pedaling his legs and windmilling his arms to gain what little control he could over his fall. Tiger hit the aluminum roof of the train flat on his belly and stretched out his arms and legs to maximize his contact with the surface. Moonlight landed on his feet with knees bent and threw himself forward, clinging like a grasshopper on a windshield. The train slowed down a little more as the curve tightened, and Tiger slid down to the end of the car. Moonlight followed him down to the small platform between the cars, and they jumped off the train on the other side of the tracks. As soon as they had their feet under them, they dashed into a neighborhood of high-rise, low-rent housing.

Abruptly, Moonlight yanked Tiger into a recessed doorway covered with graffiti. Throwing his arms around Tiger, he pulled him into a kiss that nearly drew blood. Tiger returned the desperate kiss with equal intensity, clasping Moonlight as though he meant to absorb him. Both men gasped for breath when their lips parted.

"I'm dead until I'm with you again," Moonlight said in a choked voice.

Tiger nodded and then poked his head out of the alcove to look up and down the street. "We might both be dead if we stay in one place too long."

"I think we should find a boat. Our handlers keep us ignorant except for the information we need to complete our missions, but I think I have a decent idea of what *not* to do. No airports, no trains, no buses. They're too easy for the Kagehito to check."

"And as soon as we don't report in, they'll be looking. Even sooner, if Smoke reports us missing."

"He won't."

"You sound so certain. How can you know for sure what anyone will do?"

"Smoke won't do anything to hurt us. Let's get moving."

Tiger stepped out onto the sidewalk and Moonlight kept pace with him. "At least we don't stand out too much," Tiger said as they entered a downtown area of shops and restaurants.

Moonlight glanced at Tiger's serious black suit. "We could be out for a nice dinner. You might be a young lawyer, a little square, but passionate about defending the underdog. I'd be your artistic friend from university days, in town for the weekend to attend the opera. We've come close to confessing our feelings for each other thousands of times, but something always stops us. Our careers. Our families. Society. Maybe tonight, one of us will have the courage to—"

"It amazes me the way your mind works," Tiger interrupted. "Still as full of moonshine as when I met you."

"But you like it, don't you?"

Tiger glanced down at Moonlight as they waited to cross a busy street. "I love everything about you," he said. "But I get scared that your willfulness and your... flightiness are going to get you hurt." He paused. "What am I saying? We've run. If we're caught, we're dead."

"That really puts everything in perspective, doesn't it?"

"All I know is that I love you, and I can't live without you. You say run, and I run. If we die, we die together."

"And we die free."

Moonlight touched the back of Tiger's hand as they passed the mouth of an alleyway between two restaurants. Gleaming in the dimness was the chrome of a motorcycle. Without a word spoken, both men faded into the darkness. Tiger bent down next to the bike for a few seconds and then climbed on. He thumbed a switch and the engine came to life. Moonlight got on behind Tiger and lifted his feet to the rear pegs. Tiger walked the motorcycle to the end of the alley and looked out on the street. Behind him, someone shouted, and he twisted the throttle, banking the low-slung machine to the right. Moonlight held on tight as they made the turn and zigzagged away through the traffic.

Leaning on Tiger's back, Moonlight spoke in his ear. "We can't talk to anyone we've ever met, no matter how briefly. We should go somewhere near the edge of the docks and look for jobs on a boat."

Tiger nodded and turned onto the next left-hand street. He'd had a quick look at the map in the limo and knew which direction Tokyo Bay was in. Rarely slowing down, stopping only for traffic signals, he made a Pac-Man path toward the water.

"Stay away from the big commercial area," Moonlight said when they reached the docks. "Keep going down the waterfront until we get to privately owned fishing boats. They go out really early, so it's too late to talk to anyone tonight. We'll find a place to sleep for a few hours and then look for a boat short of hands."

Tiger began assessing the buildings they passed for suitability as hideouts. Between two rows of ramshackle wooden storage sheds, he stopped the bike and waited for Moonlight to dismount. Walking the motorcycle behind a row of drums under a tarp-covered lean-to, he turned off the engine and got down from the saddle. Moonlight signaled that the bike couldn't be seen from the street and Tiger joined him.

"The closed repair shop," Tiger said. "It has an upper story."

Moonlight nodded. He'd noticed the property with the "for sale" sign in the front window. An upper story meant there was an attic for surplus inventory or maybe even living quarters.

The doors and windows were all locked, but a quick unobtrusive climb up the power pole at the back of the building got Moonlight onto the roof. It took a few seconds to smash the lock and then Moonlight was down the access hatch for the rooftop air conditioning unit. Not having a ladder handy, he hung by his hands until he lowered himself far enough to drop the rest of the way to the floor. He landed in a crouch and sprang up to find his way downstairs to the back door. Unlocking the door, he pulled Tiger inside.

"There's a bedroom upstairs," he said breathlessly.

"With a bed?"

Moonlight laughed softly and Tiger's cock stirred. As though a bell had rung somewhere, they lunged for each other, hugging, kissing, laughing, twirling around in the gloomy shop that was cluttered with broken power tools and the parts of small engines.

Moonlight backed into a workbench and Tiger lifted him to sit on the flat surface. Pushing Moonlight's knees apart, Tiger moved between Moonlight's thighs to wrap his arms around him again in a fierce embrace.

"It's worth it," Tiger murmured.

"What?"

"You're worth it. You're worth anything, any price."

"So much for years of brainwashing." Moonlight laughed again and leaned forward to touch his lips to Tiger's. "This is stronger than all our training."

"There's nothing stronger than my love for you."

"Would it be completely insane to make love right now?"

"Completely." Tiger was pulling Moonlight's shirt up to his armpits as he spoke, running his hands over Moonlight's flawless skin.

"I just want to be as close to you as I can, you know?"

"I know." Tiger took Moonlight's mouth in a kiss that left no doubt as to his intentions. He meant to possess every inch of his lover.

"Yes," Moonlight exulted as Tiger moved from his lips to devour the rest of him, one mouthful at a time. Wrapping his legs around Tiger, Moonlight pulled him in tight and pulled his head up for a kiss that should have set off fire alarms. "Do it now," he whispered when their lips parted.

With much fumbling and breathless laughter, they removed enough clothing to permit intimacy. Tiger spat several times, using the saliva to lubricate Moonlight as well as he could. He'd been hard and leaking since the first kiss and hoped the pre-cum would make up for the lack of proper lube. Spurred by his nerve-jangling excitement and Moonlight's entreaties, Tiger pushed through the tight ring of Moonlight's opening and into the lush heat beyond.

Moonlight let himself slide off the bench and onto Tiger's cock, stretching his arms out along the tool-strewn wood for balance. "I love this," he said. "I love having part of you inside me."

Tiger cupped Moonlight's ass cheeks, supporting him as he began to rock gently. "If I could stay like this for the rest of my life, I'd be happy."

Moonlight whimpered as Tiger found his prostate. "Love me," he said in a small voice. "Show me you love me."

Gladly, Tiger took up the sweet challenge. Thrusting in long, smooth glides, he rubbed against Moonlight's prostate coming and going. He sacrificed stability for stimulation, moving one hand from Moonlight's round backside to take hold of Moonlight's lolling cock.

"So good," Moonlight moaned. It *was* good. Tiger's touch always stroked him just the right way, but it was nothing physical that put Moonlight into a state of profound arousal. It was the fact that he was doing it with Tiger that elevated him to this realm of pure bliss. Only when they were together did he feel whole, and as long as Tiger was at his side, it didn't matter what the world threw at him. With Tiger beside him, he felt strong and full of hope.

"Damn," Tiger panted. "I won't last much longer if you keep doing that."

"This?" Moonlight bore down harder on Tiger's cock as it moved in and out of him.

"Bad kohai," Tiger groaned, stroking Moonlight's shaft faster.

Moonlight cried out softly as he came, sending a stream of glistening cum shooting through Tiger's fingers. The feeling that bloomed from his center was so immense that it pinned him to the bench for the duration. Trembling helplessly in the grip of the intense orgasm, Moonlight gazed into Tiger's eyes as his sheath squeezed Tiger's cock.

Tiger's eyes stung with sudden tears, and he blinked them away. He didn't want his vision blurred by excess moisture. He wanted to bask in the look of sweet fulfillment on Moonlight's beautiful face as he came. Hooking his arms under his lover's thighs, he held him securely as he thrust a few more times until his climax peaked. Ribbons of seed unfurled deep inside his beloved as he buried his length in the tight channel. Panting like a marathon winner, he looked into Moonlight's eyes as a wonderful feeling of warmth suffused him.

"We're completely crazy," Moonlight sighed.

"Completely." Tiger eased out of Moonlight and lifted him from the bench, holding him in his arms. After a long kiss, Tiger set Moonlight on his feet and tucked himself away.

Moonlight straightened his clothing and put his arms around Tiger. "That really was foolish, but I feel much better now."

"Wait until you've been wearing those underwear for another couple of hours."

"Ass." Moonlight bit Tiger's ear. "The mess is a small price for what we just shared."

"No arguments."

"Want to go upstairs and lie down for a while?"

"Yeah. We should rest even if we can't sleep. I'm not going to be able to stop thinking about them out there searching for us. Wondering when they'll find us."

"They already know where you are." Someone spoke from the front of the shop.

Tiger and Moonlight whirled toward the curtained doorway that separated the workshop from the front of the store. Instinctively, they took several steps away from each other, leaving room to fight in.

"I'm not armed."

Moonlight recognized the resonant voice. "Smoke!" he said.

The curtain swayed and Smoke came into the room. "Are you both insane?" he asked.

"That's not the most important question at the moment," Tiger said. "How did you find us?"

"Are you trying to be funny? It took me three seconds of asking myself what you would do if you ran. I followed you across the roof and saw you jump off the train, and then I got my car and drove to the nearest intersection of a street that led to the docks. At this time of night, it wasn't hard to spot you on the motorcycle, and I followed you here… at quite a distance." Smoke was comfortable with the lie. He was here to save his crèche-mates' lives, and he'd do whatever he had to.

"Crafty," Tiger said grudgingly. He was hyper-aware of the handgun in the holster under his arm and his brain kept calculating the distance between him and Smoke and all the possible scenarios stemming from him going for his weapon. "Why are you here?" he asked in honest curiosity.

"I'm only a few steps ahead of our superiors, so try not to interrupt me again."

"You're risking everything," Moonlight said.

"Yes I am." Smoke flicked a glance at Moonlight. "But I had to speak to you. To try and change your minds before it's too late. If you come back now, we can give them a story they won't believe but will pretend to swallow to save face. I don't know if you know it, but you're both very valuable properties. A few years ago, the Kagehito might have thrown you away without a second thought. Now you're highly trained operatives at the top of your field. You're two of the best ever produced by the program, and they don't want to lose you."

"Nothing you say will change our minds," Moonlight said. "We're not going back."

"You won't make it," Smoke said firmly. "Whoever's running Tiger has already put his team on alert."

Moonlight exchanged a glance with Tiger.

"They could be minutes away instead of hours," Tiger said.

"Come with me," Smoke said. "I'll speak for you."

"No." Moonlight took Tiger's hand. "I'd rather die than live one more day as a slave of the Shadow."

Smoke looked Tiger in the eyes. "Do you want Moonlight to die?" He held Tiger's gaze for several seconds. "They know where we are. They called my phone while I was following you, and I got them to agree to let me come in first to talk to you. If you don't walk out of here with me, they're going to gas us, and then come in and load our unconscious asses into a big truck with 'toxic waste disposal' written on the side. After a few days of torture, we might be allowed to die." Smoke turned his dark eyes on Moonlight. "I know you're smart people. Make the smart choice."

Moonlight shook his head. "I don't care what the Kagehito told us about being noble warriors who keep a balance between good and evil. We're killers. Killing outside the law is murder. It's evil, and I can't be part of it."

Smoke turned back to Tiger.

"I won't leave him again," Tiger said, squeezing Moonlight's hand.

"I'm not telling you to leave him." Smoke played his last card. "I'm telling you how to save his life."

Tiger looked at Moonlight.

"No," Moonlight said, reading Tiger's thoughts in the set of his features. "You can't make this decision for me. I'm not going back. I meant it when I said I'd rather die."

"I know," Tiger said. "But the thought of a world without you...." His voice trailed off. "That's the one thing I can't face. As long as we're alive, there's hope."

Smoke's head came up like a hound that hears a whistle. "They're here," he said.

Moonlight pulled away from Tiger. "I'm going," he said. "Are you coming with me?"

"It's useless," Smoke said. "They're all around this place. I expect a gas grenade any second."

"Then why aren't you running out of here?" Tiger asked.

"Tiger!" Moonlight called from the foot of the stairs. "Let's go!"

Smoke took a bulky gun from his jacket pocket and pointed it at Tiger. "It's better this way," he said as he aimed and fired.

"Tiger!" Moonlight shouted as Tiger crumpled to the ground. For a split second he hesitated, and then two men came into the shop behind Smoke. Moonlight ran up to the second story as Smoke fired at him. If he was captured, there was nothing he could do to help Tiger. As he ran onto the roof, a helicopter swooped low and dropped a gas grenade. Moonlight ran for the edge, but fell a few steps short, drugged by the needle-dart in his back.

"I'm sorry," Smoke said, kneeling next to Tiger. "But they promised me they wouldn't kill you or Moonlight. The tranquilizer in your system is going to keep you immobile, but you'll be able to see and hear. You'll come out of it around the time we get to the island."

Tiger fixed his gaze on Smoke until Smoke moved away. He didn't know what was going to happen to him, but he was sure it wasn't going to be pleasant. No matter what their masters had told Smoke, Tiger knew that they did not take slights to their authority lightly. It was possible that he'd finally suffer pain massive enough to truly test him. He just hoped he was strong enough to endure it like a man. At least he could hold onto the hope that Moonlight had eluded the net and made it to freedom.

Smoke stood to the side and watched Tiger being loaded into a plain white van by two Kagehito agents. He turned and bowed when the Hanezoku chief Karasu approached. "Lord Raven," he said respectfully, waiting for the old man to speak.

"It happened as you said it would, Smoke." Raven tilted his head to the side, regarding Smoke with eyes that gleamed as black as obsidian. "Since I arrived, my colleagues have spoken of little else but your talents. I was skeptical when they spoke so well of you. According to your trainers, you are a most exemplary addition to Feather Tribe. Praise that lavish makes me wary." Hanezoku's chief of North American operations gave Smoke a thin smile. "I have to admit though, that you've impressed me. I volunteered to come here tonight so I could watch you in action, and you don't disappoint."

"Thank you, sir."

"I'm here to assure you in person that you've already received full credit for containing these rogues. The chiefs of the Feather Tribe have heard your name and they like what they hear."

Smoke chose his answer carefully. No need for his superiors to know the motivation for his actions. "I appreciate you letting me know."

"It's a pleasure, believe it or not. I look forward to working directly with you."

"Directly, sir?"

"You've received a rather prestigious promotion this evening. You're now my personal aide."

"I'm honored."

"And so you should be. How quickly can you vacate your current residence?"

"If you can send a couple of sweepers, I don't need to go back there at all."

"No need to be dramatic. Take an hour and pack a couple of cases. I'll send sweepers to take care of the larger items. Be at the newsstand in the Delta terminal of Narita Airport by five thirty. Your passport and ticket will be waiting for you."

Smoke didn't ask where he was going. He bowed and kept his head down until Raven had walked back to his car. He went to his small apartment and packed two carry-on bags of clothing and toiletries. By six forty, he was in a first-class seat on a 747 with the eventual destination of New York City.

LIGHT stabbed Moonlight's brain like a glass dagger, and he closed his eyes again.

"You can make the pain go away."

Moonlight's heart shrank as he recognized the onmyoji's sweet voice.

"You know how," Autumn went on. "Ignore the aftereffects of the drug. You need to pay attention now."

Moonlight concentrated. He was disoriented and dehydrated, but he forced himself to focus on Autumn's mouth and the words coming out of it.

"Does he really mean that much to you?" the onmyoji asked.

Moonlight kept his mouth closed and waited for his master to continue.

"Do you have any concept of what you've done in breaking the trust between us? I sponsored you. I gave you face. You enjoyed certain privileges because of my position and my patronage. In time, you would have risen to a high post. And you chose to turn your back and run. Idiot! Did you really think you could hide from me? I can sense your presence from the other side of the world. There is nowhere that you can hide from me."

Moonlight recognized the vestiges of the drug in his system and realized he wouldn't be able to talk even if he wanted to. He could see and hear and smell and feel, but control of his muscles hadn't returned yet. Rough calculations told him he'd been unconscious for eight to twelve hours. Experience told him that the headache would last almost as long.

"I look like a fool to the Inner Council," the onmyoji said. "I *was* fooled. *You* made a fool of me. And who respects a fool? Do you begin to see the extent of the damage you've caused me because you value rutting with a killer above loyalty to your tribe?"

Moonlight could smell Autumn's sandalwood soap as the onmyoji leaned over him.

"I thought you were smarter," Autumn said softly. "How could you believe you could hide from me? But mostly I'm disappointed in myself for giving you liberties. I should kill you… but I can't. It would be too much like killing myself." The onmyoji squeezed the bridge of his nose with thumb and forefinger. "I know your fatal flaw, Moonlight. You're proud. It's not something you decided. It just is. You're better-looking, smarter, with higher ideals than everyone around you, and you don't fear anything as romantic as death. In short, you're young. I had that innocent arrogance blasted out of me when I was called to the Ryuzoku, but you…."

The onmyoji stroked Moonlight's hair and ran his fingertips down Moonlight's cheek. "I don't want to do this, but the alternative is unacceptable. I have to send you to the underworld for a while. Just until you're grateful for every crust, for every touch that isn't painful. You must learn that your morals and your desires have no meaning. You belong to the Kagehito and you do the bidding of your masters without question. When you've learned this, you can return to the land of the living."

Moonlight refused to look at the onmyoji.

Autumn drew back. "Before I leave you to begin your lessons, I assume you'd want to hear any news about your… lover. It isn't good, I'm afraid. Tiger went berserk in the warehouse and killed many of his brothers before he was brought down. He isn't dead, but his injuries are very severe. If he survives, he'll most likely be publicly executed. It's been a long time since there was a need for the traitor's death ritual." He shuddered. "A nasty business. Takes all day."

Moonlight heard the onmyoji walk eight steps, and then a door opened and closed with a hollow boom. Tears welled up and overflowed Moonlight's eyes, running from the outer corners to dampen the hair at his temples. His vision was blurry, but he recognized the ceiling and focused on that to try and distract himself from his shock. He was in the cellar of the onmyoji's house, a vaulted space that held a few wine racks and some disused pieces of furniture. He'd been here many times to fetch a bottle of wine.

Moonlight could picture it as though he was floating with his back against the ceiling. His body was lying curled on an old carpet, bound from wrists to elbows and ankles to knees with soft straps. He could see the backs of two heavy bookcases and a wardrobe that hid a few chests of clothing and other small items. He knew the yellowish light came from two oil lamps on the wall on either side of the door. Outside the door was a short hall that led to a ladder and hatch on one end and the entrance to a tunnel on the other. The tunnel door had never been open in all the years Moonlight had lived in the onmyoji's house. However, if he could free himself from his bonds, he'd have a try at opening it.

Moonlight froze at the grating shriek of metal scraping on metal. After a moment, he realized he was hearing the hinges of the tunnel door, and then he heard footsteps on the stone floor. One, two, three men had entered the cellar. Despite his training, Moonlight's heart began to pound in apprehension as the door to his cell opened, and the three men entered. The bare-chested trio was clearly Iron Tribe, their tattoos proclaiming them the survivors of many missions, with many kills to their credit. They didn't speak, didn't make any sounds beyond grunts, groans, and the occasional hoarse cry of release. They used Moonlight until they were sated and left him on the carpet still bound hand and foot. Not until the tunnel door closed again did Moonlight allow himself to weep.

"You can make the pain go away."

Moonlight cried out and rolled onto his side to see the onmyoji standing over him.

"You know how," Autumn said. "The mind is infinitely more powerful than the body."

"Don't do this," Moonlight croaked. "I beg your forgiveness. Please untie me."

"I want to. It hurts me to see something as fine as you used so roughly. But this is just the first lesson. They will come every night when they're off duty, them and others, as I choose. You'll remain bound for quite some time. When I order the wrappings removed, it will feel odd to use your hands and feet again. It will be an ordeal, but when it's over, you'll have so much to be grateful for."

"Please," Moonlight said again. "I don't need any more lessons. I understand what I did wrong."

"I know, but you're not chastened. I'll send someone to feed you and a doctor to check on you every day, but you will endure this. Unable to move, you will be nothing more than a receptacle for lust. When you've accepted that, maybe I'll untie one of your feet." Autumn shook his head. "I don't know when you'll see me again. I can't look at you like this."

"Master! Please. I know I have to be punished, but not this."

Autumn went to the door and opened it. "I look forward to the day your torment ends," he said as he left.

"No!" Moonlight flung himself across the rug, wriggling like a snake, pulling at the straps. For several minutes he writhed in desperation, fury, and sheer panic. When the adrenaline wore off, he collapsed in dazed exhaustion. His head throbbed like a rotten tooth in syncopated time with the deep ache in his lower half. He had no one now. Tiger was as good as dead. Smoke had betrayed him. And his former patron was intent on destroying him by inches.

Through that long first night, Moonlight went through many emotions as his mind replayed the escape and capture over and over. Though he had failed, he didn't regret running. His punishment only reinforced his loathing for the Kagehito and his determination to be free of them. People were not meant to be used like this, and he would never submit willingly.

 Part Eight

"How does it feel to be back after so long?" Raven glanced at his protégé's handsome profile, haloed by the helicopter window.

Smoke looked down at the island growing larger in his view. "I feel proud to be returning at the right hand of a man who's being honored for exemplary service to Feather Tribe."

"You're the perfect aide, Smoke. I never have to tell you anything twice, and you always have the right answer." The head of the Shadow People's interests in North America lowered his voice. "And you're smarter than anyone would ever believe. I'll miss you when you finally accept a promotion."

"I don't want promotions, sir. As a lowly aide, I have much more freedom to act. No one really notices the secretary, and they say all sorts of interesting things in front of me."

"You see? You're so smart that you don't need other people to know you're smart. I'll be happy to have you at my side for as long as you want to stay."

Smoke smiled as the helicopter touched down. "I appreciate that, sir," he said as he unbuckled his seat belt. His smooth face gave no hint that his stomach was churning as he followed his superior off the aircraft. They were on the other side of the island from the school, but the terrain was the same, and Smoke's memories hit him hard.

For two years, he'd been living with the guilt of betraying the only friends he had. He knew he'd done the right thing, but it hadn't turned out the way he'd thought it would. His master had assured him that Tiger and Moonlight were alive, but that was all he would say. Smoke had tried a few cautious probes of his own—after all, he was at the heart of one of the largest information webs on the planet—but learned nothing. Tiger and Moonlight had vanished, and Smoke was living in an alien culture. Seven had been killed when the getaway car he was driving was T-boned by a tanker truck running a red light, and Kite had blown up with the explosives he was rigging for a mission. Smoke had kept tabs on Key for a while, but at the moment had no idea where he was. For all he knew, Key was somewhere on this island training another crèche.

"Are you looking forward to the ceremony?" Raven asked as he and Smoke crossed the grass to the small group that waited to greet them.

"I'm interested to see what a full-dress elevation looks like, but I'd prefer a less formal affair and a different setting."

"The Great Hall is here, so changing the location is out of the question."

"I'm just being honest, as you requested when I came to work for you."

"That's really come back to bite me in the ass."

Smoke suppressed a smile at his master's use of the Americanism. They had reached the greeting committee, and it was time to play the consummate lackey.

After the amenities had been observed, the visitors were shown to rooms to change for dinner. The gathering that evening was very small compared to the banquet for two hundred that would be held the following night. A quiet meal of several courses was served to the men being honored and the leaders of their Tribes. Smoke ate with the other staff members and joined his master afterward to see if he needed anything.

"I'm tired," Raven said. "I think I should get to bed early tonight, so I'll be well rested for the ceremony tomorrow."

"That's a very good idea."

"You're young and resilient. No need for you to retire just yet." Raven leaned toward his aide, and Smoke smelled the fumes of red wine. "I've been invited to a special entertainment. Why don't you take my place?"

"Special entertainment?"

"Only the elite are invited, but Lord Pebble said he would take you with him." Raven pointed. "He's waiting with a couple of the others in the dining room. Go on. They've all had a bit to drink, and you'll be well-placed to eavesdrop."

"Of course." Smoke bowed. "I'll give you my report in the morning, unless I hear something that needs your immediate attention."

"Let's hope not. This is supposed to be a celebration."

Smoke joined the other men and accompanied them to a building that looked like a small gymnasium. Inside, they proceeded to a basement where tiers of seats descended to a fenced-off pit a little smaller than a tennis court.

"Are you much of a gambler?" Lord Pebble asked Smoke as they took their seats. "You can place a wager on one of the fighters if you like."

"Thank you, sir. I'll just watch."

Smoke looked casually around, counting seating for one hundred and fifty people. Over sixty were in attendance and more were arriving. Before the event started, every seat was filled.

Without warning, a door opened at either end of the pit and two scarred, naked men charged out. After sizing each other up, one of them threw a punch and the fight was on. It was brutal, without rules or mercy, or any weapons other than fists, feet, teeth and nails. It made Smoke sick, but he couldn't look away. He knew one of the fighters.

"Tiger," he said under his breath. "What have they done to you?"

As soon as Smoke could politely get away, he went to his room. Waking his master at this time of night was unthinkable, and anyway, he needed time to think of a way to bring up such a delicate subject. It was not impossible that Raven knew all about the gladiatorial sport and that it was something that wasn't spoken of with subordinates. Then again, this might be a local aberration, and Smoke might be putting his master in a very sticky spot. Smoke pondered many variables as the night dragged on, but he knew he couldn't leave Tiger to his fate without trying to do something about it.

In the morning, Smoke knocked on Raven's door as soon as it was permissible. When he entered, his superior was choosing a tie. Going to the case, Smoke picked out a black and gold diamond-patterned tie and put it around Raven's neck. As he deftly tied the length of knitted silk, Smoke asked if his boss had had a good night's rest.

"I slept very well. And you?"

Smoke took a calming breath and plunged into the opening. "I was too upset to sleep."

"Did you overhear something disturbing?"

"It was something I saw." Smoke cleared his throat. "Do you know what the entertainment was last night?"

"Some sort of martial arts display was my understanding."

"It was a bare-handed fight to the death."

"What?"

"Two Iron men were sent naked into a pit, and only one of them survived. Bets were being placed on this… sport."

"I won't insult you by asking if you're sure of what you saw." Raven nodded his thanks for the help with the tie. "I need a moment to think of how to deal with it. My phone." He held out his hand.

Smoke gave Raven his phone and watched him punch a number on speed dial.

Raven turned away from Smoke and had a quiet, brief conversation. When he gave the phone back into Smoke's keeping, Raven's expression was grim.

"I am told that Saigo Island is outside the world and nothing that happens here really happens. After a subtle warning to mind my own business, my friend hung up on me."

Smoke's heart sank, but he knew better than to continue with the subject.

"Smoke," Raven said. "Is there more to this than you're telling me?"

Surprised, Smoke answered truthfully. "One of the fighters was my crèche-mate Tiger."

"Ah." Raven nodded. "The teachers tell us that we aren't allowed to form sentimental bonds and yet... we are human in the end."

"I'll try harder to keep sentiment out of my thoughts."

"You misunderstand me. I'm not reprimanding you for your feelings. I think we've worked together long enough now for me to confide in you a bit more." Raven smiled faintly. "It's my heretical belief that strong emotional ties are actually beneficial to the Kagehito program. Perhaps it's because I'm older than most, and I'm growing soft and sentimental."

"That's not how I would describe you, sir."

"I'm feeling my years, Smoke. It's a sobering thing to come up against the barriers of diminished capability. No matter how fit you may be in mind and body, time takes its toll of everyone. It's funny how we never truly believe it will happen to us, and then it does. All our years seem to fall on us at once."

"I'll remember that."

"No you won't. You're twenty-five. You're strong, healthy, handsome, and frighteningly intelligent. At this point in your life, you're immortal." Raven smiled again. "Time will ambush you just like it does everyone else."

"I'm sure you're right."

"Not an easy thing, being Kagehito."

Smoke was not fooled by the lightness of his superior's tone. Raven was not making a casual remark. Instead of answering with an ego-stroking affirmative, Smoke stayed silent and waited for Raven to speak again.

"So many rules. So much formality in our interactions. It's so rarely possible for two Kagehito to just be a couple of people talking."

Again Smoke held his tongue, merely nodding in response to the obvious truth of Raven's words.

"This Iron man you're concerned about... Was he one of the two captured in the operation that began our association?"

"Yes, sir. Which brings up another concern."

"The other man who ran was also your crèche-mate."

"Yes, sir." Smoke wasn't surprised that Raven knew this detail. "I know my curiosity is a form of treason, but I need to know what happened to Moonlight."

"The Barazoku."

"Yes, sir."

"A rare calling, almost as rare as Ryuzoku. Maybe if there were female Kagehito, this would not be true."

"You're in rare form today, sir, if I may say."

"I think too much and that's the truth. Be wary of falling into that trap. If you rise to my level—and there's no reason to think you won't—just keep your eyes on the path ahead and don't stray to the sides." Raven gestured at the teapot on the tray and Smoke went to pour him a cup. "I saw Moonlight once, just a glimpse as he left the onmyoji's court. I'm not attracted to men, but he stirred something in me." Raven accepted the cup of tea and took a sip. "It's a great power the Rose Tribe wields. Few men are immune to the lure of sex."

"Moonlight is...." Smoke's voice trailed off. "When I was a mission data liaison in Tokyo, I worked with him several times. I coordinated all the mundane aspects of his Tokyo missions: cover jobs, accommodations, transportation, wardrobe, and so on. Though I saw a lot of him at that time, it's hard to describe him. You'd never mistake him for a woman, but the way he moves is so graceful that manly isn't the first thing that comes to mind."

"He reminds me of the onnagata, the actors who take female roles. While watching, you're aware that they aren't women, but you don't feel as if you're watching men dressed up as women. You're watching… something else. A sort of blend, I suppose."

"I'm sure the Barazoku receive similar training."

"Perhaps it's chauvinistic of me to consider grace a feminine attribute."

"We're Kagehito, a society of warrior monks. Some chauvinism is bound to creep in, sir."

"And of course, we must replenish our numbers by recruiting." Raven bent his arm, gold feather cuff links catching the light as he checked his watch.

"You have seventeen minutes before your breakfast meeting," Smoke said.

"Right again. How do you do that, Smoke?"

"Do what, sir?"

Raven gave his aide another of his vague smiles, playing the game that Smoke was just an ordinary valet. "It pleases me that we're able to have these casual conversations. Such a nice break from routine, but now it's over." He slipped his arms into the double-breasted jacket Smoke held for him. "Back to work."

Smoke accompanied Raven through a day of meetings, both social and business, and then returned with him to his rooms. With unobtrusive efficiency, he laid out his superior's formal robes and regalia.

"Thank you, Smoke." Raven picked up a cord of braided silk and ran his thumb over the golden medallion that hung from it. "I have a job for you tonight."

"Sir?"

"You'll have to miss the ceremony. I need you somewhere else."

"What are my new orders?" Smoke pushed aside his disappointment. There would be more honors and more ceremonies in the future.

"I've accepted a large gift, and I want you to oversee the loading of it into the helicopter."

"Of course, sir."

"Once the crate is aboard, I want you to stay with it. I'll be joining you right after the banquet for the flight back, so make sure our belongings are on board as well."

"I'll make sure of it."

"I know you will. That's why I trust you with important details despite your appallingly young age."

"I'll work on getting older." Smoke bowed and began helping his master dress for the evening.

"Yes, do that. There aren't enough old Kagehito."

A few hours later, Smoke sat talking with the helicopter pilot after seeing that Lord Raven's crate was securely stowed in the cargo area. In defiance of all safety regulations, the pilot was chain-smoking, and Smoke found the smell comforting. He had a sudden vivid memory of his father showing him how to strike a match, remembered lifting the flame to the tip of his father's cigarette... and that was all. He pushed the memory away as he'd done with the earlier disappointment and his surprise at being delegated to a flunky's errand. Like all Kagehito, Raven had a reason for everything he did—sometimes two or three.

It was only a little past ten when Raven arrived at the helipad. The hem of his robe swung around his ankles as he walked briskly to the helicopter. Without bothering to ask if everything was aboard, he gave the pilot the order to take off.

"Would you like some help?" Smoke asked when his master started untangling the chains and ribbons around his neck.

"Thank you." Raven sat back and let his nimble-fingered aide remove his medals and insignia of office. "I don't like flying over water," he said to the pilot. "Let me know as soon as we're over land again. Did you happen to…?" He smiled as Smoke produced a fresh suit of clothes from under his seat. "I should have known you'd think of it."

The flight to Narita Airport was quick, as was the loading of the crate onto the Shadow jet that waited for Raven and Smoke. The two men ate a light meal as the plane awaited permission to take off. Raven had just finished his account of the elevation ceremony and banquet when the pilot informed him that the tower had given them clearance. In less than twenty minutes, they were airborne and making the wide banking turn that would start their journey back to the United States.

"I know you're wondering why we left in such a hurry, but you're too well-trained to ask." Raven unbuckled his seat belt as soon as the captain gave permission. He beckoned to Smoke and walked to the back of the cabin. "You're also wondering why I wanted the crate here instead of the cargo space." Raven pulled loose the crowbar wedged under the wooden box's metal straps. "Open it," he said, handing the tool to Smoke.

"I'd guess it's either a statue or a couple of paintings," Smoke said as he set to work.

"No, this one isn't going into my art collection." Raven stepped closer to help when Smoke began prying the lid up.

The last nails popped free and the two men pushed the lid back onto a pair of seats. Smoke looked into the box and froze for a second. "How?" he asked his boss.

"I gave it a lot of thought before I decided the smartest thing would be to simply ask. I told the commander of Saigo Island how much I enjoyed the entertainment, and we had a sub rosa talk about the fights and the wagering." Raven clenched his jaw. "It's a fairly recent development—started about thirty years ago—but it's very popular. It will take more than one man to put an end to it. However, I did manage to get this one out."

"You just asked for him?"

"The sport is being practiced now in other places besides the island. The commander assumed I was starting an arena for Feather Tribe. He was reluctant at first to part with his top fighter, but I reminded him that people get bored when one man wins all the time."

"Still, it's hard for me to believe that they would let him go."

"I promised he'd never leave America alive."

"Now it's easier to believe." Smoke grunted as he pried off a side of the box. "I assume he's drugged."

"Heavy-duty tranquilizer guaranteed to keep him under until he's back in a cage."

"Sir?" Smoke looked up from his visual exam of Tiger.

"He's been kept behind bars, chained, and beaten when necessary, to quote the commander." Raven shook his head. "And I thought New Jersey was barbaric."

Smoke finished checking Tiger's visible bandages and sat back on his heels. The scarring was as bad as it had looked from the spectator gallery. The marks of teeth, fingernails, and whips marred the honey-colored skin, along with numerous bruises in various states of fading. Tiger's left eyebrow was bisected by a scar that had also split the skin of his cheekbone, and his nose was a little crooked.

"I'll help you get him buckled into a seat," Raven said.

"Why?" Smoke asked as they wrestled Tiger's dead weight into a chair. "Why'd you do it?"

"I could see that it weighed heavily on you and that it would trouble you for a long time." Raven shrugged. "I don't need a distracted aide."

"But the risk...."

"I thought it over very carefully before I acted. I value you, Smoke. You're the best I've ever worked with and you're going to get better. So saving this man benefits me by giving you the peace of mind to focus on your work."

"I should focus on my work out of loyalty to the Kagehito."

"Yes you should, but I've found that sometimes people need more than an abstract ideal to keep them on track. For reasons I don't need to know, you care about this man."

"Tiger," Smoke interjected.

Raven nodded as though making a mental note. "You care about Tiger, and so you will now feel a greater loyalty to me out of gratitude."

"I can't deny the truth of your words, master." Smoke gazed solemnly at Tiger's battered face. "He should probably see a doctor."

"I'd say it's imperative. Why don't you call ahead and arrange for a Kagehito doctor we don't normally use? Have him meet us in Southampton. I don't feel like going back to the city just yet, and nothing in the New York office needs my personal touch right now. Let's stay a few days on Long Island. The sea air will give me the energy I need after this trip."

"I'll get on the phone right now and arrange it."

"One more thing," Raven said as Smoke reached into his pocket. "Your other friend—the Barazoku…. The commander and I talked about the desertion, naturally, since we were both peripherally involved with the case. However, when I wondered aloud what happened to the Barazoku, it was suddenly time for the commander to be somewhere else. At the banquet, I found a note under my napkin with an invitation to meet the onmyoji in the morning to discuss my interest in the disgraced operative called Moonlight."

"The onmyoji?" Smoke frowned.

"I see you have an opinion of our stargazer."

"No, sir. Of course not. I would never presume that much. The onmyoji is the voice of the gods."

"He's definitely not of this world." Raven sat back down. "I left a note with Pebble, explaining to Autumn that I had to leave tonight and wouldn't be able to meet with him. I thanked him for the

offer of information, of course, and asked him to call or e-mail me."
He tilted his chair back and closed his eyes. "Go ahead and make
your calls."

Smoke moved farther forward so his conversations wouldn't
disturb his boss's rest, but not so far that he couldn't keep an eye on
Tiger. He was stunned that Raven had taken such risks to free a
disgraced man, but he was also immensely grateful, which his
superior had stated was the motive for the favor. Smoke didn't
believe for a second that there wasn't more to this than he was
seeing. Raven had to have another reason for his magnanimity, but
this wasn't the time to solve that particular puzzle.

As Smoke dialed the number of the liaison in New York City,
he had another flash of memory, as vivid as a slide show. Images of
Moonlight at six, thirteen, twenty-one—the boy, the youth, the man.
Moonlight, breathless with wonder as his eyes traced the arc of a
falling star. Moonlight, the exultant winner of an unofficial archery
competition. Moonlight, in white fur, sliding into the gleaming black
limousine of a Kagehito target. Moonlight, who had broken the
Kagehito rules to be Smoke's friend. Moonlight, whom he'd loved
for so long that it was a fact of life, like the need for oxygen.

The liaison answered, and Smoke explained what he needed.
After the liaison assured him that a doctor would be waiting when
Raven arrived at the Southampton house, Smoke dialed another
number. When the head of the domestic staff in Southampton
answered, Smoke informed him that Lord Raven would be staying
there for a few days. After hanging up, Smoke called the home
number of the New York office manager. He told Chisel that Raven
would be conducting business from the beach house until further
notice. After listening to a few messages that Chisel deemed urgent,
Smoke closed the phone and put it away.

Getting to his feet, he walked back and sat in the seat across
the aisle from Tiger. The flight took half a day, and Tiger never so
much as twitched an eyelid. Smoke placed a pillow around Tiger's
neck that stopped the limp lolling of his head, but other than that,
there wasn't much Smoke could do for him. There never had been.
They were friends, but Tiger had never wanted help from Smoke.

"FINALLY," Smoke said when Tiger's eyes opened.

Tiger blinked rapidly in the brightness. "Smoke," he whispered, recognizing the other man's voice. With a monumental effort, he rose to a sitting position, hands reaching for Smoke's throat. In another second, he fell back onto the mattress, wheezing for air.

"Whatever they gave you to knock you out must have been meant for elephants," Smoke said. "How do you feel?"

"Like I want to kill you," Tiger said hoarsely.

"I don't blame you. I tell myself every day that I did the right thing, but it doesn't make me feel any less guilty about turning you in."

"Moonlight?"

"I don't know. I'm trying, but I haven't been able to find out anything yet."

"I have to find him."

"I know." Smoke poured a glass of water from a metal pitcher beaded with moisture. "A doctor's had a look at you, by the way. You're a mess."

"Get away from me," Tiger said when Smoke went to help him sit up. He slid up against the headboard as Smoke set the glass on the nightstand. When Tiger's fingers stopped shaking, he picked up the water and drank it down.

"You might want to take it easy at first. I understand that the sedative they gave you can cause—" Smoke stopped talking as Tiger vomited the water back up. Grabbing a towel from the stack at the end of the bed, he tossed it at Tiger. "Small sips," he advised.

Tiger nodded curtly. "Where am I?" he asked, his voice stronger with each word.

"You're in a bedroom in a house in the Southampton area of Long Island, New York, U.S.A."

"How did this miracle come to pass?"

"My boss is a little unorthodox about what constitutes an employee bonus."

"You're still a clown."

"And you're still licking the boot that kicks you."

"You know I'm going to kill you when I'm strong enough, right?"

"Iron men are so predictable."

"You say that like it's a bad thing." Tiger sipped a little more water. "Seriously. What does your boss want with me?"

"I don't know yet, but I certainly don't believe he rescued you for my sake. No, that was a convenient excuse. He probably knew about the arena all along."

"He's a big boss, right?"

Smoke nodded. "Lord Raven to you."

"Well, whatever Lord Raven wants, I'm not staying around to find out."

"You can't escape from here. The grounds are patrolled by soldiers of your tribe."

"None of them are as good as me."

"Maybe not, but none of them have been beaten bloody recently either."

"I'll heal."

"So you intend to hang around eating my master's food until you're well enough to kill me and escape?"

"I have to find Moonlight."

"You might have to accept that he's gone."

"When I feel his cold body, I'll accept it."

Smoke swallowed, realized his throat was dry, and poured another glass of water. "I want to find out what happened to him too, but you aren't in any shape to do much of anything right now. The doctor said you look like you've been getting regular medical care, but the damage you suffered in that last fight was equivalent to being hit by a car."

"Come on, Smoke. We both know that pain is our servant, not our master."

"Don't quote Mallet to me, not even sarcastically."

"Let's talk about something else then." Tiger set the empty glass on the nightstand. "Now that you've got me here, how do you see me fitting in?"

"I admit I haven't thought it through. I saw that fight and something in me said, *enough.* I told Lord Raven, and without telling me, he arranged to get you out of there. Now I'm just trying to deal with you."

Tiger held his hands out and clenched them into fists, the corded muscles of his scarred forearms bunching. "My strength is coming back."

"You had a dislocated shoulder and several of your ribs are broken. It's amazing that you don't have a concussion, but most of you is a collage of contusions, abrasions, gouges, and bites."

"What I do in private is no one's business but mine."

"Fuck me. You made a joke." Smoke reached for Tiger's glass. "More water? And you can have a pill for the pain if you want it."

"Water."

Smoke filled the glass again and handed it over. "Can we stop posturing now and just talk?"

Tiger nodded as he took a drink.

"Here's my plan. We work together to find Moonlight."

"That's a plan?"

"We'll have plenty of time to refine it while you heal up."

"Why would I work with the man who betrayed me once already?"

"Because you know I wouldn't have done it if I'd had any other choice. They'd already found you. They would have killed you. They would have killed Moonlight. I thought it would be better if I talked to you instead of letting them go in with gas grenades and automatic weapons."

"What's done is done. I believe you believe that you had no choice. I doubt Moonlight will be as understanding as I am."

"That doesn't matter. He can spit in my face and I'll thank him, because it proves he's alive."

"I should have run with him and taken my chances."

"You'd be dead."

"And this is better?"

"It's a little better today than it was yesterday, right? You don't have to go into a pit tonight and kill anyone with your bare hands."

"I'd do it with a smile if it would get Moonlight back."

Smoke hesitated before he spoke again. "It occurred to me that he might be in the games too."

Tiger shook his head. "That wouldn't fit with the Kagehito sense of justice."

"If he's alive, we'll find him," Smoke said. "I have to go now. I actually have a real job that takes up a lot of my time, but I'll make sure you're taken care of." He stood and went to the door. "Try to rest. The doctor's going to come back and look at you again in a few hours. You're probably hungry, but you're not supposed to eat anything yet."

Tiger slid back down until his head was on the pillow and closed his eyes.

Smoke lingered in the doorway for a few moments, but Tiger didn't speak again. Closing the door softly, Smoke walked away down the hall.

"YOU have a visitor," the onmyoji said as he walked into the opulently furnished bedchamber. "Come and meet Tengu, the head of weapons research for Saruzoku Tribe." Autumn put a hand on the arm of the man beside him. "A group of his people has perfected a firearm that cannot be detected by any existing scanner. I think he deserves a reward."

Goblin cleared his throat nervously. "I've heard rumors and—"

One of the most powerful men in the Kagehito organization fell silent as the Barazoku called Moonlight emerged from behind a silk screen. "So the rumor is true," Goblin said. "You've kept the Rose Tribe's crowning jewel for yourself."

Autumn smiled slightly. "It's my feeling that Moonlight is best utilized as a reward. Sending him out into the field to be exposed to all sorts of danger seems foolish and wasteful. But tell me... have you ever seen such beauty?"

Goblin shook his head. "A rare prize," he said.

"Moonlight," the onmyoji said as Moonlight stopped in front of him. He reached out to run his hand over the glossy cap of hair that framed Moonlight's face. Cupping the young man's chin on his palm, Autumn tilted Moonlight's head up. "You were a pretty boy, but you've grown into a truly beautiful man." He glanced at Goblin. "There's more to great beauty than symmetrical features, you know. It's more about how a person carries himself."

"I see." The powerful Monkey Tribe chief was honored to meet with the man who wielded so much influence over the affairs of the Kagehito, but he had little patience for what he considered impractical matters. With an alluring courtesan standing in front of him, his first impulse was not a discussion of the nature of beauty. "Very insightful," he said.

"Insight is essential to my role." Autumn looked into Moonlight's eyes but could make no contact with the soul behind them. "I sense you grow weary of talk, Tengu. I'll go now so you may claim your reward."

"I'm grateful for your generosity." Goblin made the appropriate response as he bowed in the onmyoji's direction.

"If you need anything, just tell Moonlight," Autumn said as he left the room.

"Are you allowed to speak?" Goblin asked the Barazoku, taking nothing for granted.

Moonlight nodded.

"I'd like to hear what your voice sounds like."

Moonlight turned his gaze to a painting of a garden and recited two verses of an ancient piece of poetry before Goblin interrupted.

"Lovely," the Saruzoku chief said. "Now take your clothes off." He paused. "Is something wrong?"

"Usually, I serve tea and dance and sing for my guest before I begin to undress."

"I guessed as much from the décor and that poem. I'm not much for trappings. I'm a modern man." Goblin gestured, and Moonlight untied the sash of his robe. "I prefer having sex with women, but you...." Goblin shook his head in wonder. "You're not like anyone I've ever seen. The head of my tribe whispered to me that the hour he spent between your thighs was paradise. I'm not going to pass up a chance to find out if he was exaggerating."

"Every man is different," Moonlight said softly as he let the silk slide down his shoulders and off his arms. With the soft fabric pooled around his ankles, he began unfastening the ties at the sides of his loose trousers. The diaphanous material whispered down his long, smooth legs to drape over the crumpled robe. Stepping out of the pile of discarded clothing, he stood naked in front of the stranger.

"You really are a pinnacle of breeding," Goblin said as he walked a circle around Moonlight.

Moonlight found the compliment odd, but he didn't ask about it. He engaged as little as possible with his "guests." Each time he entertained for the onmyoji, it was a performance, and it had to be a convincing one. The wizard had use for him, but he had no illusions about how quickly he'd be punished if he didn't fill his role to Autumn's satisfaction. He found hosting the occasional dignitary far preferable to spreading his legs for the entire barracks.

"You have a beautiful ass," Goblin said, stopping behind Moonlight. "How long will it take you to get ready for me?"

"Only a few minutes, my lord."

"Then do it. Somewhere I can watch."

Moonlight went to the bed and got on his hands and knees. Dipping two fingers into the jar on the nightstand, he reached under himself as he went through the familiar mental relaxation exercise. Pushing his finger through the resistant ring of muscle, he smeared the lubricant around.

"Oddly arousing," Goblin said over the sound of his zipper going down.

Moonlight moved his finger in and out a few times before he went back for more oil. He heard Goblin rise and cross to the bed. As Goblin dropped his trousers, Moonlight got his feet on the floor and stretched himself out, belly down, across the sheets.

"I'm much more excited than I thought I'd be," Goblin said as he took his cock in hand and seated it. "I thought I'd need some help getting hard, but I'm ready. I hope you are too."

Moonlight bit his lip and focused on his breathing as Goblin drove into him in a long, straining push. He rode out the match-head moment of utter madness that always threatened to burst into flame when he was forced to submit. He'd been here before and survived it. Fighting it wouldn't get him anything but bruises. He just had to get through it and out to the other side. *Decisions were so simple now that his only goal was to keep living.*

"You don't have to pretend to like it," Goblin said. "And I can almost guarantee that it will be over quickly. You're very... tight."

Holding on to Moonlight's hips, Goblin thrust fast and hard until he came with a hoarse cry. After a few moments, Goblin's grip eased, and he took a deep, shuddering breath.

"Good," he said. "That was good."

Moonlight held himself in stillness until Goblin withdrew from him. Only then could he ease the tight control that prevented him from turning and snapping this important man's neck.

"You didn't enjoy it at all," Goblin observed. "But don't worry that I'll complain about you. I prefer it this way."

Moonlight turned over, taking a fold of the covers with him to veil his crotch. His expression neutral, he gazed up at the Saruzoku leader.

"I think you also prefer not to enjoy it," Goblin said as he pulled up his pants and fastened them. "Good. We Saruzoku like it when things fit neatly together." He narrowed his eyes as he ran them down Moonlight's supine body. "I still prefer women, but this was an experience I'd like to repeat." He raised his eyebrows at Moonlight, inviting comment.

"Your tie is crooked," Moonlight said.

Goblin straightened his tie. "Thank you." With a slight nod, he turned and left the room.

The onmyoji was sketching with brush and ink when Goblin emerged into the sitting room. Finishing a spray of pine needles, Autumn set the brush aside and stood.

The chief of the Saruzoku bowed. "Your courtesan's reputation is well-deserved. I was cynical about stories of the Barazoku, but there *is* something different about him. He roused me in a way I've not felt in some years," Goblin said candidly.

"You deserve all the rewards that the Shadow can heap upon you."

"I didn't invent the gun myself."

"No, but you provided the leadership to inspire the sort of men who did invent it."

"You should have been a Feather Tribe diplomat. You have honey on your tongue."

"I'm speaking plainly."

"Then I wonder if it's in very bad taste to ask if I could—"

"Visit Moonlight again?"

"Yes."

"Of course you may. All you have to do is excel and bring glory to the Kagehito."

"I was hoping for a more regular arrangement."

"Moonlight is not a whore, and I am not a pander."

"Of course not, but you are his master. He does your will."

"It's my will that he be kept as a prize for those who do the greatest service." Autumn paused. "Isn't it strange that the Shadow People have been working in secret for centuries, and still the world spins madly on as though we didn't exist?"

"I don't see it that way. The world would be in complete chaos if not for us."

"Are you certain there isn't something we're failing to do?"

"I'm not Dragon Tribe. I can't see what isn't there."

"Maybe we've been too soft, shown too much mercy."

"We're only human."

"But we could be more if we were only willing to—" The onmyoji stopped speaking with a self-deprecating smile. "But I shouldn't keep you here listening to my theories. You have much more important business to conduct."

"Nothing more important than paying court to you."

"Now you're flattering me. Don't waste your time. I have no real power. I can only make suggestions based on my readings."

"I've seen some examples of your influence. Let's not be modest. It seems to me that you think the Kagehito could be stronger, more efficient, and I think so too."

Autumn smiled. "You must visit again so we can discuss this further."

"Call my private number any time. Monkey Tribe is always interested in improvements."

"I've spoken with other leaders, and we aren't the only two who feel the Kagehito could be more successful."

"Perhaps I might meet with them as well. It's always pleasant to speak with like-minded people."

"I'll arrange something if you like."

"You're very gracious. And now, I should thank you for your hospitality and leave you to your art."

Autumn bowed, and in the gesture, Goblin saw an echo of the Barazoku's grace.

"It was my pleasure to have you as a guest. It's my hope that we'll meet again soon."

Goblin bowed and turned to go with the same hope burning in his brain. To say that Moonlight had aroused him was an enormous understatement. Something about that perfectly toned, sculpted male body waiting in docile submission.... Goblin shivered. He hadn't realized this kink existed inside him, but there it was. He wanted to take a strong, handsome young man who had no choice in the matter. He wanted Moonlight.

By the time the chief of the Saruzoku had been escorted to the helipad on the other side of the island, he had thought through the unexpected appearance of a new obsession. He had to have the Barazoku again. That was a priority. However, he couldn't allow his desire for Moonlight to interfere with his other obsessions with efficiency and symmetry. He would have to channel this newborn craving and let it become one of the things that drove him to excel. The onmyoji was wise; Moonlight should be a reward. Satisfied with how he'd dealt with the new facet of his life, Goblin left to take up his duties, determined to excel.

"Dogs," Moonlight said as the door opened behind him. He continued staring into the mirror as Autumn crossed the room.

"Dogs?" the onmyoji repeated.

"Yes, *dogs*. The kind that sniff for explosives. Even if the Monkey Tribe's gun can fool the scanners, I don't think it will fool the dogs. They can make it out of plastic or ceramic or whatever they want, but a firearm still requires fire, which requires powder, which the dogs will smell."

Autumn tilted his head to the side. "You're probably right. Our assassins will simply have to avoid airports with canines."

"Did I perform well, master?" Moonlight met the onmyoji's eyes in the mirror.

"Goblin was very pleased with you. Of course, you couldn't see his face while he was riding you, but I assure you that he enjoyed himself."

"You sound pleased, master."

"I've made a very advantageous bargain. You'll be seeing Goblin again."

Moonlight nodded and began drawing a brush through his hair. He wouldn't feel comfortable until after he'd bathed, but it calmed him to keep his hands busy.

"You've been very good for a long time now," Autumn said. "You've received the guests I've sent you without a fuss. I'm starting to believe that you're truly humble."

"I'm grateful for every breath I draw."

"Grateful to whom?"

"To you, of course."

"That was excellent. It would have fooled almost anyone, but not me." Autumn stopped behind Moonlight's chair and put his hands on Moonlight's bare shoulders. "I can see into your soul. You hate me."

"No, I don't." Moonlight met the onmyoji's eyes in the mirror. "I feel nothing for you."

Fine lines tightened around Autumn's eyes in a subtle frown. "You still think about him," he said softly. "Your true love. The man you ran away with. The one you couldn't live without." Autumn lifted an eyebrow. "It's funny. He's gone and yet, here you are. Still breathing. You managed to live without him after all."

Moonlight suppressed his reaction to the onmyoji's words and made himself answer calmly. "This isn't life."

"His name was Tiger, wasn't it? I heard he died with your name on his lips. A pity you weren't there to hear it, but you left him, didn't you?"

Moonlight closed his eyes. His heart was beating so hard it felt bruised and his throat had closed up. It took every ounce of willpower he had to keep from believing Autumn and to keep his tears from overflowing. It was so hard to resist the onmyoji's power.

"You see?" Autumn said. "You can still feel. Maybe if I'd had you from birth, I could have made you into a—" The onmyoji stopped speaking abruptly and eased his grip on Moonlight's shoulders. "There is still defiance in your heart, Moonlight."

"And cum in my ass."

The onmyoji laughed. "Have a bath then."

Moonlight stood and Autumn moved back to give him room.

"Wait a moment," Autumn said as Moonlight moved past him. His eyes went down to the clear imprints of fingers on Moonlight's hips. "Be sure and put something on those," he said. "Your skin is delicate, and you bruise so easily."

Moonlight nodded. "You were right." He paused. "I still think about Tiger. I should have stayed and died with him."

"But you didn't. Now go and have a nice, long soak. You did well today."

Moonlight ran the water into the big marble tub as hot as he could stand it. He lowered himself in gradually until only his head was above the surface. When he was accustomed to the temperature, he cleaned himself thoroughly with a natural sponge and a cake of hand-milled soap. Finishing by completely immersing himself, he climbed out of the tub.

Slipping into a thick cotton robe, he toweled his hair as dry as he could. He finger-combed the damp strands back from his face and wiped the condensation from the mirror. As his image appeared, he felt a chill. Who was that pale, cold creature? Moonlight blinked, and the apparition blinked back at him. Was this really what he looked like? A junkie? A wraith? A ghost haunting his own body? Would Tiger even recognize him now? Was Tiger even alive? Was the onmyoji lying or telling the truth? There was no way to know as long as he was imprisoned here.

Hot tears scalded Moonlight's eyelids, and he let them fall at last. Gripping the edge of the sink, head bent as though vomiting up his agony, he cried until the tub finished draining. After he wiped his face, he returned to the bedroom and exercised methodically for an hour. Mindlessly, he counted repetitions and gained a temporary measure of relief from his thoughts.

The onmyoji's mind was also occupied with persistent thoughts. Uppermost was the need to force Moonlight to respond to him in some way. No matter whom he sent to Moonlight's chamber, the Barazoku was submissive, and the young man's descent into passivity was most unsatisfying. Moonlight was the strongest power source the wizard had ever run across, but if he lost the power to feel, he would stop generating the energy that fed Autumn. The onmyoji needed him docile but not catatonic. He missed the fiery resistance and the storms of humiliated weeping. It was time to bring another pawn into play.

"THANK you for seeing me, Broom," the onmyoji said as he entered the commander's private office. "I know the morning is a busy time for you."

"Don't talk to me like I'm one of your pet lords," Broom said. "I don't care for courtly speech, and you know I'll see you any time you take a whim, because I'm not a stupid man."

Autumn sat. "No, you're not stupid, or I would never have taken you into my confidence."

The commander sat up a little straighter. "What does this concern?"

"The pit."

"It's very popular, as you predicted when you suggested it to me thirty years ago."

"Well, it does seem a shame to kill a criminal when you can still make use of him. Some Shadow policies are so wasteful."

"Again, I'll ask you to save that sort of talk for your lapdogs."

"Your insistence on speaking plainly is, frankly, boring."

"As is your insistence on repeating the criticism."

The onmyoji paused before he spoke again, his sculpted lips curving in a feline smile. "You give as good as you get, Broom. I've always liked that about you."

"And you generally have something of substance to discuss when you seek me out."

"I want to attend a fight, and I want to bring a special guest."

"You don't need to ask me."

"I want you to make sure that one of the gladiators is Tiger."

"I can't."

"Has he died? You should have informed me."

"Why would I inform you of a slave's death? You've made it clear that you don't want to be associated with the pit in any way."

"You knew this one was special."

"Tiger was convicted of desertion. That's not special to me."

"Did you kill him, or did he die in the pit?"

"I got rid of him. He was still dangerous. The other fighting slaves were building a cult of hero worship around him."

For just a moment, the tendons stood out in the onmyoji's neck as he gritted his teeth. When he spoke, his voice was carefully even. "Charisma. I'll never understand how the gods decide where to bestow that particular gift. Tiger's first trainer recognized it in the boy as soon as he let him out of the box. Why an unimaginative killer like that should be graced with such magnetism is unfathomable to me."

"You don't lack charisma."

"That's kind of you, but I know better. I hold a certain fascination for some, but it's not true charisma. That's very rare. Do you know how remarkable it is that Mallet had three charismatic personalities in one crèche?"

"Very?"

"Yes, very remarkable. Mallet used Moonlight to keep Tiger on track. I had planned to use Tiger to keep Moonlight in line."

"I'm genuinely sorry to disappoint you."

"Well, if he's gone, he's gone. I'll just have to be more creative."

"What is it you hope to accomplish with your training of the Barazoku?"

Autumn lifted an eyebrow. "You sound sincere. Is your interest in my plan or Moonlight?"

"Both, of course."

"You can visit him again, you know. All you have to do is ask."

Broom cleared his throat. "I think not. You have too much influence over me already."

"Ridiculous." The onmyoji stood. "I have no authority over you. We are equals here."

The commander stood also. "Is there anything else I can do for you?"

"I'll let you know," the onmyoji said as he left the office.

SMOKE knocked on Tiger's door before he opened it. Technically, Tiger was a guest, after all, and Smoke was naturally courteous. Furthermore, Smoke had no wish to walk in on Tiger in the middle of a potentially embarrassing activity.

Tiger was doing push-ups—one-handed push-ups. He ignored Smoke until he counted one hundred, and then rolled onto his back.

"The doctor told you to stay in bed for at least two more days," Smoke said.

"If I didn't listen to him, what makes you think I'll listen to you?"

"Nothing, I just thought you'd want to heal as quickly as possible."

"I can feel my muscles losing tone while I'm lying there."

"Not that I can see." Smoke allowed himself a brief, admiring glance at Tiger's chest and arms.

Tiger sat up. "Do you still train?"

"I do a half hour of tai chi when I get out of bed."

"I figured it was something like that. You still look as slinky as a weasel."

"Is that a compliment? I can't tell."

"It's just an observation. I'll bet you're still hard to beat one-on-one."

"I'm out of practice, combat-wise."

"Let me know if you want to spar."

"If I wanted to spar, Lord Raven has an entire security force that would oblige me."

"Are they any good?" Tiger cracked his knuckles.

Smoke sighed. "You really haven't changed that much since I first met you."

Tiger gave Smoke an inquiring look.

"You still have to be the best," Smoke said.

"Is there something wrong with wanting to be the best?"

"I think ambition can put blinders on you. You only see what's directly ahead of you."

"Did you come here just to lecture me?" Tiger asked as he stood up. "Because I want to take a shower before breakfast, and I'm running out of time."

"I came to tell you that I have to go into the city, and I'll be gone for several days."

"Did you tell the babysitter it's okay for me to stay up late?"

Smoke sighed again and tried a direct approach. "Why won't you let me help you?" he asked in frustration. "It's been like this since the first time we spoke. Me reaching out, you slapping my hand. Why does it have to be like this?"

"I never thought about it," Tiger lied. "It's just the way it is."

"We were friends once."

"Until you turned me and Moonlight in."

"You know why I did it."

"Doesn't mean I understand it, but I'm not a Feather. I can't think like you."

"Again, I can't tell if I'm being complimented or insulted. Maybe you have changed. You were more direct when we were kids."

"You keep coming back to our childhood. Is there something you want to say about it?"

"You remember the goat?"

"Of course."

"We saved Moonlight then, and we'll save him now. That's all I really wanted to say. I'll see you in a few days."

"He has to be alive," Tiger muttered as he turned away.

"What?"

"I said he has to be alive. I have to believe that. And I have to believe that we'll find him, wherever he is."

"Every source and connection I have is on the lookout for any information that could possibly pertain to him. We'll find him."

Smoke could think of nothing more to say, so he said good-bye again and left Tiger alone.

Tiger went into the bathroom and turned on the shower, shaving while the mirror slowly became fogged. As he performed the mundane task of removing his few whiskers, he waged the ongoing battle against imagining Moonlight in some dire circumstance. It was hard to repel the mental images and even harder to keep from screaming and charging out in search of blood. Only the fact that he didn't know where to go or who to kill kept him here. And he had faith in Smoke's abilities. The cunning Feather would find Moonlight if anyone could.

Tiger stepped into the shower and soaped his scarred body. He hoped when he found Moonlight that Moonlight would still want him, but he had to admit the possibility that Moonlight might no longer love him. He'd betrayed them out of fear. He should have stayed at Moonlight's side no matter what happened. Instead, he'd let Smoke talk him into giving up. He vowed it wouldn't happen again.

Tiger finished his shower and put on a tracksuit. After a few stretches, he went for a run around the grounds. When he returned to the house, he went to the patio, where the staff laid out breakfast every morning.

"Good morning." Raven put down his newspaper as Tiger trotted up the steps to the buffet.

Tiger bowed. "Good morning, Lord Raven."

"Please sit with me."

Tiger filled a plate and sat down opposite Raven. "I thought you'd be in the city, sir."

"Smoke is perfectly capable of handling things there, and I find myself more and more reluctant to leave this place."

"I can see why." Tiger looked out over the terraced lawn that ran down to the beach.

"I'm an old man and things don't seem as urgent as they used to. I get the sense that time is slipping away, and there was never enough of it to begin with. But somehow, it's all right. I don't feel that dull panic anymore. Regret troubles me from time to time, but it reminds me that I have a conscience, which is a comfort to me." Raven smiled at Tiger. "You have that look on your face that young people get when their elders start rambling."

Tiger swallowed a bite of melon. "You're not boring me, sir," he said.

"Smoke's right. You're a bad liar." Raven sat back in his chair. "I haven't seen you since you thanked me for taking you off Saigo. Are you managing to occupy your time?"

"Not as much as I'd like."

"Maybe you could help me."

"Of course, sir."

"It would have to be a secret from Smoke. I don't want him involved yet."

"Tell me what I can do."

"You can tell me everything you know about Saigo Island."

"Of course, but why?"

"Despite my great desire to stay on the sidelines, I've seen things that I can't ignore. The pit is a disgrace to the Kagehito way, and the fact that it exists means the rot goes deep indeed."

"Why don't you want Smoke involved?"

"He's clean, and I want him to stay that way."

Tiger nodded. "What would you like to hear about first?"

"Tell me all you know about the onmyoji."

LORD KOISHI, Pebble among his brethren, bowed to the onmyoji as he rose from his comfortable seat in the onmyoji's private sitting room. "As always, it was a delight meeting with you," he said.

"You know how much I enjoy your visits, Pebble." Autumn smiled at the chief of Feather Tribe.

"I'll implement those suggestions you made, and I'll call Talon. He'll be pleased to hear that we support him as the head of Iron Tribe's European clans, and you're right—a man of his caliber is wasted as a glorified adjuster."

"I'd be very grateful if you would. Do you have time to attend the fights while you're here?"

Pebble shook his head. "I don't enjoy them as much now that Tiger's gone to America."

Autumn froze for a split second before smiling at the other man. "Yes, it was a shame to lose him."

"I thought Raven was going to open a pit over there, but I haven't heard a word about it."

"It takes time to arrange things."

"I'm sure you're right." Pebble bowed again. "May you be healthy until we meet again."

Autumn bowed. "May your decisions be wise ones."

The onmyoji's pleasant smile held until the chief of the Hanezoku was out of sight. Autumn's lips drew back from his teeth in a silent snarl as his fingers curled into fists. He stayed perfectly still until the moment of blind fury passed and then walked briskly to his tower. Two thoughts throbbed in his brain like a heartbeat as he climbed the stairs. Tiger was alive. The commander had lied.

Autumn pushed open the door of his sanctum and went to his desk. From a hidden drawer, he took his satellite phone and dialed a number. When the new chief of the Eastern Saruzoku answered his private line, the onmyoji asked a few terse questions.

"Of course I can," Goblin answered. "I can do all of that, but I don't understand why."

Autumn took a deep breath and conquered the impulse to scream at Goblin. "If you want a reason to do me a favor—"

"No of course not," Goblin said quickly. "It's just that it's a very problematical favor. Attacking a fellow lord and concealing my involvement will take a lot of planning."

"You're good at planning."

"Don't worry. I'll do this for you. In fact, I already have an idea. Talon will be happy to have some of his Iron men do the job if I give him the right incentive. I'll let you know when you can expect delivery of your package."

"Make it soon," the onmyoji said.

"I assume a visit with Moonlight can be arranged if I deliver Tiger in person."

"You can assume that," Autumn said as he severed the connection. He put the phone away with a sense of satisfaction. He'd discovered a betrayal and taken immediate steps to resolve it. His property would be returned, and the commander would be replaced. It was a terrible shame that Broom had to go. Autumn had built a very workable relationship with the man, but now he saw that the commander considered himself superior. The commander had thought he could fool Autumn. That was a symptom of a deep lack of respect, and the onmyoji couldn't allow that. Throwing his veil over his head, he left the house.

THE onmyoji heard the light step on the basement stairs and turned from his prisoner to watch Moonlight. He was hoping to catch a reaction, however brief, to Moonlight's return to the place of his ordeal. However, Moonlight's face was as placid and remote as the moon.

"You wished to see me, master," Moonlight murmured.

"Come closer, Moonlight. I know it can't be pleasant for you to revisit this chamber, but I wanted you to see this." The onmyoji pointed to the man shackled to the wall. "You remember Commander Broom, of course."

Moonlight bowed his head, but didn't reply.

Autumn smiled. "The *former* commander was one of the first to enjoy your hospitality after you were rehabilitated. I remember you said that he was kinder than most."

"He was." Moonlight didn't want to look at the man hanging from the chains that had once held him. He preferred to forget that time, but he knew his revulsion would please the onmyoji, and so he forced himself to meet the disgraced commander's gaze.

"He can't help you," Autumn told the prisoner. "I'm sure Moonlight would like to repay your kindness, but there's nothing he can do for you. He's here for a lesson."

"Get on with it, witch." The commander's voice was a hoarse whisper.

The onmyoji put a hand on Moonlight's forearm. "You know many of my secrets, more than anyone living, and tonight you will learn another. This is the most secret of my powers and the greatest. Watch."

Moonlight watched the onmyoji put his palm against the prisoner's chest. The wizard locked eyes with the commander, and Moonlight could feel the weight of his master's will bearing down on the victim. The commander's look of steely resignation cracked and melted by degrees into abject horror. Slowly, the commander's body went limp as the light in his eyes faded, flickered, and went out. Moonlight shivered as the corpse slumped to hang lifelessly in the manacles.

Abruptly, the onmyoji's grip tightened on Moonlight's arm. The wizard hung on to keep from sagging to the floor in utter exhaustion. Mustering the vestiges of his will, the onmyoji drew some of Moonlight's life force through his fingertips to shore up his flagging energy.

Moonlight felt light-headed, and the lamps in the chamber appeared to dim. In that moment of disorientation, energy flowed back and forth between him and his master, and many things became clear. Now he knew why Autumn had singled him out and kept him close. The onmyoji was using him in more than one way.

"How long have you been sucking my energy?" Moonlight asked calmly.

Autumn drew a long shuddering breath before he answered. "Since the beginning... but I'm usually... more subtle."

"How?"

"I'm sure you'd like to know." The onmyoji let go of Moonlight, though it was clear he was still unsteady on his feet. "Just keep in mind that I can smother the spark of life in anyone I choose."

"I will, master."

"Good. Help me upstairs. Now that I've attended to personal business, it's time to serve the Shadow." Autumn didn't like Moonlight seeing him so weak, but it couldn't be helped, and he kept up a steady stream of distracting talk as they ascended the stone steps. "Our forged documents have been discovered and declared genuine. It's time I claimed the rights and powers set forth in them. For too long my position has been one of advisor. It's time I took the helm and steered our people back to greatness."

It was not the first time Moonlight had heard these words from his master, but now he could hear more shades of meaning. He realized that Autumn had repeated them so often that they had become the truth. The onmyoji *believed* he acted for the good of the Kagehito. This depth of self-delusion chilled Moonlight to the bone as he perceived the same abyss yawning before his feet. More and more, he was taking on the tasks and duties that the wizard assigned him, telling himself that he had no choice. But was he coming to enjoy wielding power over others as it had been wielded over him? Had his term of helplessness in the onmyoji's dungeon shaped him in some way he didn't yet recognize?

"By the way," Autumn said as they reached the top of the stairs, "Broom confessed several things to me. You might be interested to know that Tiger is still alive. Say the word and I'll have him brought here."

"No thank you, master." Moonlight walked the onmyoji to a chair. "Would you like some tea?"

"A restorative would be welcome." The wizard bent his head over the papers on his desk as Moonlight left the room.

Though it didn't show, the onmyoji was rejoicing. He was finally satisfied that he had control over Moonlight, and not a moment too soon. Every carefully spun line was now connected to Autumn's web, and he'd need Moonlight more than ever in the coming days.

 Part Nine

RAVEN was getting ready for bed when Smoke returned from New York, but he asked his aide to come and see him for a few minutes.

"Welcome back. How was the city?" Raven said when Smoke entered his rooms.

"It's still standing. Anything interesting happen here?"

"Hold on to your hat," Raven said.

Smoke smiled as he poured tea at the table behind his master. "I'm not wearing one."

"It's just an expression."

"Oh," Smoke said as he turned and offered Raven a cup. "You have such a flair for the native slang."

"Don't be coy. It makes you even more attractive, and I don't want to feel that way about you."

"Noted, sir. Now what's the shocking news?"

"The Commander of Saigo Island has been removed... for his habit of having forced relations with Rose Tribe initiates."

Smoke's mouth fell open. "You're joking."

"No, it's true. He's gone. The Council of Chiefs has already installed a new man called Sleepy."

"Not really, sir."

"I heard it from Pebble, so I've no reason to doubt it."

"Broom was commander when I was a novice on Saigo."

"That's why I thought you'd find the news interesting." Raven looked at his assistant over the rim of the exquisite cup. "How do you feel about his fall from grace?"

"I don't feel anything but surprise and... disbelief."

"I understand. He was a bit brusque, but he didn't strike me as...."

"Depraved?" Smoke suggested. "Perverted?"

"Exactly." Raven changed the subject. "How is Tiger?"

"Chafing and abrasive."

Raven chuckled. "He needs exercise."

"He's barely healed."

"He's been working out with the security staff for almost a week now. The captain told me he and his men have learned a few things from Tiger."

"I don't doubt it." Smoke gave his superior a wry smile. "I'm embarrassed that I didn't know what he was up to."

"You have a full schedule and Tiger is... willful, to say the least. Or so the captain reports."

"Do you want me to have a word with him? Tiger, not the captain."

"No! If I'm lucky, he'll take a position on my security staff."

"That would be like putting a timber wolf in with a pack of Dobermans. You're going to have a big vet bill." Smoke handed Raven the revised agenda for the next day. "And as soon as Tiger's able, he's going to find a way out of here so he can look for Moonlight."

"He does seem very set on it. Is it just because they were crèche-mates?"

"Of course not. They were lovers."

"Ah."

"Their bond is very strong. They were senpai and kohai."

"Well...." Raven shook his head. "It happens sometimes... this obsessive partnership."

"And why do you think it happens?" Smoke was almost successful in keeping the sarcasm out of his tone.

Raven looked up from buttoning his pajama top. "I allow you a lot of latitude because I respect your abilities," he said. "And because I know you'd never speak this way in front of anyone else. Now... are there more flaws of the system you'd like to discuss?"

Smoke took the hint. "Not right now, sir. Would you like more tea?"

Raven waved off the offer. "I'd really like a couple of shots of cheap *soju*. I got a taste for it when I did my internship at the embassy in Seoul. It must be something in my blood." He smiled at the look on Smoke's face. "You're Korean, right? So am I, at least half."

"Were you taken from your parents?"

Raven nodded. "As payment for a debt. Almost all Kagehito field operatives are recruited this way. I was one of the lucky ones who survived my term of mission service and got promoted for outstanding contributions."

"What debt?"

Raven pursed his lips in thought before he spoke again. "We don't make it common knowledge, but the Shadow funds an organization to help bright, attractive young women without means. The girls are tested for intelligence and given a physical exam. If they pass both, they're given a weekly allowance and their education is paid for. They have to sign a contract in which they agree to certain conditions concerning how they'll pay the organization back. I think you already know one of them."

"They agree to teach their children Japanese."

Raven nodded. "As many of them as possible are impregnated by Kagehito operatives. If necessary, the girls are cared for during their pregnancy, and they're monitored at intervals until their children reach the age of six. If a child is suitable, he's taken."

"Sir, when you became a lord, did you try to find your parents?"

"Why? What would be the point? No." Raven shook his head. "It would only confuse and sadden them and disappoint me. What parent wants to know that their child grew up to be a remorseless killer? And what would I do once I found them? Move in with them?" He sat on the side of the bed and let his slippers drop to the Persian carpet. "Don't swim after ships that have sailed, Smoke. You'll end up exhausted in the middle of the ocean."

"I happen to know that the cook keeps a bottle of *soju* in the kitchen liquor supply."

"I was being facetious."

"Then I'll remember to toast you with the first shot," Smoke said. "Good night, sir."

"Good night, Smoke."

Smoke shut the door to Raven's suite and went lightly down the stairs to the ground floor. He fully intended to find Tiger and have a serious talk with him about the next step in their plan to find Moonlight. It was too soon for Tiger to be completely healed, but if he was going to find ways to channel his frustration—like challenging the security team to fights—Smoke supposed that his energy might just as well be spent in searching for Moonlight.

Out of habit, Smoke turned off lights as he walked down the hall to the kitchen. Going directly to the smaller of the two refrigerators, he opened the right-hand door and pulled out a bottle of Stolichnaya. The cook did indeed keep a bottle of *soju*, but Smoke preferred vodka on those occasions when he drank. All he wanted was a couple of mouthfuls of the wintry liquid before he went to Tiger's room for a talk.

Taking the chilled bottle to the counter, he reached into an overhead cabinet for a glass. He splashed a finger of vodka into the juice glass and drank it in one swallow. Putting the glass down, he reached for the bottle again and saw an odd reflection from the corner of his eye. He dropped to the floor as the world disintegrated in a storm of light, noise, and flying debris. On hands and knees, he crawled out the rear door as fires sprang up under the rain of flaming fragments. Through the dust, he could see a gaping blast-hole in the second-story wall and guessed that someone had fired a rocket at the house.

Shaking his head did nothing to relieve the ringing, so Smoke disregarded it and gathered his thoughts. Judging from the area of worst destruction, Lord Raven had been reduced to his component atoms in the first second of the blast. Of course he would have been the primary target, but Smoke was shocked at the use of such an attention-getting weapon. Though the neighbors were distant, they would all be dialing nine-one-one by now.

Smoke had the sense that it didn't matter how quickly he moved, but he dashed to the front of the house. Through the drifting smoke, he could see the black-clad figures of the sentries racing across the grounds in this direction. He didn't wait for them, but ran in the front door. Hurrying to the east wing, he found the staircase was intact, unlike the one that used to lead up to the destroyed western end of the mansion.

Sure now that his boss was gone, Smoke went to Tiger's room, midway down the long corridor that connected the wings. The door was wedged shut by the damage the house had suffered, and it took Smoke a couple of minutes to kick it in. The room beyond looked like it had been turned upside down. Smoke found Tiger unconscious on the floor of the bathroom. Judging from the lump on Tiger's forehead, he'd fallen and collided with the sink on the way down.

Pulling Tiger's arm around his neck, Smoke hauled the other man to his feet. With an arm around Tiger's waist, Smoke half-carried, half-dragged him into the hall. Out here, the fire had made strides in claiming the building, setting red and gold flags everywhere.

"Shit!" Smoke cursed. "Wake up, man! I can't carry you down the stairs."

"Why don't you just throw me down the stairs?" Tiger mumbled. "It's what you want to do."

"Can you manage to walk if you lean on me? We need to get out of the house."

"Why are we wasting time talking about it?"

Both men nearly went to the floor as another explosion rocked the foundations.

"Come on," Smoke yelled, starting down the stairs as dust filled the air.

The two men made it down the stairs and out the front door. They kept going across the lawn until they reached the boathouse. Smoke opened the door and shoved Tiger inside.

"Why?" Tiger groaned when Smoke let him slide to the ground. "Why are you doing this?"

"You're injured."

"Just answer the question. Tell me the real reason you risked your life to get me out."

"Because he loves you."

"Bullshit! Tell me the truth," Tiger shouted and grimaced at the pain.

"You know why. You've always known."

"You're in love with Moonlight," Tiger said when he'd caught his breath.

"How could I not be?" Smoke slid down the wall to sit beside Tiger. "And he'd never forgive me if he found out I let you die."

"How would he know?"

"I'd know," Smoke said. "And I wouldn't be able to live with myself."

"You'd make a shitty adjuster."

"I'm glad to hear it." Smoke turned to face Tiger. "Do you blame me for falling in love with him?"

Tiger shrugged.

"They took us and penned us up together," Smoke said. "There was no one else our age. Who were we supposed to have feelings for?"

"They made rules against it."

"Yes, they did. They told us we weren't allowed to have sex with each other, putting the thought firmly in our heads."

"Moonlight and I never did anything until—"

Smoke lifted an eyebrow inquiringly.

"I feel like this is something that belongs to me and Moonlight." Tiger winced as he shifted to another position. "He was the Rose that came to me on the night of my manhood rite."

"The onmyoji really is a devious old fox, isn't he?" Smoke said. He would go to his grave before he told Tiger that the onmyoji had sent Moonlight to him as well. It had been a night of bittersweet joy that he would yearn after until he died, and there was no reason for Tiger to know of it.

"I'd like to have my hands around Autumn's throat right now."

"You're not afraid of his magic anymore?" Smoke tried to make light of the moment.

"Magic." Tiger made a rude noise.

"You might not believe in his magic, but he's a very shrewd observer, and he has uncanny insight into the motivations of the people around him. He'd have made an outstanding psychologist."

"He's a psycho*path*," Tiger said, putting a hand to his throbbing head.

Smoke put a finger to his lips.

Tiger listened hard and heard a subtle noise. Someone with bare feet and a talent for stealth was approaching from the dock. Rising into a crouch, Tiger gestured to Smoke to get in one of the boats.

Smoke shook his head and moved a short distance from Tiger, close enough to help but far enough away that he wouldn't hinder Tiger in a fight. Training his eyes on the slightly lighter patch of darkness at the other end of the boathouse, he was chagrined at how fast his heart was beating and at the fear-sweat that sprang from his pores. He was Kagehito; shouldn't he be a little braver?

Tiger was poised in perfect stillness, his face serene, not a trace of anxiety showing. And then a shadow blocked the doorway to the dock. Tiger uncoiled, launching himself half the length of the building in a mighty leap. The intruder charged, meeting Tiger in midair. The warriors exchanged blows as they found their footing, the sounds of flesh impacting flesh as loud as gunshots in the echoing space.

Smoke could barely follow the action as the other two men struck out with hands and feet, lunging, pivoting, ducking, and tumbling over the boards and boats. Through the torn cover of a canoe, a gleam of light along the blade of an oar caught Smoke's eye. Moving cautiously—his attention fixed on the combatants—he reached down and took hold of the shaft, drawing the paddle out of the boat. He stood up, holding the oar across his body with both hands, and waited for an opportunity. As soon as Tiger's opponent was close enough, Smoke skipped forward and bashed the intruder in the side of the head. The stranger spun on his heel, and Smoke's mouth dropped open.

"Key!" Smoke gasped just as Tiger delivered a powerful blow.

The intruder staggered, and Tiger took hold of the man's head, preparing to twist and break his enemy's neck.

"Wait!" Smoke shouted. "It's Key."

Tiger froze.

"Yeah, it's me," Key said. "But don't let that stop you."

"No," Tiger said, stepping back.

"I'm not going to stop trying to kill *you*," Key said. "I have orders."

"Ignore them," Smoke said.

Key grinned. "Very funny."

"You don't have to take their orders," Tiger said.

"Who are you talking to?" Key replied. "Of course I have to follow orders. You know how it is."

"That's not how it is for me anymore."

"You turned your back on your brothers."

"I didn't kill you," Tiger reminded him. "I love my brothers, but the Shadow doesn't own me now. I can think for myself."

"You're confused," Key said.

"And you're brainwashed," Smoke said. "I've seen the evidence of Kagehito lies."

"*We* are the only thing keeping this world from sliding into the abyss. *We* keep the rabid wolves from devouring the flocks."

"We're worse than rabid wolves," Smoke said. "They're crazed beasts, behaving as their nature dictates. We know better, but we choose to ignore our ethics when they're not convenient. For centuries, from the shadows, we've manipulated individuals and society without anyone's permission. We steal children and condition them to kill. We are what we abhor."

Key bared his teeth at Smoke. "That's traitor talk."

"There's nothing to betray," Tiger said. "We were lied to from the beginning. We owe no loyalty to the Kagehito."

"I can't believe you're saying this, Tiger." Key paused. "Honestly, I'm having trouble believing it's you. Everyone thinks you died in Tokyo a couple of years ago."

"No, I didn't die in Tokyo," Tiger said. "I *wish* I'd died, but I didn't."

"Stop being so dramatic," Smoke said. "We have a problem to sort out here."

"I don't want to kill Key."

"That's refreshing," Smoke said. "But what *are* we going to do with him?"

"We convince him." Tiger moved carefully around to stand with Smoke. "Key, let me tell you where I've been for the past eighteen months."

Key listened intently as Tiger described his punishment for trying to desert the Kagehito. "I've never heard of this pit you're talking about," Key said.

"You won't… unless you do something that really pisses off your masters."

"Like listening to you?"

"If they had made me fight in the pit to teach me a lesson, I'd understand," Tiger said. "But they staged it as entertainment. We were bet on like animals."

"That's not true."

"It's true," Smoke said. "I saw it myself." He held out his hand. "I've never lied to you, Key, not once since we've known each other, and I'm not lying now. The Shadow may have started with good intentions, but the organization is corrupt. Our masters value power for its own sake, and they'll do anything to keep it."

Tiger drew himself up and met Key's eyes. "I swear by my sword that I've told you the truth."

Key groaned. "Damn it. I could never win an argument with either of you." He looked up at the sound of sirens in the distance. "Good response time," he said under his breath.

"This is a very wealthy neighborhood," Smoke said. "And we should get our asses out of it before we're stuck here answering questions all night."

"I hesitate to suggest the very obvious." Key glanced at the double row of slips. "But there are several boats here."

Tiger was ripping the tarp off a skiing boat before Key finished his sentence. The sleek craft had two high-horsepower inboard motors, and Tiger wasted no time starting them up. Smoke untied the ropes that tethered the boat and jumped aboard with Key right behind him. Deftly, Tiger backed the boat out of the slip and turned it toward the wide exit. Smoke leaned past him and activated a remote fastened to the dash. The boathouse doors opened and Tiger gunned the motors, heedless of the wake that rocked the remaining craft against the pilings. As they headed across Long

Island Sound, they heard the popping of gunfire on the shore behind them, and Tiger pushed the throttle forward.

"SO WHAT now?" Key asked as he finished his omelet.

Smoke glanced at Tiger, but Tiger was staring at the tracks of the rain on the restaurant window. "We're going to find Moonlight," Smoke said.

"I've got news for you, brother. You can't have a crèche reunion. Two of us are gone."

"I know," Smoke said. "I've done my best to keep tabs on everyone. I appreciate all the times you helped me in the past, by the way."

Key shrugged. "It was convenient, or I would've said no. Keeping an eye on an extra person was no hardship when we were in the same place at the same time." He took a sip of his orange juice. "I was tempted to talk to Moonlight a few times, but the situation was never right. He was always surrounded by big bosses when I saw him, and I made sure he didn't see me."

"What are you talking about?" Tiger asked.

"I worked corner on a box team for a few years," Key said. "Providing security for high-ranking Feathers. There've been a lot of interesting secret meetings lately, and I have a rep for being discreet."

"Who are you working for now?" Smoke asked.

"Lord Talon."

"This is wrong. You don't sound like a teacher at all." Tiger grabbed the back of Key's neck. "What's your inner calling?"

"I'm Iron Lightning," Key said, turning so Tiger could see his tattoo. "The Denkouzoku graciously loaned me out to the Tetsuzoku when I turned out to be a better warrior than a teacher. I'm betting you're Double Iron."

Tiger nodded and Key turned to look inquiringly at Smoke.

"I haven't found my inner calling yet," Smoke said. "Don't snicker like I just admitted to being a virgin."

"None of us are *that*," Key said. "In any sense of the word."

"Our sensei made certain of it," Smoke added.

"Well…." Key took another sip of his orange juice as he glanced out the window, but he couldn't see what was holding Tiger's interest. "If you want to find Moonlight, you know who you should probably ask."

"I guess we're going back to Saigo," Smoke said. He bumped Tiger with his elbow. "Feel like playing pilot?"

"Show me the plane."

Key shook his head. "We can't just go busting in there."

"I'm well aware of how well-fortified the island is, and I have a plan. It'll take a little time, but we're going to be invited."

"Really?" Key ran a finger through the syrup on Tiger's plate and licked his finger. "How?"

"All we have to do is take over the drug trade in some random part of Tokyo."

"Get serious," Key scoffed.

"He *is* serious." Tiger turned from the window to look at Key. "And you don't have to come with us."

"Of course I'm coming with you. Now, if you're finished…?" Key stood and put two twenty-dollar bills on the table. "We've been here long enough."

The three young men left the diner, separated in the parking lot, and met up again at the edge of the small Connecticut town. Key hot-wired a station wagon from a closed used-car lot and they headed for the New York City metro area, with its many airports.

SMOKE finished outlining the plan to steal a shipment of drugs from a Kagehito-backed gang and waited for questions from Tiger or Key.

"Won't that make it awfully easy for them to catch us?" Key said. He watched Smoke glance at Tiger, and he groaned. "Fuck me. You *want* to get caught."

"It's the fastest way in," Smoke said.

"Maybe, but has it occurred to you that you'll be *in* custody?" Key shook his head. "You'll be guarded by Iron men—most likely you'll be in some kind of restraints."

"It's true that we'll have to… improvise, once we're on the island," Smoke said.

"But the hardest part is getting there," Tiger added.

"Did you consider stealing a boat and—?"

"Of course," Tiger interrupted. "But we'd trigger alarms the moment we stepped onto the compound."

"It's true," Smoke said. "The entire installation is blanketed with sensors."

"How do you know that?"

"Moonlight told me," Tiger said. "The onmyoji showed him the equipment. Monkey work operated by Feathers. That's why no one's ever escaped."

"So the best two ways I could think of to get on the island were by invitation or for punishment. No matter how high we climb in the illegal drug trade, it's unlikely that we'll get to meet any high-ranking Kagehito. However, if we piss them off, they'll send someone to deal with us."

"And why wouldn't that someone just kill us?" Key smirked.

"Because we'll show them our tattoos," Tiger said.

Smoke nodded. "The Kagehito will send a recon team that will check with their superiors before making any final adjustments. The most logical outcome would be a progression of phone calls going ever higher up the chain. Someone in the onmyoji's web will surely inform him of the rogues, and I'd wager that he opts to speak with us personally."

"He'll want more than a chat," Key predicted.

"The important thing is that he'll want to see Tiger face to face."

"You really think it's that important to the wizard?"

"I think he needs our Tiger for some reason that we don't understand. Otherwise, he'd have had Tiger killed when he tried to leave the Kagehito."

"I guess that makes sense," Key said. "But it's a big gamble."

"If you don't have anything to lose, it doesn't matter how big a chance you take," Tiger said.

Smoke put a hand on Tiger's shoulder and gave it a squeeze. "We're not asking you to go with us, Key," Smoke said. "You have a more important task ahead."

"You want me to stay alive to tell your story to the world?" Key guessed.

"Something along those lines." Smoke smiled and handed Key a flash drive. "Take this to Interpol headquarters in Lyon and make sure the right person gets it."

"Do you have a name?"

"Start with Noble Kaufmann in Organized Crime."

"France." Key sighed. "Are you sure I can't come with you and be tortured and killed?"

"This isn't something to joke about," Tiger said.

Smoke squeezed Tiger's shoulder again. "Actually, a little humor is welcome right now. It reminds me that there are still things in this world that aren't tainted and corrupt." He smiled at Key again. "And Key is one of them."

Key snorted. "What utter shit! If you knew some of the things I've done…."

"You think we haven't done the same or worse?" Smoke asked. "But everything *you* did, you did with a pure heart. You believed it was for a greater purpose."

Key looked dubious, but he put the flash drive in the pocket of his down vest and zipped it in. "If you want this fancy gizmo to go to Interpol, I'll take it there." He sighed. "It's a death sentence either way."

"I'm afraid so," Smoke said. "Whether you go with us or take the information, you'll be hunted relentlessly."

"Good. I was afraid things were going to get boring again without you two around."

Tiger laughed abruptly and leaned over to give Key a mock-punch on the shoulder. Key raised his fist and bumped it against Tiger's.

"Iron men," Smoke said with exaggerated exasperation.

TIGER slid along the outside wall of the warehouse until he reached the corner. He looked back and signaled to Smoke to move up. Darting from shadow to shadow, the two men reached the loading dock of the Kagehito-owned warehouse next door. For several minutes, they watched the sentries make their rounds on the same schedule they followed every night.

With another hand signal to Smoke, Tiger climbed the drainpipe of the neighboring warehouse and walked along the edge of the roof in a crouch. Smoke followed in the alley below, stopping behind an industrial rubbish bin. Taking out his pistol, Smoke fired several shots into the Dumpster and then ran to the other end of the warehouse. Under cover of the noise, Tiger leaped across the gap to the Kagehito warehouse and entered through a skylight. As the sentries investigated the shots, Tiger dropped to the floor in the rear of the building and opened a side door for Smoke. Hurrying to the van parked near the roll-up cargo bay door, they got in and searched for a key. Tiger slapped down the sunshade and a set of keys fell into his lap. As he cranked the engine, Smoke pushed a button on the garage door opener on the dashboard.

"Go. Go. Go," Smoke said as the door began to roll up. "But not too fast."

"Thanks for the advice. I'm not used to fucking up."

Smoke looked into the back of the panel van as Tiger inched forward, willing the door to go faster. "Damn," Smoke said. "That's a lot of blow."

"So it's coke." Tiger grimaced. "I made a bet with Key that it was heroin."

"Look on the bright side. You're probably about to die, so you'll never have to pay him."

"That's what I like about you Feathers. Always optimistic."

The second the top of the van cleared the doorway, Tiger drove out onto the concrete loading ramp.

"Easy," Smoke said as Tiger gunned the engine.

"I'm just ringing the dinner bell." Tiger revved it again and dropped the transmission into drive. Rubber barked and squealed against concrete, leaving two black streaks as the van bounced sideways at the end of the ramp and tore down the side street. Tiger looked in the side mirror as he tapped the brakes at the end of the road. He smiled as he saw a dark sedan pull around the side of the warehouse and pick up speed. "They're on us."

"Okay, don't lose them, but don't make it look too easy."

Tiger glanced over to make sure Smoke was buckled in and turned the wheel abruptly to the left. The van heeled over on two tires but made the turn, and Tiger drove straight long enough for their pursuers to catch sight of them again. Swerving and weaving, Tiger led their followers through the maze of warehouses to the docks.

"Get ready," Tiger said as he drove onto a pier.

"I'm ready."

Tiger pumped the brakes, opening his door at the same time. "Remember to tuck," he said. "Go!"

Smoke and Tiger rolled out of the van and tumbled painfully across the pavement. The van continued forward. Tiger and Smoke picked themselves up in time to watch it drive off the end of the pier, and then spun around at the sound of a car approaching fast. Pulling their weapons, they dove for the cover of a shipping container. After shooting a couple of the Kagehito soldiers so their capture wouldn't look too easy, Tiger and Smoke admitted they were surrounded and gave themselves up.

"Take it easy, brother," Tiger said when one of the men punched him in the stomach.

"Who are you calling *brother*, scum?"

"I'll bet we have the same tattoo on our backs," Tiger said.

The soldier yanked at the neck of Tiger's shirt until it tore. "I don't believe it," he said. "We're being ripped off by one of our own clans."

"It's not like that," Smoke said. "Why don't you call your superior, and we'll explain?"

"Good idea," said one of the other men. "Let the captain figure this out."

As Smoke had predicted, the first call led to several more that went steadily up the chain of command. The squad was ordered to take Tiger and Smoke to a parking structure a few blocks away. There the prisoners were transferred to a large SUV, where their hands were bound behind them before the vehicle started moving.

They were taken to a small airfield and held in a hangar for several hours before a large helicopter arrived to pick them up. At the coast, they landed again and waited a couple of more hours. When a long black car arrived, they knew the waiting was over.

"What have we here?" Iron Tribe's Chief of Enforcement walked around the kneeling prisoners. "Smoke and Tiger. Vanished into thin air, only to reappear in a drug-holding facility. I'm very interested to hear what you were up to."

Neither Tiger nor Smoke answered him.

"Are you sure you don't want to talk to me?" Talon said. "There are worse fates. For instance, I happen to know that the onmyoji is anxious to get his hands on you, Tiger."

Tiger met Talon's eyes but remained silent.

"I don't know why the onmyoji wants you," Talon said. "But I doubt it's anything you'd enjoy." He came to stand over Tiger. "When I worked with you, you were Iron Tribe's brightest young star. Now look at you. You're a traitor."

"And you're the onmyoji's tool," Tiger answered.

"I knew you'd snarl if I poked at you long enough," Talon said. "I remember you well. So full of yourself and sure you were going to change the world. You resented me for winning Moonlight's attention. You coveted him. Admit it."

"Of course I wanted him."

"Of course he did," Smoke chimed in. "Moonlight is Barazoku. Everyone wants him."

"But he wanted me," Tiger said.

"Idiot!" Smoke exclaimed. "Why make him madder?"

Talon glared at Tiger, but his voice was calm when he spoke. "As soon as the helicopter is refueled, I'm taking you to the onmyoji. If my gift pleases him enough, I'll ask him for a reward. Until then, you'd be wise to stay as quiet as possible." He gave Tiger another hard look and walked to the other end of the hangar to talk to the pilot.

"What were you thinking?" Smoke asked. "Do you want to die before you get to Saigo?"

"He pisses me off."

"Why? Because Moonlight shared his bed for a while?"

"Shut up."

"Listen to me, Tiger. Moonlight may have to sleep with whoever the onmyoji tells him to, but he's in love with you. You're the only one that has his heart."

"Talon still pisses me off."

"At least we learned something in talking to him."

"That he's a little unhinged?"

"He said he's expecting a reward. Now what does Talon want that only the onmyoji can give him?"

"Moonlight."

"Which means Talon has reason to believe Moonlight's on the island, or at least accessible."

Tiger stared at Smoke. "You're right. He's there. And we're going to get him out."

"It's a million-to-one shot."

"My kind of odds."

Smoke smiled back. "Pigheaded Iron man."

"Feather-head."

"I can't argue. Only someone without a brain would have gone along with this so-called plan."

"It's your plan."

"Only up to the point where we were captured."

"Having second thoughts?"

"Who wouldn't? In point of fact, we've run out of plan. We have no idea what we're going to do when we get to the island."

"I know what I'm going to do. I'm going to find Moonlight and take him away."

"What am I doing here?" Smoke asked the ceiling. "Surely I could have come up with a better plan than walking into the enemy's camp with no idea how I was going to get back out."

"Why *did* you come with me?"

"Because I knew you'd go by yourself if I didn't."

Tiger stared at Smoke for a long moment. "That actually made sense to me. Now I'm starting to worry."

Before Smoke could answer, the door opened and four Iron Tribe soldiers entered. None too gently, they hoisted Smoke and Tiger by their armpits and marched them out to the chopper. Shoving the prisoners into the cargo hold, the men stood guard over them as Talon got into the cockpit. Talon signaled the pilot and the helicopter took off on a heading for Saigo Island.

NO ONE spoke as the Iron box team hustled Tiger and Smoke through the gates and into the onmyoji's house. At the end of the entrance hall, the prisoners were put on their knees with shoves and kicks and held there by firm pressure on the backs of their necks. The silence continued as they waited for the wizard, and Tiger continued his subtle struggle with the cords that bound his hands. He froze along with everyone else when a figure appeared to materialize in the doorway to the left.

"I hope you have a good reason for disturbing my rest." The onmyoji's menthol voice was neutral, yet had the distinct sound of a threat. The ivory silk of his robe and veil flowed as he glided forward, and the effect was of a serpent closing in on its prey.

Talon bowed. "I thought you'd want to see these prisoners."

"Yes, I understand you thought it was important," the onmyoji interrupted. "I read my messages even when the call comes in the middle of the—" He caught sight of Tiger and paused. "Bring these men into the light," he ordered.

Talon smirked as he gestured to his men, and Tiger and Smoke were dragged to kneel directly in front of the wizard.

"Tiger," the onmyoji said. "You're still alive."

"That's more than you'd be able to say if my hands were free," Tiger answered.

Talon kicked Tiger between the shoulder blades.

"Stop!" The onmyoji held up a hand in one of his imperial gestures. "I don't want him injured."

"Right. If I was injured, I wouldn't be any good for the pit," Tiger said.

"You may go now, Talon," the wizard said.

"Are you sure?" Talon asked. "These are very dangerous men."

"Leave." The wizard's voice held a tone of command that could not be resisted.

"What of my reward?" Talon said.

"Return tomorrow and you'll have what you desire."

"So Moonlight *is* here."

The onmyoji nodded. "Now go, before you become irritating."

Talon bowed and led his men from the room.

"May I speak?" Smoke asked when the soldiers had gone.

"What do you want to say?"

"Before I die, I'd like to know that Moonlight is all right."

"Moonlight is far from all right."

"What have you done to him?"

"The worst you can imagine."

With an inarticulate cry of rage, Tiger hopped over his bound hands and launched himself from the floor. His wrists ran with blood, the flesh scored nearly to the bone, but he hadn't managed to free himself. Nevertheless, he attacked, fingers curled as though they were already around the wizard's neck.

"Tiger, no!" Smoke shouted.

The onmyoji raised his arms as if he invited an embrace as Tiger crashed into him. Both men fell to the floor, with Tiger topmost. Putting a knee into the wizard's stomach, Tiger got his hands on the onmyoji's throat and pressed his thumbs into the windpipe. Rivulets of red ran down from his wrists to soak the creamy silk of the veil.

"Stop!" Smoke screamed as he slammed into Tiger. "Don't kill him!"

Smoke's voice pierced the red haze that fogged Tiger's brain. "Why not?" Tiger growled.

"That's not Autumn," Smoke said.

"Shit!" Tiger eased the pressure of his grip. "Are you sure?"

"The onmyoji must have decoys. I would if I was him."

"He's one crafty bastard." Tiger grabbed the hem of the shoulder-length veil and yanked it up. "Moonlight," he breathed.

"Damn it," Moonlight croaked. He coughed, and Tiger moved away so he could sit up.

"Are you all right?" Tiger asked.

"Aside from having his trachea crushed?" Smoke said as he knelt beside Moonlight.

"I didn't want you to know it was me," Moonlight whispered hoarsely.

"So you would've let Tiger kill you?" Smoke shook his head. "What's happened to you? I can't believe you'd want him to live with the knowledge that he'd killed you."

"It wouldn't be for long," Tiger said as he untied Smoke's ropes.

"What's wrong with both of you?" Smoke clenched his jaw. "I can understand why you'd want to die and forget this life, but have you ever once considered the grief you'd leave to your friends? If you live, at least you have a chance for another try at it."

Moonlight shook his head. "I'm ruined... but you're not hopelessly damaged yet. Go and have a life, and I'll die happy."

"I can't believe you're saying these things," Tiger broke in. "You're the one who always had faith that we'd get free. Now we finally have a *real* hope and you're giving up? No. That's just not right."

"What do you mean by *a real hope?*"

"He means that you can impersonate the onmyoji well enough to get us off the island," Smoke said.

"He'll use every power at his command to hunt us to his last breath," Moonlight objected.

"I'd rather be on the run with you than leave you here," Tiger said.

"No. It'll be just like last time. They'll catch us and... I can't endure that again."

"Then get me and Tiger out of here," Smoke said.

Tiger whipped his head around to glare at Smoke. Smoke met the glower with an unruffled expression.

"Of course," Moonlight said. "Come with me."

"You might want a fresh veil," Smoke suggested.

Moonlight whipped off the bloodstained cloth and beckoned his friends to follow as he went down the hall. He entered his room and stuffed the veil into a chest. Taking out another length of pale fabric, he arranged it to cover his face.

"By the way," Moonlight asked as he led the way out of the building, "how did you know it was me and not the onmyoji under the veil?"

"Your imitation of Autumn is flawless," Smoke said, "but you didn't defend yourself when Tiger attacked you."

"Ah, yes. It should have been obvious to me." Moonlight started for the door when Tiger grabbed him by the arm. "We need to go," he said.

"You don't have time for one kiss?" Tiger asked.

Moonlight dropped his eyes. "I can't. Not yet."

Tiger accepted this answer and let Moonlight go. "What are we waiting for?" he said.

Moonlight led the way out of the building. The three men crossed the courtyard without seeing anyone and walked out of the gate of the onmyoji's grounds. The guards at the dividing wall bowed and stood aside to let Moonlight and his companions pass through. Moonlight strode out of the compound and down the road without hesitation.

"Where are we going?" Tiger asked. "The helipad is—"

"There's another one," Moonlight interrupted. "The commander keeps a small helicopter in case of an emergency."

"I guess you know an awful lot of inside information," Smoke said as he followed Moonlight.

"I know you're not making polite chatter, so get to your point," Moonlight answered as they entered the forest.

"You should come with us and help us bring down the Kagehito."

Moonlight laughed, and the sound was quite unlike the merry one that used to make his friends smile just to hear it. "Why don't you go throw marshmallows at a shark while you're at it?"

"Together we could do it." Smoke caught up when the path widened.

"You worked for a big boss. You should know how impossible it would be to fight the Shadow."

"With what we know between us, it's possible."

"No it isn't."

"You should listen to him, Smoke." A new voice joined the conversation as the onmyoji walked into the clearing. He glanced at the small helicopter to his right, and then turned his gaze back to the others. "Moonlight's telling you the truth."

Moonlight didn't bother asking how his master had known he was here. "Get out of the way," he said. "My friends are leaving."

"I wish I could oblige you with an evil laugh, but I'm far too angry. You intercepted my call and arranged to cheat me of—"

"Yes, I know." Moonlight moved to stand in front of Tiger and Smoke. "And you can punish me in whatever way you like after the helicopter is gone."

"You think I'd let Tiger escape again?" Autumn's wide mouth curved up at one corner in a sneering smile. "He's far too valuable to me as a hostage."

"You can't have him." Moonlight threw back his veil and met the onmyoji's eyes. "Tiger," he said, "get in the helicopter and take Smoke with you."

"Move and I'll kill you where you stand," the wizard countered.

"Almost all of our lives, Tiger and I have been used as pawns, used against one another. I can't allow it to go on."

"Still so naïve, despite all your skills and knowledge." The onmyoji held Moonlight's gaze. "The world is not made of chess pieces. There are only puppets and puppeteers. You have to choose which you're going to be." He paused. "I recommend the latter."

"You're wrong," Moonlight whispered. "And I'd still rather die than kill someone."

"No, you're not going to die. You're going to stay at my side."

"Fine, but let my friends go."

"It astounds me that you think you have anything to bargain with."

Moonlight pulled a dagger from his sash and put the point to the base of his throat. "What do you say now?" he asked.

"Moonlight, no!" Tiger shouted.

"Don't." Smoke grabbed Tiger's elbow and stopped him. "Get the chopper fired up."

"I can't let him—"

Smoke cut him off. "If the chopper isn't ready to go, we'll never get Moonlight off this rock."

Tiger gritted his teeth in frustration, but he knew Smoke was right. Turning away, he jumped into the cockpit and flipped the fuel boost and battery switches.

Smoke hovered between the helicopter and Moonlight, letting Moonlight make his play without interfering, his heart pounding with fear for him. His mind was a maelstrom of facts that were no use to him. He could think of nothing he could do to help Moonlight.

"You will not take your own life," the onmyoji told Moonlight.

"You can't be certain of that. You've warped me so badly that you can't really know which way I'll bend. I see it in your eyes. You're worried."

"I do feel a certain anxiety." The onmyoji smiled. "It's quite exhilarating. You make me feel the most interesting things. How could I ever give you up?"

"I'm not asking you to. Just let them go, and I'll stay." A drop of blood welled from beneath the tip of dagger. The bright red pearl hung against Moonlight's pale throat for a moment before it surrendered to gravity.

Autumn watched the droplet fall until it hit Moonlight's bare foot, flecking his toes with crimson. "Stop this nonsense," the wizard hissed.

"Do you accept my bargain? My life for theirs?"

"They will be dead before you breathe your last," Autumn said. "You know I can stop their hearts from here."

"*Both* of them? I don't think so. Snuffing one person's life force almost drains you. Two would probably kill you."

"Let's find out together."

The whine of the rotors warming up permeated the stillness, but neither Autumn nor Moonlight broke their eye lock. The air seemed to take on weight, freighted by the tension that wound tighter by the second, and Smoke found it difficult to breathe. He could feel a deep, subtle vibration in his bones and teeth and the thin plates of his skull. An atavistic fear rose from the depths of his limbic system, and he had to quell the urge to run.

Moonlight shredded the dense air with a scream of frustrated fury. "If you can do it, so can I," he muttered from between clenched teeth. Exerting every iota of his will, he imagined phantom fingers reaching into the onmyoji's chest and wrapping around his heart. He pictured the fingers closing, sinking into the pumping muscle, squeezing it like a sponge. Pulling in a long breath through his nostrils, he fancied he was inhaling the wizard's energy like smoke.

Autumn glared across the short space that separated him from Moonlight. "You have talent, but you don't have my experience. That was a respectable effort, but now it's my turn. I'm going to drain your energy until you're too weak to move. Then I'm going to kill Smoke. For the rest of your lives, you and Tiger will stay on this island. I'll even let you see each other from time to time, so you can replenish your energy."

"You're a fucking soulless vampire," Smoke said, surprising both Autumn and Moonlight. "When was the last time you felt human?" He moved a few steps and took Moonlight's hand. "This is my friend," he said. "Not that you'd understand what that means. People like you may win a few battles, but you'll never win the war because you reckon without the power of a bond like ours. You fucked yourself when you put us together."

"That sentimental nonsense perfectly illustrates what is wrong with the Kagehito today. The Shadow has grown weak through this addiction to emotion."

"You've got it backward," Moonlight said.

Moonlight gathered the energy that flowed into him from Smoke and attacked the onmyoji again. This time he visualized a purple-white beam of pure energy pouring from his fingertips to strike the wizard in the chest. Autumn retaliated, and Moonlight could feel the stress of the competing power streams in his every cell. The tension grew greater until Moonlight's entire body was rigid with agony, but his mind stayed focused on dominating Autumn's will. The seconds ticked by, but no matter how much energy Moonlight siphoned from Smoke, there was always more when he reached for it.

The onmyoji, however, had no way of supplementing his supply and soon realized that his protégé was simply going to wear him down. Using an extreme measure, he shut down for an eyeblink, just long enough to throw Moonlight off balance and to receive a short blast of Moonlight's energy. As the unfiltered life force flowed into Autumn, the wizard became aware of things that had been hidden from him. Throwing up an energy field for protection, the onmyoji called out.

"I yield."

Moonlight blinked. "What?"

"I don't want to fight you. I want to be your ally."

"He's finally lost his mind," Smoke muttered. He glanced at the helicopter. "Tiger's ready for us."

"Then let's not keep him waiting." Moonlight concentrated his will on Autumn.

"Stop," the onmyoji said. "You're not a killer."

"You've done your best to make me into one. Aren't you pleased now?"

"You have a greater destiny, but you'll never attain it without my guidance."

"There's nothing you can promise me that would stop me from ending your existence."

"You are Ryuzoku," the onmyoji said.

Moonlight stared at the wizard in astonishment.

"It's true," Autumn said. "You have the seeds of magic in you. I could teach you how to develop your power, to read the stars, so you could take your rightful place someday."

"Are you saying that I could be onmyoji?"

"Yes! You could have the power to steer the destiny of the Shadow People."

"And be like you?"

Moonlight's grip tightened on Smoke's hand. Focusing all his rage into a tight beam, he sent it ravening across the clearing to bore into Autumn's chest. The onmyoji staggered back, and then set himself to withstand the barrage. Moonlight felt the wizard's heartbeat falter, and his exultation strengthened his attack. He bore down harder as Autumn's pulse slowed. In his mind's eye, he could see a red gem like a flame in the mists, and its glow waned as the onmyoji grew weaker. Moonlight imagined pinching the light in the same way he'd snuff a candle. Even as he had the thought, the gem winked out of existence, the onmyoji fell to the ground, and almost every ounce of energy was ripped from Moonlight in the same instant.

Smoke sagged as the backlash hit him, but he had the strength to catch Moonlight and hold him up. Walking backward, he dragged Moonlight toward the chopper. Before he could get there, Tiger appeared and took Moonlight from him. Gratefully, Smoke relinquished Moonlight's solid weight and obeyed Tiger's shouted command to get in the chopper.

"You go with him," Moonlight whispered.

Tiger lifted Moonlight in his arms. "We're all getting out of here, even if I have to carry you all the way."

"Stupid, stubborn man."

"I thought that's why you loved me."

"Shut up. You need to save your breath."

Tiger turned his head to follow the line of Moonlight's gaze and saw Talon enter the glade with four soldiers. "Hold on," he said and made a dash for the helicopter with Moonlight in his arms.

Talon fired his pistol, emptying the clip, hitting Tiger twice. Tiger lurched as a bullet went through his calf muscle, but kept moving. Another round hit high on his left shoulder as he shoved Moonlight into the small cabin of the aircraft. As Talon reloaded and his men fired on the chopper, Smoke yelled at Tiger to fly this bitch or tell him how. Bullets punched holes in the windscreen as Tiger took hold of the throttle and the collective, and the little helicopter leapt into the air. As soon as they cleared the trees, Tiger tilted the main rotor forward and gave it more throttle, skimming the treetops and depriving the shooters of a target.

"Will this thing go any faster?" Smoke asked as he climbed into the cramped cargo area to kneel beside Moonlight.

"I'm working on it." Tiger dove the chopper down the face of a sea cliff and took it to the deck, barely clearing the tops of the waves as he hit maximum velocity. "I'll do my best to get us out of sight as soon as possible." He darted a look over his shoulder. "How's Moonlight?"

"He's conscious." Smoke pulled Moonlight's head into his lap. "How are you feeling?" he asked.

"Have you ever had a hangover?" Moonlight mumbled.

"Of course."

"Multiply your worst hangover by a thousand and you still won't be close."

"But you're alive."

"And free," Tiger called back. "We did it!"

"Yes we did," Smoke said. "We can do whatever we want... in the short time left to us."

"Maybe they won't find us, now that Autumn is gone," Moonlight said.

"We'll have to be very, very smart," Tiger said.

"Starting right now." Smoke put his jacket under Moonlight's head and went back to the navigator's seat. "We can assume that Talon radioed the mainland, and they'll be sending a chopper. Don't head straight for the coast."

"Where do you want me to go?"

"Hold on." Smoke took out his phone and connected to the Internet. "Okay." He scrolled, looked at some maps, and scrolled some more. "Head north-northeast."

"Where are we going?"

"There appears to be an island large enough to land on." Smoke did another search. "Barring that, there are at least two freighters that are big enough for a skilled pilot."

"I can land on a moving train if I have to," Tiger said.

"Good to know. Stay at this altitude, and I'll tell you when to turn."

Several minutes later, Tiger set the streamlined craft down on a reasonably flat spot on a small rocky islet. He and Smoke covered the helicopter with dead branches and vines and joined Moonlight in the dappled shade of the undergrowth. The soil was thin and the ground was hard, but the plant life was thick enough to conceal them and the chopper when a Kagehito patrol flew overhead eleven minutes later.

"I think we're safe for now," Smoke said, putting his phone away. "In a couple of hours, I'll call Key and see what I can do about getting us out of here."

"I just want to sleep," Moonlight said drowsily.

Tiger moved closer to Moonlight and pulled him into his arms. "What happened back there on Saigo?" he asked, cradling Moonlight to his chest.

"I killed Autumn."

"How?"

"My inner calling found me." Moonlight turned slightly, settling into a better fit. "The dragon in me rose up when the onmyoji tried to steal my essence permanently." His lips curved in a slight smile. "Smoke found his inner calling too."

"You're Ryuzoku?" Tiger's surprise was patent in his voice.

"So's Smoke." Moonlight rubbed his cheek against Tiger's chest. "Who would have believed…?" His words trailed off into a soft snore.

Tiger looked up at Smoke. "Dragon Tribe."

"I was really surprised," Smoke said. "When Moonlight was fighting the onmyoji, he was able to draw energy from me. When the Dragon called him, I was called too. An indescribable feeling, really."

"I know what you mean. The inner calling is a powerful thing."

Smoke nodded. "There at the end, the onmyoji recognized Moonlight's full potential, and he started trying to bargain with him. You'd have thought he'd have known better than to offer Moonlight power."

"The wizard was blinded by his belief that he was smarter than everyone else."

"Very well put." Smoke looked pointedly at Tiger's wounded leg. "Want me to do something about that?"

"I'd appreciate it. And if you could look at the wound on my shoulder?"

"I'm making a house call and you want two for one?" Smoke shook his head as he crawled back to the chopper and fetched the first aid kit.

Moonlight slept through Smoke's field surgery as the wounds were dressed. Tiger refused to let go of him, despite Smoke's complaints about making the job harder. When it was over, Tiger let out a big breath and reclined with Moonlight lying on his chest.

"Have any plans for the future?" Smoke asked to pass the time.

"I know what we're going to do first." Tiger looked over at Smoke. "Want to help?"

Tiger explained his plan, and Smoke got his phone out again. Deciding it was safe to make a call, Smoke phoned Key and gave him several instructions.

MOONLIGHT was still asleep several hours later when Smoke turned on his phone again. A troop transport chopper appeared out of the night and hovered over the islet. A ladder was lowered, and Smoke climbed on board. After a couple of minutes, a stretcher was lowered, and Tiger strapped Moonlight to it. Once Moonlight was on board, the ladder was sent down for Tiger. Wrapping his good arm around a rung, Tiger signaled the crew to pull him up.

"Good to see you," Key said. "You can have this back." He handed Smoke the flash drive.

"This looks like an official Kagehito troop transport," Tiger said.

"It is," Key said. "Smoke's phone call to me was intercepted. The crew of this ship was sent to pick me up." He held up his hands. "Don't freak out. We're not prisoners."

"What's going on, Key?" Tiger said.

"Lord Talon sent the chopper. The crew will put us down wherever we say and leave us there."

"Why would Talon do that?"

"I don't know, but you should pick a direction soon."

"Tell him where to go, Smoke," Tiger said as he sat down on the floor beside Moonlight.

SMOKE and Tiger sat on the park bench with Moonlight propped between them and watched the rising sun gild the peaked rooftops of the village. A breeze sifted through the trees, shaking loose some water and a few dead leaves that drifted down to scurry away across the dewy grass. Objects that had been dim outlines moments ago took on form, color, and mass.

"Why do you think Talon helped us?" Tiger asked.

"I don't think he helped *us*," Smoke replied. "He shot *you* twice, if you recall. I think he wanted to help Moonlight."

"I thought he wanted to keep him."

"I think he did too. I also think he may genuinely care about Moonlight. It's possible that when he realized Moonlight could actually escape the life he hated that Talon gave him the chance."

Tiger snorted. "What a fairy tale."

"You asked what I thought."

"I realize my mistake now."

Smoke looked at Tiger over the top of Moonlight's head. "Maybe he saw Moonlight kill the onmyoji and didn't want a powerful rival around, so he helped him escape. Not to mention that Moonlight probably knows that Talon killed Lord Raven."

"That sounds more believable." Tiger brushed a drop of water from Moonlight's hair. "What's it like, being Ryuzoku?"

"I feel amazingly self-assured. Like I could do anything."

A drop of condensation fell on Moonlight's left eyelid, and he blinked. Opening both eyes, he rubbed the water away and looked around. "Where is this?" he asked in a grainy voice.

"You'll know where you are in a few minutes," Smoke said.

Tiger squeezed Moonlight's shoulders and kissed his forehead. "You're free," he said.

Moonlight threw his arms around Tiger and found his lips in a kiss that ended several years of yearning. He pulled back so he could kiss Tiger again, letting his mouth wander over Tiger's face and neck. "*We're* free," he said.

"We'll have to be very quick and very clever to stay that way."

"No problem. We're together. That's all that matters." Moonlight stopped kissing Tiger abruptly. "Is this a bandage on your shoulder?"

"I got shot." Tiger shrugged and winced. "A couple of times."

"Why aren't you seeing a surgeon right now?"

"Smoke fixed me." Tiger kissed the frown from Moonlight's lips. "They were easy wounds. Through and through. He even disinfected them and put on antibiotics."

Moonlight's brow wrinkled. "Did I see Key on a helicopter?"

"Yeah."

Smoke stood up from the bench. "He decided to stay with the Shadow."

"Didn't you tell him—?"

"Of course we told him," Tiger interrupted. "He still believes in the mission."

"I envy him his faith," Smoke said.

"Blind faith is worse than none at all," Moonlight retorted.

Smoke turned to meet Moonlight's eyes. "Maybe someone should give Key a good reason to believe."

"You can*not* be suggesting what I think you're suggesting."

"We could do it," Smoke said.

"We could do what?" Tiger got up when Moonlight stood.

"We could reclaim the Shadow." Smoke took his hands out of his pockets and spread them. "Look at the resources we have between us. Moon and I are both Dragons. We have Feather and Rose Tribes' power of persuasion. We have a strong and charismatic leader to front for us." He nodded at Tiger. "Think about it—a reformation guided by the three of us."

"I'd definitely need to think about it," Moonlight said, his eyes focused on something beyond Smoke's shoulder.

Smoke turned and saw a woman coming down the road on an old yellow bicycle. She wasn't young or old but somewhere in the middle, riding carefully, mindful of the patches of slush. Her coat was years out of style, an odd pistachio color, enveloping her bird-like frame from neck to ankles. The heavy garment made the dismount a tricky thing, but she managed it with grace and aplomb, using the handbrakes, swinging a leg over, and alighting on the steps of her destination. Leaving the bicycle leaning against the rail, she unlocked the building's front door and went inside.

Moonlight left the park and walked slowly across the street to stop in front of the sign that identified the long structure as an elementary school. With Smoke and Tiger following at a distance, Moonlight went up the steps and into the building.

The woman had removed her coat and was adding wood to the cast-iron stove beside her desk. She looked up as Moonlight entered, an inquiring look on her face. Her eyes were wide-set, of an indeterminate dark gray color that Moonlight knew from his mirror, and though the skin over her fine bone structure was wrinkled now, he knew her face. As he walked forward, he smiled for sheer joy.

"Jaehan." Moonlight's mother said his name without a trace of doubt. This was her lost baby, come home at last; she would know him anywhere. Her steps quickened until she was almost running, arms spread wide to welcome her son. "My Jaehan."

Moonlight met her in the middle of the room and swept her into a hug. Her arms went around him and he smelled the familiar smell that let him know that all was right with the world. It didn't matter how long he'd been gone or what he'd done, the bond between mother and child was not strained. In that embrace, Moonlight felt joy, gratitude, and unconditional love, and his soul was finally whole again.

# Epilogue

THE Great Hall was well-lit, and the dark wood and costly fabrics of the furnishings gleamed richly. An assemblage of the Shadow's high-ranking members sat on the ancient seats around the High Table. At the head of the oblong table sat the new Commander in Chief, Lord of the Shadow, Talon of Iron Tribe.

"If we are all here, I'd like to begin," Talon said, rising to his feet. "Since my elevation—"

"Your *contested* elevation."

Talon looked down the table at Goblin, the new Chief of Monkey Tribe. "Contested by whom?" he asked calmly. He knew Goblin as a creature of the late onmyoji and didn't fear his power. Goblin was a coward at heart, and Talon was confident he could keep him at heel.

Lord Pebble of Feather Tribe broke the silence. "You were not appointed. You took power."

"Yes, I did." Talon put a hand on the hilt of his sword. "And I'll use it to make the Kagehito powerful again. It's time we came out of the shadows."

The men around the table looked uneasily at one another.

"What do you mean?" Lord Mahogany of Iron Tribe eyed his former chief enforcer with suspicion.

"I mean that we should take power," Talon said. "Why should we serve when we're superior? We should hold positions of power in the world."

"That is not our way," Pebble protested.

"Ways change," Talon said.

As if the words were a cue, the double doors of the hall opened and the leaders of the Kagehito turned toward the entrance. Three men strode through, one in the sober black suit that was a Feather's uniform, one in Iron Tribe dress black, and the third in robes of pale silk with a veil over his head. They stopped a few meters from the table as Talon drew his sword.

"How did you get in here?" the commander barked.

The robed stranger threw back his head covering. "I bewitched your guards, of course," Moonlight said.

Talon's face drained of color as he stared at the Rose. "What— what are you doing here?"

"I've come to take my rightful place at the head of the Great Council."

"You—what?" Talon's expression of surprise would have been comical at another time.

Moonlight glanced at Smoke, and Smoke stepped forward.

"The Shadow has changed in the centuries it has been in existence. New things have been learned and some things have been forgotten. By the letter of the First Laws, the man who guides the Kagehito should be a member of Dragon Tribe who has attained the rank of onmyoji. Only one who can read the stars is qualified to govern."

"Too bad there isn't a copy of the First Laws lying around," Talon said.

"Like you and everyone else, I thought all the written copies of the Law had been lost or destroyed, but in fact, a copy exists."

"Where?" Talon challenged, as curious as the other men at the table to hear what Smoke would say.

"In this very room."

Talon bared his teeth in a smile. "Now I know you're bluffing." He turned his gaze on Moonlight. "You shouldn't have come back here. I let you go once. I won't be so soft this time."

Tiger took a step forward, and Moonlight put a hand on his lover's forearm.

"Let him come," Talon sneered. "I'll show him the strength of a true Iron man."

"I'd rather not shed blood here," Moonlight said. "Gentlemen," he addressed the council. "I can easily prove that Smoke is telling the truth." His gaze fell on Goblin. "If you would, get out of your chair and turn to face the wall. Thank you. Put your hand on the bottom right corner of the block in front of your left shoulder. Yes, that one. Now push hard."

Goblin and his fellow chiefs were surprised when the block turned out to be a mere sheet of rock that pivoted inward. In the cavity thus revealed was a large box.

"How did you know of this?" Lord Pebble asked.

"Autumn told me before he died," Moonlight said.

"And where have you been since then?" Goblin asked accusingly.

"Did you miss me?" Moonlight replied softly.

Goblin turned away to hide his red face and pulled the box from its hiding place. Before he could set it on the table, Talon ordered Goblin to bring it to him. When the box was in front of Talon, he examined the latch before opening it with a blow of his sword's hilt. Inside were several scrolls wrapped in leather.

Talon gestured to Pebble. "You're a Feather," he said. "Come and look at these scrolls and tell me if they're authentic."

Pebble ran his eyes over the contents of the box, and then picked up one of the scrolls. "They're well preserved," he said, knocking a knuckle against the box. "Cedar wood." He pulled the scroll from the leather sheath by the carved ivory handle. "Workmanship is from the right period." He partially unrolled the scroll and his eyes widened. "Extraordinary," he said in a reverent tone.

"What is it?" Talon prompted.

"Ancient scripts were my area of expertise when I worked in cryptology, and this writing is absolutely authentic. Look at the little bent serifs here, like antennae on ants. This ink would originally have been a deep maroon. I can't believe the condition of the parchment." Pebble glanced at the hole in the wall. "It must have been airtight and dry as dust in there."

"Can you read it?" Talon asked.

"Probably, but these scrolls should be examined in a controlled atmosphere to prevent—" Pebble caught Talon's scowl and applied himself to deciphering the vertical lines. "This is the wisdom of Iron Dragon, as faithfully written down by his scribe, Pied Feather." Pebble looked up. "This is a collection of the sayings of the first Shadow Lord."

"Try another one," Tiger said.

"I haven't given you leave to speak at this council." Talon bristled as he locked eyes with Tiger.

"I haven't asked for any," Tiger replied. "I stand at the side of the true Lord of the Shadow as his champion. I'm ready to defend his honor against all who oppose him."

Talon's lips curled in another sneer. "The Barazoku? You're mad, or you think we are. I'll wager there isn't a man at this table who hasn't mounted him at least once."

"Tiger," Moonlight said softly, stopping Tiger in mid-stride. "Not yet."

Tiger's eyes blazed with fury, but he came back to Moonlight's side.

"Good dog," Talon said. He looked around the table. "Is there anyone here who would take orders from him?" He flapped a hand in Moonlight's direction.

"I would," said Shima, Island of Rose Tribe. "If the First Laws require it." He paused. "Also, Moonlight would have to prove he has an inner calling to the Dragon, and that he has the power and skills of a wizard."

"I stand ready to be tested," Moonlight said.

"This is outrageous," Talon said as he watched the faces of the council undergo a subtle change. "You can't be serious. Look at him!"

Tiger stiffened as Talon came closer, but Talon stopped well out of reach.

"Look at him," Talon said again, gesturing to Moonlight. "Even if you didn't know him, you can see what he is."

"Perfection," Smoke said. He ignored Talon's glare as he continued speaking. "Moonlight is the product of centuries of controlled breeding. None of you likes to talk about it, but as chiefs, you all know how carefully the mothers are selected and that only the finest Shadow warriors are sent to impregnate them. Moonlight's mother was one of the unwanted daughters of a Kagehito soldier and another unwanted female Shadow offspring. She was given up for adoption and tracked until she reached childbearing age. At that time, she was impregnated by a Shadow operative. As was Tiger's mother. And mine. We are the results of all that careful mixing of bloodlines. You can oppose us if you feel you must, but we are the future of the Kagehito, whether you like it or not."

"You're children," Talon said. "And you've disturbed this council long enough."

"Wait," Pebble said, looking up from the scroll he held. "It's right here. In essence, the law states that only the man who is able to see the—the next word is path or road—in the stars may guide the destiny of the Shadow People. Let no lesser man be given this great—"

"I don't believe you," Talon interrupted. "You're making this up because you want to get rid of me, you traitor."

"I'm only a traitor if I've given you my loyalty, which I haven't." Pebble set down the scroll and looked Talon in the eye.

"I'm the Commander." Talon turned to fix his stare on Moonlight. "Leave," he said, "and I'll let you and your friends live. Stay and I can guarantee you days of agony in a traitor's death."

"Talon." Moonlight met Talon's gaze without flinching. "I want to apologize to you."

Taken aback, Talon held his tongue as Moonlight spoke again.

"You were a good man before you met me, but I found your weaknesses and used them to twist you into a new shape. I'm sorry." Moonlight lifted his chin. "But I won't let you take the Kagehito any farther down this dark road. If that means I must depose you, I will. And though I don't want the job, I'll do it if I must."

"You think you can take anything from me?"

On the last word, Talon lunged, the tip of his sword seeking Moonlight's heart. Tiger and Smoke both surged forward as the tribal chiefs got to their feet in alarm. Moonlight stood his ground, one hand outstretched as though calling a halt. All motion ceased as everyone but Moonlight was frozen in place. Deliberately, Moonlight curled his tapered fingers into a tight fist. Talon fell to the ground, and life resumed its normal pace.

Moonlight swayed on his feet, and Tiger put a hand under his elbow to steady him. "I'm all right," Moonlight murmured. "Just a little shaky." He gathered himself and faced the council as Smoke knelt beside Talon's motionless body.

Lord Island was the first to bow to Moonlight, and the other chiefs followed suit, one by one.

"You all know that I was Autumn's student," Moonlight said. "He taught me all that he knew in preparation for this day. But I'm young, and I have no experience with being in command. So I hope I can count on this council to share the burden of rule with me and my advisors, Tiger of Iron Tribe and Smoke of Feather Tribe. Had the onmyoji planned better, my counselors might number five and all of the tribes would have been represented in them. However, Autumn went off course in pursuit of personal matters and lost his vision. The Shadow mission has become tainted, but we are going restore it to purity. One day in the future, we'll deserve the name Bright Shadow again."

Ashita, Tomorrow, the eighty-three-year-old chief of the tiny Dragon Tribe, bowed to Moonlight, and then to Smoke. "Welcome to my new brothers," he said. "I will not oppose your elevation to Shadow Lord," he told Moonlight. "May I suggest we adjourn this meeting so that Pebble can take the scrolls to his people for further study? And though you appear to have an onmyoji's powers, you need to be formally vested, young man. If everyone's agreed, shall we meet again tomorrow?"

Everyone present agreed with this suggestion and the chiefs left the chamber. Servants arrived to remove Talon while Pebble was carefully repacking the box. As Talon was carried away, Smoke appeared at Pebble's shoulder.

"Do you need any help, Lord Pebble?"

"No thank you." Pebble glanced at Moonlight, who leaned on Tiger's arm. "Is he all right?" he asked Smoke.

"It's not an easy thing for him to take a life," Smoke answered. "But he'll be fine."

"I'll be going then," Pebble said. "Until tomorrow."

Smoke bowed. "I hope it's all right if we stay for a few minutes so Moonlight can rest."

"Of course. You've been here with Raven, so you know where everything is."

Smoke's throat tightened at the casual mention of his murdered mentor. Knowing Raven's killers were dealt with brought little comfort. "Yes, I know my way around," he said. "Thank you."

"Is this to be your role?" Pebble asked curiously. "Moonlight's go-between?"

"We serve where our talents are best suited."

"Don't quote the credo to me, young dragon. You won a great victory today, but half your battle was won before you took the field. Talon had no supporters on the Inner Council, and we only needed a good reason to oust him."

"How fortunate for you that we happened to be strolling by."

"I'd also advise against taking that sarcastic tone with the councilors."

"And I'd advise you not to assume you've acquired a puppet commander."

"The lords of this council are older and wiser, with much more experience than Moonlight."

"Yes, but he could kill you just by wishing you dead." Smoke sighed. "I despise being blunt, but if it's the only way to keep you in line, I'm not above threats."

Pebble narrowed his eyes. "Get to the point."

"When we meet again tomorrow, I expect the Inner Council to declare that Moonlight be elevated to Commander-in-Chief. I expect you to show him respect, but to also be truthful and true to your beliefs. Moonlight knows he needs the Council, so don't be assholes trying to prove it to him."

"Your message is quite clear. I find nothing to disagree with in it." Pebble's gaze went back to Moonlight. "I'm not your enemy," he said as he lifted the cedar wood box in his arms. With a nod, he walked away from Smoke and out of the Great Hall.

"Unbelievable," Smoke said as he turned from shutting the doors. "I never thought it would go that smoothly. I expected a lot more opposition."

"Really?" Tiger said. "But you told us that the only logical thing the council could do was side with Moonlight."

"Well, I had to say that, didn't I? I was trying to encourage you."

Moonlight sat in the thronelike chair Talon had recently occupied and slouched wearily. "Then I won't bother asking you how you think it'll go tomorrow."

"Actually, Pebble pretty much guaranteed the council would make it official. What choice do they have, really?"

"That display of power was very convincing," Tiger said, sitting on the arm of Moonlight's chair. "I wish you had let me take care of Talon, but Smoke was right. This way had a lot more impact."

"I wish it hadn't been necessary," Moonlight said. "I'll always feel guilty about Talon."

Tiger stroked Moonlight's hair, running a hand down the back of his neck and rubbing the tight muscles. "Remember why we're doing this: so no other children will ever have to go through what we went through."

"Thank you." Moonlight reached up to stroke Tiger's hand. "The breeding program will stop. The training methods will be modified. There will be no slaves."

"In all of Autumn's scheming, I'll bet he never imagined this outcome," Smoke said.

Moonlight smiled wryly. "He had me forge all those parchments in order to get himself elevated. He created that secret chamber and hid the box. He went to all that trouble and his slave ends up as Commander."

"You beat him," Tiger said. "He tried so hard to break you, but he couldn't."

"It was a near thing." Moonlight let his head drop forward as the massage continued. "I came close to losing myself."

"From now on, you'll have us to remind you of who you are," Smoke said.

Moonlight held out his free hand, and Smoke took it. Drawing Smoke closer, Moonlight looked up at him. "I'm glad I can count on you," he said.

"So am I." Tiger put a hand on Smoke's shoulder.

For several moments they remained like that until Smoke broke the silence.

"So we never decided. What are we going to call ourselves?" he said brightly, his eyes shimmering with unshed tears. "Are we a trio? A triad? What?"

"Well, we're certainly not a threesome," Tiger said.

"You had to say it." Moonlight smacked Tiger's thigh.

"If you want me, big boy, just let me know," Smoke told Tiger.

"If the other members of the Table could hear the two of you right now…." Tiger's voice trailed off. "Pay no attention to me," he said. "I'm not known for being perceptive."

"I have no complaints," Moonlight said. "And why do we need to give ourselves a name?"

"Because if we don't, someone else will."

"Fine," Moonlight said. "If we succeed, what difference does it make what someone calls us?"

"None, I guess." Smoke looked over at Tiger.

"Am I the only one who's starving?" Tiger asked.

Moonlight realized how hungry he was and let Tiger help him to his feet. With Tiger on his right and Smoke on his left, he walked out of the Great Hall.

TSUKIKAGE, Tora, and Kemuri are remembered in Kagehito history as the Triple Dragons, though Tiger was not, in fact, a member of Dragon Tribe, he was called Iron Dragon by the men under his command. In a single lifetime, Moonlight, Tiger, and Smoke reformed the customs of the Kagehito, restoring them to the founders' original intent. Such was their power when the three stood together, a power unmatched by any that had come before them. Their like has not been seen since. However, only the stars know what the future will bring.

CONNIE BAILEY is a Luddite who can't live without her computer. She's an acrophobic who loves to fly, a fault-finding pessimist who, nonetheless, is always surprised when something bad happens, and an antisocialite who loves her friends like family. She's held a number of jobs in many disparate arenas to put food on the table, but writing is the occupation that feeds her soul.

Connie lives with her ultralight designer husband at a small grass-strip airfield halfway between Disney World and Busch Gardens. Logic and reality have had little to do with her life, and she likes it that way.

Visit her Web site at http://www.conniebailey.com/ and her blog at http://baileymoyes.livejournal.com/.

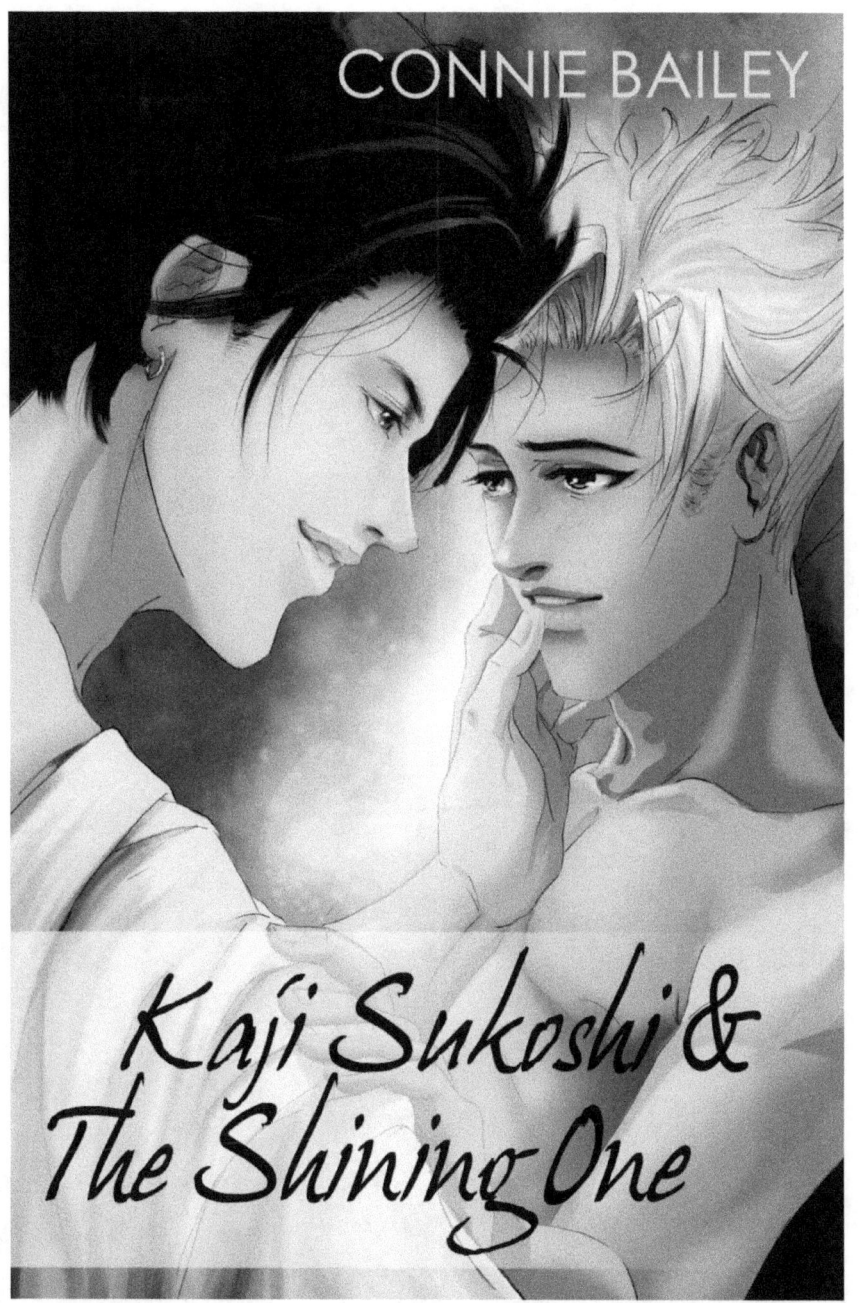

CONNIE BAILEY

Kaji Sukoshi &
The Shining One

http://www.dreamspinnerpress.com

Also by CONNIE BAILEY

Miles to Go

Connie Bailey

http://www.dreamspinnerpress.com

TRUE BLUE

Connie Bailey

http://www.dreamspinnerpress.com

www.ingramcontent.com/pod-product-compliance
Lightning Source LLC
Chambersburg PA
CBHW070057030726
47506CB00002B/493